SPECTR

SERIES 2

VOLUME 1

Also by Jordan L. Hawk:

Hainted

<u>Whyborne & Griffin series:</u>
Widdershins
Threshold
Stormhaven
Necropolis
Bloodline
Hoarfrost
Maelstrom
Fallow

"Eidolon" (A Whyborne & Griffin short story)
"Carousel" (A Whyborne & Griffin short story)
"Remnant" written with KJ Charles (A Whyborne & Griffin / The Secret Casebooks of Simon Feximal crossover)

<u>Spirits:</u>
Restless Spirits
Dangerous Spirits

<u>Hexworld</u>
The 13th Hex
Hexbreaker
Hexmaker
A Christmas Hex

"Heart of the Dragon" (short story)

JORDAN L. HAWK

SPECTR

SERIES 2

Volume 1

INCLUDING:
MOCKER OF RAVENS
DANCER OF DEATH
DRINKER OF BLOOD

SPECTR: Series 2, Volume 1 © 2015-2017 Jordan L. Hawk
ISBN: 978-1548828653

This book is a work of fiction. Names, characters, places, and incidents are products of the author's imagination or are used fictitiously. Any resemblance to actual events or locales or persons, living or dead, is entirely coincidental.

Edited by Annetta Ribken

MOCKER OF

RAVENS

CHAPTER 1

JOHN STARKWEATHER WAS not having a good night.

"Stop! Federal agent!" he bellowed. Not surprisingly, the figure currently fleeing arrest didn't obey.

Thunder grumbled off to the west, barely loud enough for human hearing to register. The oppressive heat of the July night had him perspiring even before the chase began. Now his suit stuck to his skin, and sweat ran into his eyes, stinging them with salt.

He blinked rapidly, not daring to look away in case he lost the suspect. A series of brutal murders had ripped through the homeless population, and the mauled flesh and half-eaten bodies showed all the earmarks of late-stage lycanthropes. The guy running from John might or might not be one of those responsible, but his yellow eyes, snarling mouth, and superhuman speed suggested his innocence wasn't very likely.

On a straightaway, John would have had no chance of keeping up. Fortunately, they ran through a residential district on Charleston's lower east side, not far from the waterfront. Houses loomed close against either side of the narrow street. The wildly uneven bricks making up the sidewalk would have been hazardous even without the frequent steel utility accesses jutting up through them.

Forget about keeping up—John would be lucky not to break his leg.

The suspect scrambled over a narrow iron gate between two of the old houses. Without pause, John clambered over after him, the gate's decorative swirls offering plenty of handholds. He dropped to the ground on the other side and found himself in a driveway barely wide enough for a single car. His shoes sent echoes up from the mix of bricks and pavers making up the driveway. Did the lycanthrope live here? Or had he just hoped the gate would keep John out?

Either way, the suspect had made a mistake. The driveway opened out into a tiny courtyard, surrounded on all sides by thick green hedges, which abutted the wooden siding of the houses. The smell of green growing things and damp earth flooded the small space. Gas lanterns, installed throughout Charleston's historic district, illuminated the little courtyard. A window unit air conditioner hummed to life overhead, water dripping from it into one of the hedges.

The runner stood waiting for John. The soft light of the gas lanterns revealed the acne-pocked face and scraggly moustache of a teenager.

A teenager whose eyes were a terrible, baleful yellow, and whose mouth turned up into a grin showing off inhumanly sharp teeth.

There came a scuff of claws on ancient brick from behind John. He spun, heart hammering. Two shapes made their way up the driveway behind him. Unlike the first suspect, these had made the full transition to werewolves: their bodies covered in matted fur, their lips straining around jaws filled with oversized teeth, their bestial eyes wild with the need to kill, to rend, to devour.

"You Specs think you're so smart," the teen sneered. "But you ran right into our trap."

John shook his head. "No. You ran into ours."

A dark shape dropped a heart-stopping three stories from a nearby roof. Boots thudded on the old brick paving just a few feet behind the two lycanthropes.

The newcomer surged to his feet. The gas light revealed a thin, white face, surrounded by a cloud of black hair whipped into a frenzy even though no wind stirred. Eyes black as the abyss fixed on the lycanthropes, their depths lit up by little flickers like lightning. Lips twisted back into a snarl, revealing deadly fangs.

Drakul. Or vampire, if one wasn't picky about the terminology.

"Oh shit!" the teen screamed, the NHE inside him recognizing a much larger predator. The lycanthropes were trapped, with Gray between them and the only exit. Howling madly, they both charged the drakul, who eagerly leapt to meet them.

Damn it. John couldn't risk firing on either of them without hitting

Gray. True, it wouldn't kill Gray, but it would certainly hurt him.

"Stay there!" John barked at the terrified teen crouching against the side of a building like he meant to claw his way through the siding to safety. Drawing his silver athame, John ran toward the fray.

Gray hurled himself on one of the lycanthropes. It clawed at him, but the long elk hide coat he wore foiled its grip. Gray had claws of his own; he sank them into the werewolf's shoulders, trying to get an angle to bite down on the thick vein pulsing in its neck.

Unfortunately, grappling with one werewolf left the other free to wreak havoc. It attacked Gray from the side, snarling furiously. Its claws slashed across his forehead, wrenching his head sideways. Blood flew everywhere, and Gray snarled in pain and fury. While he was distracted by the second lycanthrope, the first used the opportunity to try to sink its teeth into Gray's shoulder.

John buried his athame to the hilt in the second werewolf's back. The silver-plated blade struck bone—he'd missed the heart—but the NHE howled in agony and loosened its hold on Gray.

Gray tore free in another spray of blood. This time he managed to get a grip on the first werewolf's head, jerking it to the side hard enough to snap the vertebrae and sinking his fangs deep into the creature's throat.

Perhaps seeing its chance for escape, the second lycanthrope broke for the alleyway's entrance. John dropped his athame and brought up his Glock. His shot caught the werewolf in the hip, spinning it around.

Instead of hitting the ground, though, it surged back at him, the pain maddening it past the point of self preservation. John glimpsed jaws full of teeth and smelled the fetid breath as it bore down on him.

Then a dark shape stepped between them. Gray slammed into the werewolf, bearing it to the ground. It thrashed like a mad thing, but the drakul ignored its claws in favor of sinking his teeth deep into its throat. A few seconds later, the werewolf went still beneath him.

Gray rose lithely to his feet. Although tall, his build was slender. With all the black leather and hair, he looked like the sort of pretty goth boy John might pick up in a dance club, instead of a badass demon-killing vampire.

Or a god of storm. But John didn't let himself think about that part very often.

"John. Are you unharmed?" Gray asked in a deep voice underlain by a bass roll of thunder that rattled John's bones. He strode toward John, wiping the blood from his mouth. The wounds on his face and body had already healed, fueled by the etheric energy carried in the blood of those possessed by Non-Human Entities.

"I'm fine."

"There is one more." Gray's obsidian eyes went to the quaking teen. "It sought to lure you into a trap."

"Yeah." And that alone was odd. Ghouls might run in packs, but unlike real wolves, werewolves seldom appeared in groups. Then again, ghouls were opportunistic parasites who possessed the weak—homeless people, usually, or the desperately lonely. Summoning a lycanthrope, on the other hand, took deliberation. Which meant more than one faust in an area willfully trying to become possessed, and finding each other before an exorcist had the chance to catch them. "But he can still be exorcised."

Just because someone became possessed didn't automatically put them beyond hope. Non-Human Entities could be exorcised within forty days of the initial summoning. But any longer, and the NHE took over completely. Nothing remained but to put them down like dangerous animals.

"So I see," Gray said, not sounding at all pleased about it.

John stifled a sigh. He had joined Strategic Paranormal Entity ConTRol—more generally known as SPECTR—to protect both NHEs and humans alike. An exorcism was a victory.

Gray's interest in other NHEs, on the other hand, seemed limited as to whether or not he could eat them. Nowadays he refrained from devouring the poor souls still able to be exorcised, but John suspected he would never be entirely happy about it.

"Hold him while I work," John said as they approached the teen.

The kid tried to bolt, but Gray was far too fast. A moment later, the teen dangled flat against the wall, feet kicking as Gray pinned his shoulders to the old brick. The faust screamed, yellow eyes rolling, inhumanly sharp teeth bared. A wet patch appeared on the front of his jeans.

At one time, John would have put him in silver cuffs and dragged him back to HQ. Exorcists relied on circles and chants to sharpen their focus and give them the power to remove an NHE from a faust. Now, he simply stepped up, reached past Gray, and laid his hand on the kid's forehead.

John imagined a thick rope, covered in hooks, extending from his palm. He sank it deep into the teen, felt it snag on something, like a fish on a line.

The lycanthrope didn't want to emerge, fighting and snarling, but these days John had power to burn. He wrenched it out, caught a glimpse in his etheric sight of something like a horrid parody of a wolf, its lower half as unformed as a tadpole.

The storm front of etheric energy pouring off Gray crackled—then the NHE vanished, devoured by the drakul.

The kid went limp. Gray carefully lowered him to the ground. The etheric energy brushing John's skin vanished, folding inside even as Gray's long hair came to rest over his shoulders. A moment later, the badass vampire was gone, leaving behind just an ordinary guy.

Well, no. Nothing about Caleb was ordinary, so far as John was concerned. Caleb was smart, sexy, and brave as hell. His entire existence had changed completely last February when Gray inadvertently possessed him. Most people would have ended up curled in a ball in the corner and screaming, not hunting down dangerous NHEs at John's side.

"Oh God!" the teen gasped. His eyes—light brown now, with no trace of yellow—went wide with horror. "I didn't think it would be like that! Wh-what we did. We…oh God, did we *eat*…"

Caleb stepped hastily back while the kid emptied his stomach. "Poor bastard," he remarked.

"Yeah." Why the kid thought it a good idea to summon NHEs, John didn't know. It wasn't his business. Other people would decide whether charges would be brought; his part of the job was done. Well, almost. "Let's get him back to HQ."

Caleb reached down and hauled up the sobbing kid. "Come on, wolf boy. Hope you like orange jumpsuits."

"Caleb," John warned. For all they knew, the teen had been a victim, forced or pressured to agree to possession by his two friends. Compassion was the watchword.

"Yeah, sorry." Caleb glanced at the sky, then back at John. "Storm's got me antsy."

"Getting closer?"

"Oh yeah." Caleb's sly smile turned John's question into something far more suggestive than he'd ever intended. "So let's get this guy back to lockup, so we can wrap up for the evening. I need something to take the edge off."

Gray watches through Caleb's eyes as John finally pulls the sedan to a halt in front of their home. The storm has ridden in on the wind, and its power speaks to him, and his to it. They are one thing. Lightning sizzles in their blood.

And if Gray feels it, then so does Caleb. Gray hovers just beneath their shared skin while Caleb sucks on John's neck, the taste of salt filling their mouth from the dried sweat. His other hand is on John's crotch, massaging the stiff erection beneath the barrier of cloth. The car smells of hot skin and musk, mingled with leather and the last fading traces of John's cologne. Rain pelts on the roof. Thunder growls overhead. Gray wants to growl back, but their mouth is otherwise occupied.

The vehicle safely stopped, John turns to kiss them. His hands frame their face, and his tongue swirls into their mouth, swiping away the last traces of mint from when Caleb brushed their teeth clean of blood.

John drags his mouth free and gasps, "Inside."

Yes.

"Yeah," Caleb agrees, his voice gone ragged with the lust choking their throat.

The roar of the rain against the car roof is replaced with the drum of it against the concrete sidewalk and iron fence. John catches their hand, and they run together to the door. He swears, fumbling for the correct key as the rain soaks them both. Lightning flickers, followed by thunder a second or two later.

The night is alive around them: dark and rain and lightning and power. They could run for hours, could jump and climb, for the sheer joy of it. Of this living body.

But there are other bodies, and other things to be done for the joy of it.

"Take over for a while," Caleb suggests as they follow John through the open door.

Gray has no wish to argue. He manifests, Caleb receding to the presence watching now through his eyes, avid and hungry for what is to come. Gray pulls John to him, kissing him deep, and John moans and rubs his erection against Gray's thigh.

"Let's go upstairs," John says, when he can speak again. "I want you to fuck me until I beg to come."

As soon as they hit the bedroom, Gray seizes him. Claws snag in John's clothes, and John stiffens slightly. "Claws in, darling."

Gray leaps back, claws tight in their sheaths, putting as much space between them as the small room will allow. "I hurt you?" He would not intentionally harm John, not ever. But mortals are so fragile, and he fears making some mistake and bringing unintended pain.

John shakes his head. "No, no. Of course not. But I kind of need this suit for work, and if you rip it up, I'm making Caleb come clothes shopping with me."

"That's hitting below the belt," Caleb complains.

Perhaps it is best to let John remove his own clothes. Gray does the same, hastily unbuckling heavy boots. Before he can slide off his leather pants, the lights flicker and die.

"Damn," John says. "I like looking at you."

John cannot see in the dark, but Gray can, perfectly well. *"Other people can't see, either,"* Caleb suggests slyly. *"And the garden is nice and dark…"*

Their shared heart beats more quickly at the thought, further stiffening their cock. "Come," Gray says, and takes John's hand.

John's expression is confused, but he follows willingly. Gray pauses beside the bed just long enough to pick up the lubricant, then flings open the balcony doors and lets in the storm.

The smell of rain grows stronger: damp earth, ozone, and lush vegetation. Lightning crashes not far away, sending a tingle along their nerves. He pulls John out on the balcony with him; instantly, they are both soaked.

John moans a little when they kiss. His cock pushes hard against Gray's hip, insistent and wanting. Gray licks his lips, wanting to taste… but his fangs have a tendency to get in the way.

John takes a step toward one of the wicker chairs, but Gray has other ideas. He catches John's wrists—gently, so as not to harm him— and pulls him to the balcony railing. "Hold on," Gray says, wrapping one of John's hands around the iron.

"Um, is this safe? Metal in a thunder storm?"

We are the storm.

Caleb is still uncertain, but subsides. John doesn't question at all, simply wraps his hands around the railing and bends over it, his legs spread eagerly.

The lube is warmer than the cold rain. John moans and lowers his head as Gray pushes in. The rain is cool against their skin, but John is hot and tight and slick.

The wind howls, palmetto trees thrashing from the force. Lightning dances again, accompanied by a boom of thunder. The wild night surges through Gray's veins and along his nerves, whispering of running and hunting.

But this is better than hunting. He grips John's hips, careful not to use too much of his strength, and slides his claws free of his fingertips.

John gasps at the light pinpricks, the sound almost lost beneath the roar of rain, even to Gray's inhumanly sharp hearing.

They move together, John pushing back, Gray surging forward, and Caleb, his other self, right under their shared skin, shivering with pleasure. Gray closes his eyes and tips his head back, lets the rain kiss his face. More lightning, and the tang of ozone. His heart beats in time to the storm, or perhaps it echoes him, or perhaps they are simply one thing. John gasps out strings of words, incoherent with pleasure, "Fuck, yes, Gray, yes, don't stop."

So he doesn't, only lets the sensations wash through him: John's body tight on his, the tingle of distant lightning on his skin, the surge and power of the storm in his blood. John's movements quicken, one hand shifting from the railing to tug on his cock, his gasps and grunts coming faster.

"Gray!" he cries suddenly, body pushing back. His muscles quiver beneath Gray's hands as his orgasm takes him. Gray lets himself go as well, the storm quickening around him, the moan of wind around the cornice like a lover's cry, static gathering and gathering until it explodes in a lightning strike so close the thunder is instantaneous. Gray roars into it, the sound turning into one, white light behind his eyes as he climaxes.

For a moment, there is nothing but ecstasy, keener even than feeding on demon blood, before it slowly uncoils into a different sort of pleasure. Warmth and closeness, the smell of John's skin and semen, washing away in the rain.

"Damn," John mumbles. He's beginning to shiver, though, so Gray gathers him up and carries him inside to the bathroom to towel off.

This is something he has never known before, although he walked the earth for thousands of years. Before, he inhabited only corpses, understood the world only through the colorless memories gleaned from the decaying neurons. Pain and pleasure were distant, dull things, and love nothing but a concept.

John nuzzles against him, lips trailing affectionate kisses over Gray's collarbone as he wraps a towel around John. "This was good?" he asks John, because this is still so new.

Caleb snorts, in the space where their minds touch. *"Dude, he screamed your name so loud the neighbors probably heard it over the thunder."*

Even so. I would not take this for granted.

Oblivious to their exchange, John rewards him with a soft, contented smile. "Yeah," he says, leaning into Gray. "It was good."

CHAPTER 2

CALEB JOLTED AWAKE, a scream of denial dying in his throat.

The power had kicked back on at some point, and cool air wafted over his skin. The ceiling fan turned slowly over the bed, and the soft glow of the city lights filtered through the gauzy drapes. He took a deep breath, smelled skin and rain and John's shampoo.

No blood.

He blindly stretched out a trembling hand to John's side of the bed, too terrified to look. His palm landed on what felt like a shoulder, warm and solid.

Alive.

Oh God.

The dream haunted him, night after night, ever since the assault on Fort Sumter last March. Gorged on demons, on another drakul, the titan that was Gray's true form turned its attention to the city with the intent of going ashore and drinking the blood of every living being in Charleston. Of the southeast. Of the world.

But one thing stood in their way. One tiny mortal, shouting at them over the hurricane they'd summoned.

John.

And in the dream...in the dream, Caleb ate him. Tore him apart and feasted on his blood.

Gray stirred, a watchful tiger uncoiling from its rest. *"But we did not. I do not understand these dreams of yours. Why are you so troubled over something which did not actually occur?"*

Because it could have. They'd been so fucking close, right up against the line of turning into a monster of hunger and blood. And John would have been their first victim, because of course he wouldn't abandon anyone he loved, no matter what they'd become.

"But it did not." Bafflement. *"This is mortal foolishness."*

Ah, yes, mortal foolishness. Gray's diagnosis for everything. Because Gray wasn't human and never would be. He was a creature of the moment, who didn't cling to past grudges, or old regrets, or anything else. What was done was done. End of story.

"I am glad things happened as they did. If John had died…" Gray seldom hesitated, and Caleb sensed a flash of pain, deep and cutting. *"But he did not. Your dreams lie to you. And I do not understand why."*

Caleb let out a long sigh. *I know you don't. It's just mortal nonsense, like you said.*

"Indeed." But Gray eased up against him in the shared space of their brain, a sensation like an enormous tiger curling protectively around him. Or maybe like being wrapped in a heavy blanket woven from love and affection.

Because that was what made all of this craziness, all of the violence and pain and straight-up weirdness, bearable so far. Gray loved him. Not like he loved John—and Gray did love John, with the same guileless passion he applied to every damn thing, from hunting to fucking. But he loved Caleb in a way so complete and deep it went beyond words.

"You are my other self." As if that explained anything. *"I do not wish to feel you suffer, but I do not know how to make it stop."* A pause, as if an idea had suddenly occurred. *"You should ask John. He is mortal. He will understand this nonsense."*

One of the world's great thinkers, Gray was not. Still…*I don't want to worry him.*

"He would wish you to tell him."

Damn drakul was getting pretty good at figuring out mortal behavior. When it came to John, anyway. *I don't know. I need to think about it, okay?*

Gray didn't like it, but for once he didn't argue. Caleb lay still and watched the ceiling fan spin its lazy circles, until the alarm on John's phone went off a couple of hours later.

Caleb was still out of sorts when they pulled into SPECTR-HQ. He sipped coffee from a travel mug, although he wasn't entirely sure caffeine even did anything for him anymore, just like he couldn't get drunk or stoned. Not to say he'd tried the latter since getting possessed. No way would Agent John Starkweather be okay with his boyfriend smoking weed. Besides, there didn't seem much point in taking the risk of scoring a hit, when Gray would just fuck with their metabolism until the high went away.

"I will not allow you to damage our body. Why do you wish to do so?"

Says the drakul who routinely gets us mauled by demons.

"That is different," Gray replied loftily.

Caleb must have snorted aloud, because John said, "Did you say something, babe?"

Despite the early hour, John was bright-eyed and ready to go. His confidence in SPECTR took a big hit when it turned out the head of the Research Division was building a demon army, but the takedown at Fort Sumter alongside so many of his fellow agents had gone a long way toward restoring it.

"Just wondering how I ended up dating a guy in a suit," Caleb replied. Although "dating" probably wasn't the right word. "Let alone hanging out with him twenty-four seven."

John grinned and cast him a warm glance. His dark hair made his blue eyes stand out; Caleb would have noticed them even if they'd met before Gray decided to hop a ride. But with Gray's enhanced sight super saturating everything, their blue stood out like lasers, the most intense color Caleb had ever seen.

"And the first color I ever saw."

A line of nearly identical government-issue sedans waited to get through the security checkpoint into the SPECTR-HQ parking lot. John eased the car forward as the line crept one car length, then stopped again. "Because I'm irresistibly charming, of course. Not to mention my dazzling good looks."

"I think your modesty is what I like most about you, Starkweather." Caleb shook his head, but his mood had lightened.

It wasn't terribly unusual to see a handful of protestors cluttering the sidewalk in front of HQ. Today there were two groups, both chanting slogans and waving signs at the line of cars. Caleb's eyes skimmed over the usual signs: "God Hates Mals," "Exodus 22:18," and the ever-popular "SPECTR = SATAN."

For whatever reason, counter-protestors had shown up this morning. "God is Love," "I Love my Paranormally Abled Daughter," and "Human rights for all." Caleb doubted they'd change the minds of the other group, but it didn't hurt to start the day with a reminder that everyone didn't think he was going straight to hell.

A man in a button-down shirt peered inside the car, a slight frown on his face. Caleb wasn't sure whether he should scowl back, since the guy stood on the pro-paranormal side. He became even less sure when the man approached the sedan.

"They aren't supposed to actually interfere with us, are they?" he asked.

"What?" John turned his attention to the approaching man. "Wait. Is that...?"

Without answering his own question out loud, John powered down Caleb's window. The warm morning air blew in, bringing with it the smell of pavement still wet from the previous night's storm. The rising sun had already turned the city into even more of a sauna than usual.

"Nigel?" he called, leaning over Caleb.

The man's face split into a wide grin. Caleb sized him up, wondering if he was about to encounter one of John's ex's. The guy didn't seem John's type, though—his hair was too short, for one thing, which was a laugh given John's neatly trimmed hair. Middle-aged, with gray starting in his sandy hair at the temples and a pair of silver-rimmed glasses, he looked more like a professor than a protestor.

"John Starkweather," the man—Nigel—exclaimed, a pleased grin on his face. "Good to see you. It's been too long."

"Nigel Legare, allow me to introduce Caleb Jansen," John said. "Nigel retired from SPECTR a few years back. I learned a lot from him when I was still wet behind the ears."

Nigel snorted. "And here I thought you knew everything right out of the Academy. You certainly acted like it."

Caleb laughed. "That sounds like John."

"Hey, now," John protested.

Nigel's light-brown eyes took in Caleb's attire. "I take it you aren't an agent, Mr. Jansen?"

"Caleb, please. And no. I'm a contractor."

"So what are you doing with yourself these days?" John asked, with a pointed glance at the counter protest.

Nigel smiled. "I might have left SPECTR, but I didn't leave my paranormally abled brothers and sisters. I've been devoting most of my free time to a support group."

"Support group?" Caleb asked.

"It can be hard, being paranormally abled," Nigel said seriously. "Families reject us. Friends, sometimes. We can be fired from our jobs or denied housing on a whim. It's good to have a group of friends to talk to when things get difficult, and to cheer for us when things go well." Nigel reached into his pocket and fished out a card. "This is our group. We meet every Sunday evening. Give me a call if you'd like to stop by sometime."

A horn beeped behind them. Nigel stepped back hastily. "I'd better let you go before we get run over," he said with a wave. "It was nice meeting you, Caleb."

"So why did he quit?" Caleb asked, once they'd edged forward a car length or two.

John shrugged. "The same reason a lot of other agents leave. The job isn't easy, and he finally burned out after a bad case. I'm glad he's found something positive to focus on."

They finally reached the head of the line. As always, the guard in the security hut wore the green armband of an empath. Caleb suppressed a shiver and looked away, even as John exchanged a friendly bit of chitchat while showing his badge and Caleb's ID. Empaths couldn't sense Caleb anymore, thanks to Gray. No one could crawl around inside his head, taking a peek at his most private emotions. But they still freaked him out.

SPECTR-HQ looked relatively unassuming from the outside. In reality, most of the facility was buried deep underground, burrowing a good seven stories underneath them. Past the visitor's parking lot, the line of sedans followed a long, curving ramp to the underground garage.

John waited patiently for the cars in front of them to sort themselves out, before pulling into a space. Caleb took one last swig of coffee and abandoned the travel mug in the cup holder.

A crowd of agents waited in front of the elevator, all of them dressed in three-piece suits, like they were on the way to a photo shoot for Government Drone Monthly. Even at a distance, Caleb felt their eyes cut in his direction and heard the murmur of conversation fall silent.

Sure, he stood out. He could have gone for the whole suit-and-tie look, but since he was regularly getting up close and personal with things with claws and teeth, it only made sense to dress the part. A heavy coat of black elk leather, lined with kevlar, flapped around his calves. Thick leather pants, a soft t-shirt, and a pair of ass-kicking boots with thick tread and a half dozen silver buckles each, finished the ensemble. His hair, hanging loose down to his elbows, stood out in a sea of buzz-cuts.

Truthfully, though, even if he'd chopped off his hair and put on a suit, they'd still be giving him the side-eye and falling quiet. It just might have taken a little longer for the non-exorcists in the crowd to recognize him.

As they approached, several of the other agents seemed to recall items left in their cars and scurried off. They gave Caleb a wide berth as they did so. He pretended not to notice.

He'd had a lot of practice lately pretending not to notice.

"Morning, Jim," John said cheerfully. He seemed to think if he just acted normally, everyone else would come around. "Karl—is your daughter feeling better?"

There came a few murmurs, just enough to be polite, then silence. No one looked at Caleb.

The elevator doors slid open. The crowd shifted, and Caleb found himself the first on. John stepped in with him. A scattering of other agents shuffled in after them. Even though the elevator wasn't close to capacity, no one else got inside, and a moment later the doors closed.

Caleb folded his arms over his chest and leaned back against the stainless steel wall, trying to look nonchalant. John gave up any attempt at conversation, as they all stared at the floor numbers ticking past. As soon as the doors opened, the other agents hurried out. Caleb followed at a more leisurely pace.

A few agents had been scared of him, back when he was first possessed. Most of them were just confused as to why the district chief let a possessed guy roam free. But after Fort Sumter…

The events of the night were classified information. Of course word got out anyway, and now everyone looked at Caleb like he was one heartbeat from vamping out and eating the whole fucking office.

"They are foolish to fear us. Mortals are not food."

But drakul do eat people sometimes.

"The mad ones do. We are not like them."

No. But they might have been.

Except for the lack of windows, the cube farms, bland beige carpet, and fluorescent lights could have belonged to any office building. Caleb shook his head—he would never have imagined himself working in a fucking office, shuffling paper and trying to figure out how to unjam the copier. After everything with Forsyth and RD, he should have told SPECTR to go screw themselves. But the arrangement made John and Gray happy, so who was he to complain?

"And yet you complain about it a great deal."

As they approached the door to the office they shared, John fished out his keys. He was just reaching for the knob when the smell hit Caleb's nose.

"Garlic oil," he managed to spit out, before sneezing. Just his luck, one of the few things about vampires the folktales got right was the garlic allergy. It wouldn't injure him, but it made him damned uncomfortable. At least he didn't actually touch the shit this time, like he had earlier in the month. His whole hand had felt like it was on fire.

"Damn it." John sighed. "Hold on. I'll get a damp paper towel from the bathroom and wipe it off."

"Yeah." Caleb backed away, before the fumes sent his eyes to watering. Standing in the hall with a red face, tears and snot streaming everywhere, would give whatever asshole thought this was funny a big laugh, wouldn't it?

John cleaned it up quickly, thank God. As soon as they entered the room, Caleb kicked the door shut behind them. He wasn't in the mood to see any of the dipshits they worked with right now.

John winced as the door slammed. "I'll complain to Barillo, okay?"

Caleb flung himself into his chair. Two desks turned the office from spacious to cramped, but at least they weren't in the damned cube farm. God only knew what kind of hazing he'd get if people could get into his things. "And I'm sure it'll do just as much good as it did the first three times."

John's mouth tightened. "He can't ignore it. It's not professional."

"He's probably the one doing it," Caleb muttered. He never thought he'd miss Indira Kaniyar, but she wouldn't have put up with this shit for a second.

Of course, now she was off in Washington being the new Director of SPECTR, which left them stuck with her replacement, District Chief Michael Barillo. Caleb was starting to wish John had some ambition beyond being an ordinary field agent. If he climbed the ladder a few rungs, surely he'd get transferred somewhere else.

Not to say SPECTR would let Caleb go with him.

"They would have no choice."

John glanced at the closed door, then reached over the desks and took Caleb's hand. "Look, I know this hasn't been easy. Someone thinks he's a practical joker and doesn't realize this sort of thing stopped being funny after high school. We'll get it straightened out."

Caleb wanted to believe John. He did. But he couldn't shake the feeling what John saw as stupid jokes were just the surface of something much deeper.

John's phone rang before Caleb thought of a reply. John scooped it up immediately. "Starkweather here. Yes, sir. I'll be right there."

"Barillo?" Caleb guessed.

John nodded. "He wants to see me in his office." Funny how, even though they worked together, Barillo never called both of them in when it came time to give orders. "I'll be back soon. In the meantime, why don't you get in some reading?"

Caleb suppressed a groan. Up until last spring, he'd managed to keep his telekinesis hidden from the world. So while paranormals like John were at the state school learning about different abilities, and demons, and God only knew what else, he'd had an ordinary education, followed up by a couple of years in a community college art program. He didn't know shit about etheric theory, or how other paranormal abilities worked, or any of the things most of the agents took for granted. And on top of that, he needed to learn about SPECTR procedure so he didn't do something stupid and get John in trouble.

"Can't I just skip the studying and suck off the teacher for a good grade?" he suggested hopefully.

"Well, at least now I know how you passed math class," John said.

"I'm not bad at math!"

"Mmm hmm." John leaned over and kissed him on the hair. "I'll be back soon, okay?"

"You are terrible at math," Gray informed him as the door shut behind John.

"Shut up," Caleb muttered. "You can't even count to twenty."

"That is not true. One. Two. Three—"

"All right, all right, stop. Christ." Caleb flipped open the nearest book. "Assholes hazing me, homework, an annoying best friend. I swear I'm stuck in a bad YA novel. At least I don't have acne."

CHAPTER 3

"SIR," JOHN SAID, as soon as he stepped through the door of the district chief's office, "I'd like to file a complaint."

When the office belonged to the old chief, Indira Kaniyar, it had been a spartan place, with almost nothing in the way of decoration and even less of clutter. It still shocked John to come inside and find a desk covered in papers and mugs of half-drunk coffee, precarious piles of folders, and an overflowing in box. A glass jar of hard candy stood beside the computer monitor, the lemon yellows and lime greens glowing like individually wrapped jewels. Pictures of the new chief's family hung on the walls, a parade of smiling brown faces in graduation garb, wedding gowns, and soccer jerseys. Diplomas from the Alabama School for the Paranormally Abled and the US Department of Justice, Strategic Paranormal Entity ConTRol Academy shared the space, along with a number of commendations.

"I don't have time for it, Starkweather," Barillo replied. Unlike Kaniyar, who always projected a sense of having everything under control, Michael Barillo seemed continually harried. His coat hung over the back of his chair, and his shirt sleeves were rolled up to the elbows, the white cloth contrasting with his dark brown skin. Silver touched the temples of his short, tightly curled hair, and he absently cracked one of the candies between his molars.

"I'm sorry, sir, but I have to insist." Instead of taking the seat across from Barillo, John folded his hands at the small of his back. "Someone put garlic oil on the door knob of the office Mr. Jansen and I share. Again."

Barillo's dark eyes narrowed. "I don't have time for stupid office pranks, agent."

John reined in his temper. He'd tried to keep an upbeat appearance for Caleb's sake, but he was getting damned sick of the attitude of some of his fellow agents. "With all due respect, this isn't just a prank. It's harassment, targeting Mr. Jansen due to his unique circumstances."

Barillo's candy cracked again. He stared at John a long moment, chewing slowly. "Fine, agent. I'll have HR send out a memo reminding everyone to play nice with the drakul."

His tone left no doubt he considered it unnecessary, and this incident would probably come up one way or another at John's next review.

Fuck. Last year, John had been on the inside track for a promotion. The best damned exorcist in the southeast, on his way right up the ladder to bigger and better things. All gone now, thanks to half of SPECTR going rogue and trying to raise a demon army.

John had fought them—but he'd gone outside the lines to do it. And organizations like SPECTR didn't take kindly to that sort of thing. It was why they'd brought Barillo, a loyal SPECTR man to the core, into the Charleston office where the biggest troublemakers—John, Sean, and Tiffany—worked.

Tiffany resigned, Sean went on extended leave, and John got to watch his career swirl away down the toilet. And he tried like hell not to resent it, because if he hadn't acted, the whole southeast would be overrun with demons. Forsyth's drakul would be chewing its way through the armed forces. But knowing the consequences just made him feel even more betrayed.

"Now," Barillo said, "if we're done with your little complaint, I need to have a word with you about the arrest you made last night."

"Yes, sir." John straightened automatically. "I filed a rough outline of the take down last night, but I intend to fill in the details this morning. I can have it on your desk in an hour if you need—"

"I don't." Barillo's chair squeaked as he leaned back in it. "What I need is for you to start following procedure when it comes to exorcisms."

"Sir?"

"What is the procedure for exorcisms, Agent Starkweather?"

What the hell? "Under ordinary circumstances, the arresting agent would bring the faust back to HQ," John replied carefully. "The faust would be booked, interviewed if needed, and finally exorcised. But in my case—"

"In your case, the rules are never good enough." Barillo's eyes narrowed.

"Sir." Acid chewed at John's stomach. "With all due respect, the ability to remove an NHE in the field not only means the faust won't suffer needlessly, but the problem of disposal is taken care of on the spot by Gray."

"There is no problem with disposal," Barillo said.

John couldn't think of a reply that wouldn't get him reprimanded on the spot. He hoped like hell there wasn't a problem. Supposedly, inspections took place every month to make sure the special super hot furnaces actually euthanized the NHEs exorcised into bottles.

But those procedures had been in place before, and yet SPECTR spent decades storing the trapped NHEs instead. Building up enough demons to field an army. And someone high up—maybe even higher than the former Director—knew about it.

So maybe NHEs were being properly euthanized now. But for how long? Or were some already being diverted into warehouses within the Pentagon, or Department of Homeland Security, or whatever organization might think it their patriotic duty to someday force demons into soldiers to fight whoever they perceived to be the enemy?

"There is no problem with disposal," Barillo repeated, more forcefully. "But there is a problem with your little stunt." A look of disgust flickered across his features. "I'm aware of how you get your energy boost."

Did the disgust come from the fact John was sleeping with an NHE or because he was sleeping with a man? "It's useful," John said, struggling to pretend he hadn't noticed. "The faust doesn't have to suffer, we don't have to use supplies or an exorcism room, it's safer than bringing an NHE into HQ—"

"You bring an NHE into HQ every day," Barillo said. "One a hell of a lot more dangerous than some fucking lycanthrope. So cut the crap, agent. I don't give a damn about some stupid faust, or how much Florida water and incense you use. I don't want word getting out that being butt buddies with an NHE boosts paranormal ability, understand? Can you imagine if the press found out? You know how people are about sex. Every conservative congressman and half the liberal ones would be screaming for my head for letting it go on in my district."

John's fingers gripped each other tightly behind his back. "Gray is a special case. He's cleared to work with SPECTR—"

"Mr. Jansen is cleared to work with SPECTR," Barillo corrected him. "So long as he keeps the drakul under control and we don't have a repeat of the Fort Sumter incident."

"Forsyth would have killed us all if Gray hadn't fully manifested!"

"I've read the reports," Barillo replied sharply. "That thing scared the crap out of the most experienced agents we can field. I'm going to give their take on events a bit more weight than the opinion of someone who's doing…whatever it is you're doing with it. If it were up to me… but it isn't." He shook his head. "I'm not arguing with you, Starkweather. You *will* follow procedure when it comes to exorcisms from now on. Do you hear me?"

John wanted to argue. He wanted to yell. To rip Barillo's diplomas off the wall and hit him around the head until the district chief understood all of them owed Gray and Caleb their lives. He was out and proud, and fuck anyone who wanted him to pretend he wasn't in a relationship with both the people in Caleb's body.

But it wouldn't get him anywhere, except maybe a jail cell for assault. He took a deep breath, willing his racing pulse to calm. "Yes, sir."

"Good." Barillo pulled one of the folders off the top of the pile and tossed it across the desk. "We just got a call from the Charleston County medical examiner's office. They've got a case that looks like one of ours. Get down there and see what you can dig up."

"Yes, sir," John gritted out. He picked up the folder and started for the door.

"Oh, and Starkweather," Barillo called behind him, "pick up your new partner on the way out. She's waiting for you and Jansen at the security desk."

"New partner?" Caleb asked. "What the hell? Did you know about this?"

"No." John led the way back toward the lobby, his shoulders stiff beneath the cut of his suit. At a guess, his meeting with good old Barillo had gone a lot worse than John let on. "Barillo wants two exorcists to accompany you, the same way Kaniyar assigned Sean to us before. It's no big deal."

"Oh yeah. No big deal my boss doesn't trust me not to vamp out and start snacking on people." For all the good it would accomplish.

"What does he think two exorcists are going to do against Gray, anyway? It'd take an army to even slow him down."

"You probably shouldn't go around shouting that out loud," John said. "It tends to make people nervous."

Caleb glanced at the open office doors and lowered his voice. "What an asshole."

A tiny smile curved the corner of John's mouth. "Yeah. You'll get no argument from me."

Damn, Barillo must have really worked John over. "So do you know anything about this new exorcist?"

"Nothing other than she graduated from the Academy in May. This is her first assignment."

Great. A shiny new Spec, who would no doubt be terrified of the big, scary drakul. Bad enough he had to put up with this shit at HQ, but in the field, too? Christ.

The usual guards stood around the security checkpoint, chatting and drinking coffee since not many people came through at this time of the morning. The only other person was a tiny woman dressed in a black pantsuit with matching hijab.

Upon seeing them, a smile lit up her bronze-skinned face. "Agent John Starkweather? And you must be—" her voice went up into the octave normally reserved for boy bands. "Caleb Jansen? Oh my goodness, it's so exciting to meet you!"

"Er," Caleb said.

"It's true—I can feel the drakul even though it isn't manifesting." Her black eyes widened. "How wonderful! I can't believe they actually approved my request to work with you! I've only just graduated, and I thought it would never happen, but I applied and here I am!"

Dear God, Caleb could actually hear the exclamation points.

"Here you are," John agreed with a grin. "Do you mind telling us *who* you are?"

"Oh—I'm so sorry." Her cheeks darkened with embarrassment. "Zahira Noorzai. But you can call me Zahira—unless that's too informal? I'm not sure how the Charleston office operates compared to the Academy…"

"It's fine, Zahira. We don't stand much on formality here." The smile John gave her could have charmed a stone statue. "I'm John, as you already know, and this is Caleb and Gray."

"Gray, yes." She looked at Caleb like she thought Gray might pop out and say hello.

Ordinarily, Gray didn't pay much attention to other mortals besides John. But he stirred now. *"We will be working with this one?"*

Looks like it.

"Is it true Agent Starkweather—I mean, John—gave Gray his name?" she asked.

"Inadvertently," Caleb said, taken aback.

John cleared his throat. "We have a case. The ME is expecting us."

"A case? Already?" Zahira looked like John had just given her a present for Eid. "My first day!"

"Just your luck to end up with us," John said. "We know all the good morgues."

"Yeah," Caleb muttered under his breath as he followed John and Zahira out to the parking lot like a dour crow. "It's a fucking party every minute."

While John drove, Zahira sat in the passenger seat and interrogated Caleb.

"Is it true the drakul only inhabited dead bodies?" she asked.

John glanced in the rearview mirror and caught Caleb's eye roll. "Yes."

"Is it true he possessed you in the few seconds you were technically dead, before CPR started your heart again?"

"Yes."

"Is it true the drakul are some sort of forces of nature?" A little frown creased her brow beneath the folds of the hijab. "The reports I read weren't really very clear."

Caleb folded his arms over his chest, looking mutinous. "You're informed," John said, before Caleb could tell her to mind her own damn business. After being poked and prodded by RD, Caleb probably wasn't thrilled with any SPECTR agent asking a lot of questions.

"I read all the reports I could," she replied. "Some of it's classified, of course, and even what I did see was heavily redacted."

The hell? John would have thought any agent assigned to them would be given access to everything possible, for their own security.

Of course, he would also have assumed Barillo would want an experienced exorcist to keep an eye on them. Not a newly minted agent with the Academy shine still on her. Had Zahira somehow ended up on someone's shit list, or was she just that damned good?

"So tell us a little about Agent Zahira Noorzai," he said.

"Oh. Well." Her expression shifted from enthusiastic to uncertain.

"What do you want to know?"

"Where are you from?" He made a guess based on her accent. "Maryland?"

The relief in her laugh made him think she fielded a few too many stupid questions thanks to her hijab and skin color. "Just outside of Baltimore, actually. My parents immigrated as children in the 70s and met over here. Neither of them has any paranormal ability, but they're very proud of me."

"That's great," John said, and meant it. His own parents first sent him to a center intended to "cure" him, then surrendered custody to the state once his suicide attempt shut the place down. "Caleb and I are the only ones in our families, too."

"But you weren't registered until the drakul possessed you, correct?" she asked. Right back to Caleb.

"No," he said shortly. "And since you're probably going to ask, yes, my brother and sister-in-law were in the Fist of God, and no, I don't want to fucking talk about it."

Her face fell. "Oh. I'm sorry. I've been rude, asking so many questions."

John glanced in the rearview mirror again, just long enough to catch Caleb's wince. "No, it's...shit. I'm sorry. I didn't mean to snap at you. I didn't sleep well, and I'm kind of out of sorts."

"It's okay, Zahira," John added. "There are things you need to know if you're going to be working with us any length of time. Just try to spread the questions out a little, okay?"

The ME waited for them at the morgue. "Agent Starkweather," she greeted him. "Good to see you again."

"Dr. Sherman." They shook hands. "This is Agent Noorzai and Mr. Jansen."

If she found anything strange about Caleb's attire, she didn't show it. "This way."

"I'm afraid we haven't really been briefed on the case," John said as they followed her into the autopsy room itself. Although the tile walls and floor were made for ease of cleaning, the pervasive stench of death still underlay the sting of disinfectant.

The last time he'd stood in this room, it had been to view the remains of one Ben Jansen, suspected of being mauled to death by a lycanthrope. John had confirmed the nature of the killer, but the case stalled and went nowhere.

Until a nameless drakul jumped into Ben's corpse and walked off from the funeral home on the hunt for his murderer. And Tiffany Ward, Vigilant mole inside SPECTR, quietly deleted the incident so it never came across John's desk. Leading to Caleb doing a little amateur demon hunting in order to give his brother rest, only to find himself possessed by the drakul in turn.

Weird, how John hadn't realized at the time that he was standing at the beginning of a chain of events which would change his life forever.

A lone body lay zipped in a bag on a stainless steel gurney. "The deceased is a Mr. Gerald Keywood, aged 79," Dr. Sherman said as she pulled on latex gloves. "Mr. Keywood suffered from Alzheimer's. Last Thursday, he wandered away from the nursing facility where he resided. A groundskeeper discovered his body Friday morning in a cemetery on Meeting Street."

"Cause of death?" John asked.

"At first we assumed natural causes," she replied. "His previous conditions exacerbated by dehydration due to the heat. But when we opened him up Monday morning, we found…well. It wasn't so much what we found as what we didn't."

She unzipped the bag with a flourish. Caleb immediately took a step forward, nostrils flaring and pupils dilating. "Demon," he said, a little of Gray's bass rumble mingled in the word.

"You can smell it?" Zahira asked. Then she winced. "Sorry."

"This comes under the heading of something you need to know," John replied. "Short answer, yes."

Dr. Sherman looked interested, but evidently knew enough not to ask. Instead she peeled back the body bag, revealing the remains of the elderly man. His chest had been left open after the autopsy, and she gestured to the cavity. "Notice anything odd?"

John glanced at Zahira to see how she was holding up. A lot of new agents had trouble with their first body. And maybe she had gone a little pale, but she gamely leaned over to look. "You removed his heart?"

"Nope." Sherman folded her arms over her chest. "He didn't have one to start with."

"So if this guy was missing his heart, how could anyone have thought he died from natural causes?" Caleb asked. He wiped his mouth with the back of his hand. The scent of the demon who did this must have been strong, if it had Gray drooling.

"Because there was no outside indicator of violence." Dr. Sherman stripped off her gloves and picked up a folder. "Here are the preliminary photographs. No bruising, no cuts, and certainly no gaping hole where someone might have removed a major internal organ. And yet, when we cut him open, it was gone."

John took the photos and examined them. As Dr. Sherman had said, there wasn't much to see. Just an old man, slack in death.

"What about the arteries and veins?" Zahira asked. "Did they look hacked apart, or...?"

"Cleanly severed." Pulling on a fresh set of gloves, Dr. Sherman held up the end of the aorta for inspection. Caleb turned slightly green and hastily stepped back. "And there's a slight curvature, so it isn't even as though someone took a scalpel to it. More like the heart was removed by a giant hole punch."

Damn. This was getting weird fast. "Thank you, Dr. Sherman. We'll be in touch if we have any more questions."

Caleb led the way out. "You okay?" John asked, once they reached the street.

The full force of the July sun beat down on the pavement, raising waves of heat and drenching John in sweat in seconds. The air reeked of hot asphalt and car exhaust, mingled with dung from the many horse- or mule-drawn tourist trolleys.

"I'm fine," Caleb said. Despite wearing a hundred pounds of black leather, no sweat touched his forehead or stuck his long hair to his face. "You'd think with all the blood and gore I've seen over the last few months, I'd be pretty used to it by now."

"Death isn't something anyone really gets used to," John replied. He wanted to touch Caleb, but they were on the clock, so he just said, "So, is anyone else up for lunch?"

CHAPTER 4

THEY ATE LUNCH at a local pizza joint that catered to the hippie crowd, meaning Caleb didn't have to worry about whether or not they offered anything vegetarian besides salad. Charleston tended to favor seafood and BBQ aficionados, making a check of the menu mandatory before they went out to eat.

Plus it gave Zahira a chance to work around whatever dietary restrictions she had without embarrassing her by making a big deal out of it.

"Thoughts?" John asked once their food arrived.

"Bismillah," Zahira murmured over her Philly cheesesteak. Picking up the sandwich, she said, "It isn't a therianthrope. Or a wendigo. Or an incubus—they don't remove organs from their victims."

"It smelled like burning feathers," Caleb said, before she could run down the list of every demon known to SPECTR.

"Huh." John took a big bite out of his pizza slice and chewed thoughtfully. "So we have an NHE which removes hearts without leaving a trace, and possibly has some sort of avian connection. It ought to be enough to give us some kind of lead."

"So nothing you've heard of before?" Caleb asked. "I figured you knew all the creepy crawlies, Starkweather."

"Hey, I thought drakul were nothing but a myth," John said easily. "NHEs take on a lot of different shapes."

"Yeah." Caleb nibbled at his tofu sub. "But from what Tiffany said, the shape they take is determined by the first asshole who summons them in uncontrolled circumstances."

He glanced at Zahira to see her reaction to that particular bombshell. She'd put down her cheesesteak and taken out her phone. Her eyes had gone wide, and she looked from Caleb to John and back.

"Guess it hasn't reached the Academy curriculum yet," Caleb said.

John sighed. "We'll fill you in later," he told Zahira. "And it isn't relevant at the moment. Whatever this thing is, we need to catch it before it can kill again. So first stop is the cemetery. If there's any trace of scent left, Gray will be able to track it."

"After so many days, there's not much of a chance," Caleb pointed out.

"No." John finished off his pizza slice. "But we have to make sure."

"Just a second." Zahira tapped on her phone, then looked at them again. "Have you ever heard of a raven mocker?"

"Nope," Caleb said, but of course John was nodding his head.

"It sounds familiar. Can you give us the run down?"

She flushed slightly. "Not the official listing—I don't have access to the database yet," she said apologetically, as though it were her fault HR had fallen asleep on the job. "But from what I can pull off the internet, they're mainly mentioned in Cherokee legend. According to mythology, they go out at night and find sick or old people, and steal their hearts without leaving behind a mark. Once the heart was taken, they'd cook it, eat it, and gain however much life the person had left to them."

"Why not go after kids?" Caleb asked. "More life to get, right?"

"To stay under the radar," John suggested. "Who is going to notice if an old person dies suddenly?"

Shit. "Like Keywood. If he died in bed, no one would have thought about it twice. No autopsy."

Zahira had reached for her sandwich, but put it down again. "If so, Mr. Keywood might not be the first victim."

"Fuck," Caleb sat back, his appetite gone. "Let's get to the site and see if we can find anything to help us find the guy doing this before he kills someone else."

Caleb recognized the church where the body had been found easily enough, since he'd climbed the stucco walls and sat on top of the spire twice. He'd never really paid much attention to the church at ground level, though. The sign outside claimed two signers of the Constitution were interred in the graveyard and mentioned the clock tower was the oldest in North America. The last bit of info gave him a twinge of guilt. Hopefully the couple of claw marks Gray left in the stucco hadn't damaged anything too badly.

The cemetery was tucked into a small space beside the church. Tourists wandered the narrow paths between graves, talking excitedly and taking selfies. Due to the lack of space, the burials were really packed in, and it was hard to navigate without stepping on a grave. Some of the markers were simple slabs, their surfaces crowded with text extolling the accomplishments of those interred beneath. Others had far more elaborate headstones, and a few seemed to be aboveground vaults, pitted from rain and blackened by lichen.

The ancient oaks and magnolias kept the cemetery shaded from the summer sun. Although the heat didn't bother Caleb—one perk to sharing his body with Gray—Zahira and John both let out sighs of relief.

"The victim was found over here." John led the way to one corner of the cemetery. Low iron fences separated the family plots here from one another. Apparently even dead people couldn't stand their neighbors.

As they passed one of the above ground vaults, Gray stirred. A memory rose, colorless and almost without emotion. Dead eyes opening, the rip of the shroud, and the crack of marble falling to one side. Night and darkness, eyes altering to see clearly, a high wall of brick topped by iron. The faint scent of a demon, stirring hunger and need.

Caleb blinked rapidly, trying to focus on the here-and-now. *That wasn't in Charleston though, right?*

"No. Somewhere else." Gray was fully paying attention now, though, taking in the sights along with Caleb. *"I have walked in many graveyards over time. I always wondered why mortals went to such lengths for the dead. Why the monuments and markers, the special places set aside for no other purpose?"*

I guess so people have something to visit when they get lonely for the ones they've lost.

Gray mulled the thought over. *"Would you wish to visit your brother's remains?"*

I don't know. Not that it matters. After Gray took off wearing Ben like a cheap suit, the body went from corpse to evidence. SPECTR hauled Ben's remains away somewhere, probably to RD since Forsyth had a hard on for learning everything about drakul. No doubt there had been another autopsy, and samples taken in an attempt to figure out more about Gray.

Afterward…ghoul chow, probably, since Forsyth had a small army to keep fed. Waste not, want not.

God. Whatever he'd gotten mixed up in, Ben had deserved better. In trying to bring his brother peace, Caleb only managed to make everything even worse.

"I am sorry."

Not your fault. Gray didn't choose what body he grabbed, just found himself in the nearest available one. Of everyone involved in the cluster fuck last spring, Gray was probably the only person who could be counted wholly innocent.

"Here's where the groundskeeper found Mr. Keywood's body," John said. Caleb blinked and tried to focus on the real world in front of him, not the conversation in his head. They stood in front of a small group of aboveground vaults, each one more elaborately carved than the next, as though the families had tried to outdo one another. "According to the police report, he was found Friday morning, stretched out on top of the vault on the end here. His clothing was all in place, and given his circumstances he didn't carry a wallet. Identification was made almost immediately after discovery, since he'd been reported missing from the nursing home a few hours before."

Zahira nodded along to John's explanation. "I don't see any spirit wards. Do we know why no ghouls interfered with the corpse?"

"There haven't been any interments here for decades, at least. Possibly as long as a century." John gestured at the weatherworn monuments around them. "This isn't a normal ghoul hunting ground."

"Plus we've put a pretty good dent in the local ghoul population," Caleb added. With so many old basements and abandoned buildings, Charleston offered plenty of places for ghouls to hide. A ghoul could take an arm off with its massive teeth, but they were scavengers, not predators. Perfect snacks for something like Gray.

"Of course," Zahira said. "I should have realized. So now what?"

"Now I play bloodhound," Caleb said.

He swung over the low iron fence and landed on the vault. There came a sharp exclamation from one of the tourists, probably because a guy with flowing black hair, dressed in black leather in 98-degree heat looked a little suspicious jumping around on graves. The tourists probably figured he was some bad goth stereotype about to summon up a demon right in front of them.

"Federal investigation," John said. "Please stay back."

"May I watch?" Zahira asked.

Caleb glanced at her. "Sure. There's really nothing exciting to see, though."

Still, he felt a little awkward with her staring at him. He closed his eyes and took a deep breath. Damp earth, mingled with the heavy perfume of flowers. Hot asphalt from the street outside, human sweat, and car exhaust.

And nothing more. Damn it.

Caleb leaned down until his nose brushed the marble vault. He breathed in stone and lichen, and beyond that...nothing. Not even a trace of the body inside, long gone to dust.

"Crap." He sat back on his haunches. "I'm not picking up anything."

"It was a long shot anyway," John said. "Come back over the fence."

A small crowd had gathered, staring from a short distance away, some of them snapping pictures with their phones. Caleb resisted the urge to give them the finger.

No one said anything until they were back in the car, the AC blasting. "So what does this mean?" Zahira asked.

"It means we can't do this the easy way," Caleb said. "Big surprise there."

John maneuvered the sedan into traffic. "It would have been convenient if enough of a trail remained to track the raven mocker back to its home base. As it is, we don't have much to go on." He glanced at Zahira. "So what would you do next, Agent Noorzai?"

"Christ, John, this isn't a pop quiz," Caleb interjected.

"It's all right." Zahira straightened in her seat, as if she stood in front of a classroom. "If we didn't find anything at the end of Mr. Keywood's journey, perhaps we might find something at the beginning?"

Caleb caught John's grin in the rearview mirror. "And why would you say that, agent?"

"Because the nursing home he wandered away from is on James Island. I studied the map. An old man suffering from Alzheimer's couldn't have walked this far on his own. Even if he were still in peak physical condition, he would have had to cross the river on either the James Island Expressway or the interstate. Someone would likely have reported seeing him on either one."

"Well damn," Caleb said. Now that she pointed it out, it seemed obvious.

"Now you know why we're the agents and you're the contractor," John said, shooting him a wink in the mirror.

"Yeah, yeah. Good thing you're driving, Starkweather, because neither of us would be able to see around your swelled head to steer the car."

The next morning, they made their way to James Island shortly after the rush hour traffic subsided. From the outside, the Clear Sailing nursing home almost looked like an upscale office block. The chipper sign out front bore the logo of a sailboat heading into a sunset. Caleb wasn't sure if he found the image morbid or not, given it must be a constant reminder to the residents they drew close to the nightfall of death.

John had called ahead, and a perky blonde woman met them at the door. Everything about her screamed "marketing" to Caleb, from her perfect coif to the cosmetics that made her skin look as free of pores as a plastic doll's. Her blue eyes skipped over Caleb and Zahira, and zoned straight in on John.

"Agent Starkweather, such a pleasure to meet you," she purred as she shook his hand. Caleb barely restrained a roll of the eyes. No way was anyone involved with the nursing home *pleased* by a SPECTR investigation. "I'm Ilona Vickers."

John, of course, exuded nothing but charm. "Thank you for meeting with us, Ms. Vickers. I'm sure this won't take long."

She fluttered her eyelashes. "Oh, please, call me Ilona."

A wave of dislike caught Caleb off guard. *"Why is this mortal still holding John's hand?"*

Because she thinks she's going to blind him with her charm, and he'll be too busy looking at her to look into Keywood's death.

Gray rose sharply, his attention focused. *"This mortal believes he will have sexual relations with her?"*

Shit! No. Nothing like that. Christ, of all the things he'd expected, a jealous Gray wasn't one of them. *She's just trying to get him to think with his dick, not actually use it. You know John—it wouldn't work even if she was the right gender.*

"The right gender?"

A guy.

"I do not see what that has to do with anything."

They called Gray "he" for convenience, but etheric entities didn't have genders. It was one of the things Gray still didn't really get. *I'll explain later, okay? Let John handle this.*

Gray didn't like it, but he subsided. Caleb gestured to Zahira with his head as Ilona led them into the facility. Frowning, she hung back with him.

"Now that John has her attention," he murmured, "you talk to the staff, and I'll talk to the residents."

Zahira grinned. "Got it."

They stayed with Ilona past the check-in desk, where a receptionist in scrubs sat talking on the phone. Beyond lay a large room, which Caleb figured must be the facility's common area. The walls were painted a cheerful yellow, dotted with images of sharks, turtles, and other sea creatures. The choice of decor struck Caleb as oddly childish, more like something you'd find in a day care than a place meant for adults. Couches stood along the walls, with comfortable chairs scattered here and there. A number of seniors sat at small tables, playing cards or chess, or reliving the good old days over cups of coffee. The air smelled of disinfectant and vinegar, baby powder and chemical-laced sweat, with a trace of urine from some of the incontinent residents.

Caleb and Zahira lingered, pretending to study one of the plants adding a splash of greenery to the place. John and Ilona kept walking, no doubt to her office. Caleb half expected her to notice they were missing, but apparently John had her dazzled. *Barking up the wrong tree, Ms. Marketing.*

"John is not a tree."

No, but sometimes he sprouts wood.

"You are very strange."

"All right," Zahira said. "I'll talk to the nurse over there."

"Good idea." Caleb watched her cross the room briskly to the nurse stationed at one of the tables, obviously tasked with keeping an eye on the residents. As soon as she had the guy distracted with her badge, Caleb turned his attention to the residents themselves.

The old men arguing over cards seemed spry enough. Most weren't so animated, though. A group sat around a large television, staring at it as if mesmerized. One or two of those in the chairs read books or newspapers, but others only stared blankly into nothing, their minds gone into dementia or despair. The decrepit guy in the wheelchair seemed as lively as the potted plant an attendant had parked him beside.

Fuck. Well, if these people could take care of themselves, they wouldn't be in a home, right? What had Caleb expected?

Not this. This odd punch to the gut at the sight of lined faces and gray hair, the smells of decay and old age. Last year, it wouldn't have bothered him, not like this. Maybe because last year he knew, if he lived long enough, he'd end up this way.

Now he didn't know if he would. Gray healed everything, and there was a good chance that included the damage wrought by time. The collagen fibers in his skin would keep repairing themselves, and the cartilage in his knees would never wear away, and the pigment cells in his hair follicles would never die off.

John's would, though. Fifty years from now, he'd be old and wrinkled. And Caleb would still look twenty-six.

Unease. Gray didn't like the thought any more than he did. *"John will die."*

Some day. And maybe he'd have to stand there and watch it happen.

Or maybe some demon would eat John's head off next week, or Caleb would end up in the belly of a monster himself. There was no point in worrying about something that probably wouldn't even come to pass, let alone fifty years from now. Certainly not when he had work to do this minute.

Shaking himself, he stepped further into the room. Who to talk to? The more obviously catatonic patients were out, but maybe the guys arguing over their card game?

"Excuse me," he said. "I need to ask some—"

"What the fuck are you supposed to be?" one of the geezers snapped. "This ain't Halloween."

"Uh, no," Caleb said, startled. "I'm with—"

"Get a damned haircut," another added. "And some regular clothes. Freak."

Caleb bit down on a response that would have probably gotten him thrown out of the place. "Look, I'm here investigating what happened to Gerald Keywood. Did any of you see anything weird?"

"Yeah, I saw something weird." The third guy leaned back. "Standing right here in front of me."

"Good one, Frank," the first said. "Kids these days with their hair and their clothes. In our day—"

"You were as much of a loser as you are now," said an old woman from Caleb's side. She hooked a bony hand through his elbow. "You don't pay these assholes any mind, you hear me?"

"Yes ma'am," he said automatically.

She tugged him away from the card players. Although her shoulders stooped from osteoporosis and her hair had thinned to show the brown scalp beneath, her eyes were sharp and lively. "You can call me Miss Amy. Let's sit on the couch. I can't get around the way I used to."

Uncertain what else to do, he joined her on the couch. Miss Amy patted his forearm. "You remind me of my grandson. He's the only one of my worthless family who comes to visit me. Every week, except when he's on tour. He's in a band, you know. I tried to get them in here for the musical entertainment last month, but the stick in the muds who run this place said no. At least I can watch his videos on YouTube."

"Great," Caleb said weakly. Was there some polite way to extricate himself from the couch?

"You here with the suits?" she asked. "About Gerald wandering off?"

She might be old, but her hearing was apparently still just fine. "Yeah. I don't suppose you noticed anything strange the night he wandered off?"

"Besides him wandering off in the first place?" She snorted. "Listen, nobody who works here is going to give it to you straight. Too busy covering their own asses. But the truth is, they lock this place down tight at night."

Caleb arched a brow. "You sound like you know firsthand."

She laughed and slapped him on the arm. "Oh honey, you don't know the half of it. Tried to sneak out for some smokes a few times, and Lord, you'd have thought I'd robbed a bank, the way they carried on."

"But someone might have left a door unlocked by accident," Caleb suggested.

"True, true." She shook her head. "But Gerald's just the latest. Something weird has been going on here for the last month, easy."

Caleb straightened. Had he actually lucked out? "What do you mean?"

"Ernest Labenski, Ethan Ricks, and Doris Winstone. All of them passed on without a visit from Dr. McStubbins."

"Dr…McStubbins?" No way that could be some poor bastard's real name, could it?

"'Cause he's got a stubby tail."

Apparently Miss Amy wasn't quite as sharp as he'd thought. "A tail."

She gave him an exasperated look. "Dr. McStubbins is the therapy cat."

So much for lucking out. "How…interesting."

"Don't you look at me like I'm crazy, boy." She glared at him. "That cat knows who's going to die. Curls up with them in bed so they don't have to pass alone. Up until last month, he had a perfect prediction rate. Even when the doctors thought somebody was on their way out, if Dr. McStubbins didn't get in bed with them, they'd end up living. But this month, three people died without him. Which means they weren't supposed to die."

Could it be true?

"I am not acquainted with the precognitive abilities of felines."

"Huh," he said aloud. "Miss Amy, I think you might be on to something here."

CHAPTER 5

"A CAT," **JOHN** said flatly. "Named Dr. McStubbins."

When Caleb said he had a list of potential victims, John thought they might actually have been getting somewhere. He'd called in the names on the way back to HQ, and copies of the death certificates already waited in his email by the time they got back. Zahira still didn't have a desk assignment. Since there wasn't much space in John and Caleb's office, they'd decided to compare notes in one of the spare conference rooms.

Unfortunately, Caleb's so-called lead looked more and more like the ramblings of a crazy woman.

Caleb shrugged. "Well, yeah. But he's got a great track record."

John resisted the urge to press his fingertips into his eyes. The coffee pot in the corner gurgled happily, emitting one last puff of steam before falling silent. More to distract himself than anything, John filled three cups and passed them out. Zahira snagged the sugar and fake creamer, which caused Caleb to make a face. "That stuff is awful. Hell, I couldn't stand it before Gray turned every sense up to eleven."

"Is it true," she began, then caught herself. "Sorry."

John sat back down. "Caleb, why didn't you tell me about the cat in the first place?"

He shrugged awkwardly, black leather coat creaking with the movement. "I didn't want you to think I'd lost it."

"Too late."

Caleb flipped him off. "Look, it's the only lead we've got right now, isn't it?"

Unfortunately, Caleb was right. Ms. Vickers hadn't said a word not already pre-approved by a team of lawyers ready to contest the idea Clear Sailing was in any way responsible for Keywood's death. The staff were similarly close-mouthed with Zahira, no doubt fearing for their jobs if they let anything slip.

Still. "You realize I can't request the bodies be exhumed on the evidence of a cat."

"I know," Caleb said testily. "I'm not asking you to. Let's just look at when the possible victims died, see if we can pull out a pattern."

John laid out the printouts of the death certificates. "Fine. It looks like all three died of natural causes, between…huh. Between eight and nine o'clock in the evening."

"It might be a coincidence," Zahira pointed out. She frowned at the certificates, then turned to the calendar hanging on the wall. "Wait. They died on consecutive Thursdays."

John's heart quickened. "Three deaths in three weeks, between eight and nine, on Thursdays."

"And Keywood 'wandered away' on a Thursday," Caleb added. "Today is Wednesday. Someone else is going to die tomorrow night."

"The raven mocker might be a staff member who works that shift," Zahira said.

"Most staff would work other shifts as well," John said. "But it could be a regular visitor."

"Oh shit." Caleb sat up straight, the front legs of his chair thumping down on the carpet. "The old lady said her grandson came by every week. You don't think…?"

"Let's hope not." John stood up. "All right. Zahira, we need a warrant for information on the vics—where in the facility they died, were they seen by the same doctors, anything to link them together. Include Keywood in your search. Caleb, call the home and see if you can find out when Miss Amy's grandson comes by for visits. I'll give Barillo an update and find out how long it's going to take for Zahira to get her own desk."

"Got it." Caleb leaned back in the chair again and gave John a smirk. "I guess you'll know better than to ever doubt the power of Dr. McStubbins again."

"What is it, Starkweather?" Barillo asked. "Couldn't you just email your report like everyone else?"

John took a deep breath and reminded himself yet again that he shouldn't compare his new boss to his old one. Kaniyar had been…well, a lot of things. Hard, scary, and more than a little ruthless. But he'd known she'd always had his back.

Barillo he was less sure about. Maybe they just hadn't settled into a working relationship. Or maybe the fault was on John's part. Forsyth's monumental betrayal made him slower to trust, and Barillo might have picked up on it and responded in his own way.

"Actually, sir, I came to ask about Agent Noorzai," he said.

Barillo frowned. "Is there a problem?"

"No." The last thing he wanted to do was get Zahira on Barillo's shit list. He stepped inside and shut the office door behind him. Barillo arched a brow, but didn't say anything.

"I just had a question about her assignment to our team," John said. And yeah, he worded it carefully, because damned if he would imply Caleb was someone—something—to be watched as opposed to a full partner.

"A question," Barillo repeated.

"More than one, actually."

The district chief leaned back in his chair and folded his hands behind his head. "Let's hear it."

"Honestly, sir, I'm a little surprised you assigned someone fresh out of the Academy to our team. Not to suggest Agent Noorzai isn't perfectly capable, but standard procedure is to put new agents on the ghoul squad, or some other less hazardous duty, until they gain experience."

"You and Mr. Jansen have taken out more than your share of ghouls."

Which was true in its way—if Gray caught a whiff of ghoul coming from an abandoned building or graveyard, he'd track them immediately and eat any unable to be exorcised. A ghoul pack might take down a human exorcist, but they were no match for Gray.

But Barillo was splitting hairs and he damned well knew it. Trying to ignore the heat in his chest, John said, "Yes, sir, but that isn't our primary objective. Right now we're chasing a raven mocker. Next week it might be a wendigo, or an incubus. An inexperienced agent in a situation like this is dangerous, frankly. To her and to us."

"I see. So you're questioning why Agent Noorzai was assigned to you?" Barillo asked.

"In part." John met Barillo's gaze challengingly. "There's also the fact no one seems to have made any plans for her actually being here. She doesn't have a desk assignment, hasn't been cleared to know everything she needs to if she's to be working alongside Caleb and Gray, and you didn't even mention she'd be joining us until she arrived."

"Your point?"

"My point is the situation stinks," John snapped, his anger finally bleeding through. "After the bullshit Forsyth pulled, I have to question the motive behind this. Who ordered her here, and why? Is she really a wide-eyed newbie, or has someone above either of our pay grades sent her to keep an eye on Gray?"

Barillo dropped his arms and leaned forward. "Let's get one thing straight, Agent Starkweather. You deserted SPECTR and joined forces with a paramilitary organization. You and everyone in the Vigilant are damned lucky to have escaped being tried en masse as terrorists. Even worse, when you went off the reservation you took an extremely dangerous NHE along for the ride."

The fuck? "With all due respect," John bit out, "Forsyth ordered Caleb killed and kidnapped me, with the intention of holding me as bait to capture Gray."

"None of which is outside SPECTR's mission."

"And the fucking demon army? Was that part of our mission?"

"Do not raise your voice to me, Starkweather." Barillo slammed both palms down on the desk. "I read the reports. Agent McNamara acted within his authority to put down an NHE who, given the knowledge available, could not be exorcised. Your relationship with the faust should never have been tolerated in the first place. Putting you under arrest in order to keep the NHE from causing more destruction was perfectly lawful." He took a deep breath, nostrils flaring. "I won't deny Assistant Director Forsyth made mistakes."

"A demon army is a bit more serious than a mistake, sir," John grated. "Forsyth put NHEs into soldiers, then locked them away when their forty days ran out. He tortured them, humans and NHEs both."

"His sins don't excuse yours." Barillo leaned back again, full lips pressed into a tight line. "As far as a lot of people are concerned, you're just as much of a rogue element as he ever was. Lucky for you, Director Kaniyar disagrees with their assessment. But you don't get to be paranoid the rest of us are out to get you, when as far as we know, you're out to get us."

It hit like a punch to the gut. "That's completely unfair."

"Is it?" Barillo snorted. "Taking off with the head of a paramilitary group working against SPECTR? Fucking an NHE? Do you know how many people think the director is giving you a special pass because you're the only goddamn leash we have on that thing?"

No. Oh no. "On Gray?"

"Is there some other NHE you're screwing behind our backs?" Barillo snapped. "You came to my office looking for the truth. Fine. I'll give it to you. The reason you're stuck with a nice shiny new graduate is because no one else would take the fucking job. Oh, a few volunteered, but once they read the full reports, talked to a few agents who were actually there on the ground at Fort Sumter, they withdrew their applications. No one with any brains wants to work alongside a ticking bomb."

"Gray isn't—"

"We don't know what the NHE is or isn't. Empaths can't get a hit off it, even though they could sense Jansen before his forty days ran out. A hell of a lot of people think Caleb Jansen is solid gone, and the thing in our midst is just pretending he's still in there and in control. Just biding its time, until it can slip the leash. Or do something worse."

Sekhmet, Devourer of Evil, give him strength. It was worse than anything John had imagined. "Chief, that isn't true."

"I've got no proof either way." Barillo shrugged. "As for Agent Noorzai, her fascination with the etheric plane has interfered with her common sense. According to her instructors, she thinks we need to be trying to figure out what really separates our world from the etheric, and what NHEs are like in their natural habitat, and all that hippie-dippy crap."

"Agent Noorzai graduated top of her class," John said past the anger threatening to choke him. "She isn't stupid."

"No. But she's naïve enough to have sabotaged her career right out of the gate." Barillo shook his head in disgust. "She could have had any assignment she wanted, and she picked the one guaranteed to keep her stuck in the field the rest of her life. We didn't prepare for her arrival because you're right—she isn't stupid. No one thought she'd actually go through with it until she walked in the door."

John's mouth went cotton-dry. He tried to swallow, but his throat felt sticky. How could this have happened? He'd laid his life on the line to stop Forsyth, and this was the thanks he got?

And Caleb. Goddess, he'd thrown away his last chance at a normal life, refused exorcism. He'd sacrificed everything, and this was how people looked at him, how SPECTR saw him…

"Any more questions, agent?" Barillo asked.

The words penetrated the haze surrounding John. He shook his head and reached for the door. "No. No more questions."

"You've got to be fucking kidding me," Caleb said.

He sat across from John at their small table, dinner going cold between them. He'd known something had gone wrong as soon as John came back from Barillo's office, even though John put on a good face. He'd let it go at work, until they were back home and changed into comfortable shirts and shorts, with beers in their hands.

A part of him wished he hadn't asked. From the unhappy look on John's face, he wished the same thing.

Gray stirred, reacting to their distress. *"I do not understand. The mortals fear me?"*

"Yes," Caleb said aloud. "They're afraid of you, and they think Sean did the right thing by putting a bullet in our head and kidnapping John. They think John's in the wrong for fighting back."

A look of alarm crossed John's face. "Guys—"

"They are our enemies?" And now Gray was rising up, and Caleb's teeth burned and his fingertips itched, and shit, this wasn't really what he'd wanted. *"If they seek to harm us, we will fight them."*

"No," he said, pushing back against Gray, which was a lot like trying to shove a tiger back into its cage. "They don't want to physically hurt us. Yet, anyway."

"Whoa." John held his hands up. "Hold up a minute. Gray, *listen* to me. They weren't on Forsyth's side either, okay? But SPECTR is a government organization, and like it or not, there are rules. Those rules are in place for a reason, and I broke a lot of them."

"Are you sorry for it?" Caleb said. Or tried to say, because at the same minute Gray tried to ask, *"Do you regret this?"* and what came out was a garbled jumble.

John looked more worried than ever. "Calm down, both of you. I'm just trying to explain a different point of view, one you have to understand if we can ever get past this."

"Fuck," Caleb said, and resisted the urge to spit. "You *are* sorry, aren't you? Sorry you escaped from RD. Sorry you didn't play good little Spec while Forsyth tore down the world around us."

"Of course not!" John slammed his palms down on the table. "Damn it, Caleb, don't put words in my mouth."

"You should have—have high-fived Sean after he shot me. Left with him to get a beer," Caleb said savagely. "Then you wouldn't have had to deal with the Vigilant, or us, or any of it."

The color drained from John's face. "That isn't fair, and you know it."

"I thought I did." Caleb shoved his chair away from the table. "We're going for a run."

John rose as well. "I'll go with you."

"You couldn't keep up," Caleb shot back from the doorway. Then he was in the free evening air, the door slamming behind him.

Unfortunately, at this time of year, the sun lingered until almost nine o'clock at night. Combined with the fact it was the height of tourist season, Caleb's initial plan of running and climbing with all of Gray's speed and strength, hoping to burn off some anger, was out. No causing a fucking panic in the street, oh no. Barillo would *love* that.

Fuck Barillo. And fuck John.

Confusion and fear. *"John loves us. This has not...not changed?"*

Caleb jogged down the cobblestone street in front of the condo, before turning onto South Battery. The fierce heat of the day gave way to comparative coolness as the sun slid westward. A fresh breeze off the ocean stirred the palmettos and shepherded gulls and pelicans inland for the night.

The tight knot of anger in Caleb's chest began to loosen as he jogged. If only there were a storm, or full night, so they could really run. Or if they were in the middle of a forest somewhere, with no humans around for miles. No one to gawk at them like the freaks in a sideshow. No one to say Caleb really wasn't even around anymore, and Gray just some kind of puppet master playing them all for fools. No John, to keep making excuses for SPECTR over and over, until Caleb wanted to scream in frustration.

"John wished to come with us, when we freed him. He said he loved me."

For everyone else, the assault on RD had been a cluster fuck of horror and blood. For Gray, it had been the best damn night of his life.

He does love you. And me. Caleb's speed had started to draw some odd looks, so he slowed down.

"Then he cannot wish things occurred differently."

Impeccable logic, drakul style. *It's complicated. But you're right. I was pissed and lashed out, because...shit. Because I'm afraid we've hurt him.*

"I do not understand."

How to explain? *When Forsyth perverted everything SPECTR stood for, it nearly killed John. Seeing the agents at Fort Sumter, ready to lay down their lives to stop Forsyth, gave him back a lot of the faith he'd lost.*

"I remember."

When Kaniyar was handing out promotions left and right, and he got skipped over, he was okay with it. He understood some people would think he'd crossed a line by working with the Vigilant. And maybe...I don't know. Maybe if that was the end of it, things wouldn't be so bad. If you and I weren't there every day, reminding people of what happened. Of what John did. Of what we are.

Caleb's feet slowed. He crossed the street, passing beneath the great oaks lining this section of waterfront, until he reached the low iron rail overlooking a thin strip of marsh grass and the ocean beyond. At one time, cannons had lined the seawall, meant to protect the city if Fort Sumter and Fort Moultrie failed.

"As we should protect John. But if our presence increases the harm to him, then how can we?"

Caleb sighed and wiped his brow, pretending he actually sweated. *I don't know. I shouldn't have gotten mad at him. Shouldn't have said the things I did. He loves us, and...I don't know.*

"You hurt, to think you have brought hurt on him." Regret. "It hurts me as well."

I know. Caleb turned away from the ocean. *Let's go home.*

As they turned their steps back toward the condo and broke into a jog, a strange odor infiltrated the mélange of sweat and seafood. Gray's attention sharpened instantly, and Caleb found himself breathing more deeply, sifting through layers of scent, trying to isolate it.

Old stone and deep earth. Tilled soil warming in the sun, but underneath a whisper of dankness, of limestone caves.

What the hell?

Caleb looked around, but saw nothing out of the ordinary on the street. Cars navigated the brick road, gulls kited overhead, and tourists enjoyed the sunset.

That wasn't a demon, was it? It had lacked the edge of corruption, of something spoiled and rotting, which Caleb had come to associate with demons. Not to mention Gray hadn't started drooling.

"I do not know what it was." So Gray was as confused as him. "It was not mortal, though."

Not good. And weird. Caleb breathed deep, nostrils flared, but the scent had dissipated.

God only knew what it had been, or where it had drifted in from. *"Should we tell John?"* Gray asked.

What are we going to tell him? We smelled something weird, but we don't know what it was, where it came from, or where it went? John had enough to worry about without them piling on more.

Besides, Gray was the biggest, baddest NHE around. If they had scented something of etheric origin—and Caleb was less sure of that by the minute—it had probably caught a whiff of Gray and fled for its life. Anyway, it was gone now.

With a shrug, Caleb jogged back down the Battery, diverting only long enough to snag a large bouquet of roses from a sidewalk vendor. He had some apologizing to do.

CHAPTER 6

JOHN LOOKED UP when Caleb came back through the front door. He'd been sitting on the ugly orange couch Caleb insisted on bringing with him when he moved in, staring at the paintings on the walls.

"I'm sorry," Caleb said as soon as the door shut behind him. He thrust out a big bunch of roses in John's direction. "It's just…I'm frustrated, and angry, but not at you. At SPECTR. And I'm scared we've cost you your career, and I know how important that is to you, and…and I took it out on you. I'm an asshole."

John rose to his feet, but he didn't take the flowers. "It hurt, hearing you say those things. You know I love you. Both of you. What Sean did…"

Seeing Caleb lying there dead on the floor had been the worse moment of John's entire life. Worse even than when he'd tried to kill himself at fifteen, certain he was damned for having paranormal abilities.

"I know." Caleb scuffed at the hardwood floor with the edge of his shoe. "What can I do? What can *we* do? To make things better. Maybe if we quit SPECTR…?"

He trailed off on the unspoken question as to whether it was even a possibility.

"It'll get better." John relented and took the flowers. The heat had wilted them around the edges, but they still smelled sweet. "For both of us. People are still on edge after all the nonsense with Forsyth. They'll see what good work we're doing, and they'll forget the rest. Just give it time."

"It's like sleeping with a damn motivational poster," Caleb said, but he grinned to soften the words. "Come here."

John moved into his embrace. The fall of Caleb's long hair tumbled around them both. After a moment, etheric energy bloomed around them, accompanied by Gray's scent of desert sand kissed by rain and ancient incense. His hair stirred, crackling and shivering in an unfelt wind.

"This is very confusing," Gray said. Although he spoke the words softly, his deep voice vibrated in John's chest and bones. "I preferred when we had a clear enemy, and demons to eat, and no offices or paperwork or foolish mortals to deal with."

In other words, when they'd been on the run. "There are always foolish mortals to deal with. So long as you keep me around, anyway," John teased.

"You are an exception."

John grinned and closed his eyes. Without the visual input to contradict it, his etheric sense insisted a being much larger than Caleb's physical frame cradled him in its arms. "How are you doing?" he asked. "I know you're still getting used to everything. Being in a living body. Putting up with Caleb. I mean, that alone…"

"Caleb says you are an ass."

John laughed. "I bet he does. Seriously, though." He drew back and peered up at Gray.

Gray's eyes were black as oil slicks, but lightning flashed and flickered in their depths. Maybe those eyes should have been a clue as to his true nature from the very beginning. "I am with Caleb, and with you, so I am content," Gray said simply. "I do not care about these other mortals, save that they upset you. And I would protect you from them, but I do not know how."

"No need." John pulled Gray down for a soft kiss. "I know it's rough, but we'll get through this. I promise. I love you."

Gray's forehead rested against his. "And I love you. Caleb loves you as well, so much it frightens him at times."

Then Gray was gone, and Caleb growling angrily. "Fuck off! Damn drakul. You don't have to say every thought that comes into your head out loud."

John snickered. "Ooh, maybe I should try to get him to spill all your deep, dark secrets."

"No fair. You two are not allowed to team up against me." Caleb slid his hands beneath John's t-shirt, fingers splayed across his ribs. "And the only deep, dark secret I have is falling for a guy who wears a suit. What would my friends say?"

"Terrible things. Especially if they knew I wore the tie to bed."

Caleb swatted him on the ass. "Try it and I'll strangle you with the damned thing. Come on. Let's grab our beers, sit on the front balcony, and watch the sunset. Just like three normal guys, two of whom happen to be in the same body."

"Three normal guys," John agreed with a grin. "Grab the beers and I'll meet you out there."

The next evening, they sat in the sedan, parked in the far corner of the nursing home lot. The sun hovered low on the horizon, the air cool enough for John to shut off the engine and open the windows. Caleb watched visitors trail in and out, and hoped he wasn't the one who had to explain to Miss Amy that her grandson was possessed.

"How late are visiting hours?" Zahira asked between sips of an iced mocha.

"Until ten o'clock," John said. "So another two hours."

"But Miss Amy's grandson comes every Thursday at eight," Caleb said. "So he ought to be here any minute."

A battered van rattled into the parking lot. Once the engine sputtered off, the door opened with a loud squeak, and a man who had to be the rock star grandson climbed out. Long dreads, tattoos, and black t-shirt and jeans, paired with scuffed black boots. No wonder Caleb reminded Miss Amy of him.

"Damn it," John said. "He's too close to the building. Move now."

The original plan had been to let the guy get well in the clear before closing in on him. But that obviously wasn't going to happen now. They piled out of the car, John and Zahira moving to flank the guy if possible, while Caleb went straight. His heartbeat quickened, excitement boiling in his blood. As much as he complained about his new life, there was something just a little addictive about the hunt. About being fast and strong; about the visceral thrill of the fight. The sweet ecstasy of feeding.

Okay, maybe it was more than just a little addictive.

Gray rose to just beneath his skin, and his teeth ached. *Soon. Just hold on a minute.*

"Sir!" John's authoritative bark brought the suspect to an abrupt halt. "Federal agents. We have some questions for you."

Dark eyes went wide with fear—then the man bolted back to the van.

John swore and pulled his Glock, but there were other people in the lot. The van roared to life, belched smoke, and took off in a squeal of tires.

"Stop him!" John shouted.

Caleb bolted after the van, drawing on Gray's strength and speed. If the faust reached the street, he'd be gone, too fast for even Gray to catch. Swearing silently, Caleb leapt and ran across a line of parked cars, leaving dented hoods and shrieking alarms in his wake.

The van careened up the aisle, gunning for the entrance. Hitting the last of the cars, Caleb pushed off—

And Gray landed.

Gray sinks his claws deep into the metal roof of the van. These modern conveyances are a curse, letting demons escape from him far too easily.

Perhaps he should begin driving one as well.

"No. Absolutely not."

It matters little at the moment. The wind tears Gray's hair back as the van continues to accelerate. The road is only two lanes, and the driver swerves wildly to avoid other vehicles.

Or perhaps to shake Gray loose. His legs slide across the roof, and he tries to find grip with his boots. Each time he shifts his weight, the van lurches to one side or another, foiling him. One claw rips free, and he snarls at the pain.

They are coming up fast on an intersection, careening into the oncoming lane to avoid the cars waiting at the red light. For a moment, it seems the driver's luck will hold.

Another horn blares, accompanied by the scream of brakes. Something smashes into the van; metal crumples, glass breaks, and Gray is briefly weightless.

He hits the asphalt, bones snapping from the impact. Jagged pain tears through him, and he snarls again as the ends of bones shift and realign. Muscle knits back together, blood absorbed, and he lurches to his feet.

A tractor trailer has struck the van, leaving both inoperable. Ignoring the stares of mortals, Gray strides to the vehicle. Through the broken windshield, he can see the driver struggling with the door, which will no longer open.

Gray doesn't need doors. He thrusts his hand through the glass of the van's window and grabs the driver's collar. A moment later, he has hauled the man out and onto the pavement.

He is expecting resistance—claws and teeth and inhuman strength—but there is none. Nor is there the delicious scent of a demon. Nothing but blood and urine, and radiator fluid leaking onto warm pavement.

"Goddamn it, he's not the faust!"

There comes the squeal of tires. John has arrived along with the other mortal—Zahira, that is his—her?—name.

"Her, for Christ's sake."

Gender is a construct of mortals, who cannot even decide if there are two, or three, or five. Why they place such value on something so changeable, Gray has never understood. He lowers the mortal carefully to the ground as John and Zahira run up, guns drawn.

"This is not the demon," he says.

John doesn't back off, thrusting his gun at the terrified mortal's face. "Why did you run? Are you in league with the raven mocker?"

The mortal's lips part, eyes wide. "I don't know what the hell you're talking about! Please! The drugs aren't mine, I swear it!"

"You've got to be kidding me. He thought we were after him for drugs?"

"If he didn't have anything to do with the raven mocker," Zahira says, "then it might be at the nursing home right this minute."

"Damn it." John stands up. "Gray—go."

Gray races back the way they came, faster than any mortal could hope to travel. Normally he would try to remain out of sight, but there is no time. The raven mocker may already have come and found its next victim. Might already be gone.

He smells it the moment he enters the parking lot: burning feathers and rotten eggs, and the dry, dusty scent of birds. But the trail is faint; it has passed through here, not lingered.

The streetlights buzz to life as he slows, pacing across the lot, nostrils flared. Where is it? Should he go inside?

"We'll cause a panic."

I know this. You behave as though I have not spent five thousand years hunting amidst mortals.

"Says the guy who ended up staked more times than I want to think about."

Gray moves soundlessly, taking advantage of their dark clothing to blend into the shadows. The scent grows stronger as they cross the lot, but it does not lead in the direction of the front door. Interesting.

They continue on around the building, the trail becoming clearer. There is another, dingier lot behind the facility. A dumpster lets off the stink of food gone sour in the sun, alongside another container marked for medical waste. The scorched stench of cigarettes hangs in a cloud around the back entrance, making Gray's eyes water and nose run.

A van marked "janitorial services" sits empty near the door. Even over all the other confusion of smells, it reeks of burning feathers and rotting eggs.

Delicious.

Gray pauses in the shadows, watching. The demon isn't in the van, and there are no humans about.

"If he's a janitor, he'll be…shit. Inside. We've got to go in. Let me drive so we don't terrify some poor old lady into a heart attack."

Before, Gray would simply have waited, patient as a cat outside of a burrow, until the demon emerged. Then it would be his. The lives of mortals it might have devoured in the meantime were of no concern to him.

But they are of great concern to Caleb and John. So he falls back, and lets Caleb take over.

Caleb tried the back door, and found it locked, just as Miss Amy had said. Had Keywood somehow gotten out on his own, or had the raven mocker found him wandering the halls and taken him straight to the van?

A harsh twist and a little superhuman strength took care of that, and he slipped inside. The demon's scent saturated the small back room. It looked like a storage area, crammed with spare furniture, a hand truck, and a few outdated computers. Two doors opened off the room, one of them ajar.

Caleb followed the trail through the open door. His fingertips itched, and his teeth burned.

"It is near."

I know; I know. Caleb walked faster. *Just hold on!*

"Hey!" a sharp voice said. "What are you doing here?"

A nurse approached, scrubs straining across his broad shoulders. Caleb didn't have a badge like a real agent, but his SPECTR contractor's ID looked impressive, so he flashed it at the nurse. "SPECTR business. Where's the janitor?"

The nurse frowned. "What? No one said SPECTR was coming back."

"The janitor?" Caleb repeated urgently.

"I need to talk to my supervisor," the nurse said, backing away.

Caleb grabbed the nurse by the front of his scrubs and shoved him into the wall. "I said, where is the fucking janitor?" he demanded, Gray's bass rumble adding menace to the words.

All the color drained from the nurse's face. "S-second floor hall, last I saw him! In the hospice ward! St-stairs are over there."

"Thanks." Caleb let go. The man scrambled away, no doubt to call security, but Caleb didn't care. *If the raven mocker is in the hospice ward, he's probably found another victim already.*

"Then let us stop him."

Caleb ran up the stairs, taking them two at a time. Another nurse yelped when he emerged onto the second floor, but he ignored her. The hall reeked of the sulfur stench of eggs left in the sun, mingled with disinfectant and death. He started in one direction, then reversed as the trail thinned. The raven mocker must be here somewhere…

There.

The man stood inside one of the dimly lit rooms, at the bedside of an old woman who lay asleep or comatose, Caleb didn't know. The man's right sleeve was rolled up to the elbow, and he laid his bare hand on the woman's chest—

No. *Through* her chest. Reaching for her heart.

Gray roared.

The demon leaps back, terror shining in eyes gone black and bright as a bird's. But it is trapped in this room, with Gray guarding the only exit.

Feathers sprout, jutting through skin, and cloth rips as the body beneath changes. The stink of burning fills the air, etheric fire dancing along clumsy wings.

With a hoarse cry, like the croak of a raven, it hurls itself at the window.

No!

Gray leaps over the bed after the raven mocker as it tries to escape in a shower of broken glass. His claws sink into its legs, and it shrieks in pain. If he can hold it for just a moment longer, perhaps he can pull it back inside—

It unfurls its wings and beats at the air. Sparks fly free from the feathers, scorching Gray's skin. Wind howls through the broken window, and a moment later they're through, Gray dangling from its legs as it fights to get aloft. It twists wildly—then folds up one wing and strikes him hard in one side of the head.

He struggles to hang on, but it keeps pummeling him. The cartilage of his nose shatters, and an eye socket gives way. He tries to bite its wing, but it is too fast for him.

They drop quickly without the raven mocker's wing beats to keep them aloft. Gray hits the pavement first, one ankle snapping from the impact. Still, it isn't enough to convince him to let go. If he can only pull it down close enough, perhaps he can find an artery—

It strikes him with both wings, and claws hidden amidst the feathers come out. They rake his face, his throat, pain blazing in their wake. His grip loosens, and a moment later the raven mocker wrenches free in a shower of blood.

Gray rolls to his feel as it rockets aloft. Caleb surges almost to the surface, unleashing a burst of telekinesis aimed at the ground, propelling them upward. Their leap almost takes them high enough to grab onto the raven mocker's feet.

It twists in the air, and a clawed foot tangled in the remains of a boot catches him squarely on the chin.

His head snaps back, jaw breaking from the impact. Then they are falling, body smashing to the pavement directly in front of an oncoming car.

"Shit!" John stood on the brakes. The tires smoked and screamed, and the seatbelt went tight across his chest.

The front bumper came to a halt inches from Gray's sprawled form. John unsnapped the seatbelt and flung open the door.

"I'll call an ambulance," Zahira said as she bailed out after him.

"No, don't." John held up a hand to stop her even as he knelt beside Gray. "Are you all right?"

Gray rolled onto his stomach, then pushed himself up with his hands. He looked like hell: face bloody, jaw hanging at an odd angle, a spectacular bruise spreading over his forehead.

"What do you mean?" Zahira's voice went up an octave. "He's not all right! He needs help!"

Gray gave his head a quick shake. His jaw snapped back into place with a disturbing crunch. A moment later, he spit out the broken remnants of a fang. As the bruises faded before John's eyes, he lurched to his feet.

"I am fine," Gray said. He paused, lips parted slightly, and a new fang slid into place, replacing the broken one. "But the demon escaped."

Zahira stared at him. Gray ignored her, pacing the lot as though he thought the raven mocker might helpfully come swooping back into view.

"Gray has an incredible ability to heal, even for an NHE," John said carefully. Sometimes he forgot just how terrifying Gray could seem to someone who didn't really know him. "Look, I know Gray is kind of..."

"Amazing," Zahira breathed.

John blinked. "That...wasn't the reaction I was expecting."

"Why not?" Zahira tore her gaze away from Gray to give John a puzzled glance. "*Look* at him! You're an exorcist—can't you feel the energy?"

"Of course I can. An exorcist three counties over could sense it." Stupidly, he felt as if Zahira was sharing something only meant for him.

She took a deep breath. "And he smells wonderful."

"We aren't here to discuss Gray," John said shortly. "We need to secure the scene. Caleb!"

The storm surge of etheric energy receded, Gray folding up inside Caleb's slender body like an origami tiger. "Yeah?" Caleb asked.

"Are there any new victims?"

"No." He shook his head, long hair whispering over leather. "We interrupted him before he ate his next old lady."

At least there was that. "He won't dare come back here," John said. "Damn it. Maybe if we can get an ID on him..."

Caleb grinned. "Not a problem. He was a janitor, not a visitor. His van is still parked in the back."

CHAPTER 7

"**HERE WE ARE,**" John said midmorning the next day. They'd pulled up in front of a small house along Meeting Street, not far from the concrete river of I-26. The neighborhood had seen better days; patches of peeling paint showed on most of the houses, and few of the cars in the drives were less than a decade old. Rusted fences surrounded most of the tiny yards. Magnolias towered over the single-story homes, and the pavement was even more cracked and worn than in the historic district. They weren't far from the abandoned house where he'd first met Caleb, along the same stretch of poverty and urban blight that tourists drove through as quickly as possible.

Thanks to the van, IDing and getting an address for the raven mocker was easy enough. Kyle Quigley, 58 years old and a lifelong Charleston resident. John, Caleb, and Zahira paid a visit to Mr. Quigley's apartment in the early hours of the morning. Unsurprisingly, he'd already run for it—drawers pulled out, clothes and personal effects missing. Still, John seized the computer, just in case some lead hid within Quigley's emails or browser history.

"Mr. Quigley's daughter lives here?" Zahira asked. Although they'd had no more than a few hours sleep, snatched between the raid and reconvening at SPECTR at 8:00 am, she looked as bright and awake as ever. John remembered when he could do the same, then immediately felt old.

"Right. She was listed as next of kin in his employment records." John put the sedan in park. "It's possible he might try to hide out with her. Caleb, let me know if you smell so much as a whiff of NHE."

"I will," Caleb said. "And if he isn't here?"

"Then with any luck, she'll know where he might be."

They climbed out of the car. Not even ten o'clock and already the day was sweltering. Humidity stole the creases from John's suit and left the cloth hanging damply against his skin. They'd have afternoon thunderstorms for certain. At least it would make Gray happy.

A woman in her mid-twenties peered out a crack in the door when John knocked. "Evelyn Quigley?"

"Yes," she replied warily.

"Federal agents," he said, showing her his SPECTR badge. "Can we come inside?"

Her eyes widened with fear. "What's this about?"

"We're looking for your father."

"Daddy?" The color drained from her face. "What happened? Is he all right?"

"Can we come inside?" John repeated.

She looked at his badge, then peered at Caleb and Zahira uncertainly. "They don't look like government agents."

Whatever Zahira thought of that assessment, she didn't say, merely pulled out her badge and displayed it as well. "Oh," Evelyn said, although she seemed confused. "Sorry. With the scarf on your head, I thought you were one of them Muslims."

"SPECTR doesn't discriminate on grounds of religion, gender identity, or sexual orientation," John replied, as Evelyn unlatched the chain and swung open the door.

"Oh." She flushed slightly. "Well. Come in."

Inside the house, a lone window AC unit fought a losing battle with the July heat. Knickknacks covered the walls and tables: childlike angels, a framed cross stitch of the Lord's Prayer, half a dozen crosses in various styles, all interspersed with family photos. Evelyn's hair curled and stuck to her freckled skin. She wore a shapeless dress, worn and faded, and was heavily pregnant. "Sit down," she said, gesturing to a couple of old chairs and a couch repaired with duct tape. A calico cat lay on one chair, watching them idly. "Can I get you some iced tea?"

Ordinarily, John wouldn't have made a pregnant woman play hostess. Today, he nodded. "That would be lovely. Thank you so much."

As soon as she disappeared toward the kitchen, John turned to

Caleb. "Anything?"

Caleb nodded. "Yeah, but it's faint. He hasn't been here in a few days at least."

"Damn."

They seated themselves, Zahira and John on the couch, Caleb in a chair. As soon as Caleb sat, the calico cat leapt into his lap and began to rub her head enthusiastically on his chin.

"Patches likes you," Evelyn said when she came back in. She held a tray with four mismatched glasses full of tea on it.

"Does she like everyone?" John asked, accepting one of the glasses.

Something flickered across her face. "No."

"What about your father?"

"He stepped on her tail by accident," she said, lowering herself awkwardly into the remaining chair. "That's what he said, anyway. She used to love him, but the last few times he came over she'd growl and run. Why? What's this about? Is Daddy okay?"

Most animals had an instinctive aversion for NHEs. Or hostile ones, at least, given Patches acted like Caleb had been rubbed in tuna.

John leaned forward and met Evelyn's gaze. "We're investigating a case of possession," he said, as sympathetically as possible. "And I'm afraid your father is our primary suspect."

She put a hand protectively to her swollen belly. "No, it's…it's not possible."

"I'm afraid it is. Has anything changed about him lately? Other than the cat's behavior toward him."

"No." The words were clipped, like someone slamming a door.

John sipped his tea and tried to think what he might say to get her to be more forthcoming. There was an art to asking questions, and he sensed the straightforward approach would end with Ms. Quigley ordering them out of her house.

As he mulled possibilities, Zahira leaned forward with a smile on her face. "May I ask when you're due?"

"Oh. Um, yeah. Another month and he's ready to come out." Evelyn rubbed her belly. "I'm counting the days."

"I'm sure. My best friend was pregnant last summer, and said she thought she'd never be cool again. And her poor ankles!"

Evelyn laughed ruefully. "I haven't worn anything but flip-flops since June."

"So you're having a boy?"

"Yeah." Some of the tension eased out of the woman's face. "We're naming him Kyle, after…" She trailed off.

"After your father," Zahira finished. "He must be very excited."

"H-he is." Evelyn swallowed and looked away. "Real excited. This is his first grandchild, and…" Her voice caught.

Zahira reached across the low table between them and touched her fingers to the back of the other woman's hand. "I'm sure your father wants to be here for you both. We want that, too. But he's gotten into a bit of trouble, and he needs help. We can't help him unless we can find him."

Tears gathered in Evelyn's eyes. "He said it was a miracle."

"What was a miracle, Ms. Quigley?" John asked softly.

"The doctors said he only had six weeks to live. Maybe a little more; maybe less." Evelyn wiped her eyes. "He told them he'd hold on long enough to see his grandbaby. But he kept getting sicker and sicker. I thought…I didn't think he would make it."

"Then suddenly, he recovered," John guessed. Damn it. If not for the people Quigley killed, John would have felt sorry for the man. Looking forward to his first grandchild, only to be told he wouldn't live long enough to see it? That would be a hell of a blow to anyone.

No wonder the raven mocker answered his summons. Quigley was desperate to extend his life, and the raven mocker could help him do it. At the price of the lives of others.

Had it seemed harmless at first? Did Quigley tell himself he wasn't doing anything wrong by only preying on the elderly, who didn't have much time left anyway? Or did he simply seize on the opportunity his job gave him?

Evelyn nodded slowly. "He said God healed him. He even felt good enough to go back to work." Her gaze found John's. "And now you're saying he made a deal with some demon? It wasn't a miracle at all?"

Her eyes begged for him to say she'd gotten it wrong. "I'm afraid so," he replied, and she looked away, biting at one knuckle as if to hold back tears. "I'm very sorry. Right now, though, we need your help to find your father."

"He has an apartment…"

"We checked there, but he seems to have left. Is there anywhere he might go? Anywhere you can think of? An old hangout? A place he likes to go on weekends? Anywhere he could stay for a few days."

"N-no." She wiped at her eyes. "I can't think of anything."

So much for their only lead. John took out one of his cards and passed it to her. "If you think of anything, or if he attempts to contact you, please call me right away. Any hour of the day or night."

"I will." She blinked rapidly. "Wh-what are you going to do to him?"

"If it's possible, we're going to exorcise him," John replied. "How long ago did his miracle recovery occur?"

"A month ago? Maybe a little more?" She bit her lip. "You'd think I'd remember, but so much has been going on, and with the baby…"

"Of course." If Quigley wasn't over his forty-day limit, he had to be frighteningly close. "We'll do everything we can to help your father. You have my word."

The ride back to HQ was subdued. "Hell of a thing," Caleb said as they passed through the gate into the SPECTR lot.

"Yeah," John agreed. This was the worst part of working for SPECTR. Sometimes people's reasons for summoning NHEs seemed so stupid and short-sighted, born out of hubris or greed or plain cruelty. But then there were the cases like this one.

"If we can still exorcise him…will he die?" Caleb asked. "Or did the raven mocker cure him?"

"NHEs aren't capable of that sort of permanent change," John replied automatically.

"No. They are." Caleb tilted his head, as if listening. In the passenger seat, Zahira twisted around to look at him, as if afraid of missing any tidbit. "Gray says if he'd been exorcised, my vision wouldn't have changed back. I'd recommend everyone else stick with Lasik, though."

"Interesting. Most NHEs only make permanent changes once the forty days are up and they have full control," John mused as he maneuvered the sedan onto the ramp. "Not less than an hour after they take possession. Gray played by his own rules from the start, though, so maybe I shouldn't be surprised."

Zahira's eyes were huge, and John imagined her ears all but quivered beneath the hijab.

"When it comes to our case, if the raven mocker cured Quigley, there would be no need to keep killing," John went on. "So unfortunately, the answer is he's doomed either way. The only difference is if he dies human or not."

"Or takes more people with him before he goes," Caleb muttered. "I hate this."

Once inside, they parted ways, with Zahira going to find out if she had a cubicle assignment yet. Caleb and John returned to their office. Before John could even shut the door behind them, the phone rang.

"Starkweather," Barillo barked. "In my office. Now."

John carefully placed the phone back in its cradle, trying to avoid Caleb's gaze as he did so. Caleb wasn't having any of it, though. "What crawled up his ass? I heard him yelling over here."

"I don't know." John rubbed his eyes tiredly, wishing he'd had a bit more sleep before facing Barillo. "Why don't you round up some more coffee while I'm gone?"

"Do you want us to come with you?"

Himself and Gray, Caleb probably meant, since Zahira wasn't there. "No." John clapped Caleb on the arm as he passed, fingers tightening on the elk hide of Caleb's coat. "It's fine. Just wait here for Zahira."

"All right," Caleb said grudgingly. Then his mouth turned up in a hint of a smile. "She didn't freak out at all last night. About Gray, I mean."

"Of course she didn't," John said. No reason to mention Zahira thought Gray was "amazing." Or her opinion on how he smelled. "There was no reason she should."

"Yeah, that hasn't stopped anyone else," Caleb muttered. "Go see what Barillo wants, and I'll have coffee waiting when you get back."

As soon as John stepped into the district chief's office, Barillo rose to his feet. "Shut the door."

Not a good sign. "Sir—"

"What the hell were you thinking last night?" Barillo demanded. "Do you have any idea how much shit you've left for the rest of us to clean up?"

John blinked. "Last night? You mean at the nursing home? We followed up a lead on the raven mocker, and—"

"Caused a wreck between a van and a tractor trailer, then unleashed the drakul on an unpossessed citizen!"

Unlike Kaniyar, Barillo had never worked the field. He didn't understand how fast things could go from calm to chaotic. "That citizen was a suspect. When we attempted to confront him, he ran, which seemed to indicate his guilt. He chose to flee, and he caused the wreck. Yes, Gray pulled him out of the van, but let him go as soon as he confirmed the suspect wasn't our guy."

"And in the meantime, the actual raven mocker escaped."

John ground his teeth together. "Not exactly, sir. Even with the unintended diversion, Gray tracked the raven mocker and prevented another death. Unfortunately, the NHE is capable of flight, and escaped before Gray could apprehend him."

"Actually, you didn't prevent a death." Barillo pulled a sheet of paper from atop the pile on his desk. "You just shifted it to someone else. Ana Oliveira was at home with her family, not far from Quigley's apartment. There was a noise of wings, and the sound of a crow or raven outside. Ms. Oliveira thought a bird had been injured and went to look for it. Her body was found just a short distance away, with the heart missing."

A sick feeling pooled in John's gut. In trying to save one person, they'd inadvertently condemned another to die in her place. "It won't happen again. We've spoken to Quigley's daughter—she didn't have any immediate ideas where he might have gone, but she might still think of something. Additionally, we have an APB out on Quigley, and I'll send his picture to the local news stations. We'll find him."

"You'd better. And I want it done with as little fuss as possible. No car wrecks, no terrorizing citizens, just a nice, clean arrest." Barillo went around his desk and sat down in his chair. "Of if you have to put him down, do it quietly, away from the public eye. SPECTR is under enough scrutiny as it is."

Caleb looked up in response to a light knock on the half-open office door. Zahira stood there, balancing a couple of cardboard boxes in her arms, while trying to hold onto a small rug tucked under her elbow.

"I have a cubicle now!" she said, with far more enthusiasm than anyone had probably ever shown for a cubicle in history. Certainly in Caleb's experience.

"About time." Caleb took both boxes from her, waving away her protest. "I'm stronger than I look, thanks to Gray, and I don't get tired easily. Let me carry them."

"Thank you." She shifted her rug from under her arm. "So even when Gray isn't manifesting, he has a physical effect on you?"

"Yeah," Caleb muttered, thinking of all the trials and experiments Forsyth ran on him.

"Agent Starkweather said something about your eyes earlier," she said.

What the hell; he might as well answer. His experience with Forsyth might have left him gun shy, but honestly Zahira didn't seem the type to start summoning drakul or collecting demons. "I used to wear glasses. The first thing Gray did was fix my eyes."

She giggled. "Sorry. I'm just imagining him in those glasses with the thick black frames."

"Oh, they were! Total nerd glasses." Caleb grinned and shifted the boxes slightly. "I had the whole hippie look going, too."

"Really?" She glanced at his clothes skeptically.

"This is a uniform," he protested. "Days off, it's shorts and a t-shirt."

"Are the t-shirts tie-dyed?"

"No!" He relented. "Well, not all of them, anyway."

The buzz of conversation in the cube farm died down as they entered. He caught a flash of teeth as Zahira bit her lip. Then her shoulders went back and a determined expression crossed her face.

"Hey," Caleb lowered his voice. "It's me, not you."

She adjusted the drape of her hijab around her shoulders. "Thank you, but I doubt it."

"Then it isn't only you. Trust me." He glanced down at her. "No one's given you any trouble, have they? Because some of the people here are real dicks."

"No, no." She stopped. "Here we are. Cubicle sweet cubicle."

Caleb put the boxes on the desk. As she propped the small rug against a filing cabinet, he said, "Is that a prayer rug?"

"Yes."

He looked around uncertainly. The nearby agents who had been staring hurriedly turned back to their computers. "Listen, if you need somewhere private, where people won't be gawking at you while you're trying to pray, you can use our office. Just let us know and we'll clear out for a few minutes."

Her look of relief told him she'd worried about it. "Are you certain? Thank you."

"No problem." Caleb hadn't been big on religion even before Gray, but it seemed pretty important to Zahira. "I'll leave you to organize your stuff. If anything comes up, I'll text you."

"Thanks," she said. "I—"

"Jansen!"

Startled, Caleb turned and saw a big, burly agent walking toward them. What was the guy's name? Rodriguez. And he didn't look happy. "What?" Caleb asked.

An invisible force punched Caleb hard in the chest, sending him into the cubicle wall.

CHAPTER 8

"**THE FUCK?**" **CALEB** yelled.

Rodriguez unleashed another blast of TK, shoving Caleb onto the floor. Gray surged up, and their teeth started to shift, claws slipping free from their fingertips.

No! Shit, don't, not yet, not against another agent!

"He is attacking us!"

Let me handle it.

"Stop it!" Zahira shouted, grabbing Rodriguez's arm. "What are you doing?"

Caleb rolled into a crouch. "Do that again and we'll rip your fucking head off," he snarled at Rodriguez, Gray's deeper rumble bleeding into the words.

Rodriguez's face lost none of its angry flush. "To hell with you, Jansen, you son of a bitch! What happened to Adrian was your fault!"

"Who the fuck is Adrian?" Since it didn't look like Rodriguez was going to start knocking him around again, Caleb rose to his feet. Still, he held himself warily, ready to fight back if he needed to.

"You don't even know his name." Fury contorted Rodriguez's face, as if Caleb had delivered a personal insult. "Adrian Cortez was my nephew. Quarterback for the Cougars, wanted to go on to play college ball. Maybe NFL. He had his whole damned life ahead of him, and now he's dead because of you."

"Whoa." Caleb held up his hands. Was Rodriguez high or just crazy? "I don't know what you're talking about, so why don't you back off? I kill demons, not kids." But hadn't the guy they saved from lycanthrope possession been a teen? "Oh hell. The werewolves. The ones whose forty days were up. One of them was your cousin?"

Zahira winced. "I'm so sorry," she told Rodriguez. "But you know Caleb didn't have a choice."

"It's his fault they did it in the first place." Rodriguez wiped angrily at his eyes. *"He's* walking around after months of being possessed, like everything is fine! Of course people are going to see that and think they can do it too. What the hell is Kaniyar thinking?"

"Caleb's situation is different," Zahira said.

"Wait a minute." Caleb took a step toward Rodriguez. "How did your cousin even know about me?" There might be rumors—hell, there had to be—but this sounded like something more.

Zahira moved away from Rodriguez. "You didn't tell him, did you?" she asked. "This is classified information!"

"I didn't tell anyone but my wife," Rodriguez said defensively. "I didn't have a choice! She had the right to know why I ran for my Glock every time I heard a rumble of thunder. I didn't realize she'd told anyone, but she and her sister have always been close."

"And the kid overheard and, what, decided having the speed and strength of a lycanthrope would make him a better football player? And talked some of his teammates into it?" Caleb's hand curled into a fist. "We need to get down to the high school, right now."

"Why, so you can kill some more kids, drink their blood like you did Adrian's?" Rodriguez demanded. "Why don't you do that, huh? Or take Starkweather with you, let him show off his little trick. Has he performed it in front of you yet, rookie?"

"Trick?" Zahira asked blankly.

"Oh, he hasn't told you?" The fury drained out of Rodriguez, but his voice took on a nasty edge. "Starkweather doesn't need an exorcism circle to remove NHEs anymore."

"Don't," Caleb said, but of course no one listened to him.

"How?" Zahira glanced from Rodriguez to Caleb, then back again. "It isn't possible."

"It is if you're taking it up the ass from an NHE." Rodriguez looked like he wanted to laugh at the shock on her face. "Bad enough Starkweather is screwing a faust, but he had to go and fuck the drakul too."

Caleb's heart drummed against his ribs, and claws pricked his palm. "Go to hell, Rodriguez," he growled. Fuck, he needed to get out of here. The last thing he needed was for Gray to vamp out in the middle of the damned cube farm.

A crowd had gathered, drawn by the commotion. They parted hastily as Caleb stalked through. "You and Starkweather are a pair of sick fucks!" Rodriguez yelled after him.

Caleb gave him the one-finger salute without looking back. "Drop dead," he said. "And that goes for the rest of you, too. I should've let Forsyth eat every damn one of you."

John let out a sigh as he threw the sedan into park in front of the condo. "Long day," he said. Between the lack of sleep from the night before, getting his ass chewed out by Barillo, and an emergency trip to the high school to exorcize half the football team, he wanted to curl up on the couch and stare mindlessly at the TV until he passed out.

At the least they'd gotten there before anyone else was hurt. Due to the number of potential fausts, John had gotten permission to exorcise on site instead of bringing them all back to HQ. Of course, Barillo still wanted him to use the standard circle, candles, and incense routine, which meant a ten minute job took all afternoon.

"Yeah," Caleb said. He'd been quiet the whole ride home, staring out the window, one hand loosely intertwined with John's.

"Want to talk about it?" John offered.

Caleb climbed out of the car. Once they were in the cool interior of the condo, he shrugged off his coat and boots, then sank down on the couch. "If we'd been able to hold onto the raven mocker last night, Ana Oliveira would still be alive."

"You did everything you could." John went to the fridge and took out a couple of cold beers. "No one can ask more."

"It wasn't enough. How many more will he kill before we catch him?"

John sat down beside Caleb and handed him a beer. "It's not your fault, babe. Or Gray's. Those deaths are on Quigley, not you."

"I can't stop thinking about why he did it." Caleb shoved his hair out of his face with one hand. "It's not fair."

"No, it isn't," John agreed.

"Although at least it's a better reason for summoning demons than winning a fucking high school football game."

"Not your fault either." John put aside his beer and took Caleb's hands in his. "Look at me. You didn't do anything wrong. Rodriguez screwed up, and he'll lose his job for it, no doubt about it. At least he came clean and we got to the high school before the kids went full lycanthrope in the middle of math class."

"I guess." Caleb didn't seem convinced, but let it go. "Do you think Zahira will request another assignment?"

They hadn't taken her to the high school with them. Only one exorcist was really needed, and she had her cubicle to organize. Or so John told himself. It sounded better than being afraid to face her.

"Probably," he said heavily. "Barillo said…shit. I didn't want to upset you, but he said no one else would take the job. That's why we ended up with someone just out of the Academy instead of an experienced agent. She *wanted* the job…but they didn't tell her everything."

Caleb looked away. "Figures."

"Hey." John freed one of his hands, reached up and swept Caleb's long hair aside, so he could see Caleb's face. "I know it's been hard lately. You've had a shitty seven months by anyone's standards."

Caleb's mouth quirked into what might have been the ghost of a smile. "It hasn't been a cake walk for you, either."

"Yeah, but at least I started out with SPECTR. This is all new to you. And to Gray. It's a huge change for you both."

"Gray says all this is just mortal nonsense." Caleb shook his head. "One of his previous hosts was hung by the British Navy for being gay, so I guess he's got a weird sort of perspective."

Caleb had tried to explain what Gray's memories were like, although John wasn't entirely sure anyone else could understand. Colorless, because for whatever reason Gray didn't perceive color before possessing a living body. Stripped of emotion. Just facts recorded in decaying neurons, to be puzzled over during long hours lying in a grave, until it was time to hunt again.

Strange to think he'd fallen in love with someone who had walked the earth since the days of mud-brick ziggurats. A different order of being, the sort worshipped as a god under different circumstances. John wasn't sure he was equipped to even begin to understand Gray's perspective. But he tried.

"I'm sorry," he said.

Caleb's mouth twitched. "Yeah, well. At least SPECTR isn't going to string us up because you're banging Gray."

"Even so, I know this is hard," John said. "None of us need this crap. But the others will come around. What happened at Fort Sumter scared a lot of people, and it sucks, but eventually they'll realize none of this is a threat to them."

"Familiarity brings contempt?" Caleb asked.

"If you like."

Caleb closed his eyes. "Gray doesn't understand, you know. Why they're scared. Why you ought to be scared."

John ran his thumb gently across Caleb's jawline. "You think I should be afraid? Of what?"

"Us!" Caleb pulled back, desperation showing in his eyes. "Christ, Starkweather, don't you get it? That night on Fort Sumter, you were the only person dumb enough to come *toward* us instead of running for your life! You could have died!"

He'd never guessed Caleb felt this way. "But I didn't."

"Now you sound like Gray."

John cupped Caleb's face in both his hands, forcing his lover to look at him. "Babe...I won't pretend I wasn't afraid. But I know you, and Gray. This is all about trust, from beginning to end. From the first time you and I fell into bed together. Physically speaking, you could kill me in a heartbeat at any point while we're making love. So I either trust you'll never hurt me, or we're done. End of the line for us." He shook his head. "I had to believe in you both. And my belief, my trust, was confirmed a thousand times over. The last thing I'll ever be is afraid of you."

Tears shone on Caleb's lashes. "I hope you're right. I have dreams where we killed you, and Gray doesn't understand why, and everyone at work hates me, and people are dying because I didn't stop the raven mocker, and those stupid fucking high schoolers, and...and..."

"Shh." John put his arms around Caleb, hauling him close. "It's okay to be upset." He stroked Caleb's hair gently. "Just let it out."

"Why do you have to be so damn understanding?" Caleb mumbled into his shoulder.

"Because I love you." John closed his eyes and pressed his face into Caleb's hair. "More than anything."

Caleb sat on the balcony in the growing darkness, his belly pleasantly full of baked tofu. Comfort food, for him anyway, which John made without asking.

Poor John. He was under at least as much stress, and here he was stuck taking care of Caleb.

"It makes him feel better."

Which was actually a pretty astute observation, coming from Gray, who didn't always get the nuances of human interaction.

John slid open the balcony door. A moment later, his hands settled on Caleb's shoulders, and a kiss pressed against his hair. Caleb bent his head back over the chair and kissed John more thoroughly.

"Any news?" Caleb asked, although if there had been, John would have said something already.

"No. Nothing on the APB." John sighed. "I looked at the files again, along with everything we have on raven mockers. If there's a clue, I can't find it."

"So we wait?"

"I'm afraid so."

Waiting was something Caleb had never been good at.

"Mortals are so impatient. Sometimes you must let the prey come to you."

Gray had a patience no one human could hope to match. After decades in coffins and tombs, waiting for a staked body to decay enough to hop to the next available corpse, Caleb being upset over a few days seemed absurd to him. *But people are going to die during those days.*

"And we have no means of preventing it. There is no point to worrying about what you cannot change."

It's the mortal way.

"So I have noticed."

Well…I do have one idea for passing the time. It doesn't involve just sitting around waiting for Quigley to break cover. But I suppose if you aren't interested…

"I did not say that," Gray replied, very quickly. Caleb grinned. So much for patience.

He stretched languidly, his t-shirt riding up to expose his belly. John's eyes traveled down Caleb's form, lingering on the exposed wedge of skin. "It's been a long day," Caleb said. "Why don't we go to bed?"

A slow, sexy smile stretched John's mouth. "That sounds like a wonderful suggestion."

The air in the bedroom was much cooler than outside. The fan turned slowly above the bed, sending a gentle breeze over Caleb's skin as he stripped off his shirt. The lamp beside the bed threw a soft glow over the room, outlining the lean muscles of John's torso. Pale scars showed on his chest, the relic of a close encounter with a ghoul when he'd first been an agent. Once they were both naked, they slid into the bed, sheets thrown back.

They moved slowly, taking their time to touch and explore. Caleb ran his fingers over John's chest, feeling the texture of the scars against unmarked skin. John kissed him, then trailed a hand down Caleb's back, to the crack of his ass, and back up again. Gray hovered right under Caleb's skin, drinking it all in, making the simple touch resonate into something exquisite. John's cock pressed against their stomach, hot and hard.

"I want to taste you," Caleb whispered, voice thick with lust.

"Here," John said, and shifted position on the bed, so they were angled opposite one another, cocks at the level of each other's mouths. A moment later, his tongue teased the tip of Caleb's dick.

Caleb grasped the base of John's cock and gave it a few leisurely strokes. John groaned, the sound becoming muffled as his hot, wet mouth closed on Caleb.

Damn, it felt good.

"Then we should return the favor."

Caleb's teeth burned with Gray's nearness. But there was no danger of fangs showing up; they'd figured out just where the line was, and Gray would stay on his side of it. So Caleb slid their mouth down around John, the taste of musk and salt on his tongue. Caleb wrapped one arm around John's hip, gripping a buttock.

It was heaven, bodies pressed together, the sensation of John's mouth on his prick and his own mouth full of John's. Pleasure resonated between him and Gray, building to a keen edge of ecstasy.

There were times Gray's patience came in handy. Like while giving long, leisurely blowjobs. Or fucking, when everything was just right, and their concern for John's more fragile body provided the only constraint.

John nudged Caleb's knee, and he complied by tilting his leg up, giving John free access to whatever he might want. He tugged on Caleb's balls, sending a jolt through him. Caleb moaned and responded by redoubling his efforts on John's cock.

John's hips jerked slightly, and his thighs tensed. Gray crooned with pleasure, the sound confined to Caleb's head. Wanting this, needing it.

The warmth around Caleb's cock disappeared, and John gasped. John's dick stiffened further in his mouth, and a tremble went through John's body. Heat and salt filled Caleb's mouth, the bittersweet taste of come.

He let John's softening dick slip from his lips. "Goddess," John mumbled. Then attacked Caleb's cock like a starving man, sucking and slurping with renewed gusto.

Caleb closed his eyes and let the feeling flow over him, them. John pulled free briefly; then sucked again, the sensation accompanied by a spit-slick finger pressing against Caleb's rim. Caleb moaned at the sensation, John's mouth on his cock and finger in his ass, and to hell with patience.

He cried out, shuddering as he shot down John's throat. White flashes sparked like lightning against the inside of his eyelids.

The bed dipped as John shifted his weight. Caleb opened his eyes to find John facing him, a satisfied smirk on his lips. "Enjoy?"

"Your ego is already big enough, Starkweather," Caleb mumbled. He flung his arm and leg over John, cuddling close. "But yes, in case you couldn't tell, we enjoyed."

"Hey, I'm satisfying two men at once. I've got a reason for the ego."

"Pfft. Keep telling yourself that." Caleb kissed the nearest available bit of skin, which turned out to be John's shoulder. "It doesn't count because we're in the same body."

"But you don't want exactly the same things."

Caleb grinned against John's skin. "Stop being all logical. My brain isn't working right now."

John only chuckled and kissed him again.

CHAPTER 9

THE RINGING OF his phone brought John up out of sleep. Caleb mumbled something incoherent and tried to pull the pillow over his head. Energy shifted, from a low hum to a distinct tingle against John's skin, and a moment later Gray lay there, eyes open and watchful.

John rolled over and felt for his discarded pants. Three in the morning—no wonder Gray shifted to alert mode, whether Caleb wanted to or not. There was no such thing as good news this time of night.

He didn't recognize the number. "Hello?"

"A-agent Starkweather?" The voice was nothing more than a frightened whisper.

He sat up quickly. "Yes?"

"This is Evelyn Quigley. You s-said I could call you?"

The fear in her tone banished the last fuzziness of sleep. "Ms. Quigley, is your father there?"

"Yes. He thinks I'm in the bathroom. He's not himself. I'm scared."

Sekhmet, Devourer of Evil, watch over her. "Can you get out of the house without him realizing? Through a back door?"

"N-no. I don't...don't think so."

"All right." John swung his legs out of the bed. Gray was already up and moving—or rather, Caleb was, since apparently putting on clothes was the sort of mortal foolishness Gray preferred to delegate. "We're on our way. Just sit tight. Help is coming."

* * *

Thank Goddess, traffic was light so late at night. Even so, John felt the seconds slipping away as he drove like a maniac through the street, siren screaming as he blasted through red lights and stop signs. Caleb clung to the passenger seat with one hand, the phone with the other.

"Zahira? It's Caleb. We need your help." Caleb spoke rapidly, as if afraid to give her a chance to say no. "Evelyn Quigley just called—the raven mocker is at her house. We—oh. Okay."

He hung up. "She's on her way," he said, sounding surprised.

"She's a good agent, and this is as much her case as ours," John replied. "Zahira isn't the type to let someone else get hurt." Even if it meant working with them.

As they neared Evelyn's house, John killed the siren. No sense letting the raven mocker know they were coming. John parked a few doors down. The street was quiet, most of the houses dark at this hour. The streetlights hummed softly, and the muted sound of a television drifted from nearby. Lights shone in the front rooms of Evelyn's house, but not the back.

Zahira pulled up behind John's car and climbed out. "What's the plan?" she asked as they met on the sidewalk.

John had been wondering that himself. If only they knew the entire layout of the house.

"We don't have time to waste," he decided. "Zahira, you and I will go to the front door and knock. Caleb, you and Gray come in through the back. Be as stealthy as you can—the second the raven mocker catches a whiff of Gray, he'll run for it."

"Got it," Zahira said with a firm nod.

"Be careful," Caleb said. He slipped away down the narrow driveway separating the house from its neighbor. Thanks to his black clothing and hair, he seemed to melt away into the night.

John and Zahira climbed the front porch steps. "Get ready," John said, drawing his Glock. Zahira silently did the same.

The porch creaked under John's weight, and he winced. So much for being stealthy. The curtains blocked the windows, letting only a dim glow escape from inside, and preventing them from seeing whether anyone was even in the front rooms.

Bursting in with guns blazing might not be the best thing. If Quigley wasn't entirely gone, he might let Evelyn answer the door, if only to keep trouble to a minimum. Or, if the raven mocker had taken over completely, to get another victim.

Motioning for Zahira to stay to one side of the door, John took a deep breath and knocked.

Nothing. Silence.

Damn it.

John raised his hand again. Before he could repeat the knock, a scream sounded from inside. "Help! Help me!"

The door was unlocked. John slammed it open, hard enough to strike anyone who might have been lurking behind it. It crashed into the wall even as he and Zahira piled through. "Federal agents!" he shouted.

Evelyn lay on the floor of the living room, her body curled protectively around the mound of her belly. The raven mocker stood above her, and the stench of rotten eggs filled the small room. Greasy feathers jutted from its malformed arms, shedding sparks onto the carpet. It reached a clawed hand toward Evelyn.

"Stop!" John barked. He moved rapidly to the right, Zahira going left, both of them with their weapons trained on the raven mocker. "Step away from her now."

Was there anything left of Quigley inside? Or were they too late?

"Please, Daddy," Evelyn sobbed from the floor. "Please don't hurt me!"

The raven mocker's twisted face split into a grin. "Your father thought to live to see the child," it said in a voice like the updraft of a forest fire. "But the babe's heart will give me many sweet years instead."

John fired, but the raven mocker lunged toward Evelyn, and the shot embedded itself in the wall.

Etheric energy crackled against his skin, as a roar of anger shook the beams of the old house. The raven mocker grabbed one of the chairs and swung it, even as Gray surged from the back room. The chair disintegrated in a shower of fabric and wood, and sent Gray into the wall. Picture frames cracked and fell around him.

John fired, but the shot only caught feather. Then the raven mocker was on him.

A heavy blow from one wing numbed his arm and sent his Glock flying. The stench of scorched feathers and sulfur enveloped him as the raven mocker jerked him closer. One wing wrapped around his shoulders, claws resting against the vulnerable skin of his throat. The other...

Heat blazed in John's chest, the sensation bordering on painful. Looking down past the matt of greasy feathers, he saw the raven mocker's fingers disappear seamlessly through his shirt. Sparks shed from the wings left little scorch marks on the cotton.

The demon let out a raven-like croak, which might have been a laugh. "Don't move," it told Gray. "Or I'll rip your friend's heart out and eat it in front of your eyes."

Gray snarls, and fury trembles in his veins. Every instinct prompts him to leap forward, to sink his teeth deep into the raven mocker's neck and drink.

But the demon has John.

Gray will tear it apart.

"You can't! It'll kill John!"

The very thought makes Gray ache and sends a sick sensation through him, one he never experienced before possessing Caleb. Before falling in love with John.

Fear.

The demon edges toward the open door, dragging John with it. Wisps of smoke curl up from the carpet, from John's shirt and suit. John's face is pale, his eyes wide. Is he in pain?

"Oh hell. It's trying to get him outside, so it can fly off with him."

"Let him go," Gray orders the demon.

It croaks again, laughing at him. "So you can kill me? I know what you are."

Gray doubts it. If the raven mocker had ever encountered another drakul, it would no longer be alive.

"Unless it flew away, like it did before," Caleb points out. *"Shit, who cares? We've got to do something!"*

"Let him go, and I will not eat you." It is a sacrifice, but John is more important even than eating demons.

"As though I'd believe you," the demon says. It is almost at the door now.

"I do not lie," Gray replies. Bad enough this creature wishes to harm John, but now it must taunt him while doing so. "Mortals lie. Demons lie. I do not."

The door is directly behind it. Gray's claws slide free of their sheaths. He cannot let it take John. Perhaps, if he can move fast enough—

The roar of a gun fills the room, painful against Gray's sensitive hearing. The raven mocker lets out a shriek as blood bursts free from its right leg. Shock and pain loosen its hold, and John is free.

Gray hurls himself across the room, fangs bared and claws out. The demon crumples to one side, its leg no longer able to support its weight. With the angry cry of a bird, it flails onto the porch.

No. It cannot be allowed to escape a second time.

Wings thrash the air. Even as it rises from the ground, Gray leaps, and fastens onto its back.

John sat up, then caught himself as the world tried to spin. The sound of the gunshot still rang in his ears, and his chest felt uncomfortably warm.

"John? Are you all right?" Zahira crouched beside him. She still held her Glock in her hand, and the smell of cordite filled the air.

"I'm fine. Just dizzy." He hoped. "Good shooting."

A brief smile broke through the worry on her face. "Thanks." Then she sobered again. "The raven mocker took off with Gray on its back."

Oh hell. "We can't let it escape," he said, struggling to his feet. But if it took to the air, how could they hope to find it?

Evelyn Quigley sat up as well, or at least as much as she could in her condition. John hurried to her side. "Ms. Quigley? Don't try to move. My partner is calling 911."

Zahira took the hint and made the call while John helped Evelyn to the couch. Her eyes were wild, and her limbs shook. "Daddy was going to kill my baby," she whimpered.

Goosebumps showed on her arms despite the warmth of the night. John took off his coat and wrapped it around her shoulders. "It wasn't him any more."

"EMTs are on the way," Zahira said.

John hated leaving a pregnant woman in such a state, but any delay meant more people might die. "They'll be here in a few minutes. Just sit tight, all right?"

She nodded slowly, but he wasn't entirely sure she heard him. How must she feel, having her child threatened by the thing inside her beloved father's body? Even worse, did any part of Quigley remain, still conscious but a prisoner inside his own skull? Had he been silently screaming the whole time?

At the moment, it didn't make any difference. John gave Evelyn one last pat on the shoulder, then hurried out after Zahira.

"We have to find them," he said as they hit the sidewalk. "Tuning into the police scanner might be our best bet." It wasn't much of a plan, but it was all he had.

"Um, I have an idea," Zahira said with uncharacteristic nervousness.

John stopped beside the car. "Let's hear it."

"Gray follows the scent of other NHEs, right?" she asked. "Only it isn't just a trail of volatile molecules, is it? What he's following is the etheric disturbance they leave in their wake, and he senses it through smell."

"In part," John said. "What are you getting at?"

"Gray's incredibly powerful. That sort of energy leaves a mark on the world as he passes through, especially when he's manifesting. A trail."

John frowned. "I suppose. But it doesn't do us any good."

"But it might?" She gestured at the sky. "We're exorcists—we can sense etheric energy. Sometimes we see it, like in an exorcising circle, and sometimes it's a smell, or a feeling like touch, and sometimes it's all of the above."

With every passing second the raven mocker got further away. "Get to the point, Agent Noorzai."

She straightened sharply. "If your powers are boosted the way Agent Rodriguez seems to think, can you use your ability to follow Gray's wake?"

He started to deny it, then caught himself. Was it possible? A lesser NHE wouldn't leave much of a trail, but a being like Gray?

"It's worth a shot," he said. "Hold on a minute."

He took a deep, centering breath and pretended he was in an ordinary exorcist circle, instead of on the street with lives on the line. Deep breaths. *Sekhmet, Great Defender. Queen of the Wastelands, Eye of Ra, Lady of a Thousand Names. Steady my hand, open my eye, and restore ma'at to the world.*

Traces of etheric energy still hung like a mist around the house, almost faded beyond his ability to perceive. But as he raised his eyes to the sky, he saw it. The stars shimmered and glittered, as if reality was just the surface of a lake, and something vast had just passed underneath.

"There," he said, pointing.

"It worked?" Even Zahira seemed surprised. Then a delighted grin spread across her face. "I knew it! Well, I didn't know, but—never mind," she added hastily at his look. "I'll drive, and you can tell me where to go. Inshallah, we won't be too late."

The demon squawks a protest as Gray's claws sink deep into its shoulders. Its misshapen wings battle the air, hauling them higher even with Gray's added weight. Wind tears at Gray's hair and coat. The smell of scorched feathers and spoiled eggs rises around him, and sparks stream from its wings. He tightens his legs around its hips, preparatory to biting—

The world swings wildly, ground suddenly above them as the demon spins in the air. The lights of the city blaze in the dark, startlingly far below. Gravity tugs at Gray's body, and he tightens his grip in an effort not to be dislodged.

"Shit, it's a long way down!"

They can survive such a fall…but Gray would prefer not to experience it nonetheless.

The raven mocker straightens—but only briefly, before swooping into a dive, then back up. *"It's trying to shake us off,"* Caleb points out, rather unnecessarily in Gray's opinion.

It will not succeed.

But the wild movements mean he must concentrate on hanging on, rather than finding an angle to bite. He can only cling to the raven mocker. Embarrassment creeps through him; he is glad John isn't here to see this.

"John. God. I hope he's okay."

Worry is distracting, and the raven mocker's sudden swoop upward nearly dislodges Gray from its back. He growls, furious with it and himself. This must end; he must do something to cripple the demon's flight before it can succeed in shaking him loose.

"Look—we're heading for the Cooper River Bridge."

Light blazes before them, illuminating a vast span leaping the black line of the river. Great cables of twisted steel spread fan-like from the two huge, diamond-shaped towers. From a distance, it looks oddly delicate, as though the bridge were made of string rather than metal and concrete.

And the raven mocker is making directly for it.

Good.

They hurtle over the salt marshes along the banks of the river, then cross above the bridge itself. Headlights stream along the roadbed, traffic sparser now at this hour, but still more crowded than Gray would prefer. Not so long ago, the setting of the sun sent mortals fleeing indoors, leaving him free to hunt without the inconvenience of discovery. Now they bring day into night, never ceasing in their activity.

"Yeah, yeah, we can yell at them to get off our lawn later. Do you have a plan or not?"

I was waiting for the opportune moment.

Which is coming up fast. He feels the raven mocker tense beneath him, signaling its intent even though it doesn't mean to. When it rolls to one side, Gray flings all of his weight in the same direction.

The demon doesn't expect such a move. Rather than a controlled, if steep, bank, they tumble through the air in a spin. The raven mocker tries to right itself, but Gray bites blindly, fangs scraping across its spine.

The wound isn't serious to such a creature, but the pain shocks it into flinching. The final, inadvertent flex of wings alters their course again. One of the towers rears up ahead of them, and they slam into it with bone-snapping force.

Zahira drove rapidly through the streets, changing course whenever John ordered her to. At least this time of night there wasn't much in the way of traffic. Still, John's heart sank when the rapidly vanishing evidence of Gray's passage seemed to lead in one specific direction.

"The Cooper River Bridge," he said. "Maybe the raven mocker wants to lose us in the marshes to either side? Or go to ground on Drum Island?"

"Can you tell how far behind them we are?" she asked.

"I don't know. I've never done this before." He glanced briefly at her. Her expression was set, brows pulled tight in concentration as she maneuvered the car through the streets. Returning his gaze to the sky, he said, "I'm sorry you had to find out about...things...the way you did. Barillo doesn't want me to spread the word around. I'm under orders not to perform exorcisms outside of a circle, and...well. Even so, you were assigned to us, and I should have said something to you."

A tractor-trailer chugged slowly up the on ramp to the interstate and bridge. Zahira's mouth tightened, and she edged the car to one side, then the other, but there was no way around the slower vehicle.

"Were?" she asked, sounding confused. "Is Barillo reassigning me?"

Her question caught him off guard. "I...we...assumed you'd request a new assignment. And I understand," he added hurriedly. "I'm not angry."

"Maybe you should be." Her face creased into a scowl. "I don't know exactly what happened on Fort Sumter—it might be the sort of thing no one who wasn't there can really understand. But I like you, and Caleb, and Gray, and I like working with you."

"The trail is staying with the bridge," John said, but despite everything his heart lightened slightly. "So you don't have a problem with any of it?"

The ripples on reality grew stronger, distorting a more concentrated path across the sky. Were they closing in?

"If you're referring your personal lives, that's your business. But no, I don't have a problem with either you being gay or sleeping with Gray." She shrugged. "I'm not blind—I could see you and Caleb had a connection. And Gray…" A little grin replaced the scowl. "Don't ever tell my mother I said this, but I don't blame you at all. He's pretty freaking cute."

John laughed. "My lips are sealed. Seriously, though, I'm glad. And —"

A dark shape plummeted from atop the bridge and slammed into the trailer ahead of them.

CHAPTER 10

FOR A MOMENT, Gray tumbles free, the world spinning around him. Then he strikes one of the huge cables. Two claws snap off, snagged in the twisted steel, but his momentum slows enough for the rest to catch.

They hang from the cable, high above bridge and river. The rumble of traffic sounds from beneath, nearly lost beneath the moan of the wind around the wires. Gray hauls himself up onto the wire and balances on it, coat snapping around him in the breeze.

"Shit. Where's the demon?"

There. The creature crouches atop the tower. One wing dangles uselessly, blood and broken bone showing through the feathers. Does it need to feed in order to undo the damage? Or can it heal enough to fly away using the lives it has already stolen?

"We can't give it the chance."

Agreed.

Gray swings from cable to cable, making his way up the span toward the height of the tower. The shiny black eyes of the raven mocker focus on him, and it croaks a challenge. Sparks shed from its burning wings, blowing madly in the wind.

"I am ready for you," it caws, folding its good wing to reveal a clawed hand. "How much life, how much power, will the heart of a god give me?"

Gray balances on a cable, only feet away now. "I am drakul," he says, because apparently even demons wish to label things. "And I do not fear you."

He bursts into motion, rushing the last few feet, even as the screaming wind catches his coat and tries to tear him free of the bridge. He lands atop the tower, Caleb's telekinesis pushing them those last few critical inches.

The raven mocker is ready for them. Its hand reaches for their chest. Claws sink *through* the protective leather of their coat, through skin and muscle and bone.

And close around their beating heart.

His claws rake across the demon's face. It bites his hand, hard, teeth crunching onto bone. Agony flares through every nerve as it tugs on their heart, seeking to wrench the organ free.

Perhaps they can heal from such a wound. But there is more at play here than the physical. The heart is the raven mocker's key to the etheric, just as blood is for Gray.

This is not good. The creature might be able to kill them in this fashion.

Gray seizes the arm currently buried in his chest and bites deep.

It screams, and suddenly its hand is a solid thing, tearing a wound through chest and shredding muscle and bone. Their heart bumps against its claws, blood pouring free. But its grip loosens.

Gray kicks free from the tower, wrenching away from its hungry grasp.

And he falls.

"That was Gray!" John shouted, even as Zahira stood on the brakes.

Tires screamed, both from their sedan and the tractor-trailer in front of them. The big rig slewed sideways, broken trailer swaying violently, before the aluminum side gave way under shifted cargo. Boxes spilled free, splitting open as they struck pavement and releasing hundreds of yellow rubber duckies across the roadbed.

The seatbelt cut into John's chest, and pain flared again where the raven mocker had touched him, like a bad sunburn. More tires screamed behind them, and he closed his eyes and braced for impact.

Somehow, no one plowed into them. Clouds of smoke drifted past the window, along with the stink of hot brakes. Horns honked angrily in the distance.

When he was certain they weren't going to get hit by another car, John flung open the door and climbed out. "Stay in your vehicles!" he shouted as drivers behind them began to do the same. Zahira took out her badge and held it aloft.

"SPECTR agents!" she called. "Stay in your vehicles! Sir, that means you," she added as the truck driver climbed down from his cab.

"Look at this shit!" he shouted, pointing at the wrecked trailer. "My insurance ain't gonna cover this!"

Where was Gray? John stepped closer to the shattered trailer. A rubber ducky squeaked under his shoe. Caleb should have cushioned their fall with his TK—unless Gray had been too badly injured to relinquish control.

"Gray?" he called as he sidled up to the broken trailer, Glock in his hand. "Caleb?"

Nothing. No movement among the cracked and twisted metal of the trailer. No shift of rubber ducks, sliding away.

The raven mocker couldn't really injure Gray.

Right?

"John!" Zahira shouted. "Above us!"

John spun to see a dark shape making its way down the nearby tower. One wing dragged, clearly badly damaged. But even if it couldn't fly, it could still cling like a lizard to the concrete.

Shoving his fear for Caleb and Gray to the back of his mind, John pulled out his Glock and squeezed off three shots. All of them missed.

"Get back in the truck!" Zahira ordered the driver. But he only stood and gaped at the raven mocker, frozen like a deer in front of a mountain lion.

John sighted to fire again. Before he could take aim, the raven mocker leapt free of the tower, wings spread so it fell in a controlled glide. Zahira fired, and it jerked. But gravity was master now, and it fell directly atop the gaping truck driver.

The man crumpled to the ground beneath its weight. One clawed hand lashed out, burying itself in the man's chest, and he screamed.

John ran toward them, pulling free his silver athame. He couldn't fire without risking the driver, but if the raven mocker devoured the man's heart, it would surely heal and escape. Saying a silent prayer to Sekhmet, he lifted the athame—

The raven mocker's free hand slashed at him, ripping open his shirt and severing his tie. He jerked back, the swing of his athame going wild. The truck driver screamed and thrashed beneath the demon, and it let out a spate of croaking laughter.

Zahira joined John, chanting in what sounded like Arabic, one hand thrust out as she tried to compel the NHE. Surely she could see the forty days were up?

The raven mocker let out a corrupted laugh. "It's too late to dislodge me," it said.

"Too late to exorcise you," she agreed. "But not too late to distract you."

The side of the trailer ripped open, and Gray burst forth in a shower of yellow duckies. The front of his t-shirt was coated with blood, and bloodied skin showed beneath a hole torn in the cloth. But he was alive and moving, and John's heart stuttered in his chest at the sight.

The raven mocker shrieked and abandoned the driver. But unable to fly, trapped on the ground, it was easy prey. Gray slammed into it, claws extended, and bore it to the concrete roadbed. Growling furiously, he wrenched its head back with one hand, the other pinning it to the pavement. It croaked frantically, then shrieked as Gray's head darted forward.

Etheric energy swirled. The raven mocker's movements grew more sluggish. Gray growled, the sound muffled against flesh as he drank its blood. An odd shudder went through him, before he pulled back reluctantly. The raven mocker's head thunked to the asphalt. Dead.

Gray raised his head, mouth ringed with blood. His black eyes took in Zahira, then John. Zahira lowered her Glock, and she nodded to him once.

Then he was gone, folded back into Caleb's slim form. Caleb staggered up, wiping his mouth with his sleeve. A yellow ducky clung to his black hair, snarled amidst the locks.

John hurried to him. "Are you all right?" he asked.

Caleb glanced at the screaming truck driver. Zahira went to kneel beside the man, no doubt trying to get him to stop shrieking for a moment and calm down. "Yeah. It tried to yank out our heart. Shit, I really don't want to do that again."

Even though they were on the clock, John slid his arms around Caleb and pulled him close. "Tell Gray no more jumping off bridges. Or bridge towers."

Caleb snorted. "Not like we had a choice.'" He pulled back a little, gaze going to the remains of the raven mocker. Its body started to rot, as if Quigley died the day he summoned it. "He might have said the same."

John shook his head. "No. Quigley made a choice. Not to say any of his options were good ones, but he chose to kill other people to extend his own life. Just like those high schoolers chose to summon NHEs of their own free will. And Forsyth chose to try to handle forces he barely even understood, let alone could control. They're responsible, not you."

Caleb's gaze lingered on the body, but John sensed his focus turn inward. Gray adding his two cents, most likely. Then Caleb's brown eyes met John's, and he smiled gently. "You always know just what to say. No wonder we love you."

"Just one of many services I provide," John agreed. Sirens wailed in the distance, and he looked out over the pile up and traffic jam ensuing. "Well. A nice, quiet arrest, just like Barillo wanted."

Given it was almost dawn by the time they finished on the bridge, John didn't pull the sedan into the parking garage at SPECTR-HQ until noon the next day. Even though it was Saturday, there was plenty of paperwork to be done, and John knew they wouldn't be the only ones logging hours on the weekend.

At least Barillo wouldn't be in to chew his ass. And with any luck, come Monday morning the district chief would calm down and decide he couldn't disregard the fact the three—four—of them stopped a dangerous NHE with no further casualties.

At least, John sure as hell hoped he couldn't.

He unsnapped his seat belt, then glanced at Caleb, who had been quiet during the ride in. A little to his surprise, Caleb stared down at a small, white business card he held loosely in his hands.

"Babe?" he asked, when Caleb didn't move.

Caleb looked up, blinking. "Oh. We're here. Sorry. I was lost in thought."

John indicated the card. "What about?"

"The paranormal rights group." Caleb held up the card, as if it might make his argument for him.

"That's the card Nigel gave you?"

"Yeah. I…shit. Don't take this the wrong way, okay?" Caleb didn't meet John's gaze, instead staring at his jeans. "I just feel like I need something outside of SPECTR. A place I can go and hang out, and just be Caleb Jansen, telekinetic."

"I understand," John said.

"Do you? Because Gray doesn't see the point." Caleb sighed and rubbed at his eyes. "Not to say he thinks I'm trying to…I don't know, pretend like he isn't there, isn't important to me. But he doesn't really get anything that isn't food or fucking."

John reached over and took Caleb's hand in his. "You know that isn't true." Gray had listened to John even before they became lovers, even when he'd thought John meant to put him down like any dangerous NHE. "Gray's smart. He thinks things through."

"So do tigers." Caleb snorted. "They're smart predators, but no one's going to invite one to be on the debate team, right?"

It was a distraction, so John ignored it. "What is this really about, babe?"

Caleb bit his lip. "I just worry what you'll think."

Finally. "If Gray is okay with you hanging out with people who don't know you're possessed, then I'm not the one to say otherwise," John said gently. "And if you want to do something on your own, away from me and SPECTR, I'm fine with it."

Caleb gave him a searching look. "Are you sure? Because I love you —"

"I know." John caught Caleb's hand and brought it to his mouth, pressing a kiss against the knuckles. "You don't have to justify it, okay? We're a couple, and I'm in this for the long haul. But part of that is letting you have your own things which don't necessarily involve me."

Uncertainty darkened Caleb's brown eyes. "Yeah, but…what about you? You've dealt with plenty of bullshit yourself lately."

"True," John allowed. "Who knows, maybe I'll take up a hobby while you're at your meetings. Maybe head down to the gay club, see if I can—ow!"

Caleb punched him lightly in the shoulder. "Asshole. And, no, Gray, he isn't serious. Jesus, you need to figure out sarcasm."

There were so many weird conversational pitfalls he'd stumbled into over the last few months. But it came with being in love with Gray, and he wouldn't have it any other way. "Gray, darling, listen to Caleb. It was a stupid joke."

Gray didn't manifest, but Caleb gave a little shake of his head. *"See?* Christ, you'd think somebody who'd eaten his way across most of the world over a few millennia would be a little more confident. Okay, yes, I get this is the first time you've been in love. Even so."

John leaned in, his forehead touching Caleb's. "Tonight I'll show you guys exactly how much I want you."

"I know. And Gray does too—he's just a drama queen." Caleb kissed John softly. "Not to say I'm turning down the offer, mind you. Now let's get inside before I give into temptation and blow you right here and now. Wouldn't want to give the guards watching the security footage too much of a thrill."

When they arrived at their office, John slowed. A sweetgrass basket sat on the floor just outside, adorned with a balloon and containing several objects, one of them fuzzy.

"Is that…a gift basket?" Caleb asked incredulously.

"Let me look at it," John said. If someone had tried to haze Caleb after all he'd gone through the last few days, John would take the evidence straight to Barillo and demand something be done. And if Barillo still refused…

Director Kaniyar might still have time for a man who'd served as a loyal field agent, even if it did mean skipping way up the chain of command to talk to her. And to hell with Barillo if he had a problem with it.

The balloon floating above the basket read "Thank You." Inside sat a large teddy bear wearing a black cape and with Hollywood's idea of vampire fangs glued to the stitched seam of its mouth. John sniffed it, but didn't catch so much as a whiff of garlic. Included with the teddy were a bottle of dragon's blood scented bubble bath and a bit of body oil.

And a card, addressed to Caleb.

"Here," John said, passing the card along. He picked up the basket, unlocked the door, and led the way inside while Caleb read. "What does it say?"

John turned to see an actual grin on Caleb's face. "Dear Caleb and Gray," he read aloud, "Thank you for not letting Forsyth eat us all. Sincerely, Karl."

"Huh." John put down the basket.

"Yeah." Caleb picked up the teddy bear and shook his head. "Okay, I might be living the goth stereotype, but at least I don't have a cape."

"Not yet," John agreed. Caleb stuck out his tongue…but John noted he carefully set the teddy bear on top of their filing cabinet, in view of his desk.

"So, a soak in the tub later?" John asked, shaking the bubble bath seductively.

Caleb wrinkled his nose. "I don't think Karl realizes just how sensitive to artificial smells NHEs really are. But if it gets you naked…"

"Like you need an excuse."

"True." Caleb slid his arms around John and bent for a kiss. "So don't bother—I know what you're going to say."

"And that is?"

"First Karl, tomorrow the rest of the office. Three months from now we'll all be holding hands and singing kumbaya."

"Goddess, I hope not. I can't sing worth a damn."

Caleb only shook his head and kissed John again, his lips tender. "Point, missing it. I just mean, if you say it's going to get better…I believe you. And even if it isn't, even if every other SPECTR agent on earth hates me, I'm in this to the end with you. We are."

John swallowed against the constriction in his throat. "And I'm with you. Above all else."

"I'm glad." Caleb drew back with a grin that promised all sorts of things. "But for now, this paperwork isn't going to fill itself out."

"True enough," John agreed. And settled in to work across from his lovers, the balloon drifting like a promise above their heads.

DANCER OF DEATH

CHAPTER 1

ELISE DANCED EFFORTLESSLY to the music flowing through her ear buds. Every move was simple, her body perfect.

Grand jeté.

No pain in her ankles.

Double turn, double turn, double turn, double turn.

No pain anywhere, except for the blazing heat knotted in her chest.

Arabesque.

She held the position for a long time, without the slightest tremor in her supporting leg or the tiniest shift of weight, as though her body were made of air. As though gravity and the laws of physics bent themselves to accommodate her every desire.

The music came to an end, and she pulled out the ear buds. She should have been soaked in sweat from exertion by now, but she wasn't even breathing hard.

It was glorious.

"You are glorious," cooed the demon.

Elise crossed the room, stepping over the smears of blood covering the concrete floor. "I have to be," she said aloud. "This was my last rehearsal. Tomorrow…"

"Tomorrow, we will be perfect."

She took a deep breath and nodded. She'd had thirty-six days of practice, first alone, then *pas de deux*. Tomorrow, the show began. Three acts and a grand finale.

"And you'll have your revenge."

She smiled as she bent and picked up the corpse lying in a pool of sweat, vomit, and blood. The body was still warm, but it was July in the south. Nothing cooled off quickly here.

Not without help.

Several enormous freezers stood around the otherwise barren room, humming softly as they struggled against the summer heat. She carried the body with inhuman strength to the nearest one, opened it, and dumped the corpse on top of the others already packed inside. One mangled foot flopped out; she shoved it inside with a loud *crack*, then closed the lid.

"Maybe I should have tried to find a ghoul," she mused, clicking the padlock into place. She'd gotten into the habit of speaking aloud ever since summoning the demon. "Then I wouldn't have to worry about the power bill."

"Scavengers," the demon said with disgust. *"Brutes. We are artists, you and I."*

"Yes," she murmured as she made her way to the door. "And in four days, everyone in Charleston will know it."

They'd see she was perfect. They'd realize she was still a great dancer.

And then they would die.

"Um, hello?" Caleb called uncertainly. He stood in the doorway to the small back room of a bookstore, which looked like it normally served as the employee break room. Inside milled a group of about ten people, talking and laughing as they set out folding chairs and puttered around the donuts and soda crowded onto the short counter. "Is this Paranormally Abled Support System?"

"Caleb!" said a familiar voice. Nigel Legare emerged from the crowd, a smile on his face. "Welcome to PASS. I'm glad you decided to come."

"Um, yeah." Caleb glanced nervously at the other people in the room. They smiled at him, murmuring welcomes. He started to relax; it was a hell of a nice change from the suspicious scowls he was used to getting at work.

"They would be foolish to fear us. Mortals are not food."

And so much for relaxing. It wasn't that he wanted to forget Gray was there, exactly. But it would be nice to go ten minutes without being reminded a demon-munching vampire spirit possessed him.

"Then you are also foolish."

Hush.

Nigel shook his hand warmly. "What's your ability, Caleb?"

"TK. Telekinetic," Caleb said. After hiding his ability for most of his life, it felt weird to announce it in front of a room of strangers. But that was the whole point of coming here in the first place. To have somewhere to talk about what he was going through, away from SPECTR and everyone connected to it.

Even John.

Nigel nodded. "Here in group, we try to normalize the use of our powers. We use them as much as we can while we're here. Would you like to help Deacon set up the chairs?"

The man Nigel indicated was about Caleb's age, red haired and cute as hell. "Sure," Caleb said.

Deacon grinned. "Glad to have another fellow TK here," he said. Green eyes gave Caleb the once-over.

It looked like they had more in common than telekinesis.

"Can you lift a chair on your own? It's okay if you can't," Deacon added quickly. "We're all about working together here."

"No, I can," Caleb said. Last year he'd barely been able to nudge a paper coffee cup, but now that Gray had set up shop in his head, his TK had grown exponentially.

Deacon dragged chairs from the corner with nothing but the power of his mind. Other group members grabbed and unfolded them once they were in position. Caleb joined in, careful not to pull on the chairs too hard and send them flying into anyone.

While they worked, a pyrokinetic went around the room, lighting decorative candles. Nigel used cryokinesis to chill the soda. A woman, maybe twenty years old tops, poured the soda into cups. She wore a green armband.

Shit. Caleb had never been comfortable around empaths, even when they could sense his emotions. But once Gray's possession became permanent, a curtain had come down. Empaths couldn't pick him up at all, not even a whisper.

Like he wasn't even human anymore.

Gray stirred, like a sleepy tiger flicking an ear at an annoying gnat. *"You did not like it when empaths could sense you. Now they cannot, and yet you still are not satisfied."*

Because it's suspicious as fuck. If she realizes she's not picking up anything from me, she's going to wonder why.

"That is why we should be out hunting demons instead of wasting time with foolish mortals."

Caleb resisted the urge to roll his eyes, not wanting to weird anyone else out. *We can't. Barillo has us benched, remember?*

"How could I forget?" Annoyance and frustration flooded Caleb, spilling over from Gray. *"I have not eaten since the raven mocker. I wish to hunt; I wish to feed."*

I know, but Barillo would go ballistic.

"I do not care."

Well I do, and so does John. Christ, it's not like you can starve. Just be patient.

Soon, the group was seated in a loose circle, donuts and sodas in hand. The last conversation died away as Nigel cleared his throat.

"Welcome, friends," he said with another fatherly smile, "to this week's meeting of Paranormally Abled Support System. Just as a reminder, everything said here, stays here. Our mission is to support and lift up each other."

There was a general nodding and murmuring. Caleb shifted in the uncomfortable metal chair. He was the only one without anything to eat or drink. Gray had dialed his senses up to eleven, and he couldn't stand the chemical sweetness of soda any more. Donuts weren't much better, depending on how much high-fructose corn syrup was dumped into them.

"As you can see, we have a new member this evening." Nigel gestured at Caleb. "Caleb, would you like to go first?"

"Uh…" He'd expected Nigel to mention he worked for SPECTR, at least as a contractor. Maybe Nigel figured it was for Caleb to reveal—or not—to the group. Whatever the reason, it made him feel a little better. Like he might actually be able to blend in here and be normal. Or paranormal. Whatever. "I'm not sure what to say."

"Say whatever you want," Nigel encouraged. "Tell us what's on your mind. We're here to listen, not to judge. And if you have some good news, share that too!" He paused. "Since it's your first time here, why don't you tell us why you decided to join the group?"

"Okay." Caleb took a deep breath. "So yeah. My name's Caleb. You probably figured that out already." A smattering of laughter answered him. "I guess I came because…because I need somewhere I can just relax and be normal. I'm sick of people looking at me like I'm some kind of walking time bomb."

"I hear you," said the empath with a scowl. "I mean, I have to be touching somebody with bare skin to get even a hint of what they're feeling, but I still have to wear this stupid armband! People act like I'm going to...I don't know, scramble their brains at any second."

"Uh, yeah," Caleb said with a flash of guilt. Hadn't he used to look at empaths like that? At least he didn't have to worry about her sensing him—or rather, failing to—from across the room. "I'm not dangerous just because I'm different. But people act like I don't have any morals, or a conscience. Like I'm a monster."

Which, to be fair, he sort of was. Or rather they were, he and Gray. But that didn't mean they were going to start snacking on everyone at SPECTR-HQ, no matter what some of the agents thought.

"The paranormally abled often feel isolated, lonely," Nigel said sympathetically. Which was a laugh, because the one thing Caleb would never be again was alone.

"Alienated," said Deacon, who'd taken the seat beside Caleb.

Caleb nodded. "Yeah, that's a good word for it. Alienated."

"Do you have any support in your personal life?" Nigel took a sip from his soda. "A friend you can confide in?"

"My parents and brother are dead. And my brother got mixed up in some anti-paranormal stuff before he died." Which had indirectly led to the whole possessed-by-a-drakul thing.

"My parents were big donors to Senator Olney." Deacon offered him a rueful smile. "At least, until it turned out he was summoning demons and went to prison."

"Ouch," Caleb said. Olney had been an anti-paranormal dick, and Caleb hadn't been sorry to see him go down. "I don't want it to sound like I don't have anyone, though. My boyfriend understands. It's just... well...he thinks if I stick it out long enough, things will get better. People will realize I'm not going to go crazy and do something awful. And hell, I don't know, maybe he's right."

"Easy to tell somebody to just wait it out when you're not suffering with them," Deacon scoffed.

Caleb winced. "He's got things of his own going on." Which was true, but it sounded like a lame excuse.

Deacon looked like he had another comment, but Nigel beat him to it. "It's important to realize you aren't alone here. We've all felt alienated by society at one time or another. Sometimes refusing to engage is the right course, as your boyfriend suggests. And sometimes it's the wrong one. Only you can decide which choice is right for you."

There came a murmur and nodding of sympathetic heads. Feeling a bit like a fraud, Caleb leaned back in his chair and spent the rest of the meeting listening to the others talk. If they knew what he was having trouble coping with wasn't just the ordinary trials of having a paranormal ability, but of possession…

They'd all run screaming and never look back.

"Hey, Caleb, wait a sec," Deacon called as Caleb walked out of the bookstore.

He paused while the other man caught up. The late sunlight gleamed on Deacon's copper hair and on the thin ring in his nose. He reminded Caleb vaguely of his last boyfriend, before he'd left Charlotte and gotten mixed up in madness and death and possession.

And met John Starkweather, federal exorcist, as far from the type of guy Caleb usually went out with as it was possible to get.

"Where'd you park?" Deacon asked, falling in beside Caleb. The sidewalks in this part of Charleston were narrow and uneven, and they had to walk almost shoulder-to-shoulder.

"I didn't," Caleb confessed. "No car."

"I can give you a lift," Deacon offered.

Caleb bit his lip. "Umm…" Was Deacon hitting on him? Or just being nice?

"It's just, you know, the disappearances," Deacon said quickly, as if he knew what Caleb was thinking. "Is it safe to walk by yourself?"

"Oh yeah, I heard about that," Caleb said. Some talking head on the news last night had been going on about a higher-than-usual number of missing persons cases over the last couple of weeks. Mostly homeless people and sex workers, but otherwise there was no particular pattern.

Gray perked up. *"Perhaps it is a demon,"* he said hopefully.

Demon or human serial killer—which was worse? Then again, it might be neither. If there was any proof connecting the disappearances, the police hadn't released it. With any luck, it was nothing, just a bunch of people leaving town at the same time. Maybe going north to get away from the heat.

"And you're not worried?" Deacon asked. "Even a little?"

The real answer was no. Gray could take on just about anything. Not having to worry about getting his ass kicked by some homophobe who thought long hair and short-shorts were an affront to manhood was one of the few perks of being possessed.

"And I am another one."

Yeah, right, Caleb thought back. But he made sure to send a surge of affection along with the thought.

But Deacon was trying to be nice, and hadn't Caleb come to PASS to make friends in the first place? He wanted to feel normal, and giving each other rides when there might be a serial killer on the loose was the sort of thing normal people did.

"Yeah, a little," Caleb lied with a smile. "Thanks, man. I appreciate the offer."

Deacon grinned back and tipped an imaginary hat. "Any time."

CHAPTER 2

JOHN DUMPED THE dustpan into the kitchen trash and paused to survey the condo. There—the downstairs was picked up, dusted, and swept. He had to admit, one thing about riding a desk for the last few weeks meant far less dirt and blood tracked on the floors at the end of the day.

The dryer dinged. As he gathered the laundry into the hamper, the sound of the front door closing echoed through the condo. "How was the meeting?" he called as he carried the hamper back into the living room.

Caleb kicked off his shoes—a pair of ratty sneakers starting to come apart at the sole—beside the door. A tie-dyed shirt, thin from a thousand washings, clung to his slender frame. Long black hair hid his face for a moment as he leaned over to peel off his socks. "It was good," he said. "Everyone was nice."

"I didn't know Nigel well when he worked for SPECTR, but he always seemed like a good guy," John offered. "I'm glad it worked out for you. I guess you'll be going back?"

"Yeah." Caleb paused, chewing on his lip thoughtfully. "I felt like they understood me." He shook his head. "Which is dumb, because they don't understand anything. They can't ever know about Gray, so I spent the whole time...not lying, but letting them assume it's the ordinary discriminatory bullshit against paranormals."

"But you have faced that," John said, trying to be fair. "At least a little."

Caleb had spent most of his life under the radar. Unregistered, his TK weak enough he could pass for normal. He'd never marched in a Paranormal Pride Parade, or been refused service in a bar because of the state-required listing of his paranormal ability on his ID.

Or been sent to "therapy" by his parents, which was supposed to somehow cure him of his ability, if he only prayed hard enough.

But that wasn't a fair way to look at things, John reminded himself. Caleb had lived a paranoid life before registration, and Goddess knew he had plenty to deal with now.

"I guess," Caleb said. He paused, head cocked slightly, as if listening. "But Gray...oh fine. He wants to tell you about it himself."

Between one second and the next, Caleb's brown eyes went black as obsidian, without visible iris or white. His stance shifted, straightened, and his long black hair lifted from his shoulders, blown by a wind that touched nothing else. John's skin prickled, as if the air had taken on a static charge, and the scent of petrichor and incense washed over him.

"The meeting was boring," Gray said in a voice like the distant rumble of thunder. "Mortals talking and talking about themselves. I do not care about their problems."

John set the hamper aside. "No, but Caleb does."

"I would have preferred to hunt." Gray's lip curled, revealing a white fang. "When will we hunt again?"

John winced. Of course this was what Gray would want to talk about. "I don't know. The rest of us would rather be out in the field, too."

Although honestly, he felt far worse for Zahira than for Gray, or even himself. Even if his career was toast, at least he'd had one to start with. And Gray might be restless, but a few weeks on a no-NHE diet wouldn't actually hurt him.

But Zahira? This was her first assignment, right out of the Academy. And yeah, she'd been the one to choose it, when every other agent had flat-out refused to work with them. Well, with Gray. But she'd been determined, and if things had gone differently, the assignment might have caught the eye of someone higher up the food chain than District Chief Michael Barillo.

When they'd been barred from the field, she'd put a good face on it, and used her new clearance to delve into every scrap of information SPECTR had accumulated about the etheric plane over the years. But all the research in the world wouldn't make up for the practical field experience she was meant to be getting—and wasn't.

Gray didn't seem particularly mollified. "Perhaps."

John crossed the room. "I thought you were good at waiting," he said, settling a hand on Gray's arm. "Didn't you go years without hunting when you were staked?"

"That was different," Gray objected. "Then, there was nothing to be done. Now, there is no reason for me not to hunt."

Was that true? Or had inhabiting a living body, with all the urgency of pleasure and pain, worn away the edge of Gray's inhuman patience?

A thread of worry squirmed deep in John's belly. Of course being in a living body, being with Caleb, had changed Gray. But it *wasn't* the same sort of change that happened to other NHEs, exposed to human pain and fear and lust for the first time. Gray had a cushion of five thousand years of memories gleaned from the bodies he'd inhabited, and even if he hadn't understood them fully, even if he hadn't *felt* them, he hadn't been a total stranger to mortal existence the way a therianthrope or wendigo would be.

There was no need to worry. Gray just needed a distraction. And hell, at the moment, John could use one too.

"Still, it hasn't been all bad, has it?" he asked, leaning in closer, so his thigh brushed against Gray's.

The condo's thick walls helped keep out the summer heat, but July in Charleston was always brutal. John had stripped down to nothing but shorts and an old t-shirt while he cleaned. Caleb had donned shorts before going out, more to blend in than because he felt the heat anymore, and bare skin whispered against bare skin. Gray's nostrils flared, and John sensed the drakul's full attention settle on him.

Which could be a little disconcerting, like being stared at by a very large tiger. But in this case it was arousing, too. John slid his arms around Gray's waist, his dick swelling as they pressed together.

Gray kissed him. He didn't kiss like anyone else John had ever been with. Gray did everything with a singular sense of determination, of purpose, which stole John's breath. In that moment, it was as if he was the only thing in Gray's world, or at least the only thing that mattered.

John slid his tongue between Gray's parted lips, exploring thick fangs. Gray's hands settled on his hips, tugging him closer, and soon they ground together.

"Not all bad," Gray admitted, when their lips parted again. His long hair slid silkily over the backs of John's hands, his fingers exploring the curve of John's spine, his claws sheathed for the moment. John closed his eyes, enjoying the sensations—touch and smell and his sixth sense, the one which allowed him to manipulate etheric energy as an exorcist.

That sense insisted he stood in the middle of a storm, in the arms of something much larger and more powerful than could be accounted for by Caleb's tall, lanky body. Etheric energy crackled along his skin, arousing as hell. His breath grew erratic as his cock hardened.

"Bed?" he mumbled against Gray's mouth.

"Yes."

John led the way up the tight spiral of the iron staircase to the second floor. The setting sun tinged the light in the bedroom a summer gold. The ceiling fan spread a welcome breeze over his skin as he stripped. Gray's scent flooded the little space, especially with the windows shut, and John breathed deeply.

Naked, Gray stared at him from where he stood on the other side of the bed. His gaze fixed on John, all of his attention focused, like a big cat stalking its prey. He was beautiful and dangerous, all long hair and fangs, eyes black as oil slicks. John's heart pounded with anticipation, dick bobbing slightly in time with each beat.

A slow grin curled one corner of Gray's mouth, exposing a fang. He crawled onto the bed, his hair writhing over his pale back. His tongue flicked out, touching his upper lip, and his grin widened to reveal both fangs.

John half expected Gray to grab him, yank him down on the bed, and pin him there. Instead, Gray turned around, ass in the air, spine curved, claws catching in the comforter. "Take us."

John wasn't going to argue. He grabbed lube from the nightstand, then climbed onto the bed himself. Setting the tube aside, he ran his hands over Gray's back, bent to kiss the base of his spine. He mapped the familiar contours of skin, over rib and down hip, across a lean thigh. He ran a firm stroke down Gray's cock, cupping his balls with the other hand.

Gray shot a growl over his shoulder, teeth exposed. The low, animal sound sent a rush of blood to John's dick which left him feeling light-headed.

"So impatient," John teased.

"There is a time for patience. This is not it." Gray pushed back against him. "We want you. Now."

"Then you'll have me."

The lube felt slick and cool against heated skin. Gray growled again when John pressed in. John gasped and bit his lip hard, distracting himself. There was the tight heat of Gray's body, tugging him deeper, but that wasn't the half of it. Etheric energy shivered over John's skin, beneath the palms of his hands, against his thighs, and along every centimeter of his cock. His senses were saturated, overloaded with ecstasy, but he didn't want this to end too soon.

Gray shoved back to meet him, matching his thrusts. Another growl thrummed in the air, low and dangerous. "Is this good?" John gasped, shifting his angle slightly. "Tell me."

Gray threw his head back, and John glimpsed his face, lips drawn back from his fangs. "Yes. More."

Inspired, John thrust one hand into the seething mass of Gray's hair, knotting his fist in it. Gray snarled, but the way he arched his back and pushed against John suggested he liked it. A lot.

John tugged, gently at first, but then Gray said, "Harder. You cannot hurt us."

So he pulled harder. And Goddess, this was as insane as it was hot, fucking something like Gray. Something old and inhuman, which snarled as John pulled on his hair and drove into him, static singing along every nerve.

John shouted, control slipping. He thrust in hard, pleasure cresting, lightning dancing behind closed eyelids.

As soon as he was done coming, Gray pulled free of him. John blinked as he was pushed down against the bed. Panting and wild, Gray straddled him, and John opened his mouth for Gray's cock.

It didn't take long; a couple of sucks before salty bitterness flooded his mouth. Accompanied by something else; a flash of etheric energy, and John drank that down too.

Silence enveloped the bedroom, except for the sound of their breathing. The ceiling fan turned overhead, spreading a gentle breeze over exposed skin. John's thoughts drifted, fragmenting, until the weight of a hand resting on his belly drew him back.

He opened his eyes. Gray still manifested, lying beside him, black gaze fixed on John's face. "Let us leave this place," Gray said, his deep voice pitched softly for once. "Caleb says it is not so simple. But it could be. They cannot stop us. Let us leave, go elsewhere, where we can hunt demons. Where this sadness will disappear from your eyes."

Damn. Gray loved him, but John hadn't thought the drakul had learned to read him quite so well.

He rested his hand over Gray's. "I wish it was that easy," he said.

"But Caleb's right. It isn't. SPECTR isn't just going to let us leave." The truth was bitter on his tongue, but he owed it to Gray to speak it. "You're too powerful, darling. They can't let you wander around and just hope no one gets hurt."

Gray's eyes narrowed. "They are foolish," and now his voice wasn't so quiet any more. "I do not hunt mortals."

"I know. I do. But when things happen like Fort Sumter, or even the fight on the Cooper River Bridge, it attracts attention. You're too… you're too *big,*" he said helplessly.

Gray withdrew his hand. "You forget how long I went unnoticed. Your SPECTR believed me a made-up story, an old superstition. And yet I have always been here. These things you speak of, these battles—I would not have chosen them. I would have bided my time, hunted in silence. They were chosen for me. Because of you."

John felt as though all the air had vanished from the room. "Gray?"

But Gray was gone, hidden again beneath Caleb's skin. The etheric equivalent of rolling over and turning his back, John supposed.

"Don't mind him," Caleb said sleepily. He scooted closer, draping his arm over John's chest.

"Is it true, though?" John asked.

Caleb shrugged. "I guess. Look at it this way. Our mission is to stop NHEs from eating people, right? Gray didn't care about that before. So yeah, he wouldn't have made a big scene on the Cooper River Bridge. Mainly because it attracted attention, and it's not convenient to have people trying to chop your head off all the time. He would have waited until he could track the raven mocker to its lair and eaten it there, where no one would know. And it wouldn't have mattered how many people got their hearts devoured in the meantime."

"I suppose that makes sense," John said slowly.

"He cares now, because we care." Caleb yawned. "Look, don't let it bother you. Get a few demons in him, and he'll be fine."

"I suppose you know best," John replied. Caleb burrowed in more tightly, and within a few moments was asleep, his head resting on John's arm. But John lay awake for a long time, watching the ceiling fan spin, and wondering if Gray might have been better off never meeting either of them.

The insistent buzz of the phone dragged John reluctantly up out of sleep. Extracting himself out from beneath Caleb's arm, he rolled over and slapped the nightstand a few times before finding the phone.

District Chief Barillo's number showed on the display, along with the time. Goddess, it was fucking three in the morning. They'd been stuck riding a desk, so why was Barillo calling at this hour?

"Sir?" he mumbled into the phone.

"Starkweather!" Barillo's shout made John jump. "Got something for your team to look at."

John blinked. Were they back in the field now?

Barillo never appreciated being questioned, so John just said, "Give me the details, sir."

"There's a body in Brittlebank Park. Charleston PD says it's one of ours. Get down there and confirm, or knock it back to PD."

"Yes, s—" But Barillo had already hung up.

John shook his head and sat up. Behind him, Caleb stirred. "Was that Barillo?"

"Yeah." John switched on the lamp. "So get dressed, and I'll call Zahira. We've got a case."

CHAPTER 3

THE STREET RUNNING alongside the park blazed with flashing blue lights. As John stopped the car at the end of a line of police cruisers, Gray rose to hover just under Caleb's skin. A sensation of keen anticipation ran through them both.

"We will hunt."

Down, boy. It's not time to go off the leash yet.

Gray didn't reply, but all of his attention focused on their surroundings, his presence butting right up against Caleb's, just a hair away from manifesting. It was a little annoying, but after the last few weeks, Caleb couldn't really blame him. So he tried to ignore Gray as he climbed out of the car.

The scent of river water hung heavy on the air, combined with a marshy rot. One of the cops puffed on a cigarette, and even at a distance Caleb's nose started to itch. The sound of distant traffic drifted from the bridge over the Ashley River. Police radios barked and squawked. The surrounding area seemed quiet, though, the district more businesses than residential. Who had been wandering around out here to find a body at this time of night?

An identical government-issued sedan pulled up behind John's, and Zahira Noorzai climbed out. Despite the late hour, she looked annoyingly cheerful. "We have a case?"

"Maybe," John cautioned, although Caleb didn't think a force existed strong enough to dampen Zahira's enthusiasm. "We'll go in, have a look, and let Gray take a sniff."

John led the way to one of the officers monitoring the perimeter. A quick flash of his badge, and she said, "The body is over there by the dock. Detective Tradd is in charge of the scene."

As they made their way over the short-mowed grass, Zahira asked, "Is Barillo putting us back in the field?"

"He didn't say," John replied. "Just told us to come here and check out the scene."

"I hope so," Caleb said to Zahira. "Before Gray drives me around the bend."

"You will not let me drive," Gray complained. Caleb ignored him.

Caleb's enhanced sight easily picked out the curiosity brightening Zahira's eyes despite the dark night punctuated by flashing police lights. "Gray doesn't have to feed, right?"

"Right. I mean, it definitely makes him stronger, but he won't die if he doesn't." Caleb grinned. "Mainly, the enforced diet just makes him a pain in the ass."

Annoyance. *"You mortals are the ones who make things unnecessarily complicated. If you do not like my sensible response to your behavior, you should behave more rationally."*

"SPECTR?" a woman called. She stood just outside the inner ring of crime scene tape, looking as though she'd been waiting for them.

"Special Agent John Starkweather," John introduced himself with a handshake. "This is Special Agent Noorzai and Mr. Jansen, one of our outside experts."

That was one way to put it. The woman arched a brow, but didn't ask. "Detective Marsha Tradd. How much do you know about the scene?"

"Nothing," John confessed.

She nodded. "The body was discovered by a man who'd come to do a bit of night fishing off the pier. Caucasian female, mid-twenties, lying fully dressed near the edge of the river. Well, I say fully dressed, but her shoes are in tatters. So are her feet."

John frowned. "Was she in the water?"

"No, so it wasn't fish nibbling on her toes, if that's what you're getting at," Tradd said. Her lips pressed together slightly. "I hoped we might be getting a break on our missing persons case, but her ID doesn't match anyone reported missing. It still might tie in, of course, but I'm not holding my breath."

John nodded. "Understood. We'll take a look. Can you pull your men back while we examine the scene?"

She frowned slightly, but kept whatever questions she had behind her teeth. From what Caleb had seen, most cops didn't want anything to do with a SPECTR case. "Come on. The body is over here."

As they approached, she barked a few orders, and the forensics team and cops moved back. Tradd herself stopped a good distance from the pool of illumination created by the portable lights the crime scene unit had brought in.

The body lay centered in the stark white light. John strolled up, snapping on latex gloves as he did so, but Caleb hung back. He really fucking hated this part. Seeing the victims—or, usually, what was left of them—still filled him with a mix of nausea and horror. Would he ever get used to it? Did he want to?

Zahira glanced back at him, so he forced himself to take the last few steps closer to the body. Delaying the inevitable wasn't going to make it any easier.

Whoever the victim had been in life, she looked fragile in death. Her hair hung around her face, a few bobby pins still snarled in it, as if she'd worn it pinned up before whatever had happened. The dark strands lay across skin gone the color of a fish's belly, except around her swollen eyes and nose. Shorts and t-shirt clung wetly to her body, but Caleb's nose confirmed what Tradd had said, and the dead woman hadn't been in the river. It was sweat that saturated her clothes and hair, and tears that left slick trails on her distorted features. She'd cried for a long time before she'd died.

"Goddess," John murmured. "Her feet."

Her sneakers were held on only by their laces, the soles detached, the canvas worn through. Beneath showed feet turned purple and pulpy, their toenails gone, covered in blood and burst blisters. Bone gleamed through here and there, and Caleb's gorge rose even as he started to salivate.

Because the entire scene reeked with the stench of rancid sweat and clotted blood, of rotting bone and burning hair.

The stink of a demon.

Gray steps out of the pool of harsh light even as he surfaces. Black clothing and hair blend with the night, preventing the mortals from seeing him and panicking. River water splashes around his boots, and he breathes deep, every vein trembling, belly cramping with hunger at the delicious scent of the demon. Old memories flicker, of deep woods and high mountains. He has hunted this sort of demon before, long ago.

He pivots in place, but the area is saturated in the demon's smell. It was here for quite a while, perhaps toying with its prey. He moves along the bank, but the scent fades. The other direction yields the same results. So up, away from the river.

The trail draws him away from the demon's kill, across the short grass and amidst the brightly painted structures meant for mortal children's play. The scent is strong here, as well—did the demon lie in wait?

Flashlights cut across the swing set, throwing shadows, as John and Zahira hurry after him. He increases his pace, from a rapid walk to a jog, and then to a run. The demon may have fled already, but perhaps he might still catch it, might still feed. Might keep it from killing anyone else, and take the sadness out of John's eyes.

"It isn't that simple."

It should be.

The trail goes to the road, past a car which might have belonged to the dead mortal, cold and abandoned as the body. Then it stops.

He growls in frustration, even as John and Zahira come up behind him. "The demon left in an automobile," he says in distaste, because of course it did.

"Then if the suspect is still driving, the forty days aren't up," Zahira says. "We can perform an exorcism."

Gray wants to growl again. Hasn't he waited long enough? He doesn't wish this hunt to end in an exorcism but in feeding. But he doesn't give voice to his displeasure, because John and Caleb think he should wish to help the possessed mortal more than he wants to eat the demon.

"No, you should want to help the faust because we aren't like them. Because demons don't give a damn who they kill and hurt. And you're not a demon."

Of course I am not.

"Right. You're a lot scarier and freakier. So don't stoop to their level."

Caleb is correct, of course. "Yes," he tells Zahira and John. "You may save the mortal." He looks out over the empty expanse of cracked pavement, and the eagerness in his blood shifts. Now is the time for patience. For stalking. "But first, we must hunt the demon."

Caleb settled into a chair in the small conference room and stretched. The leather of his coat creaked, and he found himself grinning at the weight on his shoulders. After they'd been taken out of the field, he hadn't bothered dragging a hundred pounds of elk hide and kevlar into the office with him—no sense if he wasn't likely to be mauled.

It wasn't something he'd thought he would ever miss. He hadn't signed up for the SPECTR lifestyle voluntarily, after all, and he sure as hell wasn't a fan of all the blood and screaming. And yet, here he was, glad to be back in the saddle.

Maybe it was just Gray's good mood rubbing off on him.

The door swung open. John and Zahira entered, Zahira carrying files and John coffee. Since he and John shared a single tiny office, and Zahira was stuck in a cube farm, they had to use one of the conference rooms if they wanted to talk with both comfort and privacy.

"Get any more sleep this morning?" Caleb asked Zahira.

She cast him a rueful look. "It was almost time for suhur, so I just stayed up."

John glanced guiltily at his coffee. "Shit, I'm sorry."

Zahira rolled her eyes. "You're not fasting for Ramadan, are you? Then have your coffee. It's all right." She paused. "Actually, I'm curious. You follow Sekhmet, right? Is there any sort of rite or holy days that involve fasting for you?"

"Kind of the opposite," John said with a grimace. "At least in ancient times. She was a blood-drinking goddess who lost control, until Her rampage was stopped by, well, getting drunk. Her big festival in Egypt involved everyone getting shit-faced." His expression turned rueful. "And yes, in case you were going to ask, it's already been suggested at least some of the stories about Her may have been conflated with a drakul summoned directly into a living body."

"Oh." Zahira looked thoughtful. "Because of the blood-drinking?"

"And the rampaging, and the need for some last-ditch desperate ploy to stop Her. Not to say I think anyone stopped a drakul by getting it drunk."

"Alcohol doesn't affect me anymore," Caleb said sadly. "So that would probably be a 'no.' Besides, it was supposed to be dyed red so she thought it was blood, right? Maybe it *was* blood originally."

Which wasn't really a comfortable thought. Human blood wasn't nourishing for drakul…in the same way alcohol or drugs weren't nourishing for humans.

Gray stirred. *"We have not tasted John's blood for a while. Perhaps he will let us again soon."*

Not the time to be thinking about that. Caleb shifted, glad the table hid his sudden erection. *Christ.*

"Hunh," Zahira mused as she sat down. "Now we know drakul do really exist, I wonder what sort of archaeological evidence we could find for them? I know the Vigilant found a lot of stuff, but what if universities and museums begin their own research? What might we learn?"

John cleared his throat. "Let's worry about the case we have in front of us right now."

"Yeah, sorry." Zahira's light brown cheeks darkened slightly. "I ran a search on the victim's injuries and found a match. The NHE is most likely a vila."

John, of course, was nodding, but Caleb hadn't gone through the Academy. In fact, before Gray's possession brought him to SPECTR's attention, he'd actively avoided learning anything more about the etheric plane or paranormal abilities than the average school kid. "And a vila is…?"

Zahira took out her tablet and began to page through the report she'd apparently loaded on it earlier. "We get the name from Slavic legend. According to the myths, they primarily possessed young women who had been betrayed by their lovers. They would lure men into the deep forest and make them dance until they died."

"They feed on a victim's life force, similar to an incubus," John added.

"I think Gray ran into one of these before." Caleb rubbed at his forehead, trying to conjure up the flashes of memory. "The scent was familiar to him."

"Yes. But it was a long time ago." Gray considered. *"They are very fast. But I was very patient."*

"It was too fast for him," Caleb said. "But he cornered it while it slept and ate it. Then some woodsman came along and cut his head off with an ax. Which is probably a detail none of us really wanted to hear."

"I am simply being informative."

"Some myths say they're storm spirits," Zahira said, glancing up from her tablet. "Like you."

"Oh hell, no," Caleb tried to say, at the same moment Gray snarled, "They are nothing like me."

It came out as a garbled mush, and both Zahira and John looked slightly alarmed. Shit. Caleb held up his hands. "Sorry. Sorry. Gray's a little touchy about being compared to, well, *food.*"

"I didn't mean to offend. It's just, we don't even know the relationships between etheric entities, if…well." She straightened her shoulders and looked Caleb in the eye. "I'm sorry, Gray. I didn't realize."

People didn't speak to Gray directly when he wasn't manifesting. Not even John, at least not usually.

"You may tell her I forgive her," Gray said loftily, like a king granting a royal pardon.

"He accepts your apology," Caleb said. "So, what have we got? The victim jilted her lover, and the lover summoned an NHE and killed her in the park?"

It wasn't the subtlest conversational shift, but it did the trick. "Maybe." John opened the file and flipped through it. "The victim was one Kandace Danielson. She was a dancer with the Beaufain Ballet."

"A ballerina?" Caleb said. "And she was danced to death? That's… that's sick."

"You'll get no disagreement from me." John took a small sip of his coffee. "According to her roommate, she left yesterday morning to go to the ballet company's studio. She never returned home, but apparently that wasn't unusual, and the roommate didn't worry until the police showed up on their doorstep."

"It could still be a jilted lover," Zahira said slowly, staring at the files spread in front of them. "But the ballet connection…I don't know. My gut says there's more to it."

"Agreed," John said.

"I know one of the dancers with the company," Zahira went on with a concerned frown. "I met her at mosque. She probably knew the victim."

"Excellent. Hopefully your connection will make people more forthcoming when we start asking questions." John rose to his feet. "I'll update Barillo with our progress, then meet the two of you in the lobby in fifteen minutes."

"Give Barillo a kiss from me," Caleb called as John exited. He had just enough time to glimpse the obscene gesture John gave him in reply, before the door swung shut between them.

CHAPTER 4

AS THE DOOR opened on District Chief Michael Barillo's office, John took a deep, calming breath and reminded himself anger was unproductive. Yes, he'd had issues with the new district chief. Yes, Barillo had made no attempt to pretend he approved of either Caleb and Gray, or John's relationship with them. But he'd put them back in the field again, and that was progress.

"Come in," Barillo grumbled. John stepped inside, carefully shutting the door behind him. Family photos crowded the walls and desk, stacks of files perched precariously on every surface, and loose memos were scattered atop any remaining bit of space.

"You requested I keep you updated, sir," John said. "Special Agent Noorzai identified the NHE as a vila, and Gray agreed. We're going to the Beaufain Ballet's studio to question the victim's co-workers, try to find out when she was seen last and with whom."

"I'm taking a chance here, putting you back in the field," Barillo said. He unwrapped one of the butterscotch candies on his desk and popped it into his mouth. He didn't offer any to John. "I want this case closed quickly and *quietly*. Do you understand what I'm saying, Starkweather?"

John nodded. "Yes, sir."

"I'm giving you another chance because we've got our hands full. A lycanthrope running amok in North Charleston, ghoul nests popping up like mushrooms." The candy cracked loudly between Barillo's teeth. "Not to mention the rash of disappearances splashed all over the headlines. If it turns out they're legit and an NHE is behind them, we've got to get them wrapped up fast. As much as I don't like it, you've got a good track record there."

John ground his teeth silently. "Thank you, sir."

"Don't thank me. After the nonsense on the Cooper River Bridge, I'd rather you spent the rest of your career behind a desk," Barillo said bluntly. "We're not going to have a repeat of that incident, are we?"

John swallowed back a useless protest. They'd done what was necessary to stop the raven mocker, and yes, it had resulted in a bit of a spectacle. But no one else had died, and the NHE had been put down. The old district chief would have called it a win.

But Indira Kaniyar was off being the Director of SPECTR now, and it was Barillo he had to contend with.

"No, sir," John grated out.

"Good." Barillo's gaze met his. "Don't fuck this up, Starkweather. Keep the drakul on a tight leash, *don't* let this turn into front page news, and I'll think about putting you back on the streets."

John needed to keep his mouth shut. But he couldn't. "And if not? Sir?"

"There will be consequences." Barillo's eyes narrowed. "And you won't like them. Bring me the vila, in a fucking *bottle*. Got it?"

"Yes, sir." John turned away and reached for the doorknob. His fingers trembled with suppressed rage. "I understand."

"Okay," John said as he pulled into the parking lot beside the low, concrete building housing the company's studio, "we'll interview everyone who might have a lead for us. Caleb, signal me if Gray gets so much as a whiff of NHE on the premises."

Caleb nodded from the backseat. "Got it. Anything else?"

"Let Zahira and me do the talking. And don't just take off, even if the vila is right there. Let us know first, and we'll corral and handle it."

Caleb bit back a snarky reply. What had Barillo said to John? He'd been antsy as hell the whole ride up to North Charleston.

Gray stirred. *"This mortal has threatened John?"*

Barillo didn't rate a name, not from Gray. Names were reserved for the humans he deigned to notice, like John. Zahira. A handful of others.

I don't know. Just…wait and watch for now. We've got the vila to concentrate on.

A keen edge of hunger, bordering on outright lust. *"I have not forgotten."*

We can't eat it.

Annoyance. *"I have not forgotten that, either. But we can at least hunt."*

Heat waves rose from the parking lot. Zahira had texted her friend and asked her to meet them at the studio door. Technically, Caleb supposed they could just barge in and start interrogating the nearest person, but that wasn't really John's style. If they had someone to let them into the off-limits areas without having to flash their badges every few feet, they might as well use her.

When they got to the studio, the stage door swung open to reveal a tall, slender woman with dark eyes and black hair pulled back into a shiny bun. She wore a loose tank top over a leotard, accompanied by tights and pointe shoes. A light sheen of sweat showed on her olive skin. "I just got out of warm-up," she said. "What's going on, Zahira?"

"Rania Wilson, this is Special Agent John Starkweather and Caleb Jansen," Zahira said.

"Ms. Wilson," John said, shaking her hand.

"Call me Rania." Her brows pulled together. "What's going on? Why is SPECTR here?"

Zahira looked sympathetic. "I'm sorry, but we need to talk to whoever is in charge here first."

"Basil?" Rania asked with an uncertain frown. "Sure. Come this way."

She led them down a long, cool hall. Framed posters hung at intervals, advertising previous seasons of the ballet. Caleb had gone to a production of *The Nutcracker* in Charlotte one time, but that was pretty much the extent of his ballet knowledge.

Rania stopped in front of a door with *Director, Beaufain Ballet* on it. "Here we are. Do you want me to…?"

"If you don't mind," John said.

Rania nodded, still looking less than certain about the whole situation as she knocked on the door. It swung open to reveal a thin man with a deep scowl in place. "I said I would make up my mind when I make up my mind!"

Rania took a hasty step back and gestured at Zahira. "Basil Syrkus, this is my friend Zahira. She's with SPECTR," she added, before he could start yelling again.

The man's scowl flashed to confusion—then back to anger. "SPECTR? Oh for fuck's sake. Those fluttering hens have reported us?

You don't have any reason to investigate. I know my rights, and this is harassment!"

What the hell? Caleb took a deep breath, but the only reek he scented was sweaty feet. No trace of demons. So what was the director so worked up about?

"Thank you for the introduction, Rania," John said. She gave him a quick nod and scurried away, probably glad to get out of Syrkus's sight. "Mr. Syrkus, I'm Special Agent John Starkweather. I take it you're the director of the Beaufain Ballet?"

"You damned well know who I am!" Syrkus blustered.

"Agent Noorzai, would you mind taking notes?" John asked casually, glancing at Zahira. A slight twist of the head farther, and he met Caleb's gaze.

Caleb shook his head slightly. No demons here, at least not recently.

"May we continue this inside your office, Mr. Syrkus?" John suggested.

Syrkus shook his head. "No. Anything you have to say, you can say it out here."

"Very well. When was the last time you saw Kandace Danielson, and why did you think we were coming to question you about her disappearance?"

All the wind left Syrkus's sails; his skin paled, and real alarm crossed his face. "Kandace? She's disappeared? Oh God, does this have something to do with what they're talking about on the news?"

"You tell me, Mr. Syrkus. You certainly seemed to, if not expect us, be on the defensive at our appearance." John's blue eyes narrowed. "Would you care to explain why?"

"There's been a misunderstanding." Syrkus ran a hand over his face. "Come inside my office, agents. Please."

A desk took up much of the space in the small office. Plaques honoring the ballet company covered the walls. A green couch stood against one wall, and a pair of battered ballet shoes lay on the floor in front of it.

"Forgive me for my poor manners," Syrkus said. He pulled a flask from his desk and held it out toward John.

"Not while we're on duty," John said.

"Of course." Syrkus took a hefty swallow before replacing the flask in its drawer. "I didn't mean to come across as I did. Over the years, I've weathered more than my share of hate mail from the God-fearing people of South Carolina, so I assumed they'd sent you as they continually threaten. You understand."

John looked as lost as Caleb felt. "I didn't realize ballet was so controversial. Can you...elaborate?"

Syrkus gave them all a withering look down his long nose. "Not fans of the ballet?"

John shrugged easily. "I'm more of a NASCAR watcher, myself."

"A sport with its own intricate strategy, its own stories of drama played out over the course of a season." Syrkus flashed John a rueful smile. "Surprised? Perhaps you should give the ballet another chance."

"I think I will. But why are your performances particularly godless?"

Syrkus sighed. "Because my signature ballet—not performed every season, but yes, we are doing it this year—is *Giselle*." He sank down into the chair behind the desk. "It is one of the great ballets. The innocent village maiden, Giselle, is in love with Loys, a man she believes to be a peasant like herself. But no, he is in fact Duke Albrecht, having his last dalliance with a simple village girl before his wedding to a woman of his own class. Alas, his duplicity is revealed, and the girl devastated. She flees into the forest, where she is comforted by the evil spirit of a vila."

Caleb straightened sharply. Okay, no way was this a coincidence.

"Giselle's heart is weak, and she succumbs to the spirit," Syrkus went on, too enrapt with his own description to notice their surprise. "She is possessed! First she dances to death the young peasant man who was in love with her, and who exposed Albrecht's lie. Then she turns her sights on Albrecht himself. When he comes seeking her in the forest, she forces him to dance, hour after hour. But just as he is ready to succumb, she realizes the atrocity the spirit—the demon!—wishes her to commit against the man she still loves. Rather than murder Albrecht, she kills herself and the demon inside her."

"That...isn't how it works," Zahira said.

Syrkus threw up his arms. "Who cares? It is art! It is meant to uplift the human soul! To tell a tale of love triumphing over evil! But oh no, we cannot put on the play, because it will convince young women to summon vila and become possessed. Or so the clucking hens would have it." He snorted. "I think young women can make their own decisions, don't you?"

"Certainly there haven't been outbreaks of possession after every performance," John said dryly. "You're well within your rights to put on whatever ballet you want, Mr. Syrkus. Although I'm not entirely uncertain there is no connection between it and why we're here."

"Kandace." Syrkus's concerned look returned. "What happened? Is she missing? She is one of three soloists I'm considering elevating to principal dancer."

"Which means she'd play Giselle?" Zahira asked.

"That's correct."

John's lips pressed together. "I'm not certain how to say this in a way that would make it any easier, Mr. Syrkus. Ms. Danielson is dead, and she was killed by a vila."

"Everyone, please gather round," Syrkus called. "I have terrible news."

John, Zahira, and Caleb had followed the director down the hall, into the parts of the building not generally open to the public. They wound their way through a small maze of concrete-walled corridors, cheap tile floors, and doors with dancers' names posted on them with tape. The air stank of sweaty feet and hairspray. Caleb sneezed twice before they reached the studio where the dancers had gathered.

Clearly they had been rehearsing. When Syrkus spoke, the room fell silent, and the dancers stilled. John spotted Zahira's friend Rania in the group, her eyes going to Zahira and brow raised in a question.

She wasn't the only one staring at the agents, and as Syrkus spoke, informing them of the tragedy, more eyes shifted to them. Those who weren't crying, at least; several of the dancers broke down at the news of Danielson's death. Moans of "Kandace?" and "Oh God, no," echoed around the room.

When Syrkus finished his piece, he beckoned John forward. John stepped up beside him, doing his best to radiate calm authority. "Because of the manner of Ms. Danielson's death, we don't believe this was a random attack," he said. "We're looking for information as to why someone might want to hurt her. A grudge, an angry lover, any detail at all might be of help to the investigation."

One of the male dancers, his thighs distractingly muscular beneath his tights, said, "You mean someone other than Rania and Olympia?"

Gasps of horror rang out, and the entire company looked at him as though he'd said something inexcusable. "That isn't true!" Rania shouted.

The man shrugged. "She was your primary competition to dance Giselle."

"How dare you," snapped another woman, whom John assumed was Olympia.

He glanced over his shoulder at Caleb, who gave him a small shake of his head. No vila here. "No one in this room was responsible," John said, fixing the male dancer with a cold look. "We would know if anyone here was possessed."

"If you meant this as a joke, Carlos, it was in poor taste," Syrkus added with a glare at the dancer. "May I remind you Kandace is dead?"

No one else spoke up. "I'm going to leave a stack of my business cards here," John said. "If anything occurs to anyone—even something minor—don't hesitate to call me, day or night."

"Thank you, Agent Starkweather," Syrkus said. "I'm sure you'll find who did this terrible thing. In the meantime," he added, turning back to the company, "Kandace would wish the show to go on. Take five minutes to compose yourselves, and we'll restart."

The dancers began to mill around. Several fled the room, wiping at their eyes. John had hoped someone else might come forward to talk to him, once everyone's attention was scattered again, but only Rania approached.

"You're going to catch whoever did this, aren't you?" she asked Zahira.

"Inshallah, yes," Zahira replied. "I'll call you later. You have my number, right? Text or call if you think of anyone who might have wanted to hurt Kandace. Or if you just need to talk."

Rania nodded. "Yeah. I will."

They left, returning to the summer heat outside. John cranked the air vents up to full blast to combat the sweltering sedan.

"Well, that was a bust," Caleb said from the back seat. "I know it would be a weird coincidence, but maybe this doesn't actually have anything to do with the ballet company. Maybe is was just random."

"Possible," John conceded. "But one of the dancers for a company known for performing *Giselle* is murdered by a vila? And she was apparently auditioning for the part? Even if the rest of the company wasn't involved, this has all the earmarks of someone who knew Danielson and wanted her dead."

"Agreed," Zahira said. "So what next? We question the roommate?"

John nodded as he steered the car out of the lot. "Yes. Let's hope she has more for us than the company did."

CHAPTER 5

"So much for that," Caleb said as they walked through the halls of SPECTR-HQ to reach the conference room again.

The roommate hadn't been helpful—she and Danielson hadn't been particularly close, and apparently Danielson had spent her little free time studying videos of famous dancers, breaking in pointe shoes, and other ballet-related activities. Her only friends were with the company, and she had no love interest as far as the roommate knew.

"Someone has to know something," John said firmly. "I still don't believe this was a random death."

"And unfortunately the vila is still out there, so even if the first death wasn't random, the next one might be," Caleb said. He reached the door to the conference room they normally used, then stopped. "Goddamn it."

MONSTER was scrawled in huge black letters across the door.

Shit.

For a moment, John's vision flashed red and his fists tightened. He wanted to find the asshole who vandalized the door and beat him to within an inch of his life. Then he'd go to Barillo's office and scream at him for letting this shit go on, for not taking the harassment seriously.

"I'll be back," Caleb said, turning away from the door.

John took a deep breath and fought for calm. He had to keep his head together, had to be there for Caleb. "Just hold on, babe. We don't know who—"

"I'm just going to the fucking bathroom," Caleb snarled, and hell, was there a deeper rumble to his voice? "I'll be back."

He stomped away without waiting for a reply. John wanted to run after him, wanted to grab Caleb and pull him into a hug. Wanted to protect him from all the stupidity and the senseless hate.

"John?" Zahira asked uncertainly.

He sighed. "Yes?"

"I don't understand." She followed him into the conference room. "I get that Gray is a big, scary NHE. But why...this?" She gestured back at the door. "Everyone acts genuinely afraid of him, and I don't understand why."

"It's complicated," John hedged.

"If not for Gray, Forsyth would have killed a lot more people," Zahira said. "But instead of treating him like a hero, everyone seems convinced he's a bomb ready to go off." She hesitated. "Is it just some stupid prejudice? Other NHEs are dangerous, so he must be dangerous by association?"

John wanted to tell her yes. It was just a stupid prejudice, and it didn't matter how many lives Gray saved, just like it didn't matter how many people who looked like Zahira were fighting and dying against terrorists every day. Because fear had taken the place of logic.

And it would mostly be the truth. Sort of.

But the people who were the most terrified of Gray were the ones who'd been there at Fort Sumter. Who'd seen him in all his glory.

Who'd witnessed that moment of hesitation, when it had seemed like he really was going to kill them, too.

He thought about the vampire teddy bear sitting in the corner of their office, a gift from Karl Rand to Caleb in an attempt to make up for all the shitty treatment he'd gotten since Fort Sumter. "Not everyone is afraid of Gray," he replied carefully. "It's just a lot for people to adapt to. After all, we're taught our entire lives that possession equals madness and death. Our job is to stop people who are possessed, to remove NHEs from our plane of existence one way or another. And now the higher ups are asking us all to work beside one."

Zahira stared at her hands thoughtfully. Her nails were neatly clipped and covered in a clear polish. "I suppose. Maybe if we weren't so ignorant about etheric entities, people wouldn't be scared of them." A sigh of frustration escaped her. "We barely know anything about NHEs, let alone the etheric plane. We don't even know how they pass back and forth from our world to theirs, other than we have to summon them. But since summoning is completely illegal, we can't study the most basic interaction with them, not even for science, not even if we mean to send them back right away!"

John nodded, glad the conversation had shifted to less dangerous ground. "I know. After working with the Vigilant...well, I'm not sure what the law ought to be, but NHEs can be summoned safely. There should be exceptions for summonings under controlled circumstances."

"I wonder if Forsyth discovered anything useful?" Zahira sat back and crossed her arms over her chest. "Although, if he did, he certainly wasn't publishing papers on it. I'm sure all his research is locked away in a vault where no one will ever see it again. I just wish..."

No wonder she'd been so excited to work beside Gray. "Is that why you applied for this assignment? Because it was your only chance to see an NHE up close?"

She put a hand to her mouth. "Oh, no! Well, yes. But it sounds bad when you put it that way."

John grinned. "I assure you, it doesn't. Agents take assignments for a lot worse reasons, believe me."

"I don't want to sound like I think of Gray as a...a laboratory rat, though." She chewed worriedly on her lower lip. "And I understand that after being taken prisoner by Forsyth, he's wary of anyone else getting too curious."

"Honestly, I think that's mostly Caleb," John said. "He's always had a problem with authority, and Forsyth didn't help things much." He paused, an idea forming. "I tell you what—I'll ask Gray if *he* minds you asking questions. Caleb can't really object if Gray doesn't."

Of course, Caleb would most certainly object. But Gray had rights, too. Maybe not legally, but surely morally.

"Really?" Zahira clasped her hands together, eyes shining. "That would be wonderful!"

John grinned, but a little worm of guilt squirmed in his gut. Because here he was, talking about her getting a closer look at Gray when they weren't in the middle of a fight...and not telling her what had really happened that night of Fort Sumter.

What Gray actually was.

She was their partner, working with them in close quarters. Didn't she have the right to know?

Nothing like Fort Sumter would ever happen again. Those circumstances had been special—it had taken a massive amount of

NHEs to give Gray the power to fully manifest. Hundreds, at least.

And if it wouldn't happen again, then there was no need for Zahira to know about it, right?

Caleb stormed into the men's room. Thank God there was no one at the urinals; he wasn't sure he could have kept himself from flashing fangs in their direction.

Because fuck these assholes. They had him trapped—he couldn't leave because the higher ups like Kaniyar would never let him, but that didn't stop every lower-level agent from doing their damnedest to push him out. And John, acting so fucking calm, like nothing was wrong...

Caleb spun and slammed his fist into the long mirror hanging above the sinks. It shattered with a satisfying crunch, shards falling free to crash against the counter. And to hell with Barillo—if he looked the other way for the vandalism of the door, he could damn well ignore this, too.

A toilet at the end of the row of stalls flushed.

Caleb braced his hands on the counter and bowed his head. Great. Just great. He'd had a meltdown, and now someone would run to Barillo and tattle, and maybe Gray had the right idea and they should just grab John and take off...

"Caleb? Um, are you okay?" Karl Rand asked.

Some of the tension left Caleb's shoulders, and he leaned forward, resting his forehead against the broken glass. "Heh. I bet that's not a question you have to ask very often."

"Kind of a first," Karl said wryly. His shoes tapped crisply on the tiles as he crossed to a sink and washed his hands. "But, since I can't sense you, you're going to have to tell me." He let out a hiss. "You've hurt your hand."

"It'll heal," Caleb said, and indeed the cuts were already closing. Slower than they should have, since Gray hadn't fed in a while, but far faster than on anyone unpossessed.

He straightened and turned to face Karl. Karl wore a nice suit—John would be envious—and a tie which matched his green empath's armband. "Some dick wrote 'monster' on the door of the conference room we've been using," Caleb admitted. "I'm just frustrated, that's all."

Karl's mouth quirked. "I understand."

"Yeah," Caleb said, his gaze falling on the armband. "I guess you do." Bad enough most people were scared of empaths. But it had to be twice as bad to come out as a transman *and* get a full blast of what assholes felt about that delivered straight to your head. "I don't know how you put up with it."

"I have a great therapist," Karl said with a rueful grin. "Beyond that...in my experience, a lot of people spend their lives terrified of things which don't actually pose any danger to them. I don't know if it's just easier for the human brain to feel fear, if it's some kind of default you have to work against, or what. But I try to remind myself how awful it would be to live like that. Every day, choosing to spend your life afraid, when you don't have to be."

"Yeah," Caleb said slowly. "I see what you mean. I'm not sure it makes it any easier, but I see what you mean."

Karl laughed. "Well, I'm working on it too. Believe me."

"I hear you." Caleb bit his lip. "Hey, man, back when you could still sense me, before the possession became permanent...I hope I didn't make you feel bad. I didn't have the best attitude toward empaths...and I'm not telling you anything you don't already know. I was a dick, and I'm sorry."

"I've haven't been entirely comfortable around you, either, then or recently," Karl said. "So let's call it even."

"Sounds good." Caleb stuck his hand out, before remembering that wasn't something you were supposed to do with an empath. Karl looked taken aback, then grinned and shook his hand.

"You could be very popular with empaths," Karl said. "Someone we *don't* have crowding into our heads all day? If you weren't dating Starkweather..."

"Ha!" But it made Caleb think. "Listen, Karl...how much does all this bother John?"

Karl sighed. "I can't tell you, Caleb. It would be unethical."

"Yeah, sorry." Caleb felt stupid for even asking. "I wasn't thinking."

"No problem." Karl glanced at the exit. "Are you going to be okay, or...?"

"Yeah." Caleb stepped toward the door. "I need to get back to it. There's a vila out there killing people, and a few jerks here at SPECTR don't change that. But thanks for talking to me." He paused. "Hey, you want to come over some night? We'll watch the race, make John cook us dinner, and drink beer."

Karl laughed. "It's a date."

"Another day, another crime scene," Caleb said the next morning.

They'd still been dressing for the day when the call came in to John's phone. An early morning jogger had found another body, probably a second vila victim, in Waterfront Park. Now Caleb, John, and Zahira made their way through yet another scene of milling cops and forensic technicians.

Clouds had rolled in overnight, lending the sunlight a grayish hue. Seagulls kited on the stiff breeze, occasionally diving down into the waves. A few early tourists gawked from the street, held back by the police barriers.

Detective Tradd awaited them once again. "This looks like the same MO as the killer at Brittlebank Park," she said as they approached. "So I called SPECTR right away. No one's disturbed the body yet." She glanced over her shoulder. "It's in the fountain."

John nodded. "Thanks, detective. We'll take a look."

Caleb took a deep breath as he followed John and Zahira toward the circular fountain. Salt, rotting marsh grass, and fish dominated the air, but intermingled he detected the scent of old blood, of sweat gone rank and vile.

It is faint, though. Disappointment. *The demon is long gone.*

"The vila was here," he reported. "I don't think it hung around this time—the scent is pretty faded."

"Got it," John said with a nod.

"Did the vila feel more confident this time?" Zahira wondered. "Is that why it didn't linger?"

"Hard to say, but it's possible," John agreed. "Especially if the faust hasn't been possessed long, and wasn't sure about the whole 'killing people' thing to begin with. This second kill might have been easier for them to agree to."

They approached a fountain in the shape of a palmetto bush. Normally jets of water shot from the crown to fall into the basin beneath. Someone had at least thought to turn off the water, although it still pooled around the body, draining slowly from her saturated clothing and hair. The victim lay half-in the basin, as if she'd collapsed into the fountain—or flung herself in. Her legs dangled over the side, her shoes nothing but tatters, bone showing through the soles of her blistered feet. Her features were obscured beneath the water collected in the basin, but even so, Caleb's heart sank.

"She's one of the other dancers, isn't—wasn't—she?" he asked.

John nodded grimly. He leaned over the body, studying it carefully. "Olympia, I think, was the name."

Zahira hissed softly. "She was the other soloist, wasn't she?"

Caleb swore. "This was aimed at the company, then. Not at

Danielson at all—or at least, not just at her. Someone wants to take out everyone who might dance the part of Giselle."

His gaze met Zahira's. Her dark eyes had gone wide beneath her black hijab. "And that means Rania will be next."

CHAPTER 6

WHEN THEY ENTERED the studio, a hush swept across the room. The dancers were in the midst of warming up, and some remained caught in poses when they noticed the agents: arms raised, a foot resting on the barre, one leg stretched before them as they knelt on the floor.

For an instant, everything was silent. Then one of the women whispered Olympia's name. A wild murmur rose up: "Is she all right?" "Where is she?" "Maybe nothing happened to her—she's just late!"

Rania stood amidst the panicking dancers, her gaze trained on Zahira. John hoped she remained as calm when she found out she might be next on the vila's list.

"Mr. Syrkus," he said, crossing to where the director stood watching. "I'd like to speak with you privately, if I may. My colleagues will address the rest of the company."

"Privately? But..." Syrkus trailed off. "Very well, Agent Starkweather. Join me in my office."

John exchanged a look with Zahira as he followed Syrkus out. She'd break the news of Olympia's death to the rest of the company, then take Rania aside. With any luck, Rania would agree to protective custody while they figured out their next move.

Syrkus shut the door behind them, then went to his desk. "Something to drink?" he asked, pulling out the flask and two glasses.

"No, thank you," John replied, sitting down across from the desk without being asked.

"Ah yes. You're on duty." Syrkus splashed a good amount of whiskey into one of the glasses. "I hope you don't mind if I indulge."

"Go right ahead," John said. "You don't seem curious as to why we're here."

Syrkus sat down heavily in his own chair. For a moment, he looked older, the lines in his face deeply graven, as if some part of him had given up the struggle against gravity. "Olympia didn't come in this morning. I told myself she was just late. There had been a traffic jam, or her alarm didn't go off. But she's dead, isn't she?"

John nodded. "I'm afraid so."

Syrkus slugged back the whiskey in a single gulp. "Damn. So much talent; so much potential. Wasted."

"The loss of a life, especially a young one, is always tragic," John agreed. "But with her death, our investigation shifts from focusing on Ms. Danielson, to focusing on what seems to be the common thread. The Beaufain Ballet Company."

Syrkus looked alarmed. "What do you mean? Surely you aren't accusing—"

"I'm not accusing any of your dancers. Or you," John added. "My colleague, Mr. Jansen, would know in an instant if the vila had been on the premises recently."

Syrkus frowned, but didn't ask for an explanation. "So who is it? Who is doing these terrible things?"

"That's what we want to know." John leaned forward. "Think carefully, Mr. Syrkus. Is there anyone who might have a grudge against the company as a whole?"

"What do you mean?" Syrkus drew himself up slightly. "A grudge? What sort of grudge?"

"A rivalry?" John spread his hands out in a gesture of helplessness. "An angry business partner? Someone desperate to see the company fail? You could tell me far more easily than I could guess."

Syrkus's scowled. "Don't be absurd. There's nothing like that. No one who would—would *kill* to see us fail."

"Think hard. Are you sure?"

"Of course!" Syrkus rose to his feet abruptly, forcing John to look up at him. "Isn't it your job to discover these things, instead of asking the victims to solve the crime themselves? SPECTR should have protected Olympia, and now she's dead!"

John took a calming breath. "I'm sorry for your loss, Mr. Syrkus, but it's hard to predict what a faust will do if we don't know *why* they're doing it."

Syrkus snorted. "The vila is a demon. Demons don't have a *why*."

"Perhaps." John rose to his feet. "But humans do. Look to your favorite ballet, if you need a reminder."

"I can't believe this is happening," Rania said.

She sat on the floor against the wall, one knee drawn up to her chest, hugging it to her. Zahira crouched beside her. Caleb leaned against the cinder block wall a few feet away, idly admiring the legs of one of the male dancers. The company milled around, whispering to each other and casting unhappy looks in Rania's direction.

"Inshallah, it's going to be all right," Zahira said. She put a comforting hand on Rania's wrist. "We won't let the vila hurt you. We can take you into protective custody, and—"

She was cut off by Syrkus striding into the room, his face dark with anger. John followed him, and although his expression seemed impassive, Caleb knew him well enough by now to spot the tiny line on his forehead, the tightness at the corner of his mouth. Syrkus had pissed him off.

"All right." Syrkus clapped his hands for attention. "There is no delicate way to announce this, so I shall be direct. Rania, you will dance the part of Giselle this season."

Rania's eyes widened, and she rose to her feet. Someone started to applaud, then stopped quickly when no one else joined in.

Was this guy nuts? He'd already had two ballerinas murdered. Was he trying to make it three? "You can't mean to put on the ballet!" Caleb exclaimed.

"Of course I do." Syrkus scowled. "Agent Starkweather believes this vila is targeting the company. Trying to stop our production for some inscrutable reason. We must be strong, and we must honor the memories of Kandace and Olympia. So we will put on the best version of *Giselle* anyone has ever seen!"

There came a smattering of clapping this time, although many of the dancers looked alarmed. Caleb didn't blame them. Was Syrkus a complete lunatic?

Zahira looked worriedly at Rania. "Rania? Tell him you won't do it."

Rania glanced at Zahira, then at Syrkus. For a moment she hesitated…then she drew herself up, shoulders back, a study in grace and strength. "I'll do it. I'll dance the part of Giselle."

Syrkus grinned. "That's my girl. All right, everyone. Today we'll…"

Caleb tuned the rest out, turning to Rania. "You can't be serious! You're risking your life over a part?"

"This isn't just a part," Rania replied. "This means I'm being elevated to principal dancer."

"I know, but—"

"No. You don't know." Her dark eyes burned fiercely. "I've worked my entire life for this. I put on my first pair of ballet shoes when I was four. I've spent every day, every hour, every minute since working for this. And some demon isn't going to keep me from getting it."

John had joined them. "We'll do what we can to keep you safe, but you're still taking a risk. Are you sure you don't want protective custody?"

"I'm certain." Her mouth took on a firm line, and she raised her chin defiantly.

"All right." John nodded. "I respect your decision. The other two soloists weren't attacked in their homes—it looks like the vila might have followed them from the studio, then either lured or trailed them to the parks where they died."

"So step one, stay away from parks," Caleb said.

John gave him a look which suggested it would be more helpful if he'd keep his mouth shut. "My point is, your ordinary movements might draw out the vila."

"And then we catch it," Gray said unexpectedly. Caleb hadn't realized he was even paying attention. *"And eat it."*

Unless it can still be exorcised.

Caleb coughed. "That's a good idea," he said, trying to make his voice deeper to convey it was Gray's opinion, without saying anything suspicious in front of Rania.

Rania looked at him like he was crazy. "Didn't you just say the opposite?"

"You could say I'm of two minds about it."

"What do you think, Rania?" Zahira asked quickly. "We're not using you as bait, exactly…but we sort of are."

"No, that's fine." She nodded determinedly. "Anything to get this over with. I'm supposed to go out clubbing for a friend's birthday tonight—do you think that might help?" She glanced at Zahira. "I know it's Ramadan, and I probably shouldn't be out partying, but she's a good friend…"

"We'll go with you," Zahira said, with a quick look at John to confirm it. "All three of us. The vila probably won't show up around a lot of people, so we'll be safe in the club. On the way there and back, though…if it comes after you, we'll be there to put a stop to it. Permanently."

"And if it doesn't?" Rania asked, a hint of uncertainty slipping into her voice.

"Then I'll stay the night with you," Zahira promised. "I'll put up spirit wards so the vila won't be able to come into your apartment."

"Rania!" Syrkus called.

Rania winced. "Okay. That sounds good. Are you going to stay?"

"I'll go back to my place and get some things, and come pick you up after you're done here," Zahira said. "You should be safe until then, since there's so many people around."

"And there's no indication the vila's ever been inside the studio," John added. "Caleb and I will meet you at your apartment this evening. Take care of yourself, and if you get worried or change your mind, text or call Zahira immediately."

They left the dancers to their work. As they exited the building, Caleb said, "Well at least one good thing came out of all this."

"What's that?" John asked.

Caleb grinned. "We get to go clubbing."

"Are you done?" John called as he smoothed his shirt down. It had been a while since he'd gone out—shortly after he and Caleb had first met, actually, when they'd just become a couple.

Given the way Caleb was acting tonight, maybe he should have made it more of a priority. There had just been so many other things to do than go out and dance.

"Just about!" Caleb called from the bathroom down the hall. "I need you to lace me up."

The hell? John walked down the hall and stopped at the sight of Caleb checking himself out in the mirror.

He looked…delicious was one word for it. Hot as hell was another. Forget fighting the vila—Caleb would be beating off women all night, and probably a few guys as well.

Caleb wore his heavy boots—the black leather, buckles, and thick soles which made them perfect for chasing down NHEs also served well as club gear. Same for the leather pants. His light, silvery shirt looked rather familiar.

"Is that my shirt?" John asked.

"Yep," Caleb said unrepentantly. "Now help me into this thing."

The "thing" was a black leather corset from April, the same leatherworker who made Caleb's coats. "You could have gotten one that laced up the front," John pointed out as he came up behind Caleb.

"True." Caleb leaned over, brushing his ass over the front of John's pants. "But where's the fun in that?"

John laughed and went to work. There was something fucking hot about pulling the warm leather tight around Caleb's body. And when he was done...

Caleb turned around with a grin. "Like what you see, Starkweather?"

"You know I do." John rubbed at the erection rigid against his jeans. "You're going to be a hell of a distraction tonight. We're supposed to be working, but all I'll be thinking of is bending you over and fucking you the moment we get home."

Caleb's grin took on a sexy edge. "Well. We can't have you too distracted. Maybe a little taste now, hmm?"

He stepped up to John, rubbing his hand over John's erection. John pulled him in for a kiss. Caleb popped open the button of John's jeans, then tugged the zipper down.

John groaned into his mouth when Caleb's hand closed over his dick and pulled him out. "You drive me crazy," John mumbled against Caleb's lips.

"It's a short drive," Caleb teased. Then he went to his knees.

John leaned against the doorframe for support. Caleb tugged on his cock once or twice, before lapping up precome with his tongue. "Mmm. I love how you taste," Caleb murmured. Then his mouth closed over John's cock.

It felt amazing: all warmth and wetness, and the shiver of Gray's energy just underneath Caleb's skin. Not manifesting—the fangs definitely got in the way of a blowjob. But still there with them.

He looked up at the mirror, and found himself transfixed by their reflection: Caleb, dressed to fuck, on his knees, his black hair spread loose over his shoulders. John slid his hand through that hair, bunching it up, and Caleb moaned his encouragement. Caleb pulled back just long enough to say, "Fuck my mouth, Starkweather," before taking John all the way down his throat.

John gritted his teeth, clenched his fingers in Caleb's hair, and did as he was told. He looked down, found Caleb gazing back up at him, brown eyes wicked as John's dick slid over his lips. Damn, Caleb was gorgeous, and every last person in the club would be staring at him later. But he'd come home with John.

Caleb slipped one hand up, tracing John's thigh, before finding his balls and tugging. And that was it; John just had time to grunt a warning before he came. Caleb's throat worked around him, swallowing hard.

John slumped with a contented sigh. "Damn. I don't think my legs work now."

"It's just one complaint after another with you," Caleb teased. He stood up and kissed John soundly on the mouth, tasting of come.

"What about you?" John asked. "Just give me a second to recover, okay?"

"Don't worry about it. We don't have the time. You can return the favor when we get home." Caleb poured a drink of water from the sink. When he was done, he set down the glass but hesitated, studying himself in the mirror. His mouth pinched slightly, a pensive expression crossing his face.

John finished tucking himself away and zipped up his jeans. "Babe? Everything all right?"

"Yeah." But Caleb didn't look away from the mirror. "It's just... weird? Different? I was never the most butch guy around anyway."

"I never guessed," John said dryly. "So is this about the corset? Because it looks really hot, but if you're not comfortable wearing it—"

"No, I *am*. That's what's a little weird." Caleb shrugged. "I don't know. I mean Gray doesn't even have a gender, even if we do call him 'he.' That's our term, not his."

"Is there something he'd prefer?" John asked.

"No. He doesn't care one way or the other, honestly." Caleb shook his head, long hair whispering over the shirt, the corset. "Gray's been lots of different people, different genders, including in cultures that count more than two. As far as he's concerned, it's all mortal nonsense. He just *is*. And I wonder if maybe that's affecting me somehow? Like, I could put on makeup and heels and not even think about it twice, because wearing a dress or heels or whatever is just as ordinary to Gray as anything else we humans do."

Huh. John chewed on his lip a moment, not certain what to say. "Well...people do change, even when they don't have a five-thousand-year-old drakul living in their heads," he said at last. "I mean, it might be stranger if it *didn't* affect you. But...are you worried about it?"

Because if Caleb was...there was nothing they could do. Literally nothing. He'd passed up his last chance at exorcism because he'd needed Gray's power to save John.

So if there was a problem…it was John's fault, in a way.

Caleb shook his head again and turned away from the mirror. "No. I don't think so. And Gray's going through changes, too. It was just something I was thinking about, that's all." He grabbed John's hand, twining their fingers tightly together. "Come on. I want to see you shake your ass."

CHAPTER 7

GRAY WAS ON high alert the entire time they walked with Rania from her apartment to the club. They passed Marion Square, which seemed like a place the vila might ambush them, after its last two attacks. But Gray didn't so much as catch a whiff of demonic scent.

"There is still the walk back," Gray suggested hopefully. *"Perhaps it will attack us then."*

Caleb's teeth burned with Gray's eagerness. *Dial it back. I know you want some mayhem, but the rest of us would just as soon catch the vila without bloodshed.*

Rania wore a tank top and jeans. Zahira had on a bright pink hijab, a loose, long-sleeved sparkly top, and jeans. Caleb suspected her Glock was holstered beneath the loose shirt.

Caleb had hoped the club would be relatively quiet since it was a weeknight, but once inside, they had to practically shove their way through the press of bodies. The smell of sweat and booze hit him like a wall, accompanied by the nasty reek of douchebro body spray. The thumping bass punished sensitive ears, and he could feel the vibration in his chest. Okay, maybe clubbing wasn't quite as fun as it had been when he wasn't possessed.

"We should go outside. Hunt for the vila, while the mortals are in here," Gray suggested.

We need to stay close to Rania. Just in case.

They passed by the dance floor, in search of Rania's friends. Bodies shimmied and shook, some couples practically humping each other. *"We could dance with John,"* Gray countered hopefully.

We're here to work, not get off.

Gray receded, though not without letting Caleb feel his frustration. Caleb sighed and shook his head.

Rania spotted her friends and hurried over. There came a quick round of introductions; Caleb forgot the names as soon as he heard them. One of the women asked if he wanted to dance, and John gave a subtle nod.

The plan called for Zahira to stay with Rania, while Caleb and John mingled, keeping their senses open for the vila the whole time. If it got close enough to John, his exorcist's sense would pick it up, but Gray was a lot more likely to smell it from a distance.

Not that the vila would show up in the club, anyway. Nothing to do but kill time until the walk home.

After the third song, Caleb started to sympathize with Gray. Half of Rania's friends wanted to dance with him, and he'd gotten angry looks from some of the men in the club. One guy yelled that the gay club was a few blocks over, but Caleb ignored him. Christ, this wasn't some country music dive bar where he'd get his ass kicked; plenty of other people were decked out in leather and corsets, too. Although to be fair, most of those were women.

After an hour or so, Caleb headed for the bar and grabbed two bottles of water. He downed one, even though he was the only person in the club not sweating his ass off. The other he carried while he scouted around for Zahira.

He found her sitting alone at one of the tables. "Where is everyone?" he asked, putting the unopened bottle down in front of her.

"Thank you," she said—or rather, shouted over the music. She nodded in the direction of a group of dancing women, and Caleb spotted Rania among them. "Over there."

"Not your scene?" he guessed.

She absently checked the lay of her hijab over her shoulders. "One of them asked me if I shower in the hijab."

"Oh. Ouch."

"And another asked if my father knew I was here." Zahira sighed. "I know I should look at it as an opportunity to educate people, but after you're asked the same question a hundred times…"

Caleb nodded. "Yeah. That would get pretty old fast."

She opened the water and drank. "You've been popular tonight, though."

"Not why we're here," he said with a snort. "Speaking of which, I'd better circulate some more. Wouldn't want John to catch me sitting on my butt."

She grinned. "He's been popular, too."

Gray perked up. *"What does she mean?"*

"I think he's been hit on by half the people in the club," she went on.

"I do not like this. John is ours."

Calm down.

Memories flashed behind Caleb's eyes, but for once they were recent. John had sucked them off in the bathroom of a club, the one time they'd gone dancing after he and John hooked up. *"I do not wish him to do these things with anyone else."*

Pretty sure John doesn't want to, either, so quit worrying.

"Caleb?" Zahira asked. "Is everything all right?"

Shit, he'd zoned out. "No," he said, because at least he could be honest with her. "Gray's weirdly insecure sometimes."

"Oh?" she looked like she really wanted to ask more questions, but was biting her tongue to keep them back.

"Later," he said, rising to his feet. "I'm going to see how John is doing."

At least it only took a few minutes to find John. He stood in the corner, idly talking with a red-haired man. His blue eyes swept the crowd, though, and a smile crossed his face when he spotted Caleb coming toward him.

See?

The man John was talking to glanced over his shoulder, probably to see who John was looking at. His eyes widened in surprise. "Caleb?"

"Deacon?"

Deacon grinned and shook his hand. "Good to see you." His gaze took in Caleb's form appreciatively.

"I see you met my boyfriend," Caleb said with a nod to John.

Deacon laughed. "No way!"

John cocked his head, a smile hovering on his mouth. "This is Deacon from PASS," Caleb explained. "He's a TK like me."

"That's great," John said. "Deacon was just telling me..."

The smell of rancid sweat, of rotting blood and corrupted bone, slid through the scents of human perspiration and spilled alcohol like a needle through cloth.

"The demon is here."

Caleb cast around anxiously. Fuck, the vila was *here*, so where had Rania gone? Her friends were scattered, dancing and drinking, so where was she?

"Caleb?" John asked.

"Sorry, Deacon," Caleb said, knowing he must sound either rude or crazy. "We've got to go."

He plunged into the press of bodies without waiting for an answer. Where the hell was Zahira?

The scent of the vila grew stronger as they approached the bar, then veered off. He spotted Zahira's pink hijab in the crowd and made for it.

"Where's Rania?" he demanded as he approached. She leaned against one of the support columns around the dance floor, sipping on her water.

He must have communicated his alarm, because she straightened sharply. "She went to the ladies room."

Fuck.

Caleb shoved his way through the press, and was rewarded by furious shouts. He'd be lucky if he didn't end up with bouncers trying to grab him—but there was no time. Behind him, John's voice rang out. "Move aside! SPECTR Agents!"

They'd be lucky if there wasn't a panic.

The hall leading to the bathrooms was crowded with women—even more than the usual line. "What's going on?" he demanded.

"Someone locked the fucking door," a woman snapped. "There's four stalls in there, and the door's locked? Who does that shit?"

He pushed his way through, ignoring shouts of anger. Someone hit him with a purse. At the head of the line, two women were pounding on the door and yelling for whoever was inside to open up.

The air was saturated with the vila's scent.

"Out of the way!" he yelled, Gray's bass roar underlying the order. They shuffled aside, eyes wide. He took one step back, then lunged forward, slamming his shoulder into the door. The lock snapped easily beneath the impact, and he stumbled inside.

The bathroom was the usual dreary club restroom. Graffiti covered the stalls, and a low buzzing sound came from the ugly fluorescent bulb overhead. A tiny window looked out on street level, its glass covered with wire screen. Harsh chemical cleaners stung Caleb's nose, even as saliva flooded his mouth at the overwhelming scent of demon.

Two women stood inside, in the small space before the sinks. They mirrored one another's posture, arms raised, legs flashing as they spun and danced. One was Rania, her face a mask of terror, tears streaming down her cheeks, her mascara in black streaks.

The other was older, her body firm beneath a clinging leotard and tight jeans. She wore ballet shoes, up on pointe, even as Rania struggled to mimic her. As the door crashed back against the wall, the woman turned quickly. Her eyes were as yellow as an animal's.

The vila.

Gray roared.

At last.

Gray leaps forward, unhesitating, claws unsheathed and ready for battle. They will take this demon down, and—

He catches a glimpse of claws, of teeth sharper than any human's should be. Then, so fast even he can barely track the movement, the vila's foot catches him in the jaw.

The impact is stunning; his head snaps back, something cracking inside his spine with a flare of pain. The blow sends him back into the door, which has swung shut behind him. He strikes it, hits the floor, then rolls to his feet even as vertebrae pop back into alignment.

The mortal no longer dances; she is slumped to the floor beside the sinks, her eyes wide and terrified. The demon...

Is gone. The tiny window hangs open, its glass smashed and the wire screen shredded as the vila tore its way out.

The opening is slightly too small, so he simply grabs the metal frame and rips it free from the concrete, tossing it into one of the stalls. The resulting hole is still a tight fit, claws sunk into the outside of the building to help haul him through, the button tearing free of his pants.

"Good thing you possessed someone skinny."

The vila's scent is a trail on the air outside. Gray charges after it, and within moments spots the fleeing figure ahead of him.

Good.

Car brakes screech, and he hears a shout as he tears down the street after the demon. *"Remember, she can still be exorcised. We need to keep the mauling to a minimum."*

The vila is fast—and agile. It darts down an alley and springs, its jump carrying it almost to the top of an iron fire escape. It balances easily on the metal rail for a moment, before vaulting to the roof.

By the time Gray pounds up the metal stairs, the vila has leapt the gap from this building to the next. But even as it seems it will spring to a third, it comes to a sudden halt. Its head whips around, and a look of fear and panic crosses its face.

As it should be.

Gray doesn't slow, colliding with the vila and nearly sending them both off the roof. Instinct unsheathes his claws; but no, he is not to damage the creature. Growling in frustration, he wraps his arms around it, pinning its arms to its sides. It writhes like a snake, snarling its fury. If he can hold the demon until John arrives—

Something collides with the back of his head with stunning force. His grip loosens, and the vila twists free. Spinning on one foot, it kicks him in the face a second time, knocking him back into an air conditioning unit.

"What the hell happened?"

Gray blinks, but there is no one else there.

"Did she kick us? Holy shit, she kicked us in the back of the head while we were holding her."

Caleb sounds impressed despite himself. Gray is not. As he surges back to his feet, the vila dances away, its movements so graceful it seems to glide across the roof on a rail. Between one instant and the next, the vila makes the leap to the next rooftop. He gathers himself to give chase.

Then the wind shifts.

He smells old stone and cold earth, burning metal and sun-warmed soil. It is not the scent of the vila, but it is familiar.

"I remember—we smelled it the day we went jogging near the Battery. When we were arguing with John. What is it?"

I do not know. Gray breathes deep. *It is not a demon, but otherwise I am not certain.*

"Is it what scared the vila? Made her hesitate long enough for us to catch her?"

The vila.

Gray breaks into a run, following the demon's scent. Its speed has given it an advantage; though he was distracted for only seconds, it has vanished from sight. He follows the trace, from one rooftop to the next, then down to the street again.

The trail vanishes in front of a boarded-up house. A patch of damp asphalt reveals where a vehicle was parked.

"Barillo is going to kill us for losing her."

He cannot kill us, Gray corrects Caleb, but absently. Because he smells the vila all around the area of the house, even though the scent is faded.

"Maybe she parked here for a while before stalking Rania?"

No. It is too far from the street.

He follows the trail around the back of the house. A power meter hums softly in the narrow alleyway separating the back door from the next building.

"Why would a boarded-up house have the power running? Maybe if someone was restoring it, but there would be permits posted for the construction."

The door is locked, but a single kick takes care of that. The interior of the house is dark and smells of mold and rot.

And vila.

And blood.

Gray makes his way across the creaking wooden floor, until reaching a door. The padlock on the door gleams in his night vision, far too shiny to have been here for long.

"So what is it she doesn't want anyone else to find?"

The lock gives easily beneath Gray's strength. On the other side of the door, rickety wooden stairs lead down into darkness. The vila's scent is strong here, as is the rusty smell of human blood. He pauses, listening, but all he hears is an electric hum.

The stairs creak, and to a mortal, the basement would be utterly black. His sight picks out swathes of dried blood on the floor. All along the walls stand large white freezers.

A ripple of unease from Caleb. *"That...probably isn't a good sign, is it?"*

It seems unlikely, Gray agrees.

Each freezer is locked, just as the door was. Gray goes to the nearest and snaps off the lock, before lifting the lid.

It is packed with human bodies. The eyes of the one on top stare at him through a thick coating of frost.

"Oh God."

Gray carefully lowers the lid. "John will wish to see this."

CHAPTER 8

BLUE POLICE LIGHTS strobed across the old brick wall of the club's exterior. "Was there a fight?" someone asked as John walked past. A few knots of people still stood around outside, gawking and trying to figure out what had happened, but most had scattered. Or been moved along by the cops, most likely.

Gray had taken off after the vila…and he hadn't come back yet. John tried not to let it worry him. Vila might be fast, but they hunted largely through cunning, not brute force. Gray could handle a lone demon without backup. Hell, he could probably handle an entire pack of them.

No need to be concerned at all.

Rania perched in the back of an ambulance, a blanket wrapped around her shoulders. Fresh tears leaked from her swollen, red eyes. Zahira sat beside her, a comforting arm draped atop the blanket.

John met Zahira's gaze. "Is she going to be okay?" he asked with a nod at Rania.

"The EMCs said she'll be fine," Zahira replied. But her expression remained grave. "I'm so sorry. I thought she'd be safe in the bathroom…"

Rania let out another gulping sob. John crouched down in front of her. "Rania? How are you feeling?"

"Like shit," she said, rubbing angrily at her eyes. "But I'll be all right.

It only went on for a couple of minutes before..." A shudder ran through her. "What *was* that thing?"

"A vila," John said. Maybe she'd forgotten in her shock?

She shook her head. "No. Not...not Elise. It was...oh God." She closed her eyes. "It looked like Caleb."

He hesitated, caught between conflicting impulses. Rather than address the bit about Caleb, he said, "Elise?"

Rania swallowed heavily. "Elise Peyton. She's—I mean, she was—the Beaufain Ballet's principal ballerina, until she retired at the end of last season. I ran into her at the bar, and she suggested we go into the ladies room so we could catch up. It would be easier to hear in there, so I said sure. But as soon as we went in and were alone...she...she changed."

More tears. Zahira tightened her grip on Rania, even as she met John's eyes. They'd been right—there was a connection to the company. But why would a former dancer who had retired suddenly be out to destroy the women who were competing for her old job? There had to be a piece missing, somewhere.

John's phone buzzed, and he pulled it out. "Caleb," he said, and couldn't keep the relief from his voice.

"No!" Rania's eyes widened. "I saw him—he's not human! He's—he's possessed!"

"Shh." Zahira put her hands on Rania's shoulders, turning the dancer to face her. "It's all right. I know it seems strange, but Caleb helps us."

Rania blinked slowly. "But...he..."

"Just saved your life," John said shortly, and hit the button on the phone. "Caleb? Is everything all right?"

"Not even close," Caleb replied. "We followed the vila to a deserted house. She got away in her car, but...well. You need to call Detective Tradd. I think we found the missing people."

"Should I send an ambulance?" John asked.

"No." Caleb sounded tired. "Just a lot of body bags."

Elise paced the length of the cheap hotel room, back and forth, over and over. Her hands clenched and unclenched, and her breath hitched in her lungs. Alternating waves of fury and terror poured over her, until she wanted to scream, to tear things off the wall, to rip her own hair out by the roots.

"We cannot draw attention to ourselves. Not yet."

"You didn't tell me there were monsters!" Elise shouted. She grabbed the ice bucket and hurled it at the door. It bounced off and rolled beneath the pressboard desk. "You should have warned me! That thing would have...would have..."

The fear screaming in the base of her skull was more primal than anything she'd ever felt in her life. It held within it the certainty of ancient humans huddled in the dark, knowing without question there were things beyond the circle of firelight that wanted to *eat* them. Predators stronger than any human, which couldn't be placated, or reasoned with.

"But we escaped," the vila cajoled. *"We were too fast. Too clever."*

"Maybe, but tonight's show was ruined!" Elise stopped and glared at the mirror bolted to the wall. "That bitch Rania is still alive. These four nights were supposed to be my greatest performance, and now—!"

"Shh." A sensation, like arms slipping around her, except it existed nowhere but inside her own mind. *"We still have the grand finale tomorrow. Tonight was but a minor setback—a misstep during a dress rehearsal. Tomorrow... tomorrow we take the stage."*

Elise's breathing evened out as calm flowed through her. The vila was right. Tomorrow was what mattered. No one would remember what happened tonight, except as a minor footnote, a bit of trivia. It would be tomorrow's performance that would steal headlines on every news site in America.

Everyone would know her name. And the Beaufain Ballet Company would be sorry for how it had treated her.

Assuming any of them survived.

A few hours later, Caleb stood beside John and Zahira in front of Barillo's desk.

Now that they had an identity for the vila, it had been quick work to get a search warrant for her apartment. Unfortunately, the search proved a bust. Either Elise Peyton had cleared out before, or—and this seemed more likely, given all the things left behind—she'd taken off once she'd been made. She was probably sitting in a hotel somewhere, paid for in cash and under an assumed name, just waiting for the chance to murder another dancer.

"Last night could have been perfect," Barillo said, toying with a pencil as he glowered at them. "Our suspect nabbed. The missing persons case closed. The talking heads on the morning news would be singing SPECTR's praises." He tossed the pencil onto the desk. "Instead, I have a press conference in an hour to tell the good people of

Charleston there's a maniac on the loose! Do you have any idea how many antacids I've chewed just this morning? This stress is not good for me. My cardiologist is going to have a field day."

"Maybe you ought to find a quieter job," Caleb suggested.

Zahira's eyes widened, and belatedly Caleb wanted to take the words back. He didn't give a fuck about getting in trouble with SPECTR, but John and Zahira did.

"Keep your smart mouth to yourself, Jansen." Barillo fixed Zahira with his glare. "Special Agent Noorzai."

Zahira straightened sharply. "Yes, sir?"

"Why the hell did you let Ms. Wilson out of your sight?"

"With all due respect, sir," John said, "the vila broke pattern. Every time before, she came after her victims when they were isolated and alone. Zahira had no reason to think Ms. Wilson would be in danger in the ladies room of a crowded club."

"I didn't ask you for your opinion, did I, Starkweather?" Barillo growled.

Zahira fixed her gaze on the jar of candies on Barillo's desk. "I didn't think she would be in danger, sir," she said. "It was a mistake on my part."

"It damned well was." Barillo shifted back to John. "The person you were protecting almost got killed, I've got a pile of bodies on my hands, *and* the NHE got away. How the fuck did that happen?"

Knowing John, he'd cop all the blame—which wasn't fair. "It was my fault," Caleb said quickly, before John could speak. "I pursued her, but she was…was too fast."

Maybe Barillo realized it wasn't the entire truth, because his eyes narrowed. "Too fast. And I thought you were some kind of NHE sniffing bloodhound. Why the hell didn't you keep on her trail?"

"I do not like this mortal," Gray growled. Embarrassment flashed through them, although Caleb wasn't entirely sure which of them it belonged to.

Caleb felt the blood collecting in his cheeks. "I tried, but the scent faded too fast, all right? And there was something else out there. Another NHE."

John looked alarmed. "You didn't mention that before. What was it?"

"I don't know." Caleb shrugged. "Seriously, I don't. But it distracted us—me—and—"

"Stop right there." Barillo held up a hand. "Starkweather, Noorzai, out. I want to talk to Jansen alone."

John looked alarmed, but what could he do? He caught Caleb's eye as he turned toward the door, herding a downcast Zahira with him.

The door shut quietly. Caleb had never been alone with Barillo before. Hell, the man had done everything he could to avoid even setting eyes on Caleb.

So there was no way this was going to be good.

"Mr. Jansen," Barillo said. "I'm going to be upfront here. I don't like you. I don't like your attitude. I sure as hell don't like the demon in your head."

"We're not a demon," Caleb growled, and shit, now his pronouns were slipping.

Barillo noticed, of course. He shifted back, shoulders straightening. "The drakul is a demon, and your job is to find other demons."

Gray's anger swirled through Caleb's veins. *Calm down. We have to stay calm.*

"And now you're telling me you can't even do that?" Barillo went on, arching a brow. "Do I need to put in a call to Director Kaniyar?"

"No!" Shit, what would happen then? Would Kaniyar decide to drop Caleb into a hole in some black ops SPECTR facility?

Anger. *"They could not hold us."*

"It was a one time thing," Caleb said. "It won't happen again."

"Maybe." Barillo said. "Maybe you're having trouble keeping your mind on your job. Maybe you'd have less trouble concentrating if you had a partner you weren't sleeping with."

"He means to take us away from John?"

"What?" Caleb clenched his fists. "That's not fair. John had nothing to do with this!"

"Are you sure? Maybe you got distracted in the club. All hot and sweaty." Disgust laced Barillo's words.

"That isn't what happened!" Damn it, why wouldn't Barillo just listen?

"And Starkweather…fucking an NHE can't be a sign of good mental health. I ought to require he get cleared by a shrink before going out in the field." Barillo smirked. "Hell, maybe it's time to break up the dream team and assign you to someone else. For Starkweather's own good."

"No!" Caleb exclaimed—except shit, it wasn't just him, not anymore. Static crackled in the air, and he felt himself shoved back as Gray snarled, "You will not take John away from us!"

Barillo's chair hit the wall. He was on his feet now, yanking his Glock out of its shoulder holster. And oh fuck, he was going to pump them full of silver-jacketed lead, and this whole thing was turning into a disaster.

Gray, get back, now!

"He wishes to separate us from John!"

If you don't let me handle this, we'll never see John again!

Gray retreated, shocked and confused. Caleb held up hands which no longer had claws. "Stop! We're not threatening you, okay? Gray wouldn't hurt you, he just—"

"Stand down!" Barillo yelled, the Glock still in his shaking hand.

"It's all right," Caleb babbled, cautiously lowering himself to his knees. "Gray didn't mean to threaten you, I swear. You scared him, that's all. He wasn't going to hurt you."

Barillo's brown skin had taken on a horrible, grayish tinge. Sweat stood out on his brow, and his finger rested on the trigger. Caleb was acutely aware of his heartbeat pounding in his veins, of the tightness of fear around his chest, the anticipation of pain from the silver-jacketed lead.

If Barillo shot them, other agents would come running. Then their choices would either be surrender and hope Kaniyar showed them mercy, or try to escape. Which would mean a blood bath.

Barillo took his finger from the trigger and lowered the gun.

Caleb almost sagged in relief, but he didn't dare move until Barillo gave him the go-ahead.

"Let's get one thing clear," Barillo said, voice shaking. "I'd better not *ever* see the drakul again. You either keep that thing buttoned down, or I'm going to put in a call to Kaniyar. They'll lock you away so deep and so long you'll forget what the sun even looks like."

"He threatens us."

Yeah. Because we screwed up.

"Yes, sir," Caleb said, as meekly as he could.

Barillo gestured to the door. "Get the hell out of my office."

Caleb scrambled to his feet and out as fast as possible. *"We did nothing wrong,"* Gray insisted as Caleb shut the door behind them.

Yeah, we did. Caleb leaned against the nearest wall, pressing his fingers into his closed eyes. Lights danced across his vision, like distant lightning flashes. *We scared the shit out of Barillo.*

And he's not ever going to forgive us for doing it.

* * *

John looked up as Caleb walked into the conference room. He took in Caleb's pale face, his mouth pressed into a thin line. It didn't take an empath to know something had gone wrong.

"What happened?" John asked, rising to his feet. "Are you all right?"

Caleb hesitated, lips parting. Then he took a deep breath and nodded. "Yeah. Everything's fine."

Like hell. But pushing Caleb just tended to make him more obstinate, so John let it go. For now. "Barillo can be a little...abrasive," he said sympathetically.

"Yeah." Caleb dropped into one of the chairs. "Where's Rania?"

"The ballet studio," Zahira replied. "She's surrounded by people, and everyone knows to be on the lookout for Elise Peyton. I'm going to head over there as soon as we're done here."

John nodded. "Good plan. We'll make sure someone is with her twenty-four seven. When she's not at the ballet, she'll be at her apartment —no more wandering around the city."

"Yes." Zahira didn't meet his gaze. "I'm sorry I let her go off by herself. I didn't think anything would happen if she spent five minutes in the bathroom."

"It's a mistake any of us could have made," John said. Goddess knew he'd made worse when he was a rookie.

"She's seen reason about Gray, though," Zahira added with a hasty look at Caleb. "She was scared last night, but now that she's had time to think, she realizes Gray was just there to help her."

"Yeah," Caleb said, staring off into space. Damn it, something must have gone really wrong with Barillo.

If Caleb didn't want to talk about Barillo, John had plenty of other questions for him. "Caleb, you mentioned another scent? When you were chasing the vila?"

Caleb heaved a sigh. "Yeah," he said again.

"Another NHE? And you didn't mention it?"

"The whole 'freezers packed with bodies' thing seemed more important," Caleb snapped.

"And we don't want another NHE to make even more of them," John replied, swallowing back his temper. Caleb wasn't trained for this, he reminded himself. Given his background, Caleb had done amazingly well so far. But lives could be on the line.

"It's not a demon," Caleb said. He ran his hand back through his cloud of dark hair, tugging at it in frustration.

The hell?

"Not a demon?" Zahira asked in confusion.

"Gray's way of saying it's 'not food.' Demons are food, and this isn't food, so it's not a demon. Not the most helpful way of categorizing things, I know." He paused and sighed. "Yes, it makes sense if you're a drakul. Not so much for the rest of us."

"Which means what?" John asked.

"I don't know, okay?" Caleb glanced away. "But this is the second time we've smelled it, whatever it is."

John frowned. It had never occurred to him Caleb and Gray would keep secrets, certainly not about something like this. "And you didn't mention it?"

"I forgot." Caleb scowled. "Look, this was back when we were tracking the raven mocker. You and I argued, so Gray and I went for a jog along the Battery. We smelled it then. Just a whiff, there and gone. It was weird, but neither of us thought much of it. I actually wondered if we just imagined it."

John remembered that day only too well. "But you didn't."

"No. So we recognized it last night, and it distracted us. Because what the fuck *is* this thing, right?" Caleb spread his hands apart helplessly. "Then we found the bodies in the freezers, and honestly, 'I smelled something strange' seemed like a side issue."

John suppressed a sigh. "All right. Whatever it is, it doesn't seem to be causing trouble yet. I'll write it up in the report, and once we've taken care of the vila, we'll see if Gray can pick up the trail again."

"Okay." Caleb bit his lip. "Sorry. I should have said something before."

"It's all right." John glanced at the clock on the wall. "Okay. Protecting Rania and stopping the vila before it gets to her is our only mission right now."

Caleb's phone chimed. He pulled it out of his pocket and read the text. Uncertainty flickered through Caleb's eyes, before he glanced up. "It's Deacon—you met him last night."

John nodded. "I remember. From your PASS group. He seemed nice."

"He wants to know if I can get together with him for lunch. I'd tell him no, ordinarily, but..." Caleb shook his head. "I'm just...I need to get out of here."

He looked tired and frustrated. Whatever Barillo had said to him, it obviously hadn't sat well. No surprise, given Caleb had issues with authority on a good day. Maybe giving him a chance to cool off would be for the best.

"All right," John said. "You go ahead to lunch, then meet us at Rania's apartment when you're done. No sense coming back here first."

"Thanks, babe." Caleb flashed him a grateful look as he rose to his feet. "You're the best."

"And don't you forget it," John called after him. But Caleb was already gone.

CHAPTER 9

CALEB TOOK HIS time walking to lunch. Thoughts churned in his head, none of them productive.

Should he have told John about Barillo's threat to split them up? Probably. Should he have warned John and Zahira that he'd managed to make a real enemy out of Barillo? Definitely.

"So why did you not?" Gray asked. Right to the point, as usual.

Fuck, I don't know. Barillo's terror, the sight of the Glock, his threats…it all sat in Caleb's stomach like a ball of lead, too heavy to choke back up. *I feel like if I tell John, if I say the worst out loud, it will happen.*

"That is foolish." Gray told him. Then: *"We did nothing wrong."*

Yes, we did. We freaked out, and we scared Barillo. Caleb sighed. *And even if we didn't, even if you were right and we were blameless, when has that ever mattered?*

Memories flickered behind their eyes, drained of color. Old memories, from Gray's other hosts, moving too fast and too jumbled for Caleb to make sense of them.

"True," Gray admitted at last. *"The innocent are sometimes more quickly punished than the guilty. But we will not let this mortal's baseless fear take John from us."* He perked up. *"Perhaps John will agree to leave with us, if we tell him."*

I keep telling you, John keeps telling you: it's not that simple. We've done the whole "run for our lives from SPECTR" thing once already. That was hard enough, and it was only for a couple of weeks. And we had help from the Vigilant the whole time. We aren't prepared, and even if we were, we can't spend the rest of our lives fighting them.

"We will not. They will eventually disappear, just as the Inquisition, or the Roman legions, or the crusaders did."

Assuming they were immortal now. Which…Caleb didn't want to think about. *The rest of John's life, then.*

"Ah." That shut Gray up. Caleb felt him withdraw, presumably to think things over.

When Caleb finally reached the restaurant where he'd agreed to meet Deacon, he found the other man already waiting for him. Caleb flashed Deacon a smile as he slipped into the booth. "Thanks for the text, man. Your timing couldn't have been better."

Deacon grinned. "Glad to hear it."

The server approached, and Caleb did a quick scan of the lunch menu while Deacon ordered. "I'll have the black bean soup—there's no garlic in it, right? I'm kind of allergic."

"No garlic," the server assured him.

"There had better not be," Gray said once she'd left.

We'll sniff it first, okay? Caleb had learned the hard way not to just shove food in his mouth without making damn sure what was in it. Garlic wouldn't actually injure them, but it made life very unpleasant for a while.

"So," Deacon said, once the server had brought them glasses of ice tea, "I know my text probably seemed out of the blue, but I wanted to make sure you were okay after last night."

"I'm fine," Caleb said. "Sorry—I probably should have checked with you earlier."

"I figured you had other things on your mind." Deacon paused. "Listen, tell me it's none of my business if you like, but…do you work for SPECTR?"

So much for the chances of having a friend outside of work. Most of the paranormal community wasn't too fond of the agency. Caleb sure as hell hadn't been. Not to suggest he particularly was now, either.

"I'm a private contractor," he admitted. "And John is a special agent."

"It's okay," Deacon said quickly, as though he'd picked up on Caleb's reluctance. "I'm not here to judge."

Their food arrived. Caleb sniffed it carefully, just in case, but the server had been right and there was no trace of garlic. "I appreciate it," he said. "Nigel knows, too, but…"

"Don't go telling everyone at PASS," Deacon finished. "Don't worry, Caleb. I know some paranormals have a real problem with SPECTR, but even if I was one of them, it would be the organization I didn't like. Not the people in it."

"Thanks." Caleb looked down at his soup and discovered he was actually hungry. "I appreciate it."

"No problem. Like I said, I don't judge." Deacon dug into his burger.

Maybe…at least not when it came to Caleb's work situation. But if Deacon knew the truth about the rest of it—about Gray—would he be so non-judgmental? Or would he run screaming in the opposite direction?

No need to ask. Plenty of people, from SPECTR agents to Barillo to Rania, had already given Caleb the answer.

Rania lived on the second floor of one of Charleston's grand old homes that had been broken up into apartments. John parked his sedan on the street outside, then let himself in through the unlatched iron gate. The landlord had made an attempt to keep the house's appearance faithful to its original state. Roses and other flowers filled the garden running along the front, while a small fountain played softly amidst the greenery.

The lower porch creaked under his shoes as he crossed to the door. He found the buzzer with the number Zahira had given him and rang it. "It's John," he said when she answered.

"Come on up."

He climbed the stairs to Rania's apartment. "Watch out for the spirit ward," Zahira said when she opened the door for him.

He stepped over the lines of chalk, careful not to smear them with a careless scuff of his shoe. He sensed the low hum of etheric energy from the ward—powerful enough to keep the average NHE out, and at least provide a warning if one of the stronger ones broke through it. "Good work," he said, nodding to the ward. "Where's Rania?"

The apartment faced the front of the house, with a door leading out onto the upstairs porch. Zahira beckoned him to follow her onto the porch, which was guarded by another spirit ward. "She's napping—I think she took a sleeping pill." Zahira said once they were outside. "She's still pretty shaken up over last night."

"I don't blame her. Or you," John added. "You have to move past your mistakes."

"I know," she said, although he didn't know if she really believed him. She must have been working out here already, because her laptop sat on the wicker table. She sat down in one of the chairs, and he took the other one. "Listen, something really weird happened just now," she said, turning her laptop so he could see the screen. "Someone emailed me a video."

"What...?" he started, then stopped. Because even if he'd never seen the video before, a single glimpse at the paused frame was enough to make his heart sink.

"I don't know," she said, clicking play.

The video stuttered to life. It had clearly been shot from a helicopter. The picture jerked, as though strong winds buffeted the craft. The wind and rotor noise drowned out the words of the pilot and videographer, leaving behind only raw notes of panic.

Waves, whipped to a frenzy, crashed against the aging walls of Fort Sumter National Monument. Wind had shredded the remaining flags, and lightning exploded across the sky. Rain sluiced down in sheets, hammering the tiny figures scattering for cover. The tempest was on the cusp of becoming a full-blown hurricane.

And above it all loomed a titan of storm and shadow.

"Who sent you this?" he asked quietly.

Zahira shook her head. "I don't know. The address they used is from one of those anonymizer sites. The email just said it's footage of Fort Sumter, taken by a local news helicopter."

SPECTR had suppressed as much video of that night as possible. But things always got out in the end, passed around alongside whispers of conspiracy and black ops.

"I'm not sure what I'm supposed to see," she went on. "It's just a jumble of light and shadows, like some kind of weird Rorschach test." She pointed at the screen. "What *is* this, even?"

Of course she didn't know. How could she? Information about that night was supposed to be locked down tight. And yes, she'd heard about what happened, or at least a brief version of it. But seeing...seeing was different.

Seeing made things real.

He might lie. Tell her the thing on the screen was the monster summoned by Forsyth. Lie, because Caleb had already been hurt enough by the very people who should have had his back.

John paused the video. Found the best still he could, given the rain and the clouds. "Eyes," he said, pointing to twin balls of lightning.

"Wings…I guess. Sort of." Pointing to twin ragged flags of black cloud, spanning the island from one side to the next. "Claws." Each as long as a human body.

She let out a hiss as it came together for her. "I see it." She advanced the video one frame at a time. "But…what is it?"

"It's Gray."

Zahira looked up sharply, her brows drawn tight beneath her hijab. "Gray? What do you mean?"

John looked out across the garden. A breeze rustled the trees, and sent a blessed breath of coolness across the back of his neck. A burst of laughter came from the street, mingling with the soft song of the fountain below. "You asked before why everyone is so terrified of Gray. Now you know."

"But that isn't Gray. It can't be. I've seen him."

"No, you haven't." John glanced back at her. "Not fully manifested, anyway." He paused, trying to think how to explain it. "Imagine you're in a dark room. No light. While you're stumbling around, you find a big rock. You run your hands over it, trying to figure out what it looks like. It's oval, a little taller than you, and after a few minutes you come to the conclusion that somebody carved a sort of round, slightly squashed statue for some reason. With me so far?"

Zahira looked dubious. "I think?"

"Then the lights come on. And you realize what you'd been feeling wasn't just a roundish, slightly squashed sculpture. It was the toe of a colossus."

Her lips parted slightly. "Oh. Wow."

John gestured to the video. "We don't normally see Gray fully manifested, because it takes huge amounts of energy. But just because you only feel the toe of the colossus, doesn't mean the rest of it isn't still there in the darkness."

"So that's what a drakul really looks like." Zahira stared at the screen. "No wonder people made them into gods."

John ran his hand tiredly through his hair. "Yeah. And that's why other agents at SPECTR-HQ are afraid. Some of them were *there*. They stood on a tiny scrap of land in the middle of a raging storm, and they looked up and saw a power that could have swept us all away in an instant. And it scared the shit out of them."

"Barillo wasn't there, though."

"No, but he's seen the footage. And talked to those who were."

John shook his head. "I won't sit here and pretend it wasn't terrifying. If I hadn't already put my life in Gray's hands a dozen times over, if I hadn't already trusted him absolutely, I don't think I would have had the courage to face him there at the end."

The buzzer sounded inside the apartment. "I'll get it." John rose to his feet. Zahira leaned closer to the screen, forwarding through the video again, one frame at a time.

Goddess. Would she quit? Walk out right now and refuse to have anything to do with them?

"It's me," Caleb called from downstairs when John answered. "I'm coming up."

John smudged away the spirit ward—Gray would only break it, and it would have to be redrawn anyway. "Hey, babe," he said, trying to put on a calm face for Caleb. "How was lunch?"

"It was…" Caleb's words died away. Belatedly, John realized Caleb could see the computer screen from this angle. "Oh, fucking hell."

Zahira turned to him, eyes wide and slightly alarmed as Caleb strode across the room. The second spirit ward flashed and died as he passed through it without pause.

"Caleb," John said, hurrying after him.

"No." Caleb stopped and held up his hands. "You know what? I give up. Go ahead, Zahira. Be scared of me just like everybody else. Why the hell not?"

Zahira stood up. "Are you kidding? This is *amazing.*" She pointed at the video. "Gray, *you're* amazing."

Caleb just stared at her for a moment, mouth slightly open. Then Caleb was gone, and it was Gray's black eyes looking back at Zahira.

"Yes," he said, practically preening. "I *am.* You are an unusually sensible mortal."

John realized his own mouth was open now, and shut it with a snap. But Gray didn't usually pay attention to other people, unless they were in a fight, or hunting NHEs, or on the run from SPECTR. He never manifested just to talk to someone, with the exception of John.

And, okay, John hadn't realized it, but maybe that had made him feel a little special. Which was absurd, really, but he couldn't help it.

Zahira clasped her hands together enthusiastically. "I wish there was more footage, so I could get a better look. What did it feel like? Was it —" she caught herself. "Sorry—I'm being rude."

Gray cocked his head slightly to one side, as if listening. "Caleb says you wish to examine us more closely," he said. "I will allow it. And I will answer your questions, if I can."

If Zahira got any more excited, she might literally vibrate into another dimension. "Thank you! Oh my goodness, I don't know where to start!"

John sank into his wicker chair, feeling limp with relief. And a touch of guilt—he'd underestimated Zahira once before, but he apparently hadn't learned not to do it again.

Still, after everything with most of the other agents, not to mention Barillo riding their asses, he'd let himself forget there were people in their corner. Zahira and Karl. And hell, Kaniyar had been the one to put them back on the SPECTR payroll in the first place.

Gray vanished, the flood of etheric energy folding back up into Caleb. Caleb grinned at Zahira. "I think we should deal with the vila first," he said. "But…thanks. I never imagined Gray having, you know, a friend."

"I hope I am," Zahira said.

Caleb snorted. "Are you kidding? You're his second-favorite human. Well, third, I guess, since he insists on counting me for some reason." He hesitated, then shrugged. "Mine too, come to think of it."

Zahira smiled brilliantly. "Thank you, Caleb." She glanced at the broken spirit ward. "But as you said, we should concentrate on the vila right now. Decide where you and Gray want to stand watch, and I'll redraw the wards."

"I'll stay out here," Caleb said, crossing to the porch railing. "With any luck, I'll scent the vila before she reaches the yard." He cast John a grim smile. "She won't get past this team a second time. We'll take her down, and not even Barillo will have anything to complain about."

CHAPTER 10

AFTER SUNSET, ZAHIRA drank some water, and they ordered a giant vegetarian pizza for iftar. John carried a slice out onto the porch for Caleb, so he wouldn't break the spirit ward coming back inside. John and Zahira sat on the couch, watching the local news. As they finished off the last of their slices, the door to the bedroom swung open, and Rania finally emerged.

She didn't look good, her eyes puffy and her hair still tangled from sleep. She moved stiffly; had she pulled muscles last night under the vila's spell? Or hurt her feet, trying to go up on pointe in regular shoes?

"We saved you some pizza," Zahira said. "Are you feeling better?"

Rania slumped into a chair and stared listlessly at the pizza. "No, I'm not feeling better. I'm not okay."

John tried to think of something encouraging to say. "I know you're frightened, but we won't leave your side until the vila is dealt with."

"Damn Elise." Rania blinked rapidly, tears beading on her lashes. "There's a reception tonight, downtown in the historic district. A big fundraiser for the Beaufain Ballet. All the soloists and principal dancers were supposed to be there. I ought to be in the spotlight tonight. Wined and dined, and…but no, I can't, thanks to Elise." She sniffled. "The worst thing is, I'll never know if I was elevated to principal dancer because I was the best, or because the vila murdered my competition."

"I'm sorry." Zahira put a hand on Rania's arm. "It's not fair. But we're going to stop her, and you're going to be brilliant on stage."

Caleb's voice drifted in from the porch. "What I don't get is, why is Elise so pissed off? She retired from the company, right? Why does she want to come back and kill you?"

Rania let out a bitter laugh. "Retired is the polite way of saying 'forced out.'"

John set the rest of his pizza aside. "Wait. She was forced out?"

"She was old," Rania said with a shrug.

"The hell?" Caleb had come to stand just on the other side of the wards. "I saw her. She was, what, forty at the most?"

"Forty-one," Rania said. "But Giselle is supposed to be a naïve village girl, not a middle-aged woman. Besides, ballet is a lot more physically demanding than some sports. Basil felt she couldn't cut it anymore, so he allowed her to save face by 'retiring.'"

"Rania!" Zahira sat back, looking shocked. "Why didn't you mention this before?"

"Yeah," Caleb chimed in. "Like on day one, when we asked you if anyone had a grudge against the company?"

"Caleb," John said. Antagonizing Rania wasn't going to accomplish anything, even though a part of him wanted to lash out at her as well.

"Why should she have a grudge over that?" Rania demanded. "These things happen all the time, in every company. Dancers get older and can't perform, or get injured. Or hell, the director just has an eye for younger, prettier dancers. It's life in the ballet. Most of the time, former dancers just go off and open a ballet school themselves somewhere. They don't come back and try to murder their successors."

"All right," John said, his mind racing. "That explains why she was out to get the soloists, one of whom would have replaced her. But Syrkus was the one to actually decide not to rehire her for the season, correct? To make her retire? Would she be after him as well?"

"Oh hell," Caleb said. "The reception. Elise tried to kill one soloist —her potential replacements—each night leading up to it. What if tonight was supposed to be the—I don't know, the grand finale?"

Adrenaline sent John's heart thudding in his chest. "Syrkus and everyone else could be in danger. We have to get over there."

Rania curled her legs up under her, seeming to shrink in on herself. "But what about me? If you're wrong, I'll be here alone!"

"Someone has to stay here with you," John said. "Zahira—"

"Um, John?" Caleb interrupted.

"We don't have much time, Caleb."

Caleb shifted from foot to foot. "I know, but...um. Gray wasn't manifested the last time we...you know...but are you still juiced up past what an ordinary exorcist would be?"

"Yes," John said, trying to ignore the heat flooding his face.

"Then you would have a better chance of stopping the vila if we're wrong and she comes here instead," Zahira said matter-of-factly. "Caleb, Gray, and I should go check out the reception."

John wanted to protest. The vila was dangerous, and if they were right and she was loose in the middle of a crowd...

Zahira and Gray could handle it. They'd have to.

"All right," he said. "Do it. I'll stay here with Rania. Just be careful. All of you."

"When are we not?" Caleb asked. He flung a leg over the porch railing. "See you downstairs, Zahira."

"Good luck," John said. But Caleb had already dropped over the edge, vanishing into the dark garden below.

Elise slipped over the wall behind the grand old house. The scent of rain blew in from the west, but the party on the wide lawn was still in full swing. Tables covered in white cloths offered a sumptuous buffet, and the soft glow of candles transformed the space into a fairy garden.

Even from a distance, she recognized some of the people milling about: the men dressed in thousand-dollar suits, the women in designer gowns tailored to their fashionably thin forms. The movers and shakers of Charleston: corporate CEOs, state senators, the inheritors of old money and older names. All of them eager for their philanthropy to make it into the newspaper tomorrow.

Dancers were there, too; coryphees, danseurs, and of course Carlos McElroy, who would no doubt dance Albrecht again this year. No one thought *he* was too old.

"But he won't dance Albrecht," the vila reminded her. *"He has but one last dance, and that is the one we control."*

Yes. She felt them all, like little insects crawling on her skin. Everyone from the private security on the gate to the caterers to the monied guests; all of them would be hers soon enough.

"It is time for the curtain to rise."

She nodded. Timing was everything, both in the ballet and in life. She began to walk across the grass, feeling it bend softly beneath her pointe shoes.

Thank you. For this opportunity. For giving me my revenge.

"I promise you, it shall be glorious."
I know it will.

She'd worn loose clothing and a wide-brimmed hat to hide her face as long as possible. Still, she heard a gasp as she made her way through the crowd, toward the pergola where she knew her main quarry would be holding court. Candles glowed all around the pergola and lined the edges of the reflecting pool in front of it. The rising wind bent the flames and sent ripples across the water's surface, fracturing the light.

Basil Syrkus stood beneath the pergola, a glass of champagne in one hand, chatting with a white-haired society woman. Apparently an older woman was fine with Basil so long as her money was equally aged.

"We'll see how well she dances."

Perhaps warned by some instinct, Basil looked up as she approached. His eyes widened, and she felt her lips twist into a smile.

Perfect.

"Hello, Basil," she said, and tossed her hat into the reflecting pool.

Someone shouted for security, but it was far too late. Basil's face went deathly white, and the champagne fell from his grip. "El-elise," he started, then swallowed convulsively. "Don't do this. Please—"

"He betrayed you." Rage. *"We will destroy him."*

"SPECTR can still save you," he babbled. "Just surrender, and they'll get this monster out of you."

"And why would I want them to do that?" she asked, stalking slowly toward him. "Not to say it would matter, even if I did. My time is up with the vila. Just as it was up with you." She mimicked his words, spoken almost two months ago but blazing still in her heart. "'Giselle is a fresh-faced village girl, not an old woman! Perhaps you should audition for her mother.'" Elise's lips drew back from her teeth. "I gave everything to this company. To you. And now you toss me aside over a few wrinkles?"

"Elise," he said frantically, even as a dark patch spread across the front of his pants.

She raised her arms *bras en couronne*. "One more dance, Basil. For old times' sake."

Something shifted, the world taking on a new balance. It had been exactly forty days to the moment since she'd summoned the vila.

The vila rose in her triumphantly, and Elise felt herself growing smaller and smaller, pushed aside. She didn't fight it, but let herself fall away, her body no longer her own. This was what she'd wanted from the beginning, after all. Only the vila's full power could deliver a fitting grand finale.

Claws sprouted from her fingertips, and her teeth became knives. The vila reached out, and dimly Elise sensed her ensnare the security guards rushing toward them, the caterers, the well-dressed men and women.

They would pay. They would all pay.

"Join me," said the vila, and began to dance.

Caleb clung to his seat, wishing he had Gray's claws at the moment, just for a little more traction. Zahira drove even faster than John, and used her horn when the screaming siren didn't move traffic out of their way fast enough. *They must teach it at the Academy. How to Drive Like a Maniac 101.*

"It is faster than we could run," Gray pointed out. He quivered with anticipation, right under Caleb's skin, a breath away from manifesting.

Hold back. All we need is for the vila not to be there, and for you to cause a panic. We don't want a bunch of elderly ballet lovers dropping over dead from heart failure.

The reception was being held at a large historic mansion that had been converted to an event venue. The closer they got to downtown, the worse the traffic became. The car edged down George Street, passing an old church whose walls were sheathed in scaffolding. A local restoration company's banner flapped loosely in the rising wind.

Rain spotted the windshield when Zahira finally threw the sedan into park. "We're here."

Caleb scrambled out, his body thrumming with tension, partly from the oncoming storm and partly from the prospect of hunting again. Zahira led the way to the ornate iron gate letting out onto the sidewalk. There should have been security to keep random tourists from wandering inside, but instead it stood open and unattended.

That can't be good.

They hurried past the tall hedge and trees, and around the main bulk of the house. Beyond, candles and gaslights illuminated a wide lawn. The candles guttered wildly; half had already gone out in the rain.

The party should have moved indoors as soon as the first drops fell, with women anxious to protect silk dresses, men worried about their expensive shoes, the catering staff saving the canapés and champagne. Instead everyone, from security to caterers to guests, had gathered at one end of the lawn, heedless of the growing downpour.

The vila had gotten there first.

Men in suits and women in gowns, staff in black pants and white shirts, all danced in the rain. They spun, arms up, then down, balancing on one leg, then springing into the air. Mouths gaped wide in horror, though no screams seemed able to issue forth, and tears of terror streaked the dancers' faces. An old man twitched on the ground, still striving to mimic the movements of the vila despite a broken leg or hip.

The vila danced in a pergola beside a reflecting pool, illuminated by the candlelight. The sight dashed any hope that Elise's forty days weren't up. Her body bent, slender and pliable as a reed, her arms and legs inhumanly long and graceful, her hair a shimmering curtain with a life of its own.

Ah hell. We're too late.

"Then we will feed," Gray growled. The scent of old blood and rancid sweat curdled the air, and Caleb's teeth burned with hunger.

Syrkus danced at the vila's side, his movements clumsy beside her inhuman grace. His eyes bulged from his face, his pants torn where he'd fallen several times, bloody skin showing through the rents.

Zahira drew her Glock. "Stop!" she shouted. "SPECTR Agents! Release these people now!"

The vila pirouetted, coming to a halt facing them. Her yellow eyes glowed, and her lips drew back from teeth like blades. Horribly, her victims mimicked the expression.

Caleb took an involuntary step back, and Zahira let out a hiss. "Let them go," she barked. "Now."

The vila's only response was to lock eyes with Zahira, her golden gaze reflecting the light of the remaining candles. Then she slowly raised her arm above her head.

Zahira's arm mirrored the action.

Oh, hell no.

"Zahira!" Caleb shouted, starting forward, although what he meant to do he wasn't sure.

The vila pivoted gracefully on one foot, lowering her raised arm so it pointed directly at Caleb. It took him a moment to realize she mimicked holding a gun, finger poised on the trigger.

All of her victims mirrored the action—including Zahira.

Caleb barely had time to register Zahira's wide eyes, the look of horror and pleading in them, before the vila squeezed an invisible trigger.

And Zahira, her nervous system enslaved to the vila's, squeezed a real one.

Agony punched into Caleb's chest, the burn of silver-jacketed lead ripping through his lungs. The backs of his legs hit the marble side of the reflecting pool, and he collapsed into it, the water closing over his face.

CHAPTER 11

GRAY HAS HAD enough.

This vila, this *demon*, has already humiliated him once by evading him. It caused the unpleasant mortal to yell at Caleb, so now Caleb fears losing John and Zahira and everything else.

And now it dares to spread its corrupted influence over one of *his* mortals?

This will not be tolerated.

Gray rises up from the pool, soaked hair hanging in his face, water streaming from his coat. The few remaining candles gutter wildly, their reflections flickering off the ripples around him. The vila had already begun to dance again, as if it believed something so small as a bullet through the chest could kill him.

It turns—and sees him. Its yellow eyes go wide with terror.

He grins, deliberately showing it his fangs. It should be afraid.

The vila lets out a hiss, takes a step back as Gray gathers himself to leap from the pool. But even as he jumps, it grabs one of the nearest mortals and *hurls* her at Gray.

Gray acts on instinct, twisting in the air to grasp the human. They strike the ground, Gray on the bottom, his body taking the impact of the blow.

The mortal lets out a shriek, her gray hair plastered to her face by rain and sweat and tears. Gray rolls to his feet, then sets her carefully on her feet. "You are safe now," he tells her.

She falls silent and stares up at him with a kind of wonder.

"Gray!" shouts Zahira.

He turns from the elderly mortal. "The vila can no longer be exorcised," he says.

"I know." She grabs his arm. "I'm sorry—are you all right? If you're hurt—?"

"I am not hurt."

She nods, and anger sparks in the depths of her eyes. "Then…then go after her, before it's too late. Take her down."

He shows his fangs. "Yes."

Then he runs.

The scent of the vila leads him up and over the wall surrounding the house. Car tires squeal, and he glimpses the vila dancing from one vehicle to the next, even as they are in motion. He jumps after it, onto the hood of a car.

The hood crumples beneath his weight.

"Damn it, we're not as fast—or as light—as the vila is. Just run!"

Caleb may have a point. Gray springs from the car, hits the sidewalk, and stretches his legs in a flat out run. Even though he is faster than any mortal, it isn't easy to keep the vila in sight. At least the rain has largely cleared the sidewalk of mortals who might get in the way. Only a few notice him rush past; to them he is nothing more than a dark streak in a night made black by storm.

The rain threatens to wash away the vila's scent—but there, he sees it again, springing onto the wall surrounding the church undergoing restoration. For a moment it is framed there, its long hair wild, all of its weight resting on the toes of a single foot.

Then it pirouettes and leaps onto the scaffolding.

Gray may not have the vila's grace and speed, but he is still fast, and much stronger. Lips peeled back from his teeth, he vaults over the wall, Caleb's TK giving them a boost so they all but fly. His fingers wrap around the wet iron of the scaffolding, the whole structure shaking under the impact of his weight. The vila is just above him, leaping from bar to bar.

He begins to climb after it. For a moment, he loses sight of his quarry as it reaches the catwalk just below the roofline. But he is almost there, almost in reach.

The vila appears over the edge, balanced atop the guardrail. It holds an iron bar torn free from the scaffold, poised to throw.

"Oh shit, she's going to—"

The bar slams into his chest, hard enough to splinter through his sternum in front and ribs in back. His heart convulses around it, and agony consumes every nerve, weakening his grip. His foot slips, and he is falling backward.

It is a long way down.

They strike the earth with bone-breaking force. For a moment, he can only lie there, blood flooding his throat, heart quivering around the iron bar driven through him and into the ground by the impact.

"She fucking staked us!" Caleb is outraged—he has never been staked before.

Gray has, many times…but only when he wore corpses, not living flesh. It is a great deal more disturbing now that he can feel pain.

A humerus crunches back into place and heals. He grasps the rod with both hands.

Caleb flinches. *"This is going to hurt."*

Yes.

He wrenches the iron bar free in a spray of blood and hurls it away. His splintered sternum hasn't yet mended when he rolls over and stumbles to his feet.

"Hurry, before she gets away!"

It has been too long since we have fed. I cannot heal us any more quickly than this.

Broken ribs grind together, then mend. He takes a deep breath, heart falling back into its normal pace, the muscle intact again. His mouth is filled with the taste of his own blood.

No matter. The vila will not escape. Not this time.

This time he will feed.

He climbs back up the scaffolding; if she is still on the roof, he will have her. Rain gushes in a miniature waterfall off the red metal roof, the gutters overwhelmed by the sudden downpour. He springs from the catwalk to the roof's edge, claws finding purchase when his boots start to slip.

He hauls himself onto the sharply peaked roof and balances on the balls of his feet. The building, and thus the roof, forms the shape of a cross. He climbs to the top of the roof ridge, his night-sharp eyes piercing the darkness. Where is the vila?

There. It has fled down the longest roof ridge, making for the other end and escape back to the ground. But rather than flee, it has stopped and is backing up slowly.

A second figure stands at the very end of the roof, motionless. Then, between one second and the next, it is gone.

"What the hell?"

Gray does not know what it was, and does not care. He lost the vila through distraction once, and it will not happen again.

He launches into a run. The vila hears the thunder of his boots against the metal roof, and turns before he can reach it. It pirouettes, one foot snapping at his face. He avoids the kick, but the treacherous steepness of the roof sends him skidding several feet down toward the gutters before he can stop himself.

The vila presses its advantage; perhaps it realizes he will not give up the hunt until one of them is dead. Its body arcs through the air, teeth bared, one clawed hand outstretched.

He ducks beneath its arm, grabs the vila's wrist, and pulls.

The move should fling it flat to the roof, but it twists impossibly, as though its bones are no longer solid. Its feet strike the roof, and it swipes its free hand at his face. He jerks back instinctively, only to receive a knee to the stomach, the blow hard enough to rupture organs.

This fight is not going as he would prefer.

He lets go, and it leaps to the roof ridge. Blood drips from its wrist, mixing with the rain.

The vila is too quick and too flexible. So he must be cleverer.

He growls and charges. The vila springs into the air, foot snapping out and into his chest as he closes with it.

Perfect.

His claws sink deep into muscle. The vila crashes to the roof along with him. Its free foot kicks him hard in the side of the head, but he ignores the blow and sinks his teeth deep into its thigh.

Blood bursts on his tongue, and the vila shrieks in pain, its flailing becoming more frantic. The roof is slick, and gravity drags them both down the steep side, but Gray refuses to let go. Just a bit more, and—

Then they're off the edge of the roof and falling yet again.

"Damn it!" Caleb shouts.

He releases the vila, and Caleb flashes to the forefront, TK slowing their fall. The vila twists in the air, landing on its feet like a cat. Blood pours down its wounded thigh, but it gathers itself to run.

A gun goes off, the roar muted by the rain.

Zahira stands in the wet grass of the church's tiny lawn, her Glock braced in both hands. The vila stumbles, blood gushing out of its shoulder where the bullet struck. It growls, fixing its gaze on Zahira, as if it means to mesmerize her a second time.

No. He will not allow this.

Gray crashes into the vila from behind, slamming them both to the ground. It shrieks, struggling to throw him off, but he has it pinned now, and there is no escape.

His teeth find its throat, and blood sluices through the grooves on the back of his fangs and into his mouth. Ecstasy shivers through him, and he closes his eyes as he drinks deep. The vila's clawed hands fall to the side, and the last of the demonic essence fades as it goes limp.

Gray rises to his feet. Zahira's hijab hangs soaked around her face as she runs to him. "Are you all right?" she asks.

"I am."

Zahira puts away her gun and pulls out her phone. "I'm calling it in," she says, slipping beneath an overhang where she will be out of the rain.

Gray nods, but doesn't join her. Instead, he walks around the building, where the figure he glimpsed atop the roof must have descended back to the ground.

There is nothing. The rain has washed away all scent. But the stucco wall bears deep score marks, as though something with claws climbed up —or down—it earlier.

What the hell is going on? Caleb wonders.

But Gray has no answer.

Caleb and Zahira waited in the tiny office he shared with John. To pass the time, Zahira had taken down the vampire teddy bear and was playing with its cape.

"Do you have one of these?" she asked, waving it at him.

Caleb snorted. "I think I'm enough of a walking vampire stereotype as it is."

"It's the costume of your people," she said with a sly grin. "Don't turn your back on your heritage, Caleb."

"Great. My heritage is cheesy Hollywood horror flicks," Caleb said, just as the door opened and John came in. "What do you think, John? Maybe I'll start sleeping in a coffin. A crypt big enough for two?"

"Let's just stick with the bed," John replied, setting a stack of files down on his desk. "I'm glad to see the two of you were hard at work while I was gone."

Caleb stilled. He'd been trying not to think about Barillo's reaction to the events of the previous night. No one could say the vila's attack had been anything but extremely public. Gray's final takedown of it, maybe, could be considered quiet. But everything leading up to the chase had been exactly the attention-getting situation Barillo wanted them to avoid.

Gray stirred. *"Will he try to take John from us now?"*

Christ, Caleb hoped not. Because if he did…

Then I'm done with this SPECTR bullshit. One way or another.

Zahira put the bear down. "Was Barillo angry?" she asked.

"Not exactly," John said. He gave them an encouraging smile. "I wouldn't say he was *happy*, but we did stop the vila. And apparently Gray saved a state senator's elderly mother."

Caleb frowned. "The old lady the vila threw at me?"

"Is singing SPECTR's praises." John clapped him on the shoulder. "Especially those of the 'nice young man' who saved her."

"Well, there's three adjectives, none of which describe Gray in the slightest," Caleb said, but relief washed along his veins. "So her son is a senator?"

"Yep, and he's been on the news talking about the 'highly trained' SPECTR agents who handled the situation and saved his mother. And everyone else, of course." John grinned triumphantly. "So not even Barillo can find fault with us this time."

"That's great," Caleb said, and tried not to feel guilty. Because he hadn't told John everything about the last fight against the vila. If he'd mentioned the second figure on the roof, John would have felt compelled to put it in the report. And Barillo would just have used it as an excuse to harass them, despite everything they'd done right.

"So what's in the file?" Zahira asked, nodding at the folder in John's hand.

John flourished it. "Our next case. We're back in the field full time now."

"Yes!" Zahira exclaimed, pumping her fist into the air. "What is it?"

"I'll brief you both in the car."

Zahira hopped to her feet and hurried out the door. Caleb rose as well, but he lingered as he pulled his heavy elk hide coat off the back of the chair.

Because there had been someone—or, more likely, *something*—on the roof with them last night. And if he couldn't tell John about it, for fear of Barillo finding out, there was only one thing to do.

"Demon or no, we will hunt it," Gray said with grim satisfaction. *"And if it proves dangerous, we will remove it from existence."*

"Caleb?" John called from the door. "You coming?"

"Yeah." Caleb shrugged into his coat and followed John. "Let's go see what's waiting for us out there."

DRINKER OF
BLOOD

CHAPTER 1

GRAY BALANCES AMIDST the branches of a live oak, every sense attuned to the night. The warm, wet wind brings him many scents; more than he'd ever imagined existing in the long millennia spent in dead bodies. Now that he is clothed in living flesh, the world has unfolded into colors and smells and sounds.

He tips his head back, breathing deep. Spoiled fish and soured milk waft from a nearby garbage bin, accompanied by the sweet exhalations of gardenias. The August day baked the streets, and hot asphalt mixes with fading car exhaust. So many things to smell, but not the one he seeks.

"Why are we here?" Caleb asks. *"Not in general, but in this part of the city?"*

Caleb is mortal, and thus impatient. But that is all right. It is his body Gray inadvertently leapt into, during the few seconds Caleb died.

Being with Caleb allows Gray to feel these sensations, and more. Pain and ecstasy, joy and sorrow, and above all love.

They left John sleeping in their bed. They have hunted many, many demons over the last month. Lycanthropes, ghouls, and a therianthrope which took on the shape of a twisted alligator. Even Gray has not seen so many demons in such a short time, and John's body is mortal and has limitations theirs does not. He didn't stir when they slid from beneath the covers, dressed, and let themselves out the door.

What if he wakes while they're gone and wonders why they left without explanation?

Caleb's impatience is sparked now with worry. *"He won't. But if he does, I'll just tell him we were restless and went for a run."*

John would believe them, because he trusts them. And now they are breaking that trust.

"You know why. We don't have a choice. Barillo is just looking for a reason to assign us a different partner. Or worse. If John was involved in hunting this… whatever the hell it is…he'd feel duty-bound to file a report like a good little SPECTR agent. If our hunt became official, and we couldn't find it, it would give Barillo an excuse to carry out his threats. And that asshole's not getting any help from me."

Gray lets out a hiss of frustration. He loves John, but he dislikes all of the mortal rules and foolishness that John cares about so much. If only they could leave this place. Then they could hunt and copulate and live as they wish.

"You know it's not that easy. And you still haven't answered my question. Why are we here, out of everywhere in Charleston?"

I have spent five-thousand years hunting prey on this earth. Trust that I know how to track our quarry.

"Demons. You hunted demons. This thing…isn't."

Which is the problem to begin with. Mortals summon demons and become possessed. If forty days have not yet passed, an exorcist like John or Zahira can save them and banish the demon. After forty days…

Then they are food.

But this creature, whatever it might be, is not food. Its scent awakens no hunger in Gray. Yet it is not a mortal.

Three times, they have encountered its trail. Once near the condo, with no demon in sight. Then it interfered with their hunt for the vila—though perhaps not intentionally. The third time, however, had been deliberate. It had shown itself to them while they fought the vila, silhouetted against a rainy sky, then vanished.

They have caught its attention, just as it has caught theirs. It will try to track them—is already tracking them, perhaps. Which means it will likely be near the condo. But its hesitation to confront them directly suggests it will look for cover. A place to watch them without being seen. The trees offer the best places of concealment—for it and them alike.

"I suppose that makes sense," Caleb says reluctantly. *"And if we don't find it here?"*

Then we will continue the hunt another night. Patience.

Gray slips from tree to tree, then onto a rooftop. He crisscrosses the area between the condo and the street where they first scented the creature, pausing often to sift the wind. There are still many hours to go before dawn, but the longer they're gone, the more likely John will wake up and realize they left. And perhaps John will accept Caleb's excuse, but perhaps he will wait for them outside the bedroom and see they dressed not for running, but for hunting.

"You're right. Maybe we ought to call it a night."

Perhaps, Gray begins. Then the wind shifts, and he smells it. Burning metal and hot stone, mingled with the richness of broken earth. The scent belongs to nothing mortal, yet it stirs no sense of hunger within him.

Before Caleb and John, he would simply have ignored it. Assuming he could even have sensed it while inhabiting a corpse; demons had been the only smell he knew, calling him to the hunt. Likely he would have passed this one by without ever knowing it was there.

Caleb tenses, just beneath the surface of their shared skin. Gray moves slowly, carefully, following the trail but not too quickly. They do not know what this entity intends: if it is curious, or dangerous, or both, or neither.

Another smell joins that of the entity: rot. A decayed body, accompanied by the faintest traces of mange-clotted fur and sour musk.

"A lycanthrope?"

Yes. But dead.

They find the body lying in the middle of a gazebo where they have seen mortal couples wed. The scent of the not-demon lingers around it, already fading. Once he is certain the other entity isn't lurking nearby, preparing to ambush them, Gray drops to the ground and goes to inspect the lycanthrope.

The bodies possessed by demons decay quickly, as if they had died the day the demon was summoned. Little remains of the lycanthrope at this point: twisted bones, flesh going to black slime, a wretched stench. There is no way to tell how it died.

"But the entity killed it, didn't it?" Caleb is grim. *"And left it here for us to find."*

Gray straightens. The wind picks up, threading through the shifting mass of his long hair, bringing with it the last, fading trace of the creature they hunt.

Yes, he replies. *It did. This was a message.*

The moment he stepped into the Paranormally Abled Support System meeting, Caleb felt some of the tension he carried constantly these days slip away. Despite his initial uncertainty, he'd come to look forward to the meetings held every week in the back of a bookstore. Since he lived with John, PASS was the one place he could get completely away from SPECTR bullshit.

A cheery chorus of "Hi, Caleb!" greeted him when he entered. That alone was a nice change of pace from SPECTR, where people tended to greet him with scowls or suspicious looks. And sure, there were definitely exceptions: Zahira and Karl, and a few others. But PASS was the only place everyone seemed genuinely happy to see him.

"'Bout time your lazy ass showed up," said Deacon with a wink. He carefully pulled the folding chairs out of storage, using nothing but his TK. "Thought I was going to have to do this by myself."

As usual, everyone was doing whatever they could with their paranormal talent. Nigel, the group leader, chilled the bottles of soda with cryokinesis, while a pyrokinetic lit scented candles. Which was also a nice change from everyday life, where most people tried not to draw too much attention to their abilities.

The only paranormal ability the group lacked was an exorcist. Which was a good thing, because even the most half-assed exorcist would sense Gray at this close of a range.

"Sorry—wouldn't want you to break a sweat or anything," Caleb replied as he took up position by Deacon. "It might mess up your hair."

Deacon laughed. He and Caleb met for lunch once or twice a week, whenever work didn't get in the way. Deacon was his point of sanity, a friend outside of all the carnage and horror of SPECTR.

If only Caleb dared tell him about Gray. Possessed people usually meant screaming and death, and he didn't want to sabotage their friendship. Still, who knew? Maybe eventually he'd work up the courage. Introduce Gray to Deacon.

"I do not find these mortals interesting," Gray informed him. *"I do not wish to meet them."*

Your loss.

"I doubt that."

Caleb shook his head. Seeing the gesture, Deacon frowned slightly. "What's wrong?"

Crap. Caleb had gotten sloppy, talking to the voice in his head. "Just thinking about work."

"Sounds like something you should share with the group, then," put in Nigel. He was ex-SPECTR himself, and besides Deacon, the only person at PASS who knew where Caleb worked.

"Yeah, okay." As much as he could tell, anyway. Which wasn't a lot, considering Gray's involvement in most of it.

Everyone shuffled into the circle once the seats were arranged. As usual, Caleb was the only one without a donut or soft drink. "Health nut," Haylee the empath teased as she took a seat across from him.

"All that sugar is going to put you in an early grave," he shot back, though that had nothing to do with why he wasn't stuffing his face. Truth was, Gray had dialed every sense up to eleven. Soft drinks tasted like battery acid, and artificial sweeteners made him want to gag.

Just one more way he was set apart from the rest of humanity.

I do not understand why you would wish to be more like these mortals. You are yourself.

"All right, Caleb," Nigel said, settling back in his chair. "It sounds like you're having some problems at work. Is there anything you'd like to share with the group?"

"Yeah." Caleb wiped his hands on his jeans nervously. "It's been kind of crazy lately—we're really busy. So I get that tempers are short. Things have been really strained with my boss, in particular." Which was putting it lightly, given the district chief had drawn a gun on them the last time they'd been in his office. "He doesn't like my...status. You know, my paranormal status." Not quite a lie, since Gray was a part of that. "I'm on probation right now, and things have been fine for the last few weeks, but I can't help worrying it's just a temporary reprieve. That he's just looking for a reason to get rid of me."

How Barillo would get rid of him, Caleb wasn't entirely sure. Drop him in a SPECTR black ops hole, most likely. Or try to.

We will not be imprisoned again.

They'd barely escaped when Forsyth locked them up, and even that had taken outside help. *He'll try to use John against us.*

We will not allow it. Though how Gray thought they would prevent it, he couldn't guess.

"That sucks," Haylee said. "Fucking norms."

"Haylee," Nigel said reprovingly. "We do not use slurs against anyone in this space." He turned to Caleb. "Have you tried speaking to his manager?"

The Executive Assistant Director would be next up the line. Caleb had never met the guy, but he was one of the few who had managed to hang onto his position when Kaniyar took over as Director. Since he'd been the one to appoint Barillo in the first place, Caleb had his doubts. The Charleston office had been the hotbed of rebellion that brought down Forsyth; Barillo's appointment had been meant to reassure the higher-ups and Congress that the agency line would be toed from here on out. "I haven't," he admitted with a shrug. "I have a feeling it wouldn't do any good."

"At least try," Nigel advised. Everyone else nodded.

"Maybe I will." And why not? Would it really make things worse?

Nigel smiled at him, then glanced around the group. "Who wants to go next?"

"I have some news," Deacon said. "Good news. I heard from Mike last week."

The mood shifted; looks of concern appeared around the circle. "How is he?" asked Haylee. "Is he all right? Is he coming back?"

Deacon took a sip of his drink. "He's doing good. I guess he must be seeing some kind of therapist, because he said someone's been helping him come to terms with what happened. To not feel scared all the time. He wants to come back to PASS soon and share some tips with us, if that's all right."

"Of course," Nigel said. "Mike will always be welcome here."

Obviously, this Mike was someone who'd been at the group before Caleb had joined. He didn't ask, not wanting to waste the group's time. When the meeting was over, though, he made sure to leave with Deacon. "So who's Mike?"

They walked side-by-side down the cracked sidewalk. The sun had slipped below the horizon, but waves of heat still rose off the concrete and asphalt.

"That's right—I forgot he'd left by the time you came to your first meeting." Deacon shoved his hands in his pockets, his eyes fixed on the sidewalk. "Mike got jumped by some anti-paranormal assholes last spring. They beat him up pretty bad. It's taken him a while to get his head together."

"Shit." Caleb's gut twisted. At least that was one thing he didn't have to worry about anymore. If anyone tried to jump him, they'd be in for a nasty surprise—and that was even if Gray didn't manifest. "Is he going to be okay?"

Deacon shrugged. "I hope so. But things like that...they leave a mark on your soul, don't they?" He shook his head. "It didn't help that he and Nigel got into an argument. Nigel went to visit Mike in the hospital, and...well, let's just say Mike wasn't in the mood for Nigel's touchy-feely approach at the time. I think that's one of the reasons it's taken him so long to come back. He wanted to do something about it, not let things go and move on."

"Who wouldn't?" Caleb said.

"I figured you'd agree." Deacon paused. "Want me to give you a lift home?"

If they walked, they might come across the not-demon's trail. "Nah. It's a nice night. I think I'll just take a stroll."

He lingered and watched Deacon drive away. *"We should obtain a vehicle,"* Gray suggested. *"Then, when a demon tries to evade us using one, I can follow."*

Caleb snorted. *I'm not letting you drive. You don't even know how.*

There came the odd sensation of someone else shuffling through his memories. Flashes of driver's ed, making out in the old beater he'd owned at the time. The motorcycle safety course at the community college he'd attended for a couple of years. *"You know how. Therefore, I do as well."*

Huh. That was interesting. *What about what your other hosts knew?*

"Some. But it is not as…immediate."

Right. Because before Caleb, Gray had only inhabited dead bodies. No color, no scent besides the trail of demons, memories faded and worn. No emotion, really; or at least none so intense.

"It was…more peaceful," Gray admitted. *"But I prefer this. I prefer you."*

Good thing, since we're stuck together. Their forty days were long past. *Now let's get home and eat something that isn't full of high fructose corn syrup. I'm starving.*

CHAPTER 2

"**ALL RIGHT,**" **JOHN** said the next day, as he shut the door to the exorcism room behind him. "Everyone ready?"

"Ready!" Zahira chirped. After she had seen the footage of Gray fully manifested during the battle at Fort Sumter, John and Caleb had both expected her to react as badly as the rest of the agents. Instead, her enthusiasm had drawn out Gray, who ordinarily ignored everyone but John. He'd agreed to answer whatever questions she might have for him. The outbreak of possessions across Charleston had meant they hadn't had an opportunity for the interview until now.

Just because Gray had agreed to the interview didn't mean Caleb was entirely happy about it. "Do we *have* to do this in an exorcism room, Starkweather?" Caleb asked. He rubbed the toe of one heavy black boot against the silver circle set into the floor around the lone chair. The chair itself was made of solid steel, bolted to the floor and equipped with attachment points for chains. "It's not really making me feel all that comfortable, got to say."

Zahira clasped her hands together nervously. "We could go to one of the conference rooms instead."

"If we're doing this, we should get all the data we can. We chose this room because it's set up to record video, barometric pressure, and temperature," John said. "And because no one will disturb us in here, no matter what." He stepped closer to Caleb and ran a hand lightly down the back of his thick leather coat. "But if it bothers Gray…"

"Gray doesn't give a damn," Caleb muttered. He glanced at John, then sighed. "Fine. Let's get on with it. At least you could have brought us a pillow for the chair."

Caleb seated himself, slouching in the chair, his hands stuffed in his pockets. John suppressed a sigh and went to the panel on the wall, which housed the switches for the recording equipment behind a plexiglass shield. The exorcism rooms were designed to be as damage-proof and easily cleanable as possible, just in case. Nothing but stark concrete floors and walls, the steel chair where a subject would ordinarily be chained, and the silver circle to add power to the exorcism and help contain the NHE.

"We're live," he said, closing the shield back over the switches. He listed the date and time for the record, then: "Interview of the Non-Human Entity known as Gray. Class: drakul. Host: special contractor Caleb Jansen. Attending agents: John Starkweather and Zahira Noorzai."

John's eardrums ached as the pressure in the room shifted, heralding Gray's arrival. "I am ready," Gray said.

His voice was Caleb's, but not: deeper and underlain with a rumble like distant thunder. His posture had completely changed as well. Gone was Caleb's bad boy slouch. Gray sat straight, as if someone pressed a ruler to his spine, his claw-tipped hands resting lightly on the chair's arms. His black hair swirled around his shoulders in an unfelt wind, and his eyes had gone the color of a moonless night, the darkness interrupted by tiny flickers of light, like lightning on a distant horizon. The smell of ancient incense and rain-kissed sand saturated the room. John breathed deep.

Even beyond the physical changes, though, were the etheric ones. Gray loomed huge to John's exorcist senses. If he shut his eyes, he'd think he was in the presence of something much larger and stronger than Caleb's slender body. Something like a very big tiger: a predator that could kill him without a second thought.

After knowing Gray for months, he'd acquired a certain familiarity with the drakul. And yet, sometimes, it struck him anew: this being— huge and powerful and ancient—loved him. The realization stole his breath all over again.

"Thank you for agreeing to this, Gray," Zahira said, putting her hand to her chest.

"You are welcome." Gray turned his attention on her, and she shivered slightly in response. Being the center of Gray's regard could be an unsettling experience; he focused on things with a singular concentration few humans could manage. And of course Zahira's exorcist nerves were no doubt screaming the same warnings John's did. "Ask your questions."

She hurriedly referred to her clipboard, as if afraid Gray might change his mind and not answer. "You were initially summoned to our world approximately five-thousand years ago, correct?"

"Yes. But time has little meaning to me." He cocked his head. "Or it did not, before I began to truly interact with mortals. Now…things are different."

It was surely only natural that being in a living body would change Gray. And yet, John couldn't help but worry. Because the problem with most NHEs, the reason they went mad and started eating human flesh, or feeding on the life energy of those around them, came from exposure to human emotions they were unequipped to deal with. The transition from their natural state to a mortal form, subject to pain and fear, drove them mad.

Gray was different, though. He had a cushion of experience in dead bodies. He would never become dangerous, or violent to humans. John believed that to the depths of his being.

"What about before?" This was what Zahira really wanted to know, John suspected. "How did you experience time in the etheric realm?"

Gray was silent for a long moment, brows drawing together just slightly, as if puzzled. "It was not the same. I hunted. Within the storm. Swooping, diving. Prey scattered before me."

Zahira chewed on the end of the pen she was using to take notes. "So the etheric realm has a sort of ecology." She glanced at John. "And you were a predator. Did anything hunt you?"

"Of course not." Gray sounded offended by the very notion. "I am not food."

"So an apex predator, then." She scribbled furiously. "That's probably a good thing, considering how big you are."

"I don't think I'd want to imagine anything scary enough to eat Gray," John agreed wryly.

Zahira nodded. "All right, Gray. Can you tell me a bit about how you interacted with other drakul? Did you have a society? Or did you live in groups, or…?"

He hesitated, his lips parting slightly, eyes narrowing with concentration. "It has been so long, but…there was one. We hunted together for a time. The earth and the sky."

The fine hairs on the back of John's neck tried to stand up. "What do you mean?"

"I am the storm. But the other was the earthquake. I drove prey down. It drove the prey up. We ate together."

"Cooperative behavior among etheric entities." Zahira's eyes shone; John could practically see her writing the paper in her head already. "But you weren't normally social? Was the other one, um, a mate?"

Gray frowned, as if concentrating. "I do not...think so."

Something about the way he said it caught John off-guard. He'd never spent a great deal of time considering Gray's past, because Gray himself seemed to deem it irrelevant. "You don't think so?"

Gray's attention snapped to him. Dark brows had drawn down over bottomless black eyes. "It is not the same. Everything is different."

Which was the whole problem with summoning NHEs to this plane of existence in the first place. "Different how?" Zahira asked.

"Love and hate and pain and pleasure: these are mortal things. Some of the few that are not nonsense," he added. "Mortals waste their lives on so much foolishness, but to feel and experience these things is...good."

"Not for all NHEs," John reminded him. "Not for most." If the Vigilant were right, drakul ran mad when summoned directly into living bodies, capable of the full intensity of feeling both physically and emotionally. "Forsyth's drakul seemed to lose it right away, attacking his own men, feeding off anything in sight. And the Soviet experiment in the 1950s didn't work any better, considering they ended up dropping their drakul to the bottom of Lake Baikal."

"Caleb wishes to speak," Gray informed them, before vanishing. All that enormous wash of energy tucked up tight like an origami tiger, until all that remained was a low level hum, a whisper of power teasing the very edge of John's senses.

"So asking Gray about the etheric plane isn't going to get us very far," Caleb said apologetically. He lounged back in the chair, his posture far more relaxed than Gray's. "Sorry, Zahira. The problem is, etheric entities are a sort of energy, right? So they don't have brains like we do. They don't process memories or thoughts the same way. But as soon as Gray was drawn into this world and put in a body, he *had* a brain from then on. A bunch of brains, over the years. He's still a being of energy, but everything is shaped by having a physical form. Trying to bridge the gap between what he's been for the last few thousand years, and what he was before..." Caleb shook his head. "He has to really concentrate, and the things he is able to recall...I'm not even equipped to understand half of it. Like literally, I know I'm missing things because the human brain isn't built to perceive them."

"I see." Zahira frowned at her notes. "And of course, even if Gray could explain everything clearly, he's a sample size of one. There's no way to know if his experience is typical, or if other drakul would give different answers."

"You could see if the Russians want to dredge the lake for theirs," Caleb suggested.

"I think I'll skip that," she replied dryly. "So, what if—"

John's phone buzzed in his pocket. He took it out, found a text from District Chief Barillo. "Question and answer time is over for today," he said. "Barillo's got us a new assignment."

"Oh good," Caleb muttered as he rose to his feet. "And here I thought we might go an entire afternoon without murder and mayhem."

"The call came in from campus police," John said as he navigated Charleston's narrow streets. "We've got a hysterical officer and a messy dead body waiting for us at the college."

Caleb leaned his head against the window. He'd taken the backseat while John drove and Zahira rode shotgun. Tourist traffic had died off a bit from its peak, but the historic district was always stop and go no matter the time of year.

"Anything else?" he asked.

"Not right now. Apparently classes won't start back until tomorrow, so the campus itself was mostly deserted. No other witnesses." John pulled up to the curb and shut off the engine. "Here we are."

Caleb slid out of the back of the sedan and took a deep breath. Twilight had taken hold, and the air smelled of damp earth from an afternoon storm. He'd driven past signs for the college any number of times, but never thought about setting foot there before.

One glance at the big trees, draped in Spanish moss, the stately old buildings, and the make of some of the cars parked along the street, suggested this was the sort of place he could only afford with a hefty scholarship. But Charleston had other universities. He'd earned an associate's degree in Charlotte, but held back from going any farther. Mainly because he'd been hiding the fact he was paranormally abled, trying to stay under SPECTR's radar and keep from being registered.

That plan had failed spectacularly, with the introduction of Gray into his life. So why not finish his degree? Take some night classes?

"Because there are better things to do with our time," Gray countered.

Decided to quit sulking, huh? Caleb teased.

"I was not sulking. I was thinking."

Sometimes, Gray was quiet for hours at a stretch. Most mortal doings didn't interest him. If he got bored, he'd curl up in some part of their shared brain and go still, until something caught his attention again.

Today, though, his stillness had a different quality than usual. Zahira's questions about his pre-corpse hopping existence had brought on an unusually contemplative mood. *About what?*

"This existence. Love." A pause. *"I would not wish to return to the etheric plane."*

What did happen to NHEs who went back? John and the other exorcists did their best to trap NHEs in bottles, but after forty days, or in a kill-or-be-killed situation, that wasn't possible. Gray devoured the ones they fought, but the others, the ones forced out of the mortal realm when the host body was destroyed, returned to the etheric plane. Except now they were mad, twisted versions of whatever they had been before. From what little Caleb had gathered, they were thought to await another summons, to return again and again as a lycanthrope or wendigo, craving rage or flesh or whatever hellish desires their madness dictated.

Did the other denizens of the etheric plane fear them? Avoid them?

"I would eat them."

Because that's your answer to everything.

"I do not believe in needless complications."

John led the way beneath the spreading oaks to where a knot of police and EMTs gathered. "Special Agent Starkweather, SPECTR," he said, flashing his badge when they approached. "This is Special Agent Noorzai and one of our contractors, Mr. Jansen."

A woman in a campus police uniform shook his hand. "Betty O'Neal. I'm the head of campus security. Mr. Freeman is over there, near the ambulance."

"He was the responding officer?" John asked.

She nodded. "He shot at the NHE. The…" O'Neal paused and swallowed visibly. "The body is under the trees. Forensics is finished up and are just waiting for your say-so to remove it."

Caleb tipped his head back, breathing deep. Gray rose, hovering just beneath his skin, eagerly scenting the air for a trace of demon.

There. Badly faded thanks to the rain, but perhaps it would be stronger near the body.

Caleb found himself striding across toward the lawn without conscious decision. *Back off, Gray. If you manifest in the middle of a bunch of freaked-out cops, we're going to end up full of lead.*

Gray withdrew, but Caleb felt a thread of impatience. The sort of tracking they'd done the other night was one thing—that required patience. But once Gray had the scent, he didn't hesitate to act.

"Hesitation only gives the prey a chance to escape."

I'm not disagreeing. But getting shot by jumpy cops gives the prey a pretty good chance to escape, too.

The body lay beneath one of the old oak trees, starkly lit with high-powered police lights. The dead man had an athlete's build, short blond hair, and several days' worth of scruff. His shredded clothing was too soaked in gore to identify anything beyond the fact he'd been wearing khakis and a polo shirt, but the watch on one out-flung wrist looked damned expensive.

Whatever had gotten a hold of him, it hadn't made his death easy. One leg had been ripped free, and something had started to feed on it, judging by the bite marks and missing flesh.

The scent of the demon was thicker here: rot and slime, stagnant water and stinking algae. Caleb's stomach cramped in response, and saliva filled his mouth. As much as it repulsed him, it attracted Gray like a whiff of warm chocolate chip cookies. Caleb's teeth burned, need thrumming in his veins.

Zahira and John trotted up. "Therianthrope?" Zahira hazarded as she studied the body.

"No." Caleb took another deep breath. "The scent is badly faded, but it isn't a therianthrope. It smells like a swamp full of dead things."

"Can you pick up the trail?" John asked.

"I'll give it a try." Caleb paced first in one direction, then the other, then circled outward. He finally found the trail, leading deeper into campus. But after a hundred yards or so, it faded away.

"Lost it," he said, Gray's deeper growl creeping in. "But whatever it is, it must be strong for us to still smell it after a downpour."

"Damn it." John shook his head. "Campus police took too long to call us."

"What about security cameras?" Zahira peered at the trees and buildings around them. "If the NHE stopped manifesting, we might be able to identify the faust."

"We'll request them from security." John turned back to the flashing lights of the police cars and ambulance. "For now, let's talk to Officer Freeman and see what he has to say."

CHAPTER 3

THE OFFICER WHO had made contact with the NHE and discovered the murder sat in the back of one of the ambulances, wrapped in a blanket. His brown face had taken on a grayish hue, and his body shivered visibly. Given the warmth of the August evening, John guessed it wasn't an outer cold affecting him.

"Officer Freeman?" he asked. "SPECTR agents. We'd like to talk to you about the incident."

Freeman shuddered, peering at John with eyes red-rimmed and swollen. "Don't want to talk about it. Don't want to *think* about it."

John winced. Encounters with etheric entities were often horrifying. Certainly he'd had more than his share; the memory of the succubus brothel still rattled him. At least he was trained for it; probably the guard had never thought he'd find himself face-to-face with an NHE, let alone one of its victims.

"Of course you don't," Zahira said. "No one would. But we need your help to catch the NHE who did this."

"A demon." Freeman licked his lips and glanced first at her, then at John. "That's what it was. A demon straight from hell."

Now didn't seem the time to explain that demon was a badly outdated term, or that NHEs came from the etheric plane. "Can you describe to us what happened?"

Freeman took a deep breath, as if bracing himself. "I've been in this job ten years, and I never saw anything like it. Mostly I just make sure kids aren't vandalizing the campus, or that the frat house parties don't get too loud. Sometimes there are fights or what have you, but this…"

"Were you just on your normal rounds, or did you get a call about the scene?" John prompted.

"I was going around, checking to make sure all the doors were locked like they're supposed to be." Freeman licked dry lips. "Everything was fine. Quiet, you know, since classes don't start until tomorrow. Then I heard that boy screaming. Wasn't even sure it was a human at first—thought maybe it was some kind of animal, in pain."

John nodded sympathetically. "And you went to investigate?"

"I came running. Whatever was going on, I needed to put a stop to it. The rain was just starting, so visibility wasn't all that great. I thought I saw two people fighting on the ground. I shouted, and one of them looked at me…and it wasn't human."

Zahira slipped her notebook and pen out of her pocket. "Can you describe it to us?"

He swallowed convulsively. "Big. Hairless. It had purplish skin, kind of like it was bruised all over every inch of its body. There was blood on its mouth, its hands. But the worst was those yellow eyes. It looked at me like it hated me. Like it wanted me to die screaming." Freeman put his hands over his own eyes, as if to block out the memory. "I yelled again, and it ran. I had my gun out already—I must've drawn it when the screams started, I don't remember now. I shot it four times, and I know I hit the thing at least once. The bullet ricocheted off its skin, like it was made out of concrete."

That didn't sound good, not at all. Possibly Freeman was mistaken —a high adrenaline situation like this one produced false memories more easily than most people wanted to believe. Forensic analysis of any bullets found could confirm or deny it, but if he was right…well, Caleb had already said it was a powerful NHE, for its scent to have lingered so.

"I didn't try to follow it," Freeman went on. He dropped his hands slowly, eyes gazing into some horror only he could see. "Wouldn't have for all the money in the world. And besides, Derek was still screaming then. Even though his leg was off…God, that thing had been eating it in front of him! I knelt down by him, meant to stop the bleeding while I called for help. But there was nothing I could do."

"Derek? You knew the victim?" Zahira asked.

"Didn't I say? Everyone knows…knew…Derek Scheffler. Tennis star. They say he'll be playing at Wimbledon before long. Or would have." Freeman swallowed convulsively. "He was a good kid. He didn't deserve that."

"No one would." John put a hand to the man's shoulder, gave it a squeeze. "Thank you, Officer Freeman. You've been incredibly helpful. We'll find the NHE responsible and stop it, I promise you."

They left him in the care of the EMTs. As they made for the sedan, Caleb said, "What now?"

"Now we get some rest, while we wait for the security camera footage to get pulled," John said. "Then we figure out what this thing is, and exorcise it before it finds its next victim."

"All right," John said, opening up his laptop. "We have the footage from the incident last night."

He watched Caleb and Zahira take their places around the conference room table. John and Caleb's office wasn't big enough for the three of them, and Zahira was stuck in a cubicle, so they had no choice but to meet here if they wanted any amount of privacy.

Footsteps hurried up and down the hall outside the room. Every agent was working an urgent case these days, it seemed. Even the ghoul squads were overwhelmed.

Not all that long ago, they had days, maybe weeks, between cases. NHEs couldn't cross the veil from the etheric plane on their own. For reasons no one understood, it took human will to bring them from their world to the mortal plane. Which meant for some reason, record numbers of people in Charleston had decided to start summoning demons.

Why, John didn't know. The heat, maybe. Maybe when autumn came in, people would regain their senses.

It was illogical, but he clung to the hope anyway, because otherwise they were in trouble. Agents had already worked long enough hours to start making mistakes. If this stretched on much longer, those mistakes would become fatal.

Zahira and Caleb crowded in on either side of him as John located the relevant file and brought it up. He fast-forwarded to the time stamp, then slowed the video to half speed.

"There's the victim, who has been confirmed as Mr. Derek Scheffler. Business major. The shining star of the tennis team, just as Officer Freeman said." John stopped the video, then forwarded it one frame at a time. Scheffler entered the frame, looking as though he was in a hurry to get out of the rain.

The picture wasn't the best in the dim light, and the shadows of the trees made it even harder to see the NHE as it dropped from the branches and bore its victim to the ground.

"It was waiting for him," Caleb said. "Ambush."

"Waiting for him, or waiting for anyone who wandered past?" Zahira countered.

"That's a good question. I've asked for his student records, but since Mr. Scheffler was the victim and not a perpetrator, I doubt we'll get them." John continued to advance the video. Thankfully, there was no audio to accompany the violent attack, and the rain obscured some of the details.

Within a short time, Freeman entered the frame, gun drawn. "There," John said, stopping the video and pointing. "He shoots the NHE point blank. Forensics confirms they found a ricocheted bullet on the ground nearby."

Caleb leaned back in his chair. "Great. A bulletproof NHE. I swear, these cases just get more fun by the day."

John ignored Caleb's griping. "That should make it easier to narrow down what...yes, Zahira?" he asked, given she was almost bouncing in her seat.

"I've already made a list of NHEs with impenetrable skin," she said in a rush. "There aren't many, and all of them are very powerful. Stony-coats, trolls, and grendels."

"Well done," John said.

"You get the gold star for the day," Caleb said. "Just like every other day. Good thing you're here to pick up my slack."

Zahira's bronze skin darkened, but a smile hovered on her lips. "Someone has to."

"Ouch." Caleb put a hand to his chest. "Staked through the heart."

"All right, you two. Going by the footage, it isn't a troll," John said, bringing the conversation back on track.

"Agreed." Zahira straightened in her chair, all business now. "And a stony-coat would have eaten the liver and nothing else. What we've got is a grendel."

"Like in the poem?" Caleb asked. "You mean that was real?"

"For a given value of real," Zahira said. "There isn't a lot of information on them, but I've put together what little I found for us to review."

John rubbed his eyes. Even though he'd gotten a decent night's sleep last night, the pace of the last few weeks was wearing on him. "This isn't good. It would take a powerful exorcist to summon something like that."

Caleb frowned a little. "Because your talent isn't really exorcism, right? It's manipulating etheric energy."

"Correct. Exorcism is the only legal application of our talent, so that's the description most commonly used." John stared at the footage on the screen. The grendel was nothing but a dark blob, thanks to the rain and the dim lighting. "Ordinary people can summon NHEs using the correct rites to breach the veil. But the more powerful the NHE, the more energy manipulation it takes. Forsyth needed a whole team to bring the drakul through. And that was with the human sacrifice."

Zahira paled. Caleb glanced at her. "Yeah, that's how they brought Gray through, too. It was bad." He paused. "Gray would like me to remind you he didn't ask for it."

"Of course," she said immediately. "He's not to blame."

"Since we're unlikely to get copies of Scheffler's student records, I'm going to try to set up a meeting with his parents," John said, deliberately moving the conversation along. Very little seemed to disturb Gray, but he knew from experience this was one of the things that did. The fact people—children—had died to bring him here, their throats cut by some priest long gone to dust, upset him now that he had access to a full range of emotions. "Just in case this wasn't a random killing. In the meantime, we'll scope out the college. If the victim *was* random, the faust is probably familiar with the campus, and felt comfortable enough to make his first kill there."

"Are we thinking a student?" Caleb asked. "Faculty?"

"Or a groundskeeper, or member of the janitorial staff," Zahira pointed out. "Or someone who works in the IT department."

"Way to narrow down the list of suspects," Caleb said with a wry twist of his lips.

"Then you'll love my next suggestion," John said, even though he knew the opposite was true. "If we can't find the grendel, we need to find the exorcist who summoned it. Which means going down the list on the registry."

Caleb's eyes widened. "Wait. You mean using the damn paranormal registry to go out and harass a bunch of people just trying to live their fucking lives—"

"More people are going to die, Caleb." John's hands clenched on the armrests of his chair. "I know you aren't in favor of the registry—"

"I spent my life trying to stay off the damned thing, yeah. And this is exactly why." Caleb scowled, and John could practically taste the shift in etheric energy. Gray must be rousing in response to Caleb's fury. "Now you're talking about hauling in innocent people who haven't done anything wrong, just because someone *might* have—"

"An exorcist was involved." John returned Caleb's glare. "One of them might even be the grendel himself. Either way, they're our only solid lead, assuming we can't pick up the grendel's trail on campus."

Caleb clearly wasn't going to let this go, no matter how much logic John threw at him. "And what if it's someone from out of town? Visiting for a couple of weeks? Here on business? They won't even show up on the local registry. You'll be wasting—"

"Caleb, *enough!*" John slammed his hand down on the table. Out of the corner of his eye, he saw Zahira jump. "This is not a discussion. I'm the lead investigator, and I'm telling you this is what we're going to do. Understand?"

Caleb's eyes narrowed and his lips pressed tightly together. Then he nodded. "Yeah," he said, not bothering to disguise the bitterness in his voice. "I understand, all right."

Caleb stomped into the condo on John's heels, his hands shoved into his coat pockets and his shoulders stiff with suppressed tension. They'd spent hours roaming the campus, sniffing the air like some sort of supernatural bloodhound, and what had it got them? Nothing.

Which meant tomorrow John started going down his list. Interrogating poor bastards unlucky enough to have the same talent John had.

And what happened to them when a SPECTR agent showed up at their job, or in the middle of class, wanting to talk to them? Would the normals just shrug it off, or would they look at the exorcist with suspicion? Ask themselves why a Spec would be coming around if the exorcist hadn't done anything wrong?

"I know you're mad," John said. The rattle of keys and click of the deadbolt accompanied his words. "And I understand why. I do. But more people are going to die if we don't find the grendel. And we don't have much in the way of leads."

"Yeah," Caleb muttered. He stripped off his heavy coat and tossed it carelessly over the back of a chair, even though he knew it annoyed John when he did that. "I get it."

He could sense Gray watching. Gray didn't like it when they argued. Well hell, neither did Caleb.

"I do not know who is in the right. Or if it matters," Gray explained.

Of course it matters.

John followed Caleb across the room, removing his coat and tie as he did so. "Then stop taking it out on me. I didn't create this system, but I can't refuse to use it if it might help save lives."

Caleb flung himself down on the couch. "It's so damned hypocritical. Normals are the most likely to summon demons in the first place. Normal, male, white, 17-30 years old. But no one's putting them on a fucking registry."

John sat by him. "I know."

He sounded so tired that Caleb finally looked at him. Really looked. There were dark circles under his eyes, and his usual cocky grin was absent. Had been absent, ever since they started running themselves ragged after every fool who thought possession was the answer to their problem.

"I'm sorry," Caleb said. He put his hand on John's. "I've been a dick to you today. Again. I don't know why the hell you don't dump me."

John offered him a wan smile. "Because I love you. Asshole."

"I do not wish John to be sad." Gray considered. *"I do not wish any of us to be sad."*

Me neither.

"I'm a jerk," Caleb said. He swung around to straddle John's lap. Cupping John's face in his hands, he tilted John's head back to stare down at him. "And I'll try better not to be, because you're everything to me. To us. Gray doesn't want you to be sad, and my attitude hasn't helped. I'm sorry. All the rest of this…it doesn't matter, so long as we're with you."

"Same," John said softly.

Caleb leaned forward, his long hair tumbling down like a shining black curtain around them, blotting out the rest of the world. He kissed John, starting off soft and sweet, then deepening into something hungrier. Something to show John he loved him, needed him, appreciated him.

John slid his hands down Caleb's back, cupping his ass through his jeans. Caleb murmured encouragement, grinding his hips down against John's hardening erection.

"Let me make it up to you," Caleb said. He leaned back, just far enough to see John's face. "Do you want to fuck us? Or would you rather we fuck you? Get a little of that etheric energy boost?" Because at least John got one obvious perk for putting up with Caleb.

"I am more than a perk," Gray corrected him. *"Although you are right. I am worth putting up with you."*

Oh, very funny.

"I don't care about that," John said. He frowned just a little. "You know that, right? I'm here for you, both of you, not for some increase in my paranormal ability."

"And you're the only reason we haven't taken off for parts unknown," Caleb said. Which wasn't exactly the truth, since he didn't know how he'd stay off SPECTR's radar if they did make a run for it. "The great sex is a pretty good bonus, though."

John grinned up at him. "Show me, then."

Caleb stretched back and stripped off his shirt, making sure to give John a good look at his body. Gray hovered right under his skin now, and his anticipation resonated with Caleb's, reflecting back and forth into something exquisite.

John tugged him forward to lick one of Caleb's nipples. It sent a jolt through him, an echo back from Gray enhancing the sensation further. "You're so hot," John mumbled against their skin.

"And don't you forget it." Caleb climbed off John's lap, just long enough to shuck off his jeans and underwear. John hastily stripped as well, clothing ending up in a messy pile on the floor.

Caleb straddled his lap again, pressing his cock against John's. John wrapped his hand loosely around them both, the stroke of his thumb smearing precome over the heads. It drew a moan from Caleb, and Gray writhed from the pleasure.

He gripped the back of the couch, rolling his hips forward and up, rubbing their cocks together. John rested his head back, his lips parted and face flushed with lust. "Yeah," he growled. His free hand gripped Caleb's hip, urging him faster.

It felt so good, bodies sliding against each other. Caleb's heightened senses were aware of every inch of velvety skin pressed against his own, of the musky scent of John's desire, of the soft gasps of pleasure riding every breath. He rubbed against John, driving them higher, and all the while Gray hovered right on that line between manifesting and not.

"You like this, don't you?" John said.

"Fuck, you've no idea," Caleb growled. His prick ached, and his balls tingled, and he didn't know how long he could hold back.

"Then tell me."

Caleb closed his eyes, his thoughts scrambled with pleasure and the echo of pleasure. "It's so intense. We're so aware—of you, of us, of—"

His sense of Gray sharpened unexpectedly. Nerves fired, insisting he was being held from behind. His fingers were on his own nipple, though he hadn't deliberately moved his arm, pinching hard.

Caleb's eyes flew open in shock, his back arching as he came. John's hand tightened on his hip, and a moment later, more warm spunk coated Caleb's cock.

"Fuck," Caleb whispered. He slumped forward, bracing himself on the couch pillows. A second, long shiver went through him, not quite an orgasm, but something close. "Christ."

John's hand slid from his hip to his arm. "Are you all right? You had a weird look on your face for a minute there."

"Yeah." Caleb swallowed. "Gray got...creative."

Smugness. *"You are welcome."*

How did you even do that?

"The same way you use your telekinesis when we fight."

At first, they'd had to completely hand over control of their shared body for Caleb to use his TK. But they'd gotten better at it, switching back and forth so fast it was almost seamless.

"Huh," he said aloud. "Well, that was weird, but good-weird." He ran his hand along the line of John's jaw, then kissed him. "So, did I remind you why you put up with me?"

"That depends." John kissed him back. "Are you making dinner?"

"And doing the dishes." Caleb climbed off him and stretched.

John watched with an appreciative look. "Then I suppose I'll keep you around."

CHAPTER 4

CALEB WOKE TO the sound of John's phone ringing, shortly before dawn.

He rolled over, yanking the covers above his head while John answered. Good thing he and Gray hadn't tried sneaking out tonight.

"Sure," John said to whoever was on the other end. "We'll be right there." A moment later, he poked Caleb in the back. "Time to wake up."

"I don't want to." Caleb kept the covers tight over his head. "Why can't things ever go wrong at a decent hour?"

"NHEs do it just to annoy you personally," John replied. "That was Special Agent Ericsson. He was on call tonight. The police brought him in for a homicide, and he thinks it might be related to the grendel case."

Gray perked up at that. *The demon?*

Yes, the damn demon. Caleb sighed and threw the covers back. "Fine. But if it isn't the grendel, Ericsson owes us breakfast."

A little over half an hour later, they parked in front of one of Charleston's grand old homes on Short St. Like many of the city's 19th century houses, it was built side-on to the road, with the main bulk of the house facing a private courtyard. Hanging baskets bedecked the upper and lower porches, swinging in the breeze. Red and blue lights strobed off the beige siding, and a large SUV with Strategic Paranormal Entity ConTRol stenciled on the side blocked the narrow driveway.

Zahira pulled up just as they climbed out of the sedan. The three of them made their way past an unhappy Charleston police officer and into the small walled garden in front of the house. A fountain gurgled softly amidst the antique iron garden furniture.

Inside, the place was as opulent as Caleb had ever seen. Someone had spared no expense to decorate with period-appropriate furnishings; it felt more like a museum than a home. Crystal chandeliers cast soft light over the ornately carved marble fireplaces and gilded picture frames.

Two SPECTR agents stood at the foot of the stairs. "Ericsson," John said, "what have you got for us?"

One of the agents turned to them. He had to crane his head back to look up at John, and Caleb practically towered over him. "Starkweather," he said shortly. "Barillo says you're chasing a grendel. Figure this mess is yours."

"Fill us in, then," John said.

Ericsson glanced past John to Zahira. His eyes darted to Caleb, then away again, as if he hoped Caleb might disappear if he didn't look too close. "The victim is one Brice Wilkinson. Retired, but his husband still works and was away on business. He tried to call and text Wilkinson a couple of times over the last two days but couldn't reach him. Apparently Wilkinson was bad about forgetting his phone, so it didn't raise any alarm bells. The husband gets home just before midnight, goes upstairs to the bedroom, and finds Wilkinson dismembered and partially eaten."

A shudder ran through Caleb. What a thing to come home to. If he found John dead...

Gray roused sharply. *"Why do you think of such things?"*

It's a little thing called empathy.

"I do not like it."

Caleb frowned. Very little disturbed Gray—five-thousand years had given him perspective if nothing else. Except when it came to John. *I can't help it.*

Gray refused to be mollified. *"We would never allow harm to come to John. Do not waste time imagining it."*

"Any idea when the victim was killed?" John was asking. Caleb forced himself to concentrate on the conversation outside of his skull, rather than the one inside.

"The ME will have a better idea, but judging by the smell, I'd say at least a day." Ericsson made a face. "It might just be a therianthrope killing, but the bite marks look wrong. Too human. Could be a wendigo, but I'm kind of hoping we don't have a grendel *and* a wendigo on the loose at the same time."

"You and me both," John said fervently. "We'll take a look."

He started up the stairs. Zahira followed, and Caleb came last. The agents stepped well back as he passed, and a shudder ran through Ericsson.

"I hate it when that thing gets too close," Ericsson said to the other agent, once Caleb was halfway up the stairs. He kept his voice down, but Caleb's hearing was sharper than that of anyone unpossessed. "Makes my skin crawl. Be glad you can't feel it."

"I don't need to feel it," the other replied, also murmuring. "Just looking at that freak is bad enough."

Caleb's hands clenched. If they realized he could hear them, it would only make things worse, though. So he pretended not to, even as acid etched holes in his stomach.

Instead, he let himself be distracted by the stink of rot and dried blood, which wafted down from the second floor. "Left," he said, when John hesitated at the top of the stairs. John gave a quick nod and went in the direction Caleb indicated.

The master bedroom was no less ostentatious than the other rooms. An antique canopy bed dominated the space, the curtains tied back. Blood spattered the rich carpet, the wallpaper, and the mirror in a gilded frame hanging above the small fireplace.

The window was open, which meant the full heat of the day had its chance to work on the body. Flies buzzed in an angry cloud. Caleb looked at the shape in the bed—then hastily turned his back on it. Fuck, he'd never get used to this shit.

"Gray?" Zahira asked. "Did the grendel do this? Can you tell?"

"There's no smell of demon—I mean, NHE—left," Caleb said, without bothering to ask Gray first. "Just blood and…things."

The open window.

"Hold on." Caleb crossed the room, then bent down, almost pressing his nose against the sill.

The scent was faint. If they'd been closer to the bay, Caleb might have put the trace of rotting marsh grass and stagnant water down to nature. "It's really faded, but yeah. This was the work of the grendel."

John poured another cup of coffee and told himself caffeine was almost as good as a full night's sleep. His eyes felt gritty, and a part of him longed to stretch out on top of the conference room table and just take a nap.

Instead, he forced a smile on his face as he turned back to his small team. "Nectar of the gods," he said, lifting the cup.

"Then the gods have some awfully low standards," Caleb said. He leaned back, chair tilted precariously on its rear legs. Out of everyone at SPECTR, he was the only one who didn't seem worse for wear after the last few weeks. No bags under his eyes, or zombie shuffle to the coffee maker in the morning.

Thanks to Gray, no doubt. What were their limits? Gray's presence might have altered him, but surely Caleb still needed REM sleep to keep sane. Probably, anyway. Whatever the case, he certainly didn't need as much sleep as an ordinary person.

Zahira hid a yawn behind her hand. "Here's the file on the victim," she said, waving it in the air. "I haven't had a chance to look yet."

She handed it to John while she went to pour her own coffee. John sat down and smacked Caleb's leg. "Feet on the floor, Caleb."

"Fine." Caleb's chair came down on the front legs with a loud *thunk*. "So let's have the run down on the victim."

John opened the file. Wilkinson had been handsome in life, with iron gray hair, a fit body, and a face suspiciously free of wrinkles. "Brice Wilkinson," he said, as Zahira settled in across from him. "Sixty-six years old, born in Charleston. Retired, and his last job was...shit."

Caleb perked up. "What?"

"He worked at the college." John glanced up, saw Zahira had paused with her coffee halfway to her mouth. "He held a couple of different positions, but for the last ten years he worked as the Dean of Student Affairs."

"One victim a current student, and the other the former Dean of Student Affairs." Caleb's brown eyes had gone thoughtful. "So maybe this is pointing us toward a student, and away from faculty?"

"If nothing else, it does seem to confirm the college is the focus of the grendel's attention," Zahira agreed.

"When did he retire?" Caleb asked.

"At the end of the spring semester." John scanned rapidly down the page. "I don't see any other obvious connections between him and Scheffler."

"So if we find the connection between Scheffler and Wilkinson, that might narrow our list of suspects," Caleb said. "Considering I doubt most students could pick any of the deans out of a police lineup, there must be something."

"True." John downed the rest of his coffee, despite the acid chewing at his stomach. "All right. I'll continue with the exorcist interviews, focusing on any with a connection to the college, no matter how slim. You two go find the current dean and see if they're willing to help. Or if they even can, given we still don't have permission from Scheffler's parents to access his student records."

Zahira sipped her coffee. "Do you think that's suspicious? Surely they should be eager to do anything to help bring his killer to justice."

"Hard to say." John rubbed at his aching eyes. "Grieving people don't always act rationally. Given their son was the victim, they might just see it as a waste of time when we should be focusing on the killer."

"Maybe." Caleb frowned, his eyes unfocussed. "But when there's a death in the family, there is one thing some people will go to almost any lengths to protect."

"What?" John asked.

Caleb glanced at him. "Reputation. Either his...or theirs."

John considered a long moment...then nodded. "You have a good point. All right. Let's head out and see what we can find."

Caleb smelled the ghoul almost the moment they stepped out of the condo. Rot and grave dust, and his belly cramped with hunger that had nothing to do with the take-out they'd grabbed after a long, pointless day.

The new dean had answered all of Caleb and Zahira's questions with an air of polite regret. She could speak in generalities, of course, but couldn't comment on any specific interactions between the former dean and Scheffler, without running the risk of violating privacy laws. What had happened to them both was deeply troubling—frightening, even— but without a court order, her hands were tied.

A court order they didn't have, and didn't seem likely to get. More and more, Caleb was beginning to think he'd been right with his guess, that someone with money and influence was protecting their reputation. Whether that reputation belonged to Scheffler, the college, or someone else, he had no idea.

As a parting shot, the dean had suggested they find the grendel quickly, before panic could spread among the students. As if they weren't working their asses off trying to do just that.

Well, if he couldn't find the damned grendel, maybe he and Gray would have more luck with the not-demon. They'd left John dozing on the couch, worn out after a long day of harassing other paranormals with no more results than Caleb and Zahira had gotten. After dinner, Caleb had lied to John, told him Deacon had texted him about getting a beer, and not to wait up.

The lie sent a twinge of guilt through him, but surely it was better than sneaking out after John was asleep. Unfortunately, it also meant he had to leave the condo in street clothes, without the protection of his kevlar-lined coat and ass-kicking boots.

And now here, on the very street where they lived, was a fucking ghoul.

Gray roused, and Caleb's teeth burned. *"Good."*

No, not good. After all these months, the area had to be saturated with Gray's etheric scent. A regular person wouldn't notice, but a ghoul's superhuman nose would surely have picked up on it, the way a mouse would smell a fox's den. Prey didn't just waltz right up to its predator's burrow, not unless it was particularly stupid. Or controlled by a brain parasite; hadn't he read something about that on the internet?

"You are wasting time while the ghoul gets away. What does it matter why it came here? It will not live to regret its mistake."

Fine. Caleb broke into a jog. There were still a few people wandering around on the streets, but Waterfront Park looked empty, and the trail led straight there.

But why? Ghouls were scavengers. Was there a dead body in the park?

A subtle shift in the wind, and he smelled it. Hot metal and burning stone, black earth heaved up into the sun, ancient rock and water.

The not-demon.

It had killed the lycanthrope they found last week. Was it after the ghoul now as well?

"No! The ghoul is ours to eat."

Caleb broke into a run, spurred on by Gray. The drakul hovered right under their skin, pushing for control. *Hold up, until we see what's going on.*

The ghoul came into view, flattened against the railing overlooking the marsh, as though it had tried to squeeze through and escape into the tall grass below. But the ghoul wasn't alone.

Another figure stood there, bracketing the ghoul between itself and Gray. The faint light from the city glowed off shoulder-length hair so pale it bordered on white. The figure had a slender build, shorter than Caleb, and the breeze off the bay ruffled its hair and billowed the long coat it wore despite the sultry heat of the night.

Caleb slowed, heart pounding. This was what they'd been tracking all along. The not-demon.

But what the hell was it?

It—he?—looked human. But it couldn't be, not with that scent.

The not-demon turned his attention from the ghoul to them. Its eyes were like volcanic glass, lit from within by an orange glow, as though lava boiled deep inside. Its mouth widened in a grin, and ivory fangs flashed in the night.

Fangs. Oh hell. No wonder it didn't smell like food. It wasn't a demon at all.

It was another drakul.

CHAPTER 5

GRAY FLASHES FORWARD, Caleb falling back in an instant.

Another drakul.

He has never met another like himself, not in all his long wanderings on the mortal plane. The mortals who called themselves the Vigilant claimed others existed, but even those were meant to be possessors of corpses. As Gray had been, before Caleb.

This one inhabits a living body.

"Oh shit, this is bad."

Caleb's panic flares along their nerves, but Gray ignores it, focusing instead on the creature in front of him. It does not seem insane, as those who enter living bodies directly from the etheric plane are supposed to be. As Forsyth's drakul was.

Could it be…like him? Could it have taken a host that returned to life unexpectedly, as Caleb did?

The ghoul whimpers. It reminds Gray that this drakul has been hunting on *his* territory, in *his* city. It has interfered with *his* hunts.

Gray's lips twitch back, and he lets out a warning growl.

But the other drakul doesn't seem intimidated. Instead, it stares back at him with something almost like joy spreading over its face.

When it speaks, its voice is the grinding of rock on rock, deep and powerful. The sound of the world breaking.

"It *is* you."

"What the hell? Do you know this thing?"

Gray has no answer for Caleb; he is equally confused. "What do you mean?" he asks the other.

"It is you," it repeats, and steps toward them, one claw-tipped hand outstretched.

Gray jerks back with a warning snarl. "Come no closer. Who are you? Why are you here?"

For a moment, the joy fades, and the other looks almost...lost. "Do you not remember me?" it asks. It holds out its hand again, etheric energy flaring. "Scent is a thing of this world." Its volcanic glass eyes remain on him, steady. "As is flesh. But our essence remains."

Uncertain, Gray reaches back, and the edges of their energy touch.

Something cracks open—recognition, memory, from the time before he came to this world. Swooping and diving and hunting. He drives the prey down from the sky, and the other drives prey up from the earth.

The other. This one.

"Yes," Gray says, and the words reverberate through him like a shockwave. "I remember."

"Wait, stop!" Caleb exclaimed, and held up his hands.

For a moment, Gray fought him for control. *"You saw the memories. I know this one."*

The sky and the earth. The storm and the earthquake.

And shit, that was *not* something Caleb wanted to think about now. The sheer destructive power standing in front of him, waiting to be unlocked...

I know, he told Gray. *But he's on this side of the veil now, and you damned well know what that means.*

Because etheric entities didn't tend to fare well in the mortal realm, experiencing things like pain and terror and hunger for the first time. Whatever their natural psychology was, it didn't equip them for human existence. They went mad, twisted by whatever mortal summoned them. A man dying of hunger might turn an entity into a wendigo. An NHE summoned in rage, to become stronger and punish the enemies of the faust, would twist into a therianthrope.

But those were low-level entities. Even something like the grendel, as powerful as it was, was way down the food chain from a drakul.

When drakul ran mad, entire civilizations remembered.

"I'm Caleb Jansen," he said, and was grateful his voice didn't shake.

"Let me talk to your host."

Because that right there should tell them if this drakul was solid gone. True, it hadn't been rampaging around Charleston yet—there would be too high of a body count for them to have missed—but if it had taken over and swept away whatever poor bastard it possessed, they were in serious trouble.

For a moment, Caleb didn't think the other drakul would comply. Then suddenly, it was gone, all that energy sucked inside and folded up, and Caleb found himself facing an ordinary man.

Well, not ordinary, exactly. Not with those cheekbones that could cut glass, and eyes like blue chips of ice. Not to mention the dimple that appeared in his cheek when he gave Caleb a grin. "Sorry about that," he said. Was that just the trace of an accent? Russian, maybe? "Dru's terrible at explaining things. I thought maybe another drakul would understand him better, but apparently not."

At least the guy sounded sane. "Dru?"

"Drugoy. It's what I call him. But where are my manners?" He thrust a hand out at Caleb. "Yuri Azarov, at your service."

This is pointless. I wish to speak to the other. Gray tasted the name. *Drugoy.*

It isn't pointless. Hush and let me do this.

"Caleb Jansen," Caleb said, shaking his hand. Yuri's grip was firm but not overly so, his palm cool and dry against Caleb's. "Sorry, but let's cut to the chase. How long have you been possessed?" If it was less than forty days, they could still help him. Drakul couldn't be easily exorcised, but John had made damn sure the Vigilant's ritual was entered into SPECTR archives. Just in case.

Seeing them distracted, the ghoul tried to bolt. Yuri kicked it, almost casually. Its body impacted the iron railing with a wet crunch, and it collapsed into a whimpering heap.

"Around sixty years, give or take," Yuri said, as though there'd been no interruption. "One loses track."

"Sixty..." Caleb trailed off.

Sixty years. And he looked in his mid-twenties at best.

Caleb had wondered from the start. Gray continuously healed their shared body, and Caleb always knew there was a good chance that would include the damage done by time. But he'd tried not to think about it, because of all it implied. That if they survived SPECTR and demons and every other damned thing, their big reward would be watching John grow old and die.

He felt as though he'd been punched by something powerful, everything breaking apart inside.

Yuri frowned and quickly reached out, putting a hand to Caleb's arm. "Are you all right?"

"I've...I've only been possessed a few months." Caleb swallowed. "I didn't know..."

To his surprise, Yuri laughed. "Then I have good news, friend. You'll never have to worry about gray hair and wrinkles. You have what people throughout history have spent their whole lives searching for. Immortality." His laugh faded, and he frowned. "That's not cheering you up."

"It's...just a lot to process." Because no way was he telling this guy about John.

Why are you not listening? I know this other drakul.

You hunted with him on the etheric plane five-thousand years ago. I don't know what that even means in terms of human relationships. But I'm not risking John because you think this drakul hasn't changed in all that time.

"You were looking for us," Caleb said. "Because Dru recognized Gray. But how? Gray didn't recognize him. Not until their energy touched."

"Gray," Yuri said slowly. Rolling the name over his tongue, even as a deeper edge crept into his voice. "We saw you on the television at Fort Sumter, before the feed was cut."

God-damned Forsyth. Still causing trouble for them long after death. "Oh."

"We knew there was another living drakul. That we weren't alone anymore." Yuri glanced away, out over the water, then back at them. "Just for that, we would have come to you no matter what. But Dru was certain there was something familiar about the pattern of the drakul's energy, when it was fully manifested. Gray's, that is, not the one you were fighting." Yuri cocked his head to one side. "What happened to him, anyway?"

Well, if anyone would understand, it was probably Yuri. "We ate him."

Yuri laughed again and held up his hands, as if to ward them off. "Well, then, a good thing we brought you dinner!" He gestured to the whimpering ghoul.

Caleb frowned. "That was for us?"

Between one moment and the next, Yuri was gone, and it was Dru who watched Caleb. His energy rolled over Caleb's skin: immense, utterly different from even something like the grendel. Was this how Gray felt to an exorcist like John? "To prove to you we can hunt together again. Just as I kept the vila from fleeing, so you could catch her. I wished to show you. To remind you." A slow smile spread over his face, revealing fangs. "Gray."

Gray pushed at Caleb impatiently, and he reluctantly gave way. "You wish to hunt together again?" Gray asked. Because of course *that* was what he would focus on.

"I do." Dru's fangs flashed. "But Yuri says Caleb has many more questions. That this is natural for humans, to ask and ask and ask."

"Mortal nonsense," Gray agreed.

Dru tipped his head to one side, long, pale hair tumbling gracefully across his shoulder. Listening to Yuri? "Tomorrow evening. There is a bar at Queen St. and Prioleau. Yuri will buy the drinks."

Tell him I agree.

"Caleb agrees."

"Good." Dru hopped onto the rail, balancing with inhuman ease on the round metal bar. "Enjoy your dinner."

Then he dropped over the side into the marsh, and was gone.

"John's going to freak when he finds out about this," Caleb muttered aloud. Gray, not one to pass up a free meal, had happily polished off the ghoul. Now Caleb wandered idly, his head too full of everything that had happened to even consider going back to the condo.

Another drakul. Another *living* drakul, the possibility of which had scared the shit out of the Vigilant, and for damned good reason.

"No," Gray said vehemently. *"They did not have good reason. They feared us, and for what?"*

You do remember the part where we almost ate everyone on Fort Sumter, right?

"But we did not."

Because of John.

Gray brushed the thought aside. *"They feared us before, when we had done nothing. SPECTR fears us now, even though we saved them. We cannot tell them about Drugoy and Yuri."*

Caleb remembered how Ericsson and the other agent had talked about them. As though he and Gray were just things. There'd been no attempt to understand, to get to know them. Just revulsion.

He could imagine how Ericsson and those like him would react to Dru easily enough. Caleb and Gray roamed free thanks to the role they'd played stopping Forsyth. Yuri and Dru didn't have even that much to protect them.

SPECTR would see them as something to be destroyed at all costs. And if Caleb and Gray didn't go along, they'd be on the chopping block too.

There was only one potential problem. *I don't know if John's going to agree to hide Yuri and Dru. He'd do anything for us, but concealing something as potentially dangerous as another living drakul? That's huge. John's going to feel it's his duty to report them.*

"*Then we will not tell John.*"

Caleb came to a halt. The wind blew through the live oaks and rustled the palmettos: hot and sticky with humidity. *You want to keep this a secret?*

"*We kept our search for them from John, did we not?*"

Because it might cause John trouble. Especially with Barillo.

"*And has that changed?*" Gray countered.

Fuck. Caleb chewed on his lip uncertainly. He'd always thought that once they figured out what the not-demon was, they'd either take care of it themselves or ask John for guidance.

"*We did not realize it would be another like us. We did not realize it would be…him.*"

Yeah, and that's something else that bothers me. Caleb shook his head. *What are the odds that the* one *drakul we meet is your ex?* Or whatever Dru had been to Gray.

"*I have seen much stranger coincidences in my time on this earth.*"

Maybe.

Shit. Gray was right. If they told John, he'd definitely call in SPECTR. Best case scenario, Yuri and Dru would be forced to flee Charleston. And the one person who could answer Caleb's questions— the one who really *understood* what it was like to live this way—would be gone.

You're right. Caleb couldn't pass up this chance. Just one conversation with Yuri, and he'd already learned that he'd better be happy with looking twenty-six forever. God only knew what else Yuri could tell him, things Caleb hadn't even thought to consider yet. *We won't tell John. Not now, anyway.*

"*I am glad you are finally seeing sense.*"

Yeah, yeah. Don't let it go to your head. Caleb took a deep breath and started walking again. And tried to ignore the little worm of guilt squirming in his chest.

* * *

"What is this all about?" asked the young man who answered the front door of the apartment not far from campus.

Not far, and yet a world away. Given the shabby exterior and cracked parking lot, John wondered if he might be a scholarship student. The digging he'd been able to do into the campus online suggested they set aside a handful of places each year for "poor and underprivileged students."

"Arthur Inverness?" John asked. At his nod, John flashed his badge. "SPECTR. I'm Special Agent Starkweather, and this is Agent Rand. Can we come in?"

Inverness's gaze went to the green arm band on Karl's suit, which identified him as an empath. Even though Inverness was a registered exorcist himself, a look of fear and revulsion flickered across his face. John clenched his jaw and worked to keep his own emotions calm. Karl knew better than anyone how badly empaths were treated; he didn't need John giving him a second dose of anger to deal with on top of his own.

"Sure," Inverness said warily. He took a step back, beckoning them into the dim interior. A whiff of garbage drifted from the overflowing can in the kitchen directly off the main room. Pizza boxes covered most of a coffee table, and posters of bands and scantily clad women papered the walls. "My roommates aren't here right now."

"You're the one we want to talk to," John replied as he took a seat on the couch Inverness indicated. The couch's springs were long worn out, and cigarette holes showed on the worn brown upholstery. Karl settled beside him, and Inverness took a chair several feet away, perching nervously on the very edge.

"What's this about?" Inverness fished out his wallet. "I've got my registration card, and I filled out the change of address paperwork before I moved to Charleston."

"You're an exorcist, correct?" John asked, though he knew the answer already.

Inverness showed him the registration card with its purple band around the edges. "That's right. What's this about?"

No sense beating around the bush. Certainly not with Karl there to let him know if Inverness told the truth or not. "Have you ever summoned an NHE?"

"No!" Inverness's face went white, and he almost dropped his wallet. "Did someone say I did? Because they were lying."

"He's telling the truth," Karl said.

"That's right!" Inverness exclaimed. His fear of Karl's empathic ability had, predictably, turned to gratitude. "Listen to him. I haven't summoned any demons, or banished any, or had anything to do with the damned things."

Inverness's talent was undoubtedly much smaller than John's. Far too weak to do anything useful with, or else he would have been snapped up by SPECTR as a teen. Still, an exorcist's gifts weren't like telekinesis, or pyrokinesis, or any of the rest. They had no other real practical application beyond interacting with NHEs.

What would it be like, to let the gift rot inside, unused? To know it had to remain that way, or else someone with a badge and a gun would come knocking on your door?

John thrust the thought aside. "I'm glad to hear it," he said. "I don't suppose you know anyone who has recently summoned or interacted with an NHE?"

"No," Inverness said vehemently. "Wait—is this about the... whatever it was? The thing I sensed? How the hell did you know?"

John glanced at Karl, who looked equally baffled. "What did you sense?" John asked.

Inverness slumped back and ran a hand over his jaw. "Fuck, I don't know. I was out on the Battery with my parents. Place was packed with tourists, but they'd never been to Charleston, so I wanted to show them the sights. And that's when I felt...it."

John leaned forward. The Battery wasn't anywhere near the campus, but that didn't mean the grendel hadn't been roaming around. Or that Inverness hadn't brushed up against some other faust. "Can you describe what you sensed?"

"Something big." Inverness swallowed. "That was my first impression. That there was...I don't know, a predator nearby, like a grizzly or something. I can barely manipulate etheric energy at all, and I've never sensed an NHE from a distance before. I don't know what the fuck it was, but you'd better believe I grabbed my parents and ran."

"I see," John said, though he didn't. It could have been the grendel, but he doubted it now. Someone with Inverness's level of talent wasn't likely to sense an unmanifested NHE, even one as powerful as a grendel.

Could it have been Gray? The Battery wasn't far from the condo. "When was this? Do you remember the date?"

"Sure. Weekend before last. Saturday, because that's the only full day my parents were here."

Not Gray, then. They'd spent that weekend on Isle of Palms, tracking the alligator therianthrope.

So what had it been?

"I didn't report it, because I didn't know what to say," Inverness went on. "I don't know what it was, or who the source was in the crowd. I figured it was best to just forget about it and leave it to you Specs." He frowned. "So that's not why you're here?"

John rose to his feet. "I'm afraid not. One last question: did you know either Derek Scheffler or Brice Wilkinson?"

"Derek? He's the guy who was killed the other day, right?" Inverness shook his head. "Never met him. And I've got no clue as to the other one."

Karl nodded, and John made his way to the door. Inverness trailed after them. "Thank you for your help." John took out his card. "If you sense anything else out of the ordinary, call this number, day or night."

Once they were back in the car, John said, "So no lies?"

Karl shook his head. "He believed every word he told us, at any rate." He hesitated. "What do you think he sensed on the Battery?"

No doubt Karl had picked up John's concern over that part of the story. "I have no idea." John cranked the car. "But the way things have been going lately, I'm afraid it's nothing good."

CHAPTER 6

CALEB AND ZAHIRA sat in the back of a small lecture hall, while sobbing students shared their memories of Derek Scheffler.

While John interviewed more exorcists, Caleb and Zahira had returned to campus, for yet another fruitless day of searching for any sign of the grendel. When they'd spotted a flyer for a memorial for Scheffler being held by the frat he'd belonged to, the opportunity had seemed too good to pass up.

Unfortunately, no one in Scheffler's family seemed to be in attendance. The coach had already refused to talk to them, citing student privacy regulations. But that didn't mean they couldn't talk to Scheffler's friends.

A few of Scheffler's tennis teammates spoke, along with Scheffler's girlfriend, but mostly the memorial consisted of his frat brothers reminiscing over the good times. Or some sanitized version thereof, where they spent all day helping little old ladies across the street and didn't even know what the word "kegger" meant. They all looked rich as fuck—even their haircuts probably cost a few hundred bucks a pop.

Zahira listened intently, then leaned over and whispered to Caleb, "I say we talk to the best friend. Hunter Pochron."

"What does he hunt? Is it demons?"

The only thing this guy hunts is sorority babes. Pochron had spoken first, identifying himself as the one to organize the memorial. He had perfect brown hair, kissed by the sun, and teeth so white Caleb worried the people in the front row would be struck blind.

When the memorial finally ended, everyone began to shuffle out. Pochron lingered, shaking hands and conversing sorrowfully. Once the crowd thinned out, Zahira led the way to the front.

"Hunter Pochron?" she asked.

He turned, got a good look at them both, and his smile faded. "Who are you?"

From what Caleb had seen of the student body, there weren't many brown-skinned women in hijabs, let alone long haired goths, roaming around campus. Certainly not together. Zahira pulled out her badge. "Special Agent Noorzai, SPECTR. This is Mr. Jansen. We have a few questions for you."

Pochron glanced at the others around them and nodded. "I'll catch up with you guys at the bar." He turned back to them. "We figured that would be a good place to keep swapping stories about Derek."

"I'm sure it's what he would have wanted," Caleb said.

"Exactly," Pochron agreed. "So why do you need to talk to me? Have you found the killer?"

"We're pursuing every available lead," Zahira replied. "Even the most unlikely ones." She took out her notebook. "The memorial was lovely, by the way. It sounds like Mr. Scheffler will be missed by a great many people."

Pochron's eyes grew misty. "Yeah. Derek was the best, you know?" He looked away, clearly struggling to hold in tears. "The sort of guy who'd do anything for a friend. And when he was on the court…he was going to be one of those players where even people who don't care about tennis know his name. The next Roger Federer."

Caleb resisted pointing out he'd never heard of Federer. "Right. So he was a great guy. Everybody loved him."

Pochron nodded. "Yeah. He was so much fun to be around."

"So he didn't have anyone who would want to do him harm?" Zahira asked.

Pochron's expression shifted into one of disapproval. "Of course not."

"And he never got in any sort of trouble?" Caleb asked.

"Didn't you hear what I said?" Scheffler took a step back from them. "I don't know what you're trying to imply, but Derek was the best. He sure as fuck didn't deserve what happened to him."

"No one's saying he did," Zahira replied soothingly. "We're only looking into every possible option."

"Wasting taxpayer money is what you're doing." A sneer crept over his lips. "Investigating Derek, instead of going out and finding his killer. Do you know who my father is?"

Caleb bit his tongue; John would be proud of his restraint. Zahira kept her face carefully neutral as well. "We have to look into all possible lines of investigation, sir. Lives are at stake. Did Mr. Scheffler know the former Dean of Student Affairs? Mr. Wilkinson?"

Pochron's expression darkened. "Fuck off. I've got nothing more to say to you people."

"If you change your mind," Zahira began and held out a card.

Pochron tore it out of her hand and threw it on the ground. A moment later, he'd stormed out, leaving them alone in the lecture hall.

Caleb exchanged a look with Zahira. "Methinks he doth protest too much."

"Agreed." A furrow appeared between her brows. "Then again, people do have a tendency to get defensive about the dead. Anything that suggests they weren't a perfect angel can feel like disrespect."

"I get that," Caleb said. His own brother had been part of an anti-paranormal hate group. Not the way he'd wanted to remember Ben.

But it is the path he chose. Surely it would be disrespectful to deny what he wished to do.

Yeah, that's not how it works. People don't want to remember uncomfortable facts. Especially about someone they loved.

"Ah. Mortal nonsense."

They left the lecture hall and descended the steps from the academic building. Pochron was still in sight, striding rapidly away with his hands shoved in his pockets. The evening air was just starting to cool off, and the campus seemed mostly deserted. Not many night courses at a swanky place like this.

"So what next?" Caleb asked. They crossed a brick patio with a large gazebo in the center. The gazebo's concrete dome was held up by thick pillars; it looked like the sort of place students would relax between classes.

"We report back to John, and hope he had better luck," she said.

Right. Then Caleb had to come up with some excuse to slip away. Yuri would be waiting for him, and that wasn't an appointment he could afford to miss. One good thing about John going off with Karl to harass anyone registered as an exorcist: Caleb hadn't had to spend the day feeling guilty about hiding Yuri and Dru.

The scent of marshy rot and old blood came to him on the breeze.

Caleb froze, nostrils flaring. Zahira glanced at him worriedly. "What's wrong?"

"It's here," Caleb said. "The grendel."

Zahira instantly went on alert. "Where?"

Caleb shook his head, scanning the area as he did so. Oh hell, Pochron—the guy might be a douche, but they had to warn him there was a killer in the area.

Except Pochron was no longer in sight.

Shit. Maybe he'd just turned off or gone behind a tree during the seconds Caleb had glanced down at Zahira. "Just follow us," he said, and broke into a run.

The grendel's scent grew stronger and stronger. *"It is near."*

Caleb's teeth burned, and his fingertips ached, Gray riding the fine line of manifestation. The wind kicked up, but it wasn't the only thing that sent his long hair unspooling behind him like a black spill of ink. *Hold on, Gray, damn it. If Pochron sees you, he'll freak out and cause even more trouble for us.*

"Where is it?" Zahira called behind him.

"I don't know." The scent was overwhelming, saturating the air. So where the hell was the thing?

Caleb stopped, turning around in circles, and felt Gray's impatience clawing at the underside of his skin.

"We've got to be right on top of it," he said, baffled. Zahira cast about, her Glock drawn and ready.

"Where is it?" she asked again.

"Shh. Be still and pay attention."

To what?

"Everything."

Caleb did as Gray ordered. He stood motionless, letting the world come to him. The wind kissed his cheek, rubbing together the branches of the live oak above. Beneath the rattle of leaves and groan of bark against bark, there came a sort of wet smacking sound.

Oh hell. It was right above them.

Caleb looked up, just in time to see something large and dark hurtling down toward him.

The demon's weight smashes Gray into the ground.

Anger surges through him as he manifests—this creature has dared to ambush him, as if he were its prey.

Normally, demons flee him unless cornered. Even the least cunning among them have an instinct for survival. He believed the grendel would run if it scented him, or at least attempt to conceal itself.

In not doing so, it has made a deadly mistake. Its last, if he has anything to say about it.

The grendel tries to bite, but his thick, kevlar-lined coat resists the maw full of misshapen teeth. He twists, gets a hand free from beneath himself, and drives his claws into its shoulder.

Or tries to. His claws fail to pierce its rough, purplish hide by even the smallest amount.

"*Oh fuck,*" Caleb says. Gray cannot disagree.

The grendel's strength is immense, and it pins him to the ground. One of its hands grips his other wrist, grinding the bones together until they shatter. Gray bellows in pain, then kicks it, hard.

Its grip loosens, so he kicks it again, this time using Caleb's telekinesis in conjunction with the blow. Together they heave it off him. The moment it is away from him, Zahira fires.

Her bullets do no more damage than his claws. One bounces off the creature's skin; the hot lead strikes Gray in the leg, tearing a hole through denim and into flesh.

The grendel rises to its full height, the top of its head brushing the lower limbs of the tree. It is taller than the average human, its body hairless and muscular. Skin the color of a ripe eggplant covers it, and its eyes burn a hateful yellow. Its mouth splits in a grin, revealing uneven teeth, and it reaches into the tree above it to yank down Pochron's ravaged corpse.

"*Is it...taunting us?*" Caleb asks. "*But that doesn't make any sense. Does it?*"

It does not matter. We will kill it either way.

Zahira has abandoned the useless Glock and begun to chant. But the demon is too strong; her exorcist's power can find nowhere to hook into its essence.

Gray's wrist straightens, bones mending, and he leaps for the demon. Even if he can't break the skin with his claws, perhaps he can still use his strength to hold it down. If they can find some way to contain it, they can summon John. Surely he can exorcise it.

The demon's fist slams into Gray's face like a sledgehammer, breaking bone and striking him to the earth. Pain and rage snap through him, and he snarls, staggering back to his feet. Before he can regain his footing, the grendel rushes him.

The grendel's punch buries itself in his stomach, rupturing vital organs, snapping ribs, and heaving him through the air. For an instant, all is weightless pain—until his back smashes into the brick wall of the academic building.

They collapse into a heap at the base of the wall, broken skull and back screaming in agony. There is a blinding flare of light, parts wrenching back into place. Fear bubbles up from Caleb.

"Oh hell, he's too strong for us."

They open their eyes; blinking against the damage their body fights to heal. The grendel stalks across the brick patio toward Zahira. She backs away slowly, still chanting, her useless Glock thrust out in front of her.

No. Zahira is their mortal. This demon will not take her from them.

Gray roars as he comes to his feet. Blood fills his mouth, spills from pulverized organs, but they will not let the grendel have her.

Their distraction works; the grendel turns away from Zahira and back to them.

"We've got to take this thing down."

Agreed. But he hesitates. *Perhaps it can be exorcised. But I cannot see how to stop it without damaging the host.*

Caleb's resolve rushes through them both. *"It's him or us. Whether or not the forty days are up, we've got to kill this fucker now."*

Gray springs at it, even as it rushes him again. His claws can't puncture the gnarled skin, but they catch on it long enough for him to grapple with the demon. He drives his head forward with all his strength to sink fangs into its flesh.

Both fangs snap against its skin, sending a spike of agony through their skull. The only blood that fills their mouth is their own.

The grendel lets out a croaking laugh. Its huge hands close on Gray's throat and thigh, ragged nails biting deep as it hoists him above its head.

Then, with a shout of triumph, it hurls him into the nearest pillar of the gazebo.

Concrete shatters under the impact, as do bones. With a low roar, the entire structure collapses on top of them, burying them in rubble and dust and darkness.

"That fucking sucked," Caleb said. He sat on the steps leading up to the academic building, his skin smeared with dried blood and dust, his hair a clotted snarl. The sight of fading purple on his cheek twisted John's heart. He was almost glad he hadn't been here to see the full extent of the damage. If Gray was still healing bruises, it must have been bad.

The campus was on lockdown, and SPECTR agents swarmed the area, but had yet to find any trace of the grendel. Forensics had set up around the tree where the grendel had stashed its second victim. Hunter Pochron.

"Alhamdulillah, it decided to run," Zahira said tiredly. "My bullets did nothing against it, and it was too powerful for any attempts to drain or slow it using etheric energy."

John nodded. "It must have decided continuing the fight wasn't worth it, even with Gray down."

"No." Caleb rubbed at his face, then winced when he pressed on the bruise. "Ouch. Damn it."

"I'll see if the EMTs have any ice packs," John said. He touched Caleb's shoulder, though what he really wanted to do was pull Caleb into his arms and never let go.

"We're fine." Caleb waved him off. "But, no, I don't think it ran off because of anything we did. It left because it got what it wanted."

John sat back on his heels. "What do you mean?"

"It *laughed*." An edge of dark thunder rumbled beneath the word, Gray's displeasure bleeding into Caleb's voice. "Most demons piss themselves when Gray shows up. And why wouldn't they? He's coming to fucking *eat* them. But this thing grabbed Pochron while we weren't looking, set up an ambush, then deliberately showed us his body like it was taunting us with it. Then it fought us to a standstill and walked off."

John frowned. "What do you mean?"

"It wasn't just not scared—it took delight in beating us. Beating Gray." Caleb ground his teeth. "Yes, you *were* beaten. For fuck's sake, five minutes ago I coughed up a chunk of our liver. We didn't win this, so quit sulking."

"It's okay, Gray," Zahira said. "We all have our off days."

"And the grendel won the battle, not the war," John added. "We have to figure out how to get through its skin. There might be some way of softening it—Florida water, or incense, something that interacts with etheric energy. Has Gray ever fought one before?"

"If he had, we wouldn't have ended up buried under the gazebo," Caleb said. The bruise had finally vanished from his cheek. "I guess you were right about them not being that common. There have to be more of them than there are drakul, though, since it takes a lot less energy to summon them, comparatively speaking." He paused, an odd look crossing his face. "Maybe another drakul out there has killed one."

"Which doesn't really help us, since we don't know where any are to ask them," John pointed out.

Caleb stared down at his hands. "Yeah. So, how did they kill the one in Beowulf? I was a crap student in high school."

"Beowulf pulled its arm off," Zahira said doubtfully. "That seems... unlikely, to say the least."

"I think we can agree that was just embellishment on the part of the poet," John said. Which was a damned shame, because they needed *something*. "I'm going to have to research this. As far as I know, no grendel's been seen in at least a couple of centuries, maybe longer."

"Maybe a little research first would have helped," Caleb muttered.

John's shoulders sagged. "You're right. I assumed Gray could take on anything we came across. I left it all on your shoulders, instead of doing my part of the job."

"Oh, don't be that way." Caleb bumped his knee against John's leg. "And you're right—Gray's normally up to just about anything. And he'd like me to assure you, the next time he meets the grendel, he's going to eat it. Not that he has a plan to make that happen, of course."

"Then I'll do my best to get him that plan." John patted Caleb's arm, then rose to his feet. "Zahira, do you mind driving Caleb home? I need to go back to HQ and report to Barillo."

"Sure," she said.

Caleb looked up at him, brown eyes dark. "You want us to come with?"

"No." John forced a smile onto his face, so none of the trepidation he felt could show. "You go home and take a shower. You've got some liver in your hair."

"Ha ha," Caleb muttered. "Go on, then. Have fun with Barillo."

"Always," John lied. Then he turned away and started across campus to his sedan, and tried not to give away the deep sense of worry growing steadily in his gut.

CHAPTER 7

JOHN STEPPED INTO District Chief Barillo's office. Although a part of him would have liked to have brought Caleb, so Barillo could get the report from someone who had actually been there, he hadn't even dared suggest it.

John still wasn't sure exactly what had happened between Barillo and Caleb in July. Barillo had dismissed the rest of them and kept Caleb behind, presumably for the sort of ass-chewing he regularly gave John. John had worried about leaving them alone together, simply because Caleb's "screw the man" attitude would only make Barillo angrier.

But when Caleb rejoined them, he'd said everything had gone fine. Except he'd been paler than usual, and there had been an uncharacteristic look of worry—or was it fear?— in his eyes.

"Sir," John said, doing his best to project respect. Like it or not, they all had to deal with the district chief. As the old saying went, honey attracted more flies than vinegar.

Barillo's dark eyes assessed John. Lines of strain had begun to show around them, and there was noticeably more gray in his short, tightly curled hair than before.

The outbreak of NHEs had worn on them all. Before, the district chief usually had gone home at five, though he was always on call. Now, John couldn't remember the last time he'd seen the man leave before eight, if not later.

"Starkweather." Barillo scowled. "I've read your preliminary report. Am I to understand that Special Agent Noorzai and Mr. Jansen let some kid get eaten right in front of them?"

Shit. "No, sir. Let me explain. They were interviewing Mr. Pochron about the first victim, Mr. Scheffler."

Barillo held up a hand. "Let me stop you right there. Why the hell were they interviewing Pochron?"

"Both Scheffler and Wilkinson were connected with the college. I don't think their deaths were just random. Neither was Pochron's." John forced his spine straight. "In light of this latest death, if we could get a warrant for their student records—"

"Absolutely not." Barillo leaned back in his chair. "Let me spell things out for you, Starkweather. This college? Their alumni go on to be congressmen and CEOs. You go requesting records, and the media's going to think the college has something to hide. Trust me when I say, any damage to their reputation will *not* be looked upon kindly by a large number of very wealthy people."

John ground his teeth in frustration. "With all due respect, sir, how am I to investigate if I can't follow our best lead? Scheffler and Pochron were best friends, at least according to Pochron, and now they're both dead. As is the former Dean of Student Affairs. If we're to keep anyone else from dying—"

"Here's an idea," Barillo broke in. "How about your demon-sniffing vampire keeps a hold of the grendel next time. Don't you think that would be a good way to keep anyone else from dying? As opposed to, say, harassing grieving friends and relatives?"

Oh hell. John sent a swift prayer to Sekhmet before answering. "Mr. Jansen and Agent Noorzai attempted to apprehend the NHE, but its skin proved impenetrable to all of their weapons. There's nothing anyone could have done that would have resulted in a different outcome, not with the knowledge we have now."

"Good try, Starkweather, but they failed. And you're trying to cover up their failure with this obsession with student records."

John wanted to lash out. To make Barillo understand how badly Caleb had been hurt. To fucking *get* what it was like out there in the field, instead of playing armchair quarterback later on.

"The grendel is a very dangerous NHE," John said frostily. "We haven't seen its like in a long time, and no one knew just what to expect. Its immense strength and impenetrable skin allowed it to effectively fight off Gray, without sustaining injury to itself."

Barillo flinched at the mention of Gray. He reached out, took a candy from the jar on his desk, and slowly unwrapped it. "Seems to me your pet demon lets NHEs get away on a regular basis."

"That isn't so," John snapped. "The raven mocker could fly, and the vila—"

He caught himself. That time, Gray had been distracted, by something he still hadn't adequately explained to John. Could the mystery NHE have anything to do with what Inverness had sensed in Battery Park? Caleb had said they'd originally scented the entity not far from there.

The wrapper crinkled as Barillo balled it up between his fingers. "That *thing* gets to run loose in exchange for being useful. But honestly, I'm starting to think it isn't half as useful as I was led to believe it would be."

Fuck. This wasn't good. John felt as though a sword hung over his head, suspended by a thread as he sought the words that would keep it from falling. Except it wouldn't fall on his neck, would it? It would descend on Caleb and Gray. "No SPECTR agent could have done half as good a job," he said carefully. "I'm one of the top field agents in the southeast—I'm not saying that to brag, but to point out I couldn't have brought in either the raven mocker or the vila without Gray's assistance. Certainly not without a larger loss of life."

Not to mention Forsyth would have eaten his way through the low country, and they'd all be dead now if Gray hadn't been there. But Barillo had already made it clear that any talk about Forsyth was off the table.

"And maybe that says it all right there, agent." Barillo popped the candy in his mouth and steepled his fingers together. "You used to be one of the top agents. Now you've come to rely on your little demon friend as a crutch. And you're letting us all down in the process."

Fury stole John's breath. His fists clenched, and his gut churned. "I assure you, I've done my utmost to serve this agency and this country," he grated out. "As have Mr. Jansen, Special Agent Noorzai, and Gray. I would defend our actions to anyone."

"Would you?" Barillo sat back in his chair. "Get out of here, Starkweather. Scheffler and Pochron were good kids. Let them rest in peace, instead of trying to dig up dirt. Hear me?"

John's throat was almost too tight to speak. "Yes, sir."

He walked swiftly back to the office he shared with Caleb, careful to keep his face expressionless until the door was firmly shut behind him. Fury still trembled in his veins, and when he unclenched his hands, he saw his nails had made bloody crescents in the palms.

Sekhmet, guide and protect him.

He took a deep breath, then another, and tried to focus. Past the anger, past Barillo's half-veiled threats, to the last thing the district chief said.

"Scheffler and Pochron were good kids. Let them rest in peace, instead of trying to dig up dirt."

Except John hadn't been trying to dig up any dirt. He'd only wanted the student records, to see what sort of connections he could make between them and Wilkinson.

Which suggested there *was* dirt to find on them…and that someone was leaning on Barillo to keep it from getting out.

"You came," Yuri said with a smile. He looked utterly at ease, sitting at a table in the rooftop bar, dressed in a stylish jacket and shirt. The breeze ruffled his long, pale hair. Night had fallen, and Charleston spread out before them, a city of gleaming lights.

"Of course I did," Caleb replied, dropping into a seat by him. Gray hovered close to the surface, eager for a glimpse of Dru. *Later. Let me handle this.*

"Order what you like." Yuri beckoned to a waiter. "My treat."

Caleb had left John on the couch, falling asleep over his tablet. He'd lied—again—claiming Deacon was going through a bad breakup and needed a friendly ear. It was the second night in a row he'd used the same excuse, but John had only waved a tired hand at him.

Even if he hadn't been meeting Yuri, he would have probably found some excuse to get out of the condo. Their defeat at the hands of the grendel had left Gray edgy and angry all evening.

If only the alcohol would do anything to settle their nerves. "I miss getting drunk," Caleb said, once the waiter left.

"That is foolish of you."

Hush.

"I'm Russian. Imagine how I feel." Yuri winked at him. "Dru says hello, by the way. He's very glad you came."

"As am I."

"Gray says the same."

The waiter brought Caleb's drink: some hideously expense whiskey, served neat. Once they were alone again, Yuri raised his glass. "To new friendship."

Caleb clinked his tumbler to Yuri's. "To friendship."

"Now," Yuri said, leaning back in his chair with a contented sigh, "I'm sure you have many questions. Ask away."

Caleb winced. "I don't mean to come across as suspicious…"

"It's only natural. And you wish to protect Gray, of course." Yuri gazed out over the city. "How long have you been together? You said only a few months, but Dru's been in this world for a great deal longer. And if Gray left the etheric plane first…"

Oh hell. He'd hoped—really hoped—that their story was the same. That Dru had the same cushion of memories gleaned from dead bodies, and that was what had kept them from running mad. "Gray spent thousands of years hopping from corpse to corpse," Caleb said, in what he hoped was a casual tone. "Didn't Dru?"

Confusion flashed over Yuri's face. "Corpses?"

Caleb had thought it couldn't be true. Because everything he'd been told—everything he'd seen, when it came to Forsyth at least—said drakul summoned directly into living bodies went mad just like so many other NHEs.

Unless the Vigilant were wrong. Unless it wasn't as clear cut as they'd thought.

"Here's the thing," Caleb said. "I know who you are."

Yuri cocked his head, brows drawing down. "What do you mean?"

"I've seen the classified files." Caleb pinned Yuri with his gaze. "You're Russian. Possessed sixty years ago. You're the Lake Baikal vampire, aren't you?"

Yuri stared off at the city. For a moment, he was utterly motionless, not even breathing. The stir of his hair in the breeze was the only thing about him that even seemed alive.

Then he turned and gave Caleb a dazzling smile. "Fascinating! How did you find out?"

The sudden shift caught Caleb off guard. Though not enough to blurt out the answer. "So it's true?"

Yuri tossed back his drink and signaled the waiter for another. "It's a long story, my friend, but…yes. Depending on the accuracy of whatever you heard, naturally."

"Why don't you tell me what the real story is, then?" Caleb asked.

"I was a lieutenant in the Soviet army." Yuri accepted his fresh drink from the waiter, eyes lingering on the man as he returned to the bar. "I competed with many others to have the honor of being host to something—I didn't know what, just yet—that would protect my homeland and keep it safe."

"Sounds like Gray's original host," Caleb said. People really didn't change much, no matter the era. "Except the priests strangled her before summoning Gray."

Yuri shuddered delicately. "Did they? How horrible. I can't imagine how awful it must have been for him, trapped in dead flesh."

"It didn't bother him." Supposedly, Gray had been better off for it. That was what everyone believed, that it was the cushion of memories gleaned from dead flesh that had allowed him to adapt to a living body without going insane.

And yet here was Yuri, smiling and friendly. Dru wasn't exactly frothing at the mouth, either; he didn't strike Caleb as any more murderous than Gray.

"We have been misled, it seems."

Yeah. I'm starting to think you're right.

Caleb cleared his throat. "I heard...I mean, the reports said something went wrong. They trapped you." Encased in tons of steel and concrete, more like. Except, again, here was Yuri, clearly not at all trapped at the bottom of a mile-deep lake.

Yuri shook his head. "Don't believe everything you read, Caleb. Imagine for a moment that you're an officer facing execution because Dru and I escaped. Wouldn't you make up some story about averting disaster, paint yourself as a hero of the people, and hope no one ever discovered the truth?"

"Yeah, I guess. When you put it that way." Caleb hesitated. "You escaped?"

"When I realized my superiors didn't have our best interests in mind." Yuri waved a dismissive hand. "But that is the past. What is important now is that we've found you. You can't imagine how often I've wanted someone to talk to, someone who understood."

Poor bastard. Caleb was half crazy after just a few months of it. "Believe me, I can. Not being able to tell anyone..." Outside of SPECTR, anyway.

"But we have each other now," Yuri said. "So tell me—does Gray feel like any moment not spent hunting is wasted, and never tires of reminding you of the fact?"

Caleb laughed. "God, yes. Or going on about mortal foolishness." He lowered his voice to imitate Gray. "'They are not food, why are they running and screaming? Mortal nonsense.'"

"It is," Gray objected.

Yuri grinned. "Of course. And *you're* the one stuck dealing with the screaming humans, because he decides it's not worth his time. And the constant complaints about food! 'It is cold blood, Yuri, we cannot eat that.'"

"I'm really surprised Gray isn't bitching about the alcohol right now."

"I have resigned myself to your attempts to poison us."

"Never mind—spoke too soon." Caleb downed the rest of his drink and leaned back. Something inside him seemed to uncoil, for the first time in weeks. Months, maybe.

Yuri understood. Of course John had tried to be supportive, but Yuri *knew* what it was like.

Caleb had a dozen different questions. How long Yuri and Dru had been in the states. What sort of life they'd had over all these years. Where they normally lived, and if they had any friends who knew the truth about them.

But all that could wait. Right now, he could just sit back and enjoy. Without having to worry about saying the wrong thing, or accidentally frightening Yuri, or anything else.

It was a feeling he could get used to.

"So," Yuri said, "have I satisfied you for the moment? Because if so…what say we go somewhere more interesting?"

Caleb lifted a brow. John was waiting for them, but… "Sure. Why not?"

Yuri paid for the drinks, then led the way back down to the street. They crossed East Bay, and Yuri ducked casually into a narrow alleyway between an art gallery and a restaurant.

Caleb felt the whisper of etheric energy and smelled Dru's scent even before he turned to them. His eyes glowed in the dim light, hot orange trapped within a shell of volcanic glass. Dru tipped his head to one side, grin exposing his fangs. "Yuri says…try to keep up."

In a blink he was up the side of the building, claws sinking into old brick. His coat flared out behind him, before he vanished onto the rooftop.

Caleb laughed. "Oh, it's on," he said. And fell back even as Gray surged forward.

CHAPTER 8

THEY RACE EACH other across the rooftops. Pleasure sings along Gray's nerves: the pure sensation of muscles moving, of breath whispering through lungs, of simply being alive in the night. Drugoy's hair is a pale flag in the moonlight, beckoning him on. The lights of the city blaze on their left: neon in every color, yellow gaslight in front of historic buildings, cold green street lamps. To the right, the river is nothing but a dark ribbon, broken up by the occasional boat.

Drugoy had a head start, but Gray's legs are longer. They leap over air conditioning units and ductwork, dash over terra cotta tiles, and all but fly across the gaps between buildings. Cars stream beneath them as they clear one street, then the next, the mortals utterly oblivious to them passing overhead.

Drugoy glances once over his shoulder, hair streaming into his face, his mouth shaped into a wicked smile that reveals an edge of fangs. Then he leaps the longest gap yet, across a small parking lot.

Testing them.

"Then we'll just have to show him what we've got."

Gray follows easily. Drugoy's next jump is farther still, from building to the branch of a sturdy old oak, to the roof of a stately home. The branch springs beneath Gray's weight as he follows, claws digging into a downspout to gain the roof.

"We almost missed that one"

But we did not.

"No." Delight bubbles up from Caleb; the simple joy of running and jumping, of a living body responding effortlessly to every command. *"We didn't."*

Another leap, stretching their body to its fullest. They are racing north up the peninsula, nearly to the concrete river of US 17 pouring off the interstate to bridge the Cooper River. Drugoy darts across the roof of a boarded up building, and for a moment Gray thinks he will try to jump the four lanes of Meeting Street.

Instead, he comes to an abrupt halt at the very edge.

Gray can feel Caleb just beneath the surface of their skin, leaning forward eagerly. *"Let's do what Yuri asked, and show them what we've got."*

Gray doesn't slow, let alone stop. He has just enough time to glimpse Drugoy's eyes widen, before they push off the roof with every ounce of strength in their legs.

And with Caleb's TK.

And it is like flying, if only for a few seconds. Headlights rush past beneath them, the night city spread out all around, and a bubble of wild exultation wells up from Caleb.

Then their boots hit the flat roof of another boarded up business. Gray turns and flashes his fangs triumphantly at Drugoy.

Drugoy tips his head in acknowledgement, before dropping from the roof to the sidewalk. A man nursing a bottle in a brown paper bag gapes, but the drakul pays him no mind. A few moments later, he joins Gray on the roof. "You are still one with the sky," he says, and the admiration is something of a balm over the irritation left behind by the earlier fight with the grendel. "How did you do that?"

"Caleb is telekinetic."

"Ah." Drugoy cocks his head slightly. Listening to Yuri, perhaps. The wind catches his hair; it doesn't thrash of its own accord the way Gray's does. But Drugoy is the breaking of the earth, not the shattering of the sky.

It is impossibly strange, standing here with another drakul. He had never considered before if he would even wish such a thing. Never wondered what it would be like, to exist in this mortal world with another of his kind.

"I know where a lycanthrope pack is," Drugoy says.

Hunger sharpens Gray's attention. "You have not eaten them?"

"This city has been a rich feast. There has been no need."

"It is not always like this," Gray says. "There were not so many demons, when I first came here." And of course he isn't free to simply hunt as he will, the way Drugoy is.

"Let's keep that to ourselves for now."

"Shall we hunt them?" Drugoy asks. The light in his eyes shifts slowly, as though a river of lava moves behind them.

Gray's claws slide from their sheaths in anticipation. "Yes."

"Then follow me."

They pass like a pair of ghosts through the grassy marshland beneath the steel and concrete overpasses. Scattered apartments and businesses lay beyond, but Drugoy remains away from them, leading the way toward the river. Soon they stand on a decaying road of cracked pavement, arrowing off into low, unkempt fields and marsh. A sagging gate halfheartedly blocks further access, weathered KEEP OUT signs barely visible on it beneath a growth of vines and grass. In the distance, Gray can just make out a long, low concrete building with a corrugated metal roof.

"What was this place? Some kind of government facility? Because this is a lot of land to just leave to waste."

Does it matter? They are not here to worry about mortal nonsense. They're here to eat demons.

Drugoy springs over the gate easily, and Gray follows. The pavement is almost gone on this side of the fence, the wilderness taking over again. This is always the way of things; he has seen it again and again. Mortals building their temples and palaces, believing they are the pinnacle, the end point of history. Then they fall, and are subsumed by desert and forest, until no traces remain to even suggest they existed at all.

"What a cheerful thought. Thanks."

You tell me to hush often. Now I am telling you.

Caleb does as asked, and falls silent. Gray and Drugoy move cautiously up the road, drawing closer to the dilapidated building. Drugoy's footfalls are utterly soundless, as if the earth swallows the vibrations before they can spread.

Gray smells the demons even before Drugoy halts. The hot summer wind carries on it the delicious scent of matted fur and scabrous mange, and his stomach cramps with hunger.

"You come in from the roof," Drugoy says, his voice a low rumble. "And I shall come from ground level and block their escape."

Memories shift and shiver, more insubstantial even than those of dead hosts. "As we did before."

"Yes."

Drugoy melts away into the night. Gray approaches the building cautiously. The sound of faint growls and crunching bone comes from within. The pack is feeding.

A telephone pole sags at one corner of the structure. It is but the work of a moment to scramble up the cracked wood and onto the metal roof.

It groans beneath their weight, and Gray freezes. Listening. The sounds below die away, the pack uncertain. Scenting the air, no doubt, but the breeze is brisk off the river, and he is still downwind. After a long moment, one of the werewolves barks, and there comes the wet rip of flesh being stripped from the bone.

Gray moves slowly across the roof, testing each step. Caleb hovers, just at the edge of consciousness, for once not distracting from Gray's focus. Rust has eaten a small hole in the metal, and they crouch to press an eye to it.

All is darkness within, but they can see perfectly well in the night. The interior of the structure is utterly destroyed. Claw marks show on support beams, wires have been ripped free from the walls, and a detritus of rotting flesh, gnawed bones, and filth covers the concrete floor. The mouth-watering stench of the lycanthropes rises up, and his fangs ache, hunger biting at his spine.

There are four of them, their muzzles coated in blood as they finish off the last morsels of whatever unfortunate mortal became their victim tonight. *"I wonder if SPECTR has any idea they're out here?"*

Doubtful. As Drugoy said, there are many more demons here than there were before. But no matter; they will deal with these creatures. John would be pleased, if they dared tell him.

Caleb seems less certain of that, but subsides.

There comes a crash from below, accompanied by the shattering of the wood boarded up over the door. The werewolves leap up, snarling— then whining in fear as Drugoy steps in. Two rush at him, but the other two back away, ready to flee.

"That's our cue."

Gray grasps the edge of the rusty metal and peels it free. Then he drops through the hole, directly onto one of the lycanthropes.

The werewolves panic, caught between the two drakul. Gray seizes the one he knocked to the floor, yanking it to him. It bites, teeth slashing his face, but he ignores the flare of pain and buries his fangs in its neck.

The pleasure he was denied earlier with the grendel sings through him. Feeding in a living body is utterly unlike anything he had experienced before. Blood pours into his mouth through the grooves on the back of his teeth, and energy races into him, suffusing every cell. The werewolf struggles, but weakly now. Gray sucks harder, wringing every drop of etheric energy, of blood, from its body, until it goes still.

He tosses the body aside. Drugoy has another werewolf pinned beneath him on the floor. His pale hair spreads around him as he feeds, and an odd feeling of shame flashes from Caleb, as if they have accidentally witnessed something intimate.

The other two lycanthropes have fled through the broken window in the back wall, which they no doubt used to get into the building to start with. Drugoy finishes his werewolf, glances at the window, then at Gray.

It takes no more communication than that.

Within seconds, they race across the marshy flats, boots sinking into the muck. The fleeing werewolves run ahead, having gone to all fours on the uncertain ground. The drakul spread out, flanking them, giving them no direction to run in except that of the river.

One becomes helplessly mired in the stinking mud. Drugoy falls on it, and Gray leaves him behind. The last werewolf stops when it reaches the water, turning back on him. Its yellow eyes are wide with panic, and its misshapen mouth works, seeming oddly confused. As if it does not quite understand how this happened.

Even so, it tries to fight. Gray ignores the damage from its claws in favor of subduing it quickly. The wounds seal as they feed, and it is with a feeling of regret that he drops the corpse. A shame there aren't more for them to hunt.

"Greedy," Caleb says. But for once, that is the only complaint he offers.

Drugoy crosses the water-logged ground with a confident step, as though the mud doesn't quite cling to his boots. His chin is covered in blood, his pale hair flecked with it. Gray looks down, finds his own clothing and skin slicked with mud and blood.

Drugoy drops into a crouch beside him. They both sit in silence, staring out over the river. There is no need for mortal chatter, no need to ask what the other is feeling, or whether he enjoyed the hunt. There is only this moment of quiet existence.

Caleb, of course, must break it eventually. *"We should ask them. For help."*

"There is a grendel," Gray says aloud. "I fought it today. But its skin cannot be broken, and...I could not kill it. And I do not know where it is hiding now."

Drugoy tilts his head slightly. Long hair slides gracefully over his shoulder, like a spill of moonlight. "Then we shall hunt it together."

John woke at the brush of etheric energy against his back. He'd gone to bed alone, after drifting off twice on the couch, waiting for Caleb to come home.

Now, a familiar weight dinted the mattress by him, and a warm hand rested on his hip. He didn't have to open his eyes to know Gray was manifesting. John took a deep breath, smelled ancient incense and petrichor...accompanied by grapefruit shampoo and sandalwood soap.

"Did you guys take a shower?" he asked.

Gray tucked in closer against John's back. His lips brushed John's shoulder, and his hand traced little circles on John's hip. "Yes. There was a werewolf."

That brought John fully awake. He rolled over on his back. The room was dark, save for the light leaking in from street lamps outside, and the faint, ghostly flashes of lightning deep within Gray's eyes. "A werewolf? Was anyone hurt? Why didn't you call?"

Gray's hand slid distractingly up John's belly. "There was no need." He kissed John's shoulder again, nuzzling inward toward his neck. "We smelled it on the way home. It fled into the marsh. I ate it."

Damn it. "You'll have to file a report. I mean, Caleb will. Barillo—"

Gray silenced him with his mouth. John kissed him back automatically, and Gray moved to straddle his thighs. His hair slithered around them, his skin hot from the shower.

John's prick responded. He put his hands to Gray's shoulders, not sure if he wanted to pull him closer, or push him back and bring up the lycanthrope again.

Fuck it. The body was off rotting in the marsh. There'd be no way of identifying the human host, no way to link it to any particular murder the way things had been going lately. Why give Barillo any more ammunition to use against Caleb and Gray, when nothing good could possibly come of it?

Gray let out a purr of pleasure when John ran his hands down Gray's back, to his ass. He kissed John's neck again, then lower, over his collar bone, and down. John closed his eyes and let his lover do as he wished, drinking in the sensations.

"What do you want?" Gray murmured against his belly. His breath felt warm against John's skin, and his hair slithered over thighs and cock like black silk.

"Fuck me. Like this. Turn on the light so I can see you."

The mattress shifted again, as Gray leaned over to reach the nightstand. John grabbed his pillow and shoved it beneath his hips.

Then everything was slickness and heat, and the faint prick of not-quite-sheathed claws as Gray gripped his hips. Gray's hair rippled in an unfelt wind, and his parted lips showed the tips of his fangs. Every movement was one of controlled power, and John didn't bother to hold back his moans as Gray pushed into him.

He gripped Gray's shoulder with one hand, cupped Gray's face with the other. Gray turned his head, pressing lips into John's palm—then licking the vein of his wrist.

"Let me taste you," he growled.

"Oh hell, yes." Not because the act itself did anything for John, but the effect it had on Gray...

Gray's fangs were meant to do damage; biting was out of the question. Instead he let go of John's hips and dragged a claw along the vulnerable skin of his forearm. Just a scratch, the flare of pain almost lost beneath the pleasure of being fucked. Blood beaded along the edge of the wound. Gray licked it—then with a groan, fastened his mouth over the cut and sucked.

His cock seemed to stiffen even further, and his thrusts became harder, more urgent. His eyes half-closed in ecstasy, the swirl of etheric energy prickling along John's skin.

"You look so hot," John gasped. He grabbed his aching prick, stroking in time to Gray's strokes. "Fuck—I'm going to come; come with me, please—"

Gray shuddered. Etheric energy sang along John's nerves, flooding into his body, and he shouted incoherently as he came.

For a long moment, there was nothing but the sound of their breathing, gradually slowing. Then Gray stretched out half on top of him, arms and legs tucked around John. Holding him close.

John felt boneless, sleep threatening to suck him back down. He resisted its pull long enough to murmur, "I love you."

"Even if I ate the werewolf without permission?"

John blinked. He'd almost forgotten about it in the haze of sex. "Of course. And to hell with reporting it. I trust you guys."

Gray didn't reply for a long moment. Then he nuzzled John's hair. "Good."

CHAPTER 9

THE NEXT AFTERNOON, John settled back in his chair at SPECTR and chewed on the end of a pen. Stalking around the campus, hoping for a whiff of the grendel, hadn't worked. Interviewing every exorcist he could find had resulted in no new leads, either. The bodies were piling up, and they'd hit dead end after dead end.

The case had stalled, no doubt about it. The college still refused to turn over the records of the two student victims, and his requests to interview the parents had been vetoed by their lawyers. Ordinarily, he would have pushed harder on those fronts, but Barillo's warning replayed over and over again in his mind.

"What next?" Zahira asked.

Caleb was off fetching lunch, leaving John and Zahira to stare at the facts of the case, laid out on the conference room whiteboard, accompanied by images of the three dead men.

"I'm not sure," John admitted. "We're running into a brick wall here. I'm certain the college is hiding something, but I don't know how to find out what. And honestly, it might not even be related to the case. Say Scheffler was busted for underage drinking, and Wilkinson helped make it go away, even though Scheffler should have been booted off the tennis team. People might want to keep something like that quiet, especially since it's nothing to do with their deaths."

She sipped her coffee. "What about the internet? Have you searched for anything there?"

"There's nothing but the usual news articles about the deaths. Memorials for Scheffler from teammates and coaches." John rubbed at his eyes. Sekhmet, he was tired. "I don't think there's a single article without someone throwing around 'Wimbledon,' though whether he was really that good or not I've no idea. According to everyone, both the student victims were saints who walked on water."

"No speaking ill of the dead," Zahira said.

"At least, not when they're rich athletes."

"Did you try the school newsletter?" she asked. "It might at least have photos the news outlets don't. Something might show up."

John blinked. "No. It didn't occur to me." Goddess, he was slipping. "Is it online?"

"Everything is online now." Zahira opened her laptop. "Let's see… here's the college website…and here's the archive of the newspaper."

John leaned in close to watch as she ran the search. It brought up several memorial articles, followed by a long list of tennis scores. Just as he was about to give up, John saw an innocuous headline buried among the rest. *No Charges in Late Night Fight on Campus.*

"What's that?" John asked, pointing.

Zahira brought up the article.

Three students were involved in a fight on campus the night of April 11. Officer Freeman responded to the complaint and broke up the fight. According to campus police, the incident was minor, and no charges will be filed. Drugs and alcohol were not involved.

"Well, that was barely worth the pixels it took to display it," John said. "But why did a search on Scheffler's name even bring it up? It doesn't mention him."

"Hold on. Let's take a look at the source code for the page." Zahira brought it up in the browser. "Here—look. In the metadata."

Three names were listed: Officer Freeman, Derek Scheffler, and Hunter Pochron. "It was edited," John guessed. "The original article was longer. Named names. And someone ordered it scrubbed."

"Except they forgot the metadata," she agreed.

Was this the secret the college wanted to keep? It seemed pointless. Despite the assurance that no alcohol was involved, John didn't have any trouble imagining three college guys getting into a minor tussle over something stupid. Though it was odd the third person hadn't been named—or maybe he had been, but was left out of the metadata by accident, or because he wasn't well known on campus like Scheffler and Pochron.

"Maybe even a minor fight with no charges would have been enough to get Scheffler kicked off the tennis team," John reasoned aloud. "Except he was the golden boy, so instead it was buried."

"But he's dead now," Zahira argued. "If this had any bearing on the case, wouldn't someone have mentioned it? It doesn't sound worth keeping from us."

"Maybe it wasn't really a fight," John said grimly. "What if they were doing something a lot worse, something that should have been mentioned to the police but wasn't? Like summoning a demon."

"But if the grendel was summoned in April, it would have started killing in May at the latest," she argued. "The timeline doesn't work."

"Damn it." John tossed his pen at the wall. It bounced off and rolled under the desk. "Still, this has to be the connection. Wilkinson would have gotten involved as Dean of Student Affairs."

Zahira stared at the laptop, as if the code would suddenly spell out the key to the murder. "Officer Freeman was the responding officer to this incident and Scheffler's murder, both. Do you think it's a coincidence?"

"Probably." After all, the college's security force was fairly small. If Freeman had the evening shift regularly, it made sense he would have responded to both events.

Even so, he'd know the truth behind the so-called "fight." If they could persuade him to tell them what happened, even off the record, they might finally get somewhere. "Zahira, call campus security. See what time Freeman starts work, and if we can arrange an interview with him this afternoon."

While Zahira dialed, the door opened and Caleb stepped inside, arms laden with sandwiches and drinks. He'd been unusually quiet all day, but now he offered them a smile. "So you solved the case while I was gone, right?"

"Not quite, but we might be on to something." John took the sandwiches while Caleb distributed ice tea. "Veggie wrap for you, lamb gyro for Zahira, and…"

He trailed off at the serious look on her face. "Thank you," she said into the phone, and hung up.

Caleb had paused in the midst of putting an ice tea in front of her. "Trouble?"

Her dark eyes met John's gaze. "Officer Freeman was supposed to start work an hour ago. He hasn't shown up."

"Shit." John grabbed up his drink. "Come on. We'll eat in the car."

John knew something was wrong the moment they pulled up in front of the small bungalow where Officer Freeman lived.

There was no obvious disturbance from the outside. No smashed-in front door, or bloody handprints on the siding. More of a feeling, like a buzz in the fillings of his teeth, or a subsonic noise vibrating his bones.

His etheric sense had grown far keener thanks to Gray. Was that the root of this certainty?

"The grendel," he said, even as he parked the car. "It was here. Is here, maybe; I don't know."

Caleb put away his phone. "I texted Nigel to let him know I might be late to tonight's PASS meeting," he said, even though John hadn't asked. A moment later, he was gone, and Gray manifested instead.

"All right," Zahira said, peering out the window cautiously at the bungalow. "What's the plan?"

This was a neighborhood. Older, but not run-down, probably full of children. If the grendel went on a rampage here, the death toll could be horrendous.

Might already have been, if they were too late.

"I'll go in the back," he said. "Zahira take the front. Gray, do whatever seems best to you at this point."

How they were going to stop a NHE that had already out-fought Gray, he didn't know. But they had no choice but to try. "Bullets don't work," he reminded them, and drew his athame. "This probably won't either, but if I channel enough etheric energy into it, it might at least hurt. If I can get a toehold, I'll try to exorcise the grendel right here." Which went against Barillo's express orders, but to hell with that. Even the district chief would have to see they couldn't drag a grendel back to HQ for a traditional exorcism. "Gray, give me thirty seconds to get around the back before you do anything."

"Be careful," Gray cautioned as they exited the car. "I would not have this demon harm you."

"Neither would I," John muttered. Gripping his athame, he made his way around the back of the house, his eyes on the windows as he passed. Nothing stirred inside that he could see.

Not a good sign.

A canal of sorts ran behind the house, leading in the direction of the

Ashley River. In the distance, he could see an earthen dam separating it from the river delta proper. A scummy film of green algae hid the water's surface. Its rank smell almost overcame the trace of blood drifting from the bungalow.

The back door hung off one hinge, the wood shattered. Every sense alert, John slipped inside, the athame held in front of him like a shield.

A broken television lay in the living room, smeared with blood. Bits of hair and flesh coated the walls and floor, accompanied by white slivers of bone. Amidst the carnage, he saw two sets of clothing: shredded shirt and pants, and a house dress whose original color could no longer be determined. A photo on the wall showed Officer Freeman's smiling face, accompanied by a woman who must have been his wife.

The grendel had feasted, far past any human capacity, leaving almost nothing of its victims behind. The etheric charge in the air didn't shift; just a remaining trace, left behind when it abandoned the site of its latest slaughter.

Gray growled. John jumped; he hadn't noticed Gray's entrance. The drakul crouched in an open window, his lip curled to reveal a fang. "The demon is gone. I will track it, if I can."

John lowered his athame. "Do that," he said, without much hope. "Make sure it didn't go into any of the neighboring houses."

Zahira entered from the front, Glock drawn but lowered. Her eyes took in the scene of carnage, and she murmured something that might have been a prayer. "I'll call the morgue."

"Thanks." John started out the back. "I'll follow Gray, just in case." But in his gut, John knew the grendel had left once it got what it came for.

Three students, involved in a fight, two of them now dead. One security guard, also dead. No charges filed, and the dean who had helped cover up the matter murdered as well.

They had to find out the identity of the third student, no matter who was leaning on Barillo to cover up what really happened that night. Because unless John was mistaken, the unknown student was either the next victim...or the one who had summoned the grendel in the first place.

"Are you sure you don't need me to stick around?" Caleb asked.

They were back at SPECTR-HQ. Zahira and John had spent the last hour heating up the phone lines, leaving voicemails, and pushing hard for anyone at the college to talk to them. Barillo wouldn't be happy when word got back to him…unless they could catch the grendel before that happened.

Which was why Caleb had been surreptitiously texting Yuri, not just on the way to the Freeman residence, but after. Surely two drakul could not just find the grendel, but figure out some way to kill it.

John shook his head. "Go to your PASS meeting. No sense in sitting around here. If we have a breakthrough, I'll give you a call."

"Okay. If you're sure." He leaned down and pressed a kiss to John's forehead, since the door to their office was closed. "We love you."

"Love you, too." John smacked him on the ass. "Now get out of here and let me get back to work."

Caleb left HQ on foot. The plan was to walk to the bookstore where PASS had its meetings, drop in for a half hour or so and kill time while the sun went down. Then he'd duck out early. Yuri would pick him up outside, they'd head over to the college, and let Dru and Gray do their thing.

"I do not understand why we must go to the meeting to begin with. Those mortals are boring. I do not care about them."

Well too bad, because I do. Deacon was his friend, but so were Nigel and Haylee and the rest.

"We have John and Zahira. And now we have Drugoy and Yuri. They are all much more interesting."

I need these people. I need something that isn't demons and killing, all right? Caleb let his anger and annoyance rise to the surface, making sure Gray got a good dose of it. *Yes, I want to spend time with Yuri and Dru. But they're still a part of all…this. All the craziness. Just let me have something for myself.*

Gray subsided—not happy, no, but letting it go for the moment. Caleb stuffed his hands in his pockets and walked the rest of the way in relatively peaceful silence. The tourists were out in force, even with the spike in NHE activity, and jammed the cracked and uneven sidewalks. Caleb wove through the press, drawing a number of strange looks as he'd left his elk hide coat on. At least he didn't really sweat anymore.

The closed sign was up on the bookstore, and the door locked, so he tapped on the window. The owner came from amidst the shelves and let him in. "They've already started," he said with a nod toward the back room.

"Thanks," Caleb said. He made his way through the shelves to the employee door…then slowed.

The air smelled of old books, of dust and paper and the sweat of the tourists who had come in earlier. From the back room drifted sugary donuts and spilled soda.

But overwhelming all of them—overwhelming everything—was the smell of demon.

The grendel was here.

Caleb stilled, his heart drumming against his ribs. Gray surged forward, hovering just under their skin, twisting and frantic. *"It is here!"*

There was no tang of blood, and the murmur of voices came from the back room. *It hasn't manifested. Whoever the faust is, their forty days isn't up yet.*

Which meant maybe—*maybe*—they had a chance of keeping this from becoming a bloodbath. But they had to keep from panicking the faust for it to work. *So stay down and let me handle it.*

How he was going to handle it, exactly…well, he'd work it out as he went along. Hopefully.

Trying to keep his expression calm, Caleb entered the room. The group had already gathered in the circle and started the meeting. Caleb didn't recognize the person currently talking. What had Deacon said, about a returning member? Mike, was that the name?

He was slender and small-boned, and like Haylee wore a green empath's armband. "I kept having the nightmares, though," he was saying. "Every time I closed my eyes, I saw them over me. Laughing. And the security guard…he saw how bad it was, but did he stand up for me? No one in authority cared what happened to me. The dean swept it under the rug. The coach even threatened me, said if I told anyone, he'd make my life difficult. Like it was such a picnic already."

"Fuckers!" Haylee said, glaring. "I'd like to put a boot in their face."

"We're listening to Mike now, Haylee," Nigel reminded her gently. "Mike, you said you found something that helped you cope. Would you like to share it with the rest of us?"

Mike took a deep, shuddery breath. "I did. I realized that I—that all of us—have to look for our own protection. To find our own justice. And there is a way, if we just accept it." A slow smile crept over his face. "It feels so good, knowing I'll never have to be afraid again."

Oh hell. "You ought to be afraid," Caleb said from the doorway. "The demon inside you is just waiting for time to run out. As soon as the forty days are up, you're gone."

Every eye turned to him, and several people gasped or muttered. Nigel looked shocked. "Caleb! That's a terrible accusation to make. I'm afraid you're going to have to apologize, or else leave PASS."

Fuck. "Look, Mike, is it?" Caleb held out his hands. "Deacon said you got jumped by some anti-mal assholes. Scheffler and Pochron, right?"

Damn it, he wished John was there. He'd know exactly what to say. How to keep Mike calm and evacuate the rest of the group at the same time.

Mike frowned and looked around. "Who is this? Why is he attacking me?"

"You're being an asshole yourself, Caleb," Deacon said sharply. "I don't know what's gotten into your head, but—"

"Mike is possessed. I work for SPECTR—we've been tracking his kills." Caleb swallowed. "I really, really need the rest of you to get out of here. Now."

"SPECTR?" Haylee sat forward, her eyes narrowed. "Fucking hell, you're a plant! They sent you to try and get dirt on us."

"No!" Caleb shook his head frantically. "Nigel knew where I worked from the start, okay? I just didn't want to say anything, because…because I knew you might not want me to be part of the group. But I swear—"

"He's the one who's possessed!" Mike put one hand to his empath's armband, eyes going wide. "I can't read him at all, not even a little."

"Mike," Nigel said, now clearly alarmed. "Your talent isn't that strong. Everyone needs to just settle down."

"No!" Mike pointed a shaky finger at Caleb. "He's a monster!"

Deacon rose to his feet. "Look, I don't know what's gotten into the two of you, but you'd better explain right now."

He reached out toward Mike. Acting on instinct, Caleb lunged for him, meaning to drag Deacon back away from the grendel.

Mike shouted and snatched up the bagel knife from the table. Caleb jerked back, but the blade laid open his cheek to the bone.

"Oh my God!" Haylee shouted. "What are you…?"

But it was no longer Caleb she shouted at, but Gray.

CHAPTER 10

GRAY IS ANGRY.

This grendel has bested him, has *laughed* at him, and now it taunts him in this way?

This must end. It *will* end.

The mortals begin to scream.

"Call 9-1-1!"

"It's a monster!"

"God, no!"

No—these are not just mortals. *"I need these people,"* Caleb said, and now the sound and sight of their terror slices far deeper than the knife.

These humans are foolish, but Gray will not allow them to hurt Caleb. He will simply explain.

"Do not be afraid," Gray says, holding out a hand. They scramble away from him, chairs overturning. Nigel's face is white as milk, and the female empath—Haylee—has tears streaming down her face. "I am no threat to you. I am only a danger to the demon."

He starts toward the grendel, confident it will leave behind its mask of humanity. Then these others will see.

Instead, it cries, "Oh God! It's coming for me! Someone help!"

"Mike, run!" shouts the red-haired mortal. Deacon. Caleb's friend. "We'll protect you!"

"You are Caleb's friend," Gray says. "There is no need to—"

A metal chair slams into the side of Gray's head, hard enough to send him to the floor. Caleb finally seems to break out of the paralysis gripping him. *We have to get out of here.*

"Save Mike!" Deacon shouts. "That thing wants to kill him, but we can hold it back!"

Then suddenly Gray is besieged by mortals. More chairs strike him, and the pyrokinetic sets the ends of his hair on fire. Nigel lays frost on Gray's skin, even though his face is wrung by fear.

"No." Caleb's thought is faint with shock and horror, with grief. Every fear he has had, that they would turn against him, is coming true.

He had feared it—but Gray understands now he did not truly believe it. That someplace deep inside, Caleb nursed the hope this would not happen. That he would tell them about Gray and somehow they would understand after all.

Mortals often fool themselves. Gray knew this, but he did not know how badly it would hurt.

"Take my car—get out of here." Deacon flings his keys across the room and into the grendel's hand. With a last, mocking look over its shoulder, it flees.

"You are letting it escape!" Gray roars, and the air is thick with the stench of fear. But still the mortals attack him, some now holding chairs or other implements in their hands, striking him. He tries to force his way through without hurting them, but Nigel stabs a silver athame deep into his side. Blood sprays when he wrenches it free, and the other humans take encouragement and began to hit Gray in earnest.

"They want to kill us." Caleb feels dazed, remote, and Gray does not like it.

"You are making Caleb sad," Gray snarls. "Do you not understand? I have always been here. We are one. You have never known Caleb without me, but I have never harmed you. This is foo—"

A metal chair smashes into his mouth, breaking teeth and cutting him off. And all the while, the grendel is getting farther and farther away. Probably laughing at Gray the entire time.

"Enough!" he roars, and bursts upwards, flinging them off him. Bones break as they strike the walls and floor, but he does not care. These mortals have hurt Caleb, and that he will not tolerate.

They are starting to flee now, those who can walk. Haylee comes at him again, the bagel knife in her hand.

He slaps it aside, hears her wrist fracture at the blow. Grabbing her arm, he hoists her up, so her feet dangle about the floor.

"Stop this at once," he growls.

"Fuck off, demon," she says, and spits at him.

He never cared before, when mortals defied him. When they staked him to the ground, or chanted at him, or lit candles they thought would hold some power over him. It did not matter, save that it was inconvenient, and he avoided them when he could.

This matters. This mortal, who spoke to Caleb, who knew him, turning on him because of Gray.

"Let her go, Gray. The grendel is getting away. And this won't...it won't change anything."

Gray lowers her to her feet. "I am no demon," he says, and turns his back on her. She doesn't try to come after him.

He pauses in the doorway leading to the sidewalk. Night has fallen, but there are too many mortals about. The grendel is gone, in a vehicle.

There comes the deep growl of a powerful engine, and a sleek, black motorcycle pulls up to the curb. "Gray?" Yuri asks in surprise. "What happened?"

He lets go, folds back so Caleb can come to the fore. "The grendel," Caleb says, his voice rough with suppressed emotion.

Yuri's lips curl back from his teeth. "Where?"

"Here—but it's gone now." Caleb takes a deep breath. "But don't worry. I think I know where it's going to strike next. We just have to get there in time to stop it."

Zahira and John hurried through the lobby of the college's athletics building. Night had fallen outside, and their footsteps echoed through a silent building that felt deserted.

John hadn't expected the tennis coach to be the one to finally return their calls, willing to talk. But there had been real fear in the man's voice when he'd asked them to meet him as soon as possible in his office. A curved staircase led up to the second floor, where the offices were located.

The day's heat had collected upstairs, and the coach's balding head shone with sweat when he opened the door at John's knock. "Mr. Kent? Special Agents Starkweather and Noorzai. We spoke on the phone."

"Come on in." Kent gestured to a pair of chairs in front of his desk. The office was nicely appointed, with an expensive looking desk and custom-built cabinets holding a wide variety of trophies. Kent dropped into his own chair, grabbed up a small towel emblazoned with the college logo from a drawer, and wiped his brow. "'Scuse me. I wrapped up my workout early to meet you, but I'm still hot from the shower."

"Mr. Kent, can you tell us why you needed to speak to us so urgently?" John asked. "You suggested you knew something about the string of murders."

"When I heard the guard was dead…" Kent trailed off and shook his head. "I didn't want to think it had anything to do with the mal."

John stiffened at the slur, but only said, "Can you elaborate?"

"Yeah, but…" Kent shifted uncomfortably. "You've got to understand. About Derek."

"What is it we need to understand?" John asked, keeping a tight rein on his impatience.

"Derek was a good kid. A great athlete. He had his whole life ahead of him." The coach put the towel away, the chair creaking under him with every movement. "He didn't deserve to have all that taken away from him over one little mistake."

Cold pooled in John's stomach. He let it seep into his voice. "Mr. Kent, what exactly did Mr. Scheffler do?"

"He was just a rowdy boy." The coach tried a we're-both-guys smile. "You know how it is, right?"

"I know that Mr. Scheffler was nineteen and hardly a 'boy,'" John replied. "I suggest you stop making excuses for him and tell us what this is about."

"You'll protect me, right? From the demon?"

John wanted to scream with frustration. Zahira leaned forward slightly. "That's our duty as SPECTR agents, sir," she said.

"Duty. Right." Apparently reassured, Kent said, "There was this other kid, English major I think. A mal—one of the ones who have to wear the armbands. He was in one of Derek's classes. Well, I'm sure I don't have to tell you, Derek didn't feel right about that. Having to sit there in class with one of them."

Zahira offered only a blank, expressionless stare. John did the same. After a few moments, the coach shifted uncomfortably and cleared his throat. "Right. Well. Derek and Hunter had maybe had a beer or two. Not a lot, just a little something to take the edge off. They were crossing campus and ran into the kid. And there was a fight."

"You mean Scheffler and Pochron jumped him," John said, struggling to keep his anger from showing. By the look on the coach's face, he failed.

"It was a mistake, okay? And Freeman made sure the kid got to the hospital."

"They put him in the hospital?" Zahira asked. Out of the corner of his eye, John saw her hands clench in her lap.

"Just for a few days," Kent protested. "Look, it was a dumb thing for them to do, sure, but not bad enough to throw away their whole lives over. The dean, me, a few other people, went by and talked the kid out of pressing charges. After all, fighting is against the student code of conduct. If the kid went to the police, he'd just get thrown out too, or at least lose his scholarship."

John didn't want to believe what he was hearing. "You threatened him?"

"No! Just reminded him about the no fighting rule, that's all."

"He was the *victim!*" Bile coated the back of John's throat. He longed to lunge across the table and slam Kent's head into the display case behind him.

The coach's face flushed even redder. "He spent a few days in the hospital and didn't finish one semester. So what? Compared to everything Derek and Hunter had to lose, who would have been the *real* victims if charges were filed? Derek would have been forced off the team, and both of them would have had a criminal record for the rest of their lives."

"Mr. Kent," Zahira said, her voice far calmer than John could manage at the moment, "do you remember the name of the student they assaulted?"

"Mike something. I'm sure I can look it up." Kent glanced back and forth between them. "Can you protect me?"

"Why did you wait so long to come to us?" John demanded. "If you'd said something immediately—"

"Well, how was I to know?" Kent scowled at him. "I thought maybe Derek and Hunter had gotten involved in something else. You know how wild boys can be. They liked to blow off steam sometimes. But when you said the security guard was dead…that's the only time they got in trouble on campus. And I thought…what if I'm next? What if this maniac has a grudge against me, too?"

Sekhmet give him strength. A part of John wanted to just get up, walk away, and let Kent fend for himself. What else had the man helped cover up in his years as coach? What other destruction had he turned a blind eye to, in order to preserve those whose futures he deemed more important?

The sound of shattering glass echoed up from the ground floor.

* * *

Yuri leaned low over the bike's gas tank. His pale hair blew back into Caleb's face, and Caleb squinted and ducked low himself.

The bike roared through the streets, darting around cars and blowing through red lights, Yuri's every move one of confident control. Caleb clung to his waist and wished South Carolina's helmet laws applied to riders over the age of twenty-one. They screamed down the yellow line in between rows of cars, barely missed the rear end of a horse-drawn tourist trolley, and passed close enough to pedestrians crossing the street that Caleb could have knocked the cigarette from a startled man's lips.

No unpossessed human driver could have done it: the way Yuri was pulling from Dru's enhanced reflexes, as though he'd been born with them...

"And yet you will not allow me to drive a vehicle."

If any cops saw them, Yuri left them behind in the dust. The very fact he didn't seem to care about causing a scene made Caleb wonder. This was exactly the sort of thing that would get SPECTR's attention.

"Perhaps he is more concerned with helping us."

Damn. If that was true, and SPECTR ended up after Yuri and Dru because of it...

They just had to take out the grendel. Then Yuri and Dru could lie low elsewhere. If any questions arose, Caleb would just act dumb, or...

Who was he kidding? Of course questions were going to arise. Nigel or Deacon or someone had already called 9-1-1. There was already a SPECTR team on the way, responding to reports of an attack.

For all he knew, John was en route to the bookstore. Maybe thinking Caleb had lost it, that he and Gray had snapped and turned into the monster everyone else thought they were.

"No. John would never believe such a thing."

Gray was right, about that at least. But the look on Nigel's face...on Haylee's...

They thought we were going to kill them. And he shouldn't blame them, not really, because how could they know that Gray was different?

Except somehow...some way...he'd stupidly hoped they'd understand if they ever found out. That they'd listen. Or that Deacon would, if no one else.

A mixture of sorrow and affection emanated from Gray. In the shared space of their brain, he wrapped around Caleb. *"I am sorry."*

It isn't your fault.

"I did not like the mortals, but I love you. I do not wish you to be sad."

I know. I love you, too.

"That is a given."

The bike decelerated sharply. Blinking, Caleb looked up and found they were on the street outside the athletics building.

The two students who had beaten Mike were dead, along with the dean. But he'd named the coach, before Caleb's arrival at PASS interrupted him, so it had seemed likely he'd be the next victim on Mike's list.

And now it looked like Caleb's guess had been right. The glass of the front door was shattered, the metal frame hanging half-off its hinges. The scent of rot and slime overwhelmed even the tang of car exhaust and human sweat on the sidewalk.

"He's already here," Caleb said.

"Yes." Yuri swung off the bike and stared up at the building. "You two go to the roof. We'll follow the trail from the front door."

"Same as with the werewolves?" Caleb asked.

Yuri's eyes turned to fractured, black glass, lit from within by the hellish glow of a lava flow. "Why alter what has always worked?" Dru asked in his bass rumble. "Now come. Let us put an end to this demon and feast on its blood."

John bit back a curse. Kent's face went utterly white. "Wh-what was that?"

John ignored him. "Zahira, stay here with Mr. Kent and call for backup. I'll go investigate."

Ordinarily, she never questioned an order from him. But this time, she said, "Are you sure? If it is the grendel..."

She didn't finish with the obvious. That it was unlikely John could take it on, no matter how much his powers were expanded thanks to Gray.

Certainly a part of him wanted her at his back. But, like it or not, they had a civilian to protect. "I'm sure. Call Caleb first, though." If he didn't have his phone switched off in the PASS meeting.

And even if he didn't...it would take time for him to get across town. Time in which the grendel might tear John limb from limb.

He slipped out of the room, heard Zahira close and lock the door behind him. His gun wouldn't do much good, so he drew his athame. Of course, his damned Florida water was in the trunk of the car, along with all of his other gear. They'd expected an interview, not to find themselves face-to-face with a powerful NHE.

He went as quietly as he could, every sense extended, including his sixth one. There was no further breakage of glass, no sound of claws on the floor. Nothing.

The stairs let out onto the first floor. Glass carpeted the lobby, the door dangling by its hinges. A second door stood open; John was almost positive it had been closed before. The sign beside it advised it led to the weight room, lockers, and steam room.

What was it Kent had said about wrapping up his workout early? If the grendel knew his ordinary routine, it might have expected to find him there.

All but holding his breath, John stepped through the door. The weight room was empty, the space reeking of old sweat and grungy carpet. Doors to the locker rooms opened on the other side. John went to the men's, offered up a quick prayer, and opened it.

Rows of lockers, painted in the school colors, blocked his view of most of the room. He stepped inside, pulse pounding in his throat. Only silence greeted him.

He made his way down the aisle between two rows, wincing as his shoes scuffed on the worn concrete. The door to the steam room stood open, and he stepped toward it.

Etheric energy. At his back.

He spun, athame out like a shield. The grendel stalked down the aisle behind him: eight feet of misshapen muscle and distorted limbs, like the parody of a prize fighter. The fluorescent lighting made its bruise-colored skin seem even more unnatural. As it approached, its scent of rotting marshland and rancid sweat rolled over him like a wave.

Even though it was still several feet away, he aimed his talent at it, visualizing a barbed rope sinking into it to drag free the NHE. But nothing happened; either he was too far away, or it was too strong for him to exorcise alone without a circle.

Its mouth widened, showing off uneven teeth. Grinning at his failure.

He was going to die here.

CHAPTER 11

JOHN BROKE AND ran.

The grendel followed, its long strides eating up the distance. It was between him and the entrance; his only refuge was the dead end of the steam room.

He slammed the door behind him and threw the lock. The grendel struck it, and the frosted glass exploded inward.

John pressed his back against the tiled wall and swapped athame for gun. Glass popped and cracked as the grendel's foot came down on it, but none of the shards pierced the skin. Its grin became even more maniacal, the jaw opening impossibly wide, ready to devour him alive.

John fired. The bullet struck the steam head as the grendel passed by.

A jet of scalding steam burst forth. The grendel let out a shriek of agony, stumbling back and clawing blindly at its eyes and skin.

Bullets and knives might have no impact, but it could still be hurt. John clung to that bit of information as it staggered out of the steam room, howling its pain. As soon as the doorway was clear, he yanked his coat up to protect his face and hands, and ran.

Out. Past the steam and the grendel. Now if he could just make the lobby, he could either delay it, or—

The grendel's screech of fury shattered one of the fluorescent bulbs overhead. A fist slammed into John's back, sending him crashing into the lockers. Something snapped in his nose, and warm blood splattered across the metal and onto the concrete.

Training was the only thing that kept him moving. He'd ended up on the floor, so he rolled onto his back, gun aimed even though he was still dazed. The grendel loomed up over him; he fired, knowing it would do no good, until only a click rewarded the pull of the trigger.

The grendel didn't so much as flinch. The right side of its face was flushed almost black, and it wasn't grinning any more.

John had only a split second to sense what felt like a wall of etheric energy, rushing from the direction of the door. A figure cannoned into the grendel, sending it flying to the side. The grendel crashed into the lockers, crushing the metal from the force of its impact. The second figure rolled into a crouch.

Pale hair hung about its shoulders. Its eyes were black glass, lit from within by a hellish glow. The scent of burning metal and broken stone flooded the air. Even before it bared its fangs at the grendel, John knew exactly what it must be, because no other NHE he'd met exuded that level of etheric energy.

It was a drakul. And it wasn't Gray.

John's mind spun in circles, because this wasn't possible. But there were the flashing fangs, the claws. And most of all, the overwhelming feeling that he was in the presence of something huge, a titan that would rip apart the very earth beneath him.

The grendel scrambled to its feet—but it moved more slowly now, as though something inside had broken. Its yellow eyes were wide, jaw slack. A sound issued forth, neither words nor growl, as though something inside it struggled to recall human speech.

The faust? If it wasn't past forty days, could they still talk him down? Save him?

The drakul roared, a sound so loud John had to cover his ears. The concrete around the drakul's feet shattered, cracks racing away across the floor, as if in response to its fury.

It leapt at the grendel, fangs and claws bared. But the thick hide refused to yield; there came a loud snap, and the drakul spit out a stream of blood.

The grendel seemed to have recovered. It struck the drakul a heavy blow, sending the slim body flying across the locker room. The drakul slammed into a row of shelves holding fresh towels, which came crashing down to the floor along with it.

Its way cleared, the grendel fled for the door. Growling in frustrated anger, the drakul flung aside the towels and chased after it.

John forced himself to his feet. Warm blood filled his mouth, and he spit out a gobbet before starting after them. Goddess, a grendel was bad enough, but a drakul…

Maybe its body was a corpse. A very fresh one. It hadn't looked that way, but maybe he was wrong.

Sekhmet, please let him be wrong.

The drakul caught up with the grendel in the lobby. The grendel snarled and fought back, raking broken nails over the drakul's pale face, laying the flesh open to the bone. The drakul ignored the wounds and latched onto the grendel's arm, growling furiously.

Gray leapt from the top of the lobby stairs like an avenging angel. His leather coat flared around him, and his hair spread like a dark halo. He landed half-on the grendel, dragging it to the floor. His arms wrapped around its torso, trapping its other arm.

The other drakul's boots literally seemed to dig into the floor as it wrenched the grendel's arm violently in the opposite direction.

There came a horrible tearing and cracking. Splits appeared in the grendel's bruise-colored skin, and it screamed in agony. Its cry only seemed to spur the drakul on; they redoubled their efforts, and with a final *pop* the grendel's arm ripped free.

Blood fountained out in a great torrent. The other drakul fastened on the wound as the grendel collapsed. Gray shoved in beside it with a growl, and they feasted together on the dying NHE.

John stood very still, his hands shaking and the metallic taste of adrenaline flooding his mouth.

The wounds had sealed in the other drakul's cheek. It was alive.

Swallowing hard, he took a step forward, then another. The other drakul looked up. It rose to its feet, blood smeared across its chin, and those hotly glowing eyes fastened on him.

No. Fastened on the blood dripping slowly from his nose.

It moved toward him.

Then Gray was there between them. He shoved John back, putting himself in between with a roar that shook the air. "Ours!"

The other drakul's energy collapsed like a wave front, folding back into the slim figure of a young man with white-blond hair and eyes like an arctic morning. "Sorry about that." He stepped back, hands up and an easy grin on his face. "We didn't realize he was one of yours."

One of yours. What the fuck did that mean?

The sound of sirens approached, and blue and red lights flashed over the building's facade. The other drakul glanced casually at Gray. "I believe that's our cue to depart. Coming?"

Gray's energy retreated. "No," Caleb said. "This is…SPECTR is my job. I'm sorry, Yuri. Just—just go."

Yuri.

Caleb knew him.

Yuri flashed him a smile. "Don't look so sad, Caleb. I'll catch up with you later."

He was gone in the blink of an eye, vanishing outside and into the night with preternatural speed. Caleb sighed and wiped the blood off his lips.

Thoughts and feelings pinballed through John, too many to name or process. But one foremost of all.

Betrayal.

"That was another drakul," he said, voice shaking. "And you knew him."

Guilt flashed over Caleb's face. He scratched the back of his neck, his gaze dropping to the rotting body of the grendel. "Yeah. He's—they're—what we smelled before. The not-demon."

"You went looking for it. Without me."

"All those times I was supposedly getting a beer with Deacon." Caleb shrugged, a lift of one shoulder. Brushing off the lie, as if it didn't matter. "And we found them."

"And you didn't tell me." John clenched his fist, resisting the impulse to shake Caleb. "You knew there was another living drakul in Charleston, and you *didn't tell me.*"

"Of course I didn't," Caleb snapped. "Because you'd want to get SPECTR involved, even though Yuri and Dru aren't a danger to anyone."

"That isn't your determination to make!"

Caleb stepped up to John, glaring down. "Like hell it isn't." His voice was cold and tight with anger. "I love you, John. We both do. But Yuri and Dru have things to teach Gray and me. Things about living in this world as a drakul. Things we need to know."

John took a deep breath. "I understand, but you can't just—"

"No, you don't understand!" Caleb flung his arms out in frustration. "You can't."

It hurt. "Caleb—"

"No!" Caleb stabbed a finger in the direction the other drakul had vanished. "If nothing else, Yuri and Dru don't deserve to get caught in the same trap Gray and I are in."

John felt as though the grendel had hit him a second time, knocking all the wind from his lungs. He knew Caleb wasn't happy, knew Gray was restless. But this... "You feel trapped?"

"SPECTR isn't going to let us go," Caleb said. "Not *ever*. What do you think?" He shook his head. "John...please. I'm begging you. *We're* begging you. Don't tell anyone about them."

John hesitated. He knew what he had to do. What duty required him to do. Caleb said the drakul wasn't dangerous—but wasn't such an entity dangerous by its very nature? Gray might not hurt anyone unless he had no other choice, but other living drakul didn't have such a good track record.

As far as he knew, anyway. Maybe there were more of them out there. Ones who hadn't made it into the legends. Maybe the Vigilant had been wrong about that part.

But the way the other drakul had looked at the blood on John's face...

One of yours. What the hell did that mean?

Caleb's pleading eyes vanished, replaced by Gray's black gaze. "Please," he said, his deep voice pitched soft. "I knew him once, John. Beyond the veil. Do not betray Drugoy to SPECTR."

John closed his eyes. "All right."

Caleb, John, and Zahira stood in front of Barillo's desk. The morning shift was starting, and the long night showed on them all. Caleb glanced at John out of the corner of his eye. Though not exactly swaying on his feet, John's normal professional exterior was worn around the edges. His coat was wrinkled, his tie was loose, and blood stained his dress shirt. The EMTs had slapped a white bandage across his badly swollen and bruised nose. But it was the haunted look in his eyes that worried Caleb most.

Dru and Yuri had scared John. Just like almost everyone at SPECTR, not to mention his so-called friends at PASS, were scared of Caleb and Gray.

Of all the reactions Caleb had expected, he'd never imagined fear would be one of them. Concern, yes, even worry. But not personal fear. Not from John.

It left a bitter taste he couldn't quite swallow away.

Gray stirred. *"But he agreed not to tell anyone."*

There was that, at least. Despite his fear, John had still chosen them over SPECTR. Just as he had before, when he'd planned to botch Gray's exorcism and free him. Caleb should have remembered that, should never had doubted John would always have their back no matter what.

Barillo leaned forward in his chair. He looked as tired as the rest of them, the wrinkles multiplying around his dark eyes. Ordinarily he wouldn't have called Caleb in with the others, not since Gray had accidentally frightened him. The fact that he had now left Caleb uneasy. "Do you three have anything to say for yourselves?"

"Sir," John said, "we—"

"Save it, Starkweather." Barillo's eyes narrowed. "This was a cluster fuck from start to finish. The one thing I asked you to do, was to not dig up any dirt. Now there are dead bodies all over the landscape, and the coach is blabbing to the press that the college helped cover up a crime just to keep a star athlete in the game. The last thing anyone wanted was reporters poking their noses where they don't belong. I've got congressmen on the phone chewing my ass out, and senators demanding answers from Director Kaniyar."

"The college has been covering up criminal activity by students, and we're supposed to feel sorry for them?" Caleb asked incredulously.

"I don't give a fuck how you feel about them, Jansen. You should feel sorry for me, because I have to deal with the shit. And now, so do you." Barillo's eyes narrowed. "Want to tell me about these reports that your demon is off the leash terrorizing citizens."

"I did not—"

Shut it.

Surprisingly, Gray fell silent. Maybe for once he'd realized Caleb knew more about how to handle Barillo than he did.

"We were trying to protect them from the grendel," Caleb said, before John could jump in. If anyone was going to get blamed for this, it might as well be him.

"Protect them? By sending two of them to the emergency room?"

"They attacked us," Caleb said. "They didn't realize their friend was a faust. I had to get away from them so we could keep the grendel from killing anyone else."

"Sir," Zahira said, "if Gray hadn't been there, the grendel would certainly have killed John, then come up to the office and killed Mr. Kent and me as well. He saved lives."

"I didn't ask what you think, Noorzai." Barillo didn't take his eyes off Caleb. "This has gone on long enough. Between the politicians breathing down my neck, and civilians screaming you tried to kill them, I ought to just drop you in a hole. But, because I'm such a damned nice guy, I'm giving you one last chance, Jansen. Screw this up…and let's just say you won't like the consequences."

"This mortal threatens us."

Yeah. So stay down and let me handle this.

"I understand," Caleb said aloud.

"You'd better." Barillo said. "Effective immediately, I'm breaking up the dream team. You'll be partnered with a new pair of exorcists. Let's see if your performance improves when you aren't fucking the boss."

John's indrawn breath was audible. Caleb didn't dare look at him; didn't dare so much as move. Not with Barillo watching so closely.

"He seeks to take us away from John?" Gray's anger lashed, dangerously close to the surface.

No. Just while we're here at HQ. And on the job, but we'll still be living with him. Fear began to spread along Caleb's nerves. *Damn it, Gray, stop. If you manifest now, that's it. Then they will take us away, and we'll never see John again.*

Gray withdrew, but just barely. Caleb took a deep breath, and made sure his relief didn't show on his face.

"Hear me?" Barillo prodded.

Caleb swallowed. "Yes."

"Yes what?"

The smirk on Barillo's face made Caleb want to leap over the desk and throttle him. "Yes, sir."

"Good." Barillo settled back, clearly pleased with himself. "Go clean out your desk—you won't be sharing an office with Starkweather anymore. Noorzai, you're on ghoul squad now. And Starkweather, we still don't know who the exorcist was who summoned the damned grendel. Find him, and maybe we can use him to distract the press."

"Yes, sir," Zahira said, subdued. John only nodded mutely.

They left Barillo's office, Caleb first. Once they were down the hall, Zahira burst out: "It's not fair! He's being completely unreasonable."

"You'll get no argument from me," Caleb agreed, not looking back.

When John didn't say anything, Zahira said, "John? Are you…all right?"

"No," John said. "I'm really not."

Caleb stopped at last. John looked…lost. Tired and uncertain, and maybe this had been one too many shocks to the system in too few hours.

John had always been there for them. From the first moments in the house where Caleb had died, when he'd tried and failed to exorcise Gray. No matter what else was going on, John had been the one thing they could count on without question.

So now it was time to return the favor.

Caleb put his hand on John's shoulder, squeezing gently. "It's going to be okay," he said, meeting John's blue gaze. "Sure, things are going to be tough for a while, but we'll get through this."

Because they weren't alone anymore, were they? If things truly went south, they had an ace up their sleeve in the form of Yuri and Dru. They had another drakul, who had safely stayed out of SPECTR's notice for decades. Who could teach them how to do the same.

John stared at him searchingly for a long moment. Then he smiled, not much, but a little. "You're right. Thanks."

Caleb gave him one last squeeze before letting his hand drop. For John's sake, he'd put up with whatever bullshit Barillo dished out. For now.

But if Barillo tried to punish John…

"Then he'll have us to deal with."

Caleb ran his tongue over his teeth, feeling the points. *Yes. He will.*

SHARE YOUR EXPERIENCE

IF YOU ENJOYED this book, please consider leaving a review on the site where you purchased it, or on Goodreads.

Thank you for your support of independent authors!

AUTHOR'S NOTES

DANCER OF DEATH:

Giselle is a lovely ballet, which I encourage anyone to see performed, live or on video. The plot as relayed in this book has been adapted to fit the SPECTR universe. In the original, Giselle dies from a broken heart and is resurrected as a wili—also known as a vila. Her sister-wili attempt to dance Albrecht to death, but Giselle protects him until the clock strikes 4 am, the time when the power of the wilis is broken. She then retreats to the peace of the grave.

DRINKER OF BLOOD:

Thanks to Liz Jacobs, for assistance in helping me figure out the proper form of Drugoy (Russian for "Other").

ABOUT THE AUTHOR

JORDAN L. HAWK grew up in North Carolina and forgot to ever leave. Childhood tales of mountain ghosts and mysterious creatures gave her a life-long love of things that go bump in the night. When she isn't writing, she brews her own beer and tries to keep her cats from destroying the house. Her best-selling Whyborne & Griffin series (beginning with *Widdershins*) can be found in print, ebook, and audiobook.

If you're interested in receiving Jordan's newsletter and being the first to know when new books are released, plus getting sneak peeks at upcoming novels, please sign up at her website, jordanlhawk.com.

Made in the USA
Middletown, DE
22 April 2018